THE
EMPTY THRONE

BOOKS BY BERNARD CORNWELL

1356
THE FORT
AGINCOURT

The Saxon Tales
THE LAST KINGDOM
THE PALE HORSEMAN
THE LORDS OF THE NORTH
SWORD SONG
THE BURNING LAND
DEATH OF KINGS
THE PAGAN LORD

The Sharpe Novels (in chronological order)
SHARPE'S TIGER
Richard Sharpe and the Siege of Seringapatam, 1799
SHARPE'S TRIUMPH
Richard Sharpe and the Battle of Assaye, September 1803
SHARPE'S FORTRESS
Richard Sharpe and the Siege of Gawilghur, December 1803
SHARPE'S TRAFALGAR
Richard Sharpe and the Battle of Trafalgar, 21 October 1805
SHARPE'S PREY
Richard Sharpe and the Expedition to Copenhagen, 1807
SHARPE'S RIFLES
Richard Sharpe and the French Invasion of Galicia, January
    1809
SHARPE'S HAVOC
Richard Sharpe and the Campaign in Northern Portugal,
    Spring 1809
SHARPE'S EAGLE
Richard Sharpe and the Talavera Campaign, July 1809

SHARPE'S GOLD
Richard Sharpe and the Destruction of Almeida, August 1810

SHARPE'S ESCAPE
Richard Sharpe and the Bussaco Campaign, 1810

SHARPE'S FURY
Richard Sharpe and the Battle of Barrosa, March 1811

SHARPE'S BATTLE
Richard Sharpe and the Battle of Fuentes de Onoro, May 1811

SHARPE'S COMPANY
Richard Sharpe and the Siege of Badajoz, January to April 1812

SHARPE'S SWORD
Richard Sharpe and the Salamanca Campaign, June and July 1812

SHARPE'S ENEMY
Richard Sharpe and the Defense of Portugal, Christmas 1812

SHARPE'S HONOR
Richard Sharpe and the Vitoria Campaign, February to June 1813

SHARPE'S REGIMENT
Richard Sharpe and the Invasion of France, June to November 1813

SHARPE'S SIEGE
Richard Sharpe and the Winter Campaign, 1814

SHARPE'S REVENGE
Richard Sharpe and the Peace of 1814

SHARPE'S WATERLOO
Richard Sharpe and the Waterloo Campaign, 15 June to 18 June 1815

SHARPE'S DEVIL
Richard Sharpe and the Emperor, 1820–1821

The Grail Quest Series

THE ARCHER'S TALE

VAGABOND

HERETIC

The Nathaniel Starbuck Chronicles

REBEL

COPPERHEAD

BATTLE FLAG

THE BLOODY GROUND

The Warlord Chronicles

THE WINTER KING

THE ENEMY OF GOD

EXCALIBUR

The Sailing Thrillers

STORMCHILD

SCOUNDREL

WILDTRACK

CRACKDOWN

Other Novels

STONEHENGE

GALLOWS THIEF

A CROWNING MERCY

THE FALLEN ANGELS

REDCOAT

THE
EMPTY
THRONE

A NOVEL

BERNARD
CORNWELL

HARPER

An Imprint of HarperCollins*Publishers*

HarperCollins books may be purchased for educational, business, or sales promotional use. For information, please e-mail the Special Markets Department at SPsales@harpercollins.com.

Published in Great Britain in 2014 by HarperCollins Publishers.

FIRST U.S. EDITION

Map copyright © 2014 by John Gilkes

Library of Congress Cataloging-in-Publication Data has been applied for.

ISBN: 978-0-06-225071-1

15 16 17 18 19   DIX/RRD   10 9 8 7 6 5 4 3

For Peggy Davis

Contents

Map
xii

Place-Names
xiii

Prologue
1

Part One
The Dying Lord
27

Part Two
The Lady of Mercia
95

Part Three
The God of War
187

HISTORICAL NOTE
295

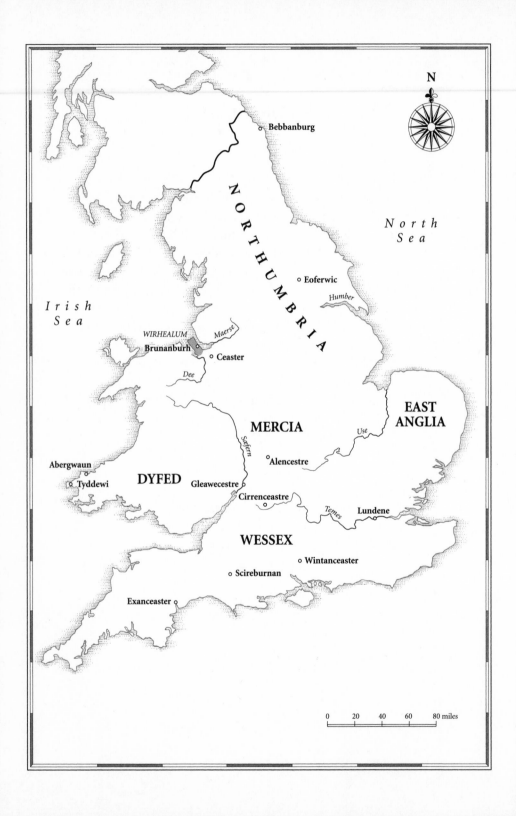

PLACE-NAMES

The spelling of place-names in Anglo-Saxon England was an uncertain business, with no consistency and no agreement even about the name itself. Thus London was variously rendered as Lundonia, Lundenberg, Lundenne, Lundene, Lundenwic, Lundenceaster and Lundres. Doubtless some readers will prefer other versions of the names listed below, but I have usually employed whichever spelling is cited in either the *Oxford Dictionary of English Place-Names* or the *Cambridge Dictionary of English Place-Names* for the years nearest or contained within Alfred's reign, AD 871–899, but even that solution is not foolproof. Hayling Island, in 956, was written as both Heilincigae and Hæglingaiggæ. Nor have I been consistent myself; preferring the modern form Northumbria to Norðhymbralond to avoid the suggestion that the boundaries of the ancient kingdom coincide with those of the modern county. So this list, like the spellings themselves, is capricious.

Abergwaun	Fishguard, Pembrokeshire
Alencestre	Alcester, Warwickshire
Beamfleot	Benfleet, Essex
Bebbanburg	Bamburgh Castle, Northumberland
Brunanburh	Bromborough, Cheshire
Cadum	Caen, Normandy
Ceaster	Chester, Cheshire
Cirrenceastre	Cirencester, Gloucestershire
Cracgelad	Cricklade, Wiltshire
Cumbraland	Cumbria
Defnascir	Devonshire
Eoferwic	York
Eveshomme	Evesham, Worcestershire
Fagranforda	Fairford, Gloucestershire

Fearnhamme	Farnham, Surrey
Gleawecestre	Gloucester, Gloucestershire
Lundene	London
Lundi	Lundy Island, Devon
Mærse	River Mersey
Neustria	Westernmost province of Frankia, including Normandy
Sæfern	River Severn
Scireburnan	Sherborne, Dorset
Sealtwic	Droitwich, Worcestershire
Teotanheale	Tettenhall, West Midlands
Thornsæta	Dorset
Tyddewi	St. Davids, Pembrokeshire
Wiltunscir	Wiltshire
Wintanceaster	Winchester, Hampshire
Wirhealum	The Wirral, Cheshire

THE
EMPTY THRONE

PROLOGUE

My name is Uhtred. I am the son of Uhtred, who was the son of Uhtred, and his father was also called Uhtred. My father wrote his name thus, Uhtred, but I have seen the name written as Utred, Ughtred or even Ootred. Some of those names are on ancient parchments which declare that Uhtred, son of Uhtred and grandson of Uhtred, is the lawful, sole and eternal owner of the lands that are carefully marked by stones and by dikes, by oaks and by ash, by marsh and by sea. That land is in the north of the country we have learned to call Englaland. They are wave-beaten lands beneath a wind-driven sky. It is the land we call Bebbanburg.

I did not see Bebbanburg till I was grown, and the first time we attacked its high walls we failed. My father's cousin ruled the great fortress then. His father had stolen it from my father. It was a bloodfeud. The church tried to stop the feud, saying the enemy of all Saxon Christians was the pagan Northmen, whether Danish or Norse, but my father swore me to the feud. If I had refused the oath he would have disinherited me, just as he disinherited and disowned my older brother, not because my brother would not pursue the feud, but because he became a Christian priest. I was once named Osbert, but when my elder brother became a priest I was given his name. My name is Uhtred of Bebbanburg.

My father was a pagan, a warlord, and frightening. He often told me he was frightened of his own father, but I cannot believe it because nothing seemed to frighten him. Many folk claim that our country would be called Daneland and we would all be worshipping Thor and Woden if it had not been for my father, and that is true. True and strange because he hated the Christian god, calling him "the nailed god," yet despite his hatred he spent the greatest part of his life fighting against the pagans. The church will not admit that Englaland exists because of my father, claiming that it was made and won by Christian warriors, but the folk of Englaland know the truth. My father should have been called Uhtred of Englaland.

Yet in the year of our Lord 911 there was no Englaland. There was Wessex and Mercia and East Anglia and Northumbria, and as the winter turned to a sullen spring in that year I was on the border of Mercia and Northumbria in thickly wooded country north of the River Mærse. There were thirty-eight of us, all well mounted and all waiting among the winter-bare branches of a high wood. Beneath us was a valley in which a small fast stream flowed south, and where frost lingered in deep-shadowed gullies. The valley was empty, though just moments before some sixty-five riders had followed the stream southward and then vanished where the valley and its stream turned sharply west. "Not long now," Rædwald said.

That was just nervousness and I made no answer. I was nervous too, but tried not to show it. Instead I imagined what my father would have done. He would have been hunched in the saddle, glowering and motionless, and so I hunched in my saddle and stared fixedly into the valley. I touched the hilt of my sword.

She was called Raven-Beak. I suppose she had another name before that because she had belonged to Sigurd Thorrson, and he must have given her a name though I never did find out what it was. At first I thought the sword was called Vlfberht because that strange name was inscribed on the blade in big letters. It looked like this:

† VLFBERH † T

But Finan, my father's friend, told me that Vlfberht is the name of the Frankish smith who made her, and that he makes the finest and most expensive blades in all Christendom, and it must be Christendom because Vlfberht puts the crosses in front of and inside his name. I asked Finan how we could find Vlfberht to buy more swords, but Finan says he is a magic smith who works in secret. A blacksmith will leave his furnace for the night and return in the morning to find that Vlfberht has been in the smithy and left a sword forged in the fires of hell and quenched with dragon's blood. I called her Raven-Beak because Sigurd's banner had shown a raven. She had been the sword Sigurd carried when he fought me and when my seax had ripped his belly open. I remember that sword-stroke so well, remember the resistance of his fine mail suddenly giving way and the look in his eyes as he realized he was dying and the elation I felt as I dragged the seax sideways to empty his lifeblood. That had happened in the previous year at the battle at Teotanheale which had driven the Danes out of central Mercia, the same battle in which my father had killed Cnut Ranulfson, but in killing Cnut he had been wounded by Cnut's sword, Ice-Spite.

Raven-Beak was a good sword, I thought her even better than Serpent-Breath, my father's blade. She was long-bladed, but surprisingly light, and other swords broke against her edge. She was a warrior's sword, and I carried her that day in the high wood above the frosted valley where the stream ran so fast. I carried Raven-Beak and my seax, Attor. Attor means venom and she was a short-sword, good for the crowded work of a shield wall. She stung, and it was her venom that had killed Sigurd. And I carried my round shield on which was painted the wolf's head, the emblem of our family. I wore a helmet crested with a wolf's head, and a coat of Frankish mail above a leather jerkin, and above it all a cloak of bear fur. I am Uhtred Uhtredson, the true lord of Bebbanburg, and I was nervous that day.

I led the war-band. I was just twenty-one years old and some of the men behind me were almost twice my age with many times my experience, but I was the son of Uhtred, a lord, and so I commanded. Most of the men were well back among the trees, only Rædwald and Sihtric were with me. Both were older, and both had been sent to offer me advice or, rather, to keep me from headstrong stupidity. I had known Sihtric forever, he was one of my father's trusted men, while Rædwald was a warrior in the service of the Lady Æthelflaed. "Maybe they're not coming," he said. He was a steady man, cautious and careful, and I half suspected he hoped the enemy would not appear.

"They're coming," Sihtric grunted.

And they did come. They came hurrying from the north, a band of horsemen with shields, spears, axes, and swords. Norsemen. I leaned forward in the saddle, trying to count the riders who spurred beside the stream. Three crews? At least one hundred men, and Haki Grimmson was among them, or at least his banner of a ship was there.

"One hundred and twenty," Sihtric said.

"More," Rædwald said.

"One hundred and twenty," Sihtric insisted flatly.

One hundred and twenty horsemen pursuing the sixty-five who had ridden through the valley some moments before. One hundred and twenty men following Haki Grimmson's banner that was supposed to show a red ship on a white sea, though the red dye of the wool had faded to brown and stained the white sea so that it seemed as if the high-prowed ship was bleeding. The standard-bearer was riding behind a big man on a powerful black horse and I assumed that big man was Haki. He was a Norseman who had settled in Ireland, from where he had crossed to Britain and found land north of the River Mærse and thought to make himself rich by raiding southward into Mercia. He had taken slaves, cattle, and property, he had even assaulted the Roman walls of Ceaster, though that assault had been beaten off easily enough by the Lady Æthelflaed's garrison. He was, in short, a nuisance, and that was why we were north of the Mærse, concealed among winter-bare trees and watching his war-band pound south on the frost-hardened track beside the stream.

"We should . . ." Rædwald began.

"Not yet," I interrupted him. I touched Raven-Beak, making sure she moved in her scabbard.

"Not yet," Sihtric agreed.

"Godric!" I called, and my servant, a twelve-year-old boy named Godric Grindanson, spurred from where my men waited. "Spear," I said.

"Lord," he said, and handed me the nine-foot-long ash pole with the heavy iron spearhead.

"You ride behind us," I told Godric, "well behind us. You have the horn?"

"Yes, lord." He held up the horn to show me. The sound of the horn would summon help from the sixty-five riders if things went wrong, though I doubted they could offer any real help if my small war-band was attacked by Haki's grim horsemen.

"If they've dismounted," Sihtric spoke to the boy, "you help drive their horses away."

"I should stay close to . . ." Godric began, plainly about to plead that he should stay by my side and so join the fight, but he stopped abruptly when Sihtric backhanded him across the face.

"You help drive the horses away," Sihtric snarled.

"I will," the boy said. His lip was bleeding.

Sihtric loosened the sword in his scabbard. As a boy he had been my father's servant, and doubtless he had wanted to fight alongside the grown men back then, but there was no quicker way for a boy to die than trying to fight a battle-hardened Norseman. "Are we ready?" he prompted me.

"Let's go and kill the bastards," I said.

Haki's war-band had turned west and ridden out of sight. They were following the stream that flowed into a tributary of the Mærse some two miles beyond the valley's sharp westward turn. There was a small hill where the two streams joined, nothing more than a long grassy mound like the graves the old people placed all across the land, and that was where Haki would die or be defeated, which, in the end, amounted to the same thing.

We spurred down the hill, though I was in no hurry because I did not want Haki's men to look behind and see us. We reached the stream and turned south. We did not hurry, indeed I slowed down as Sihtric rode ahead to scout. I watched as he dismounted and as he found a place from where he could see westward. He was crouching and holding up one hand to caution us, and it was some time before he ran back to his horse and waved us on. He grinned at me when we joined him. "They stopped a ways down the valley," he said, his voice sibilant because a Danish spear had taken his front teeth at the battle at Teotanheale, "then unslung their shields." They had ridden beneath us with their shields strapped on their backs, but Haki obviously expected trouble where the valley ended and so had taken the time for his men to prepare for a fight. Our shields were already on our arms.

"They'll dismount when they reach the valley's end," I said.

"Then form a shield wall," Sihtric said.

"So there's no hurry," I finished the thought and grinned.

"They might hurry," Rædwald suggested. He was worried that the fight would start without us.

I shook my head. "There are sixty-five Saxons waiting for them," I told him, "and Haki might outnumber them, but he'll still be cautious." The Norseman would have almost twice as many warriors as the waiting Saxons, but those Saxons were on a hill and already formed into a shield wall. Haki would have to dismount his troops a good distance away so he was not attacked while his men formed their own shield wall, and only when they were formed and when the horses were safely led away would he advance, and that advance would be slow. It takes immense courage to fight in the shield wall when you can smell your enemy's breath and the blades are falling and stabbing. He would advance slowly, confident in his numbers but careful in case the waiting Saxons had laid a trap. Haki could not afford to lose men. He might reckon he could win the fight where the stream joined the larger river, but he would still be cautious.

The Irish Norse were spreading into Britain. Finan, my father's companion, claimed that the Irish tribesmen were too formidable an enemy, and so the Norse were being pinned to Ireland's eastern coast. Yet on this side of the sea, the land north of the Mærse and south of the Scottish kingdoms was wild land, untamed, and so their ships crossed the waves to settle in the valleys of Cumbraland. Cumbraland was properly a part of Northumbria, but the Danish king in Eoferwic welcomed the newcomers. The Danes feared the growing power of the Saxons, and the Irish Norse were savage fighters who could help defend Danish-held land. Haki was merely the last to arrive, and he had thought to enrich himself at

Mercia's expense, which is why we had been sent to destroy him. "Remember!" I called to my men. "Only one of them is to survive!"

Leave one alive, that had always been my father's advice. Let one man take the bad news home to frighten the others, though I suspected all Haki's men were here, which meant the survivor, if there was one, would take the news of the defeat to widows and orphans. The priests tell us to love our enemies, but to show them no mercy, and Haki had earned none. He had raided the lands around Ceaster and the garrison there, sufficient to hold the walls, but not sufficient to hold the walls and send a war-band across the Mærse at the same time, had appealed for help. We were the help, and now we rode westward beside the stream, which grew wider and shallower, no longer hurrying over rocks. Stunted alders grew thick, their bare branches bent eastward by the unending wind from the far sea. We passed a burned farm-stead, nothing left there now except the blackened stones of a hearth. It had been the southernmost of Haki's steadings and the first we had attacked. In the two weeks since we had come to Ceaster we had burned a dozen of his settlements, taken scores of his cattle, killed his people and enslaved his children. Now he thought he had us trapped.

My stallion's motion made the heavy golden cross that hung about my neck beat against my chest. I looked southward to where the sun was a clouded silver disc in a fading sky and I sent a silent prayer to Woden. I am half a pagan, maybe less than half, but even my father had been known to say a prayer to the Christian god. "There are many gods," he had told me so often, "and you never know which one of them is awake, so pray to them all."

So I prayed to Woden. I am of your blood, I told him, so protect me, and I was indeed of his blood because our family is descended from Woden. He had come to earth and slept with a human girl, but that was long before our people crossed the sea to take Britain. "He didn't sleep with a girl," I could hear my father's scorn as I rode, "he gave her a good humping, and you don't sleep through that." I wondered why the gods no longer came to earth. It would make belief so much easier.

"Not so fast!" Sihtric called, and I stopped thinking about gods humping girls to see that three of our younger men had spurred ahead. "Fall back," Sihtric called, then grinned at me. "Not far, lord."

"We should scout," Rædwald advised.

"They've had long enough," I said, "keep riding."

I knew Haki would dismount his men to attack the waiting shield wall. Horses will not charge home into a shield wall, instead they will sheer aside, so Haki's men would form their own shield wall to attack the Saxons who were waiting on the long low mound. But we would come from their rear, and horses will charge into the back of a shield wall which is never as tight as the front rank. The front rank is a wall of locked shields and bright weapons, the rear rank is where the panic starts.

We turned slightly northward, clearing the spur of a hill, and there they were. The sun slanted bright from a gap in the clouds to light the Christian banners on the hilltop and glint from the blades waiting there. Sixty-five men, just sixty-five, a tight shield wall of two ranks on the hill crest beneath the cross-blazoned flags, and between them and us was Haki's shield wall, still forming, and nearest to us and off to our right were his horses under the guard of boys. "Rædwald," I said, "three men to drive the horses off."

"Lord," he acknowledged.

"Go with them, Godric!" I called to my servant, then hefted the heavy ash-shafted spear. The Norsemen had still not seen us. All they knew was that a raiding party of Mercians had penetrated deep into Haki's territory and the Norsemen had pursued them, thinking to slaughter them, but now they would find they had been lured into a trap. "Kill them!" I shouted and put my spurs back.

Kill them. This is what the poets sing about. At night, in the hall, when the hearth smoke thickens about the beams and the ale-horns are filled and the harpist plucks his strings, the songs of battle are sung. They are the songs of our family, of our people, and it is how we remember the past. We call a poet a scop and scop means someone who shapes things and a poet shapes our past so we remember the glories of our ancestors and how they brought us land and women and cattle and glory. There would be no Norse song of Haki, I thought, because this would be a Saxon song about a Saxon victory.

And we charged. Spear held tight, shield close, and Hearding, my horse, brave beast, was pounding the earth with hard hooves, and to my left and right the horses galloped, the spears held low, horse breath steaming, and the enemy turned, astonished, and the men at the rear of their shield wall did not know what to do. Some ran toward their horses and others tried to make a new shield wall to face us and I saw the gaps opening and knew they were dead men already. Beyond them, on the mound, the waiting Saxon warriors were fetching their own horses, but we would start the slaughter.

And we did.

I fixed my eyes on a tall, black-bearded man wearing fine mail and a helmet crested with eagle feathers. He was shouting, presumably to call men to lock their shields with his own shield that was painted with a spread eagle, but he saw my gaze, knew his fate and braced himself with his eagle-shield raised and his sword drawn back, and I knew he would strike at Hearding, hoping to blind my horse or shatter his teeth. Always fight the horse, not the rider. Wound or kill the horse and the rider becomes a victim, and the shield wall was breaking, scattering in panic, and I heard the shouts as men tried to rally the fugitives and I leaned into my spear, aiming her, then touched Hearding with my left knee and he swerved as the black-bearded man swung. His sword cut across Hearding's chest, a savage enough cut that drew blood, but it was not a killing blow, not a crippling cut, and my spear went through his shield, splintering the willow boards and thrusting on to break his mail. I felt her blade shatter his breast-bone and I let the ash shaft go and drew Raven-Beak and turned Hearding back to drive Raven-Beak's blade into another man's spine. The blade, made by a sorcerer, broke through mail as if it were tree bark. Hearding crashed between two men, spilling them both to the ground and we turned again, and the whole field was a chaos of panicked men among whom the riders spurred to kill, and more riders came from the mound, our whole force killing and shouting, and above us the banners waved. "Merewalh!" a high voice called sharply. "Stop the horses."

A handful of Norsemen had reached their horses, but Merewalh, a hard warrior, led men to kill them. Haki still lived, surrounded now by thirty or forty of his men, who had formed a shield barrier about their lord, and those men could only watch as their comrades were cut down. But some of our men were down too. I could see three riderless horses and one dying horse, its hooves beating as it lay in a mess of blood. I turned toward it and cut down at a man who had just struggled to his feet. He was dazed and I dazed him more with a slash across his helmet and he went down again, and a man bellowed from my left, swinging an ax two-handed, and Hearding twisted, lithe as a cat, and the ax-blade glanced from my shield, we turned again and Raven-Beak sliced once and I saw the blood bright. I was shouting, exhilarated, screaming my name so that the dead would know who had sent them to their doom.

I spurred on, sword low, looking for the white horse called Gast and saw him fifty or sixty paces away. His rider, sword in hand, was spurring toward Haki's shield-guarded remnant, but three other horses swerved into Gast's path to check his rider. Then I had to forget Gast because a man swung a sword at me with an overhead slash. The man had lost his helmet, and half his face was smothered with blood. I could see more blood seeping at his waist, but he was grim-faced, hard-eyed, battle-forged, and he bellowed death at me as he swung, and I met the sword with Raven-Beak and she split his blade in two so that the upper half speared into my saddle's pommel and stayed there. The lower half tore a gash in my right boot and I felt the blood welling as the man stumbled. I thrust Raven-Beak down to shatter his skull and rode on to see Gerbruht had dismounted and was thrashing an ax at a dead or nearly dead man. Gerbruht had already disemboweled his victim, now he seemed intent on separating flesh from bone and was screaming in rage as he slashed the heavy blade down to spatter gobbets of flesh, blood, shattered mail, and splintered bone onto the grass.

"What are you doing?" I shouted at him.

"He called me fat!" Gerbruht, a Frisian who had joined our war-band during the winter, shouted back. "The bastard called me fat!"

"You are fat," I pointed out, and that was true. Gerbruht had a belly like a pig and legs like tree trunks and three chins under his beard, but he was also hugely strong. A fearful man to face in a fight and a good friend to have beside you in the shield wall.

"He won't call me fat again," Gerbruht snarled, and drove the ax into the dead man's skull, splitting the face and opening up the brain. "Skinny bastard."

"You eat too much," I said.

"I'm always hungry, that's why."

I turned my horse to see that the fight was over. Haki and his shield companions still lived, but they were outnumbered and surrounded. Our Saxons were dismounting to kill the wounded and strip the corpses of mail, weapons, silver, and gold. Like all the Northmen, these warriors liked arm rings to boast of their prowess in battle, and we piled the rings, along with brooches, scabbard decorations, and neck chains onto a sword-ripped, blood-soaked cloak. I took one arm ring from the corpse of the black-bearded man. It was a chunk of gold, incised with the angular letters the Norsemen use, and I slipped it over my left wrist to join my other rings. Sihtric was grinning. He had a prisoner, a scared boy who was almost a man. "Our one survivor, lord," Sihtric said.

"He'll do," I said. "Cut off his sword hand and give him a horse. Then he can go."

Haki watched us. I rode close to the remaining Norsemen and stopped to stare at him. He was a squat, scar-faced man with a brown beard. His helmet had come off in the fight and his straggly hair was dark with blood. His ears stood out like jug handles. He stared back, defiant. Thor's hammer, shaped in gold, hung at his mail-clad chest. I counted twenty-seven men around him. They made a tight circle, shields outward. "Become a Christian," I called to him in Danish, "and you might live."

He understood me, though I doubted Danish was his language. He laughed at my suggestion, then spat. I was not even sure I had told him the truth, though many defeated enemies were spared if they agreed to conversion and baptism. The decision was not mine to make, it belonged to the rider mounted on the tall white horse called Gast. I turned toward the ring of horsemen who now surrounded Haki and his survivors, and the rider of the white horse looked past me. "Take Haki alive, kill the rest."

It did not take long. Most of the bravest Norsemen were already dead and only a handful of experienced fighters were with Haki, the rest of them were youngsters, many of whom shouted that they surrendered, only to be cut down. I watched. Merewalh, a good man who had deserted Lord Æthelred's service to follow Æthelflaed, led the attack, and it was Merewalh who dragged Haki out of the bloody heap, stripped him of his sword and shield, and forced him to his knees in front of the white horse.

Haki looked up. The sun was low in the west so that it was behind Gast's rider and thus dazzling Haki, but he sensed the hatred and scorn that looked down on him. He shifted his head till his eyes were in the rider's shadow, so now, perhaps, he could see the polished Frankish mail, scrubbed with sand till it shone like silver. He could see the white woollen cloak, edged with a weasel's silky, white winter fur. He could see the tall boots, bound in white cord, and the long sword scabbard dressed with polished silver, and, if he dared raise his eyes higher, the hard blue eyes in the hard face framed by golden hair held by a helmet polished to the same high sheen as the mail. The helmet was ringed with a silver band and had a silver cross on the crown. "Take the mail from him," the white-clothed rider on the white horse said.

"Yes, my lady," Merewalh said.

The lady was Æthelflaed, daughter of Alfred who had been King of Wessex. She was married to Æthelred, the Lord of Mercia, but everyone in Wessex and in Mercia knew she had been my father's lover for years. It was Æthelflaed who had brought her men north to reinforce Ceaster's garrison, and Æthelflaed who had devised the trap that now had Haki on his knees in front of her horse.

She looked at me. "You did well," she said, almost grudgingly.

"Thank you, my lady," I said.

"You'll take him south," she said, gesturing at Haki. "He can die in Gleawecestre."

I thought that a strange decision. Why not let him die here on the pale winter grass? "You will not go back south, my lady?" I asked her.

It was plain she thought the question impertinent, but she answered anyway. "I have much to do here. You will take him." She held up a gloved hand to stop me as I turned away. "Make sure you arrive before Saint Cuthbert's Day. You hear me?"

I bowed for answer, then we tied Haki's hands behind his back, mounted him on a poor horse, and rode back to Ceaster where we arrived after dark. We had left the Norsemen's bodies where they fell, food for ravens, but we carried our own dead with us, just five men. We took all the Norse horses and loaded them with captured weapons, with mail, with clothes, and with shields. We rode back victorious, carrying Haki's captured banner and following Lord Æthelred's standard of the white horse, the banner of Saint Oswald, and Æthelflaed's strange flag which showed a white goose holding a sword and a cross. The goose was the symbol of Saint Werburgh, a holy woman who had miraculously rid a cornfield of marauding geese, though it was beyond my wits to understand why a job any ten-year-old could have done with a loud voice was considered a miracle. Even a three-legged dog could have rid the field of geese, but that was not a comment I would have dared make to Æthelflaed, who held the goose-frightening saint in the highest regard.

The burh at Ceaster had been built by the Romans so the ramparts were of stone, unlike the burhs we Saxons built that had walls of earth and timber. We passed under the high fighting platform of the gateway, threading a tunnel lit by torches and so into the main street that ran arrow straight between high stone buildings. The sound of horses' hooves echoed from the walls, then the bells of Saint Peter's church rang out to celebrate Æthelflaed's return.

Æthelflaed and most of her men went to the church to give thanks for the victory before gathering in the great hall that stood at the center of Ceaster's streets. Sihtric and I put Haki into a small stone hut, leaving his hands tied for the night. "I have gold," he said in Danish.

"You'll have straw for a bed and piss for ale," Sihtric told him, then we shut the door and left two men to guard him. "So we're off to Gleawecestre?" Sihtric said to me as we went to the hall.

"So she says."

"You'll be happy then."

"Me?"

He grinned toothlessly. "The redhead at the Wheatsheaf."

"One of many, Sihtric," I said airily, "one of many."

"And your girl in the farm near Cirrenceastre too," he added.

"She is a widow," I said with as much dignity as I could muster, "and I'm told it's our Christian duty to protect widows."

"You call that protecting her?" he laughed. "Are you going to marry her?"

"Of course not. I'll marry for land."

"You should be married," he said. "How old are you?"

"Twenty-one, I think."

"Should be long married, then," he said. "What about Ælfwynn?"

"What about her?" I asked.

"She's a pretty little mare," Sihtric said, "and I dare say she knows how to gallop." He pushed open the heavy door and we walked into the hall that was lit by rushlights and by a huge fire in a crude stone hearth that had cracked the Roman floor. There were not enough tables for both the burh's garrison and for the men Æthelflaed had brought north, so some ate squatting on the floor, though I was given a place at the high table close to Æthelflaed. She was flanked by two priests, one of whom intoned a long prayer in Latin before we were allowed to start on the food.

I was scared of Æthelflaed. She had a hard face, though men said she had been beautiful as a young woman. In that year, 911, she must have been forty or more years old, and her hair, which was golden, had pale gray streaks. She had very blue eyes and a gaze that could unsettle the bravest of men. That gaze was cold and thoughtful, as if she were reading your thoughts and despising them. I was not the only person who was scared of Æthelflaed. Her own daughter, Ælfwynn, would hide from her mother. I liked Ælfwynn, who was full of laughter and mischief. She was a little younger than I was and we had spent much of our childhood together, and many people thought the two of us should be married. I did not know whether Æthelflaed thought that a good idea. She seemed to dislike me, but she seemed to dislike most people, and yet, for all that coldness, she was adored in Mercia. Her husband, Æthelred, Lord of Mercia, was acknowledged as the ruler of the country, but it was his estranged wife people loved.

"Gleawecestre," she now said to me.

"Yes, my lady."

"You'll take all the plunder, all of it. Use wagons. And take the prisoners."

"Yes, my lady." The prisoners were mostly children we had taken from Haki's steadings during the first days of our raiding. They would be sold as slaves.

"And you must arrive before Saint Cuthbert's Day," she repeated that command. "You understand?"

"Before Saint Cuthbert's Day," I said dutifully.

She gave me that long, silent stare. The priests flanking her gazed at me too, their expressions as hostile as hers. "And you'll take Haki," she went on.

"And Haki," I said.

"And you will hang him in front of my husband's hall."

"Make it slow," one of the priests said. There are two ways of hanging a man, the quick way and the slow, agonizing way.

"Yes, Father," I said.

"But show him to the people first," Æthelflaed ordered.

"I will, my lady, of course," I said, then hesitated.

"What?" She saw my uncertainty.

"Folk will want to know why you stayed here, my lady," I said.

She bridled at that, and the second priest frowned. "It is none of their business . . ." he began.

Æthelflaed waved him to silence. "Many Norsemen are leaving Ireland," she said carefully, "and wanting to settle here. They must be stopped."

"Haki's defeat will make them fearful," I suggested carefully.

She ignored my clumsy compliment. "Ceaster prevents them using the River Dee," she said, "but the Mærse is open. I shall build a burh on its bank."

"A good idea, my lady," I said and received a look of such scorn that I blushed.

She dismissed me with a gesture and I went back to the mutton stew. I watched her from the corner of my eye, seeing the hard jawline, the bitterness on the lips, and I wondered what in God's name had attracted my father to her and why men revered her.

But tomorrow I would be free of her.

"Men follow her," Sihtric said, "because other than your father she's the only one who's ever been willing to fight."

We were traveling south, following a road I had come to know well in the last few years. The road followed the boundary between Mercia and Wales, a boundary that was the subject of constant argument between the Welsh kingdoms and the Mercians. The Welsh were our enemies, of course, but that enmity was confused because they were also Christian and we would never have won the battle at Teotanheale without the help of those Welsh Christians. Sometimes they fought for Christ, as they had at Teotanheale, but just as often they fought for plunder, driving cattle and slaves back to their mountain valleys. Those constant raids meant there were burhs all along the road, fortified towns where folk could take refuge when an enemy came, and from where a garrison could sally out to attack that enemy.

I rode with thirty-six men and Godric, my servant. Four of the warriors were always ahead, scouting the road margins for fear of an ambush, while the rest of us guarded Haki and the two carts loaded with plunder. We also guarded eighteen children, bound for the slave markets, though Æthelflaed insisted we display the captives before the folk of Gleawecestre first. "She wants to put on a show," Sihtric told me.

"She does!" Father Fraomar agreed. "We have to let the people in Gleawecestre know that we're defeating Christ's enemies." He was one of Æthelflaed's tame priests, still a young man, eager and enthusiastic. He nodded toward the cart ahead of us that was loaded with armor and weapons. "We shall sell those and the money will go toward the new burh, praise God."

"Praise God," I said dutifully.

And money, I knew, was Æthelflaed's problem. If she was to build her new burh to guard the River Mærse she needed money and there was never enough. Her husband received the land-rents and the merchants' taxes and the customs payments, and Lord Æthelred hated Æthelflaed. She might be loved in Mercia, but Æthelred controlled the silver, and men were loath to offend him. Even now, when Æthelred lay sick in Gleawecestre, men paid him homage. Only the bravest and wealthiest risked his anger by giving men and silver to Æthelflaed.

And Æthelred was dying. He had been struck by a spear on the back of the head at the battle of Teotanheale and the spear had pierced his helmet and broken through his skull. No one had expected him to survive, but he did, though some rumors said he was as good as dead, that he raved like a moonstruck madman, that he dribbled and twitched, and that sometimes he howled like a gutted wolf. All Mercia expected his death, and all Mercia wondered what would follow that death. That was something no one spoke of, at least not openly, though in secret they spoke of little else.

Yet to my surprise Father Fraomar spoke of it on the first night. We were traveling slowly because of the carts and prisoners and had stopped at a farmstead near Westune. This part of Mercia was newly settled, made safe because of the burh at Ceaster. The farm had belonged to a Dane, but now a one-eyed Mercian lived there with a wife, four sons, and six slaves. His house was a hovel of mud, wood, and straw, his cattle shed a poor thing of leaking wattles, but all of it was surrounded by a well-made palisade of oak trunks. "Welsh aren't far away," he explained the expensive palisade.

"You can't defend this with six slaves," I said.

"Neighbors come here," he said curtly.

"And helped build it?"

"They did."

We tied Haki's ankles, made sure the bonds on his wrists were tightly knotted, then shackled him to a plow that stood abandoned beside a dung-heap. The eighteen children were crammed into the house with two men to guard them, while the rest of us found what comfort we could in the dung-spattered yard. We lit a fire. Gerbruht ate steadily, feeding his barrel-sized belly, while Redbad, another Frisian, played songs on his reed-pipes. The wistful notes filled the night air with melancholy. The sparks flew upward. It had rained earlier, but the clouds were clearing away to show the stars. I watched some of the sparks drift onto the hovel's roof and wondered if the thatch would smolder, but the moss-covered straw was damp and the sparks died quickly.

"The Nunnaminster," Father Fraomar said suddenly.

"The Nunnaminster?" I asked after a pause.

The priest had also been watching the drifting sparks fade and die on the roof. "The convent in Wintanceaster where the Lady Ælswith died," he explained, though the explanation made me no wiser.

"King Alfred's wife?"

"God rest her soul," he said and made the sign of the cross. "She built the convent after the king's death."

"What of it?" I asked, still puzzled.

"Part of the convent burned down after her death," he explained. "It was caused by sparks lodging in the roof-straw."

"This thatch is too wet," I said, nodding toward the house.

"Of course." The priest was staring at the sparks settling on the thatch. "Some folk say the fire was the devil's revenge," he paused to cross himself, "because the Lady Ælswith was such a pious soul and she'd escaped him."

"My father always told me she was a vengeful bitch," I ventured.

Father Fraomar frowned, then relented to offer a wry smile. "God rest her soul. I hear she was not an easy woman."

"Which one is?" Sihtric asked.

"The Lady Æthelflaed won't wish it," Fraomar said softly.

I hesitated because the conversation was now touching on dangerous things. "Won't wish what?" I finally asked.

"To go to a nunnery."

"Is that what will happen?"

"What else?" Fraomar asked bleakly. "Her husband dies, she's a widow, and a widow with property and power. Men won't want her marrying again. Her new husband might become too powerful. Besides . . ." his voice died away.

"Besides?" Sihtric asked quietly.

"The Lord Æthelred has made a will, God preserve him."

"And the will," I said slowly, "says his wife is to go to a nunnery?"

"What else can she do?" Fraomar asked. "It's the custom."

"I can't see her as a nun," I said.

"Oh, she's a saintly woman. A good woman," Fraomar spoke eagerly, then remembered she was an adulterer. "Not perfect, of course," he went on, "but we all fall short, do we not? We have all sinned."

"And her daughter?" I asked. "Ælfwynn?"

"Oh, a silly girl," Fraomar said without hesitation.

"But if someone marries her . . . ," I suggested, but was interrupted.

"She's a woman! She can't inherit her father's power!" Father Fraomar laughed at the very idea. "No, the best thing for Ælfwynn would be to marry abroad. To marry far away! Maybe a Frankish lord? Either that or join her mother in the nunnery."

The conversation was dangerous because no one was certain what might happen when Æthelred died, and that death must surely be soon. Mercia had no king, but Æthelred, the Lord of Mercia, had almost the same powers. He would dearly have loved to be king, but he depended on the West Saxons to help him defend Mercia's frontiers, and the West Saxons wanted no king in Mercia, or rather they wanted their own king to rule there. Yet, though Mercia and Wessex were allies, there was little love between them. Mercians had a proud past, now they were a client state, and if Edward of Wessex were to proclaim his kingship there could be unrest. No one knew what would happen, just as no one knew who they should support. Should they give allegiance to Wessex? Or to one of the Mercian ealdormen?

"It's just a pity that Lord Æthelred has no heir," Father Fraomar said.

"No legitimate heir," I said, and to my surprise the priest laughed.

"No legitimate heir," he agreed, then crossed himself. "But the Lord will provide," he added piously.

Next day the sky darkened with thick clouds that spread from the Welsh hills. By mid-morning it was raining and it went on raining as we made our slow way south. The roads we followed had been made by the Romans and we spent every subsequent night in the ruins of Roman forts. We saw no marauding Welsh, and the battle of Teotanheale had ensured that no Danes would harass us this far south.

The rain and the prisoners made it a slow journey, but at last we came to Gleawecestre, the capital city of Mercia. We arrived two days before the feast of Saint Cuthbert, though it was not till we were inside the city that I discovered why Æthelflaed had thought that date so important. Father Fraomar had spurred ahead to announce our arrival, and the bells of the city's churches were ringing to greet us, and a small crowd was waiting at the gate's arch. I unfurled our banners: my own wolf's head, the flag of Saint Oswald, Æthelred's white horse, and Æthelflaed's goose. Haki's banner was carried by Godric, my servant, who dragged it on the wet road. Our small procession was led by one cart of plunder, then came the child prisoners, then Haki who was tied by rope to the tail of Godric's horse. The second cart brought up the rear, while my warriors rode on either side of the column. It was a petty display. After Teotanheale we had dragged over twenty wagons of plunder through the city, along with prisoners, captured horses, and a dozen enemy banners, but even my small procession gave the citizens of Gleawecestre something to celebrate and we were cheered all the way from the north gate to the entrance of Æthelred's palace. A pair of priests hurled horse dung at Haki and the crowds took up the sport as small boys ran alongside jeering at the man.

And there, waiting for us at Æthelred's gate, was Eardwulf, the commander of Lord Æthelred's household troops and brother to Eadith, the woman who slept with Lord Æthelred. Eardwulf was clever, handsome, ambitious, and effective. He had led Æthelred's troops against the Welsh and done much damage, and men said he had fought well at Teotanheale. "His power," my father had told me, "comes from between his sister's thighs, but don't underestimate him. He's dangerous."

The dangerous Eardwulf was in a coat of mail, polished to a bright shine, and wearing a dark blue cloak edged with otter fur. He was bare-headed and his dark hair was oiled sleekly back to be tied by a brown ribbon. His sword, a heavy blade, was scabbarded in soft leather trimmed with gold. He was flanked by a pair of priests and by a half-dozen of his men, all wearing Æthelred's symbol of the white horse. He smiled when he saw us. I saw his eyes flick toward Æthelflaed's standard as he sauntered toward us. "Going to market, Lord Uhtred?" he asked.

"Slaves, armor, swords, spears, axes," I said. "Do you want to buy?"

"And him?" He jerked a thumb toward Haki.

I twisted in my saddle. "Haki, a Norse chieftain who thought to make himself rich from Mercia."

"Are you selling him too?"

"Hanging him," I said, "slowly. My lady wanted us to hang him right here."

"Your lady?"

"Yours too," I said, knowing that would annoy him, "the Lady Æthelflaed."

If he was annoyed he did not show it, instead he smiled again. "She has been busy," he said lightly, "and is she planning to be here as well?"

I shook my head. "She has work in the north."

"And I thought she would be here for the Witan in two days," he said sarcastically.

"Witan?" I asked.

"It's none of your business," he said tartly. "You are not invited."

But the Witan, I noted, was to be held on Saint Cuthbert's feast day and that was surely why Æthelflaed had wanted us to arrive before the great men of Mercia met in council. She was reminding them that she fought their enemies.

Eardwulf walked to Haki, looked him up and down, then turned back to me. "I see you fly the Lord Æthelred's banner."

"Of course," I said.

"And in the skirmish where you captured this creature," he nodded toward Haki, "did you fly it there too?"

"Whenever my lady fights for Mercia," I said, "she flies her husband's banner."

"Then the prisoners and the plunder belong to Lord Æthelred," Eardwulf said.

"I'm ordered to sell them," I said.

"Are you?" He laughed. "Well now you have new orders. They all belong to Lord Æthelred so you will give them to me." He gazed at me, daring me to contradict him. I must have looked belligerent because his men half lowered their spears.

Father Fraomar had reappeared and darted to the side of my horse. "No fighting," he hissed at me.

"My Lord Uhtred would not dream of drawing a sword against Lord Æthelred's household warriors," Eardwulf said. He beckoned to his men. "Take it all inside," he ordered, indicating carts, plunder, Haki, and the slaves, "and do thank the Lady Æthelflaed," he was looking at me again, "for her little contribution to her husband's treasury."

I watched his men take the plunder and slaves through the gateway. Eardwulf smiled when it was done, then gave me a mocking smile. "And the Lady Æthelflaed," he asked, "has no desire to attend the Witan?"

"She's invited?" I asked.

"Of course not, she's a woman. But she might be curious about the Witan's decisions."

He was trying to discover whether Æthelflaed would be in Gleawecestre. I half thought of saying I had no idea what she planned, then decided to tell the truth. "She won't be here," I said, "because she's busy. She's making a burh on the Mærse."

"Oh, a burh on the Mærse!" he repeated, then laughed.

The gates closed behind him.

"Bastard," I said.

"He had the right," Father Fraomar explained, "the Lord Æthelred is the husband of the Lady Æthelflaed, so what is hers is his."

"Æthelred's an unwiped pig-sucking bastard," I said, staring at the closed gates.

"He is the Lord of Mercia," Father Fraomar said uneasily. He was a supporter of Æthelflaed, but he sensed that her husband's death would strip her of both power and influence.

"Whatever the bastard is," Sihtric put in, "he won't offer us any ale."

"Ale is a good idea," I growled.

"The redhead at the Wheatsheaf, then?" he asked, then grinned. "Unless you're going to learn more about farming?"

I grinned back. My father had given me a farm north of Cirrenceastre, saying I should learn husbandry. "A man should know as much about crops, pasture, and cattle as his steward knows," my father had growled to me, "otherwise the bastard will cheat you blind." He had been pleased at the number of days I spent at the estate, though I confess I had learned almost nothing about crops, pasture, or cattle, but I had learned a great deal about the young widow to whom I had given the farm's great hall as her home.

"The Wheatsheaf for now," I said and kicked Hearding down the street. And tomorrow, I thought, I would ride to my widow.

The tavern's sign was a great wooden carving of a wheatsheaf and I rode beneath it into the rain-soaked courtyard and let a servant take the horse. Father Fraomar, I knew, was right. The Lord Æthelred did have the legal right to take whatever belonged to his wife because nothing belonged to her that was not his, yet still Eardwulf's action had surprised me. Æthelred and Æthelflaed had lived for years in a state of warfare, though it was war without fighting. He had the legal power in Mercia while she had the love of the Mercians. It would have been easy enough for Æthelred to order his wife's arrest and captivity, but her brother was the King of Wessex, and Mercia only survived because the West Saxons came to its rescue whenever enemies pressed too hard. And so husband and wife hated each other, tolerated each other, and pretended that no feud existed, which was why Æthelflaed took such care to fly her husband's banner.

I was daydreaming of taking revenge on Eardwulf as I ducked through the tavern's door. I was dreaming of gutting him or beheading him or listening to his pleas for mercy while I held Raven-Beak at his throat. The bastard, I thought, the sniveling, pompous, grease-haired, arrogant bastard.

"Earsling," a harsh voice challenged me from beside the Wheat-sheaf's hearth. "What rancid demon brought you here to spoil my day?" I stared. And stared. Because the last person I had ever expected to see in Æthelred's stronghold of Gleawecestre was staring at me. "Well, earsling?" he demanded, "what are you doing here?"

It was my father.

PART ONE

The Dying Lord

One

My son looked tired and angry. He was wet, covered in mud, his hair was like a damp haystack after a good romp, and one of his boots was slashed. The leather was stained black where a blade had pierced his calf, but he was not limping so I had no need to worry about him, except that he was gaping at me like a moon-struck idiot. "Don't just stare at me, idiot," I told him, "buy me some ale. Tell the girl you want it from the black barrel. Sihtric, it's good to see you."

"And you, lord," Sihtric said.

"Father!" my son said, still gaping.

"Who did you think it was?" I asked. "The holy ghost?" I made room on the bench. "Sit beside me," I told Sihtric, "and tell me some news. Stop gawping," I said to Uhtred, "and have one of the girls bring us some ale. From the black barrel!"

"Why the black barrel, lord?" Sihtric asked as he sat.

"It's brewed from our barley," I explained, "he keeps it for people he likes." I leaned back against the wall. It hurt to bend forward, it hurt even to sit upright, it hurt to breathe. Everything hurt, yet it was a marvel that I lived at all. Cnut Longsword had near killed me with his blade Ice-Spite and it was small consolation that Serpent-Breath had sliced his throat in the same heartbeat that his sword had broken a rib and pierced my lung. "Christ Jesus," Finan had told me, "but the grass was slippery with blood. It looked like a Samhain pig slaughtering, it did."

But the slipperiness had been Cnut's blood, and Cnut was dead and his army destroyed. The Danes had been driven from much of northern Mercia and the Saxons gave thanks to their nailed god for that deliverance. Some of them doubtless prayed that they would be delivered from me too, but I lived. They were Christians, I am not, though rumors spread that it was a Christian priest who saved my life. Æthelflaed had me carried in a cart to her home in Cirrenceastre and a priest famed as a healer and bone-setter tended me. Æthelflaed said he pushed a reed through my ribs and a gust of foul air came from the hole. "It blew out," she told me, "and stank like a cesspit." "That's the evil leaving him," the priest had explained, or so she said, and then he plugged the wound with cow dung. The shit formed a crust and the priest said it would stop the evil getting back inside me. Is that true? I don't know. All I know is that it took weeks of pain, weeks in which I expected to die, and that some time in the new year I managed to struggle to my feet again. Now, almost two months later, I could ride a horse and walk a mile or so, yet I had still not regained my old strength, and Serpent-Breath felt heavy in my hand. And the pain was always there, sometimes excruciating, sometimes bearable, and all day, every day, the wound leaked filthy stinking pus. The Christian sorcerer probably sealed the wound before all the evil left and sometimes I wondered if he did that on purpose because the Christians do hate me, or most of them do. They smile and sing their psalms and preach that their creed is all about love, but tell them you believe in a different god and suddenly it's all spittle and spite. So most days I felt old and feeble and useless, and some days I was not even sure I wanted to live.

"How did you get here, lord?" Sihtric asked me.

"I rode, of course, how do you think?"

That was not entirely true. It was not far from Cirrenceastre to Gleawecestre, and I had ridden for some of the journey, but a few miles short of the city I climbed into a cart and lay on a bed of straw. God, it hurt climbing onto that cart's bed. Then I let myself be carried into the city, and when Eardwulf saw me I groaned and pretended to be too weak to recognize him. The slick-haired bastard had ridden alongside the cart telling silky-tongued lies. "It is sad indeed to see you thus, Lord Uhtred," he had said and what he meant was that it was a joy to see me feeble and maybe dying. "You are an example to us all!" he had said, speaking very slow and loud as if I were an imbecile. I just groaned and said nothing. "We never expected you to come," he went on, "but here you are." The bastard.

The Witan had been summoned to meet on Saint Cuthbert's feast day. The summons had been issued over the horse-seal of Æthelred and it demanded the presence in Gleawecestre of Mercia's leading men, the ealdormen and the bishops, the abbots and the thegns. The summons declared that they were called to "advise" the Lord of Mercia, but as rumor insisted that the Lord of Mercia was now a driveling cripple who dribbled piss down his legs it was more likely that the Witan had been called to approve whatever mischief Eardwulf had devised. I had not expected a summons, but to my astonishment a messenger brought me a parchment heavy with Æthelred's great seal. Why did he want me there? I was his wife's chief supporter, yet he had invited me. None of the other leading men who supported Æthelflaed had been called, yet I was summoned. Why? "He wants to kill you, lord," Finan had suggested.

"I'm near enough dead already. Why should he bother?"

"He wants you there," Finan had suggested slowly, "because they're planning to shit all over Æthelflaed, and if you're there they can't claim no one spoke for her."

That seemed a weak reason to me, but I could think of no other. "Maybe."

"And they know you're not healed. You can't cause them trouble."

"Maybe," I said again. It was plain that this Witan had been summoned to decide Mercia's future, and equally plain that Æthelred would do everything he could to make certain his estranged wife had no part in that future, so why invite me? I would speak for her, they knew that, but they also knew I was weakened by injury. So was I there to prove that every opinion had been aired? It seemed strange to me, but if they were relying on my weakness to make sure that my advice was ignored then I wanted to encourage that belief, and that was why I had taken such care to appear feeble to Eardwulf. Let the bastard think me helpless.

Which I almost was. Except that I lived.

My son brought ale and dragged a stool to sit beside me. He was worried about me, but I brushed away his questions and asked my own. He told me about the fight with Haki, then complained that Eardwulf had stolen the slaves and plunder. "How could I stop him?" he asked.

"You weren't meant to stop him," I said and, when he looked puzzled, explained. "Æthelflaed knew that would happen. Why else send you to Gleawecestre?"

"She needs the money!"

"She needs Mercia's support more," I said, and he still looked puzzled. "By sending you here," I went on, "she's showing that she's fighting. If she really wanted money she'd have sent the slaves to Lundene."

"So she thinks a few slaves and two wagon-loads of rusted mail will influence the Witan?"

"Did you see any of Æthelred's men in Ceaster?"

"No, of course not."

"And what is a ruler's first duty?"

He thought for a few heartbeats. "To defend his land?"

"So if Mercia is looking for a new ruler?" I asked.

"They'll want someone," he said slowly, "who can fight?"

"Someone who can fight," I said, "and lead, and inspire."

"You?" he asked.

I almost hit him for his stupidity, but he was no longer a child. "Not me," I said instead.

My son frowned as he considered. He knew the answer I wanted, but was too stubborn to give it. "Eardwulf?" he suggested instead. I said nothing and he thought a moment longer. "He's been fighting the Welsh," he went on, "and men say he's good."

"He's been fighting bare-arsed cattle raiders," I said scornfully, "nothing else. When was the last time a Welsh army invaded Mercia? Besides, Eardwulf isn't noble."

"So if he can't lead Mercia," my son said slowly, "who can?"

"You know who can," I said, and when he still refused to name her, I did. "Æthelflaed."

"Æthelflaed," he repeated the name and then just shook his

head. I knew he was wary of her and probably frightened of her too, and I knew she was scornful of him, just as she scorned her own daughter. She was her father's child in that way; she disliked flippant and carefree people, treasuring serious souls who thought life a grim duty. She put up with me, maybe because she knew that in battle I was as serious and grim as any of her dreary priests.

"So why not Æthelflaed?" I asked.

"Because she's a woman," he said.

"So?"

"She's a woman!"

"I know that! I've seen her tits."

"The Witan will never choose a woman to rule," he said firmly.

"That's true," Sihtric put in.

"Who else can they choose?" I asked.

"Her brother?" my son suggested, and he was probably right. Edward, King of Wessex, wanted the throne of Mercia, but he did not want to just take it. He wanted an invitation. Maybe that was what the Witan was supposed to agree? I could think of no other reason why the nobility and high churchmen had been summoned. It made sense that Æthelred's successor should be chosen now, before Æthelred died, to avert the squabbling and even outright war that sometimes follows a ruler's death, and I was certain that Æthelred himself wanted the satisfaction of knowing that his wife would not inherit his power. He would let rabid dogs gnaw on his balls before he allowed that. So who would inherit? Not Eardwulf, I was sure. He was competent, he was brave enough, and he was no fool, but the Witan would want a man of birth, and Eardwulf, though not low-born, was no ealdorman. Nor was there any ealdorman in Mercia who stood head and shoulders above the rest except perhaps for Æthelfrith who ruled much of the land north of Lundene. Æthelfrith was the richest of all Mercia's noblemen after Æthelred, but he had stood aloof from Gleawecestre and its squabbles, allying himself with the West Saxons and, so far as I knew, he had not bothered to attend the Witan. And it probably did not matter what the Witan advised because, in the end, the West Saxons would decide who or what was best for Mercia.

Or so I thought.

And I should have thought harder.

The Witan began, of course it began, with a tedious service in Saint Oswald's church, which was part of an abbey built by Æthelred. I had arrived on crutches, which I did not need, but I was determined to look more sickly than I felt. Ricseg, the abbot, welcomed me fulsomely, even trying to bow which was difficult because he had a belly like a pregnant sow. "It distresses me to see you in such pain, Lord Uhtred," he said, meaning he would have jumped for joy if he was not so damned fat. "May God bless you," he added, sketching a plump hand in the sign of a cross, while secretly praying that his god would flatten me with a thunderbolt. I thanked him as insincerely as he had blessed me, then took a stone bench at the back of the church and leaned against the wall, flanked there by Finan and by Osferth. Ricseg waddled about as he greeted men, and I heard the clatter of weapons being dropped outside the church. I had left my son and Sihtric out there to make sure no bastard stole Serpent-Breath. I leaned my head on the wall and tried to guess the cost of the silver candlesticks that stood at either side of the altar. They were vast things, heavy as war axes and dripping with scented beeswax, while the light from their dozen candles glinted from the silver reliquaries and golden dishes piled on the altar.

The Christian church is a clever thing. The moment a lord becomes wealthy he builds a church or a convent. Æthelflaed had insisted on making a church in Ceaster even before she began surveying the walls or deepening the ditch. I told her it was a waste of money, all she achieved was to build a place where men like Ricseg could get fat, but she insisted anyway. There are hundreds of men and women living off the churches, abbeys, and convents built by lords, and most do nothing except eat, drink, and mutter an occasional prayer. Monks work, of course. They till the fields, grub up weeds, cut firewood, draw water, and copy manuscripts, but only so their superiors can live like nobles. It is a clever scheme, to get other men to pay for your luxuries. I growled.

"The ceremony will be over soon," Finan said soothingly, thinking that the growl was a sign of pain.

"Shall I ask for honeyed wine, lord?" Osferth asked me, concerned. He was King Alfred's one bastard and a more decent man never walked this earth. I have often wondered what kind of king Osferth would have made if he had been born to a wife instead of to some scared servant girl who had lifted her skirts for a royal prick. He would have been a great king, judicious and clever and honest, but Osferth was ever marked by his bastardry. His father had tried to make Osferth a priest, but the son had wilfully chosen the way of the warrior and I was lucky to have him as one of my household.

I closed my eyes. Monks were chanting and one of the sorcerers was wafting a metal bowl on the end of a chain to spread smoke through the church. I sneezed, and it hurt, then there was a sudden commotion at the door and I thought it must be Æthelred arriving, but when I opened one eye I saw it was Bishop Wulfheard with a pack of fawning priests at his heels. "If there's mischief," I said, "that tit-sucking bastard will be in the middle of it."

"Not so loud, lord," Osferth reproved me.

"Tit-sucking?" Finan asked.

I nodded. "That's what they tell me in the Wheatsheaf."

"Oh no! No!" Osferth said, shocked. "That can't be true. He's married!"

I laughed, then closed my eyes again. "You shouldn't say things like that," I told Osferth.

"Why not, lord? It's just a foul rumor! The bishop is married."

"You shouldn't say it," I said, "because it hurts so much when I laugh."

Wulfheard was Bishop of Hereford, but he spent most of his time in Gleawecestre because that was where Æthelred had his deep coffers. Wulfheard hated me and had burned down my barns at Fagranforda in an effort to drive me from Mercia. He was not one of the fat priests, instead he was lean as a blade with a hard face that he forced into a smile when he saw me. "My Lord Uhtred," he greeted me.

"Wulfheard," I responded churlishly.

"I am delighted to see you in church," he said.

"But not wearing that," one of his attendant priests spat, and I opened my eyes to see him pointing at the hammer I wore about my neck. It was the symbol of Thor.

"Careful, priest," I warned the man, though I was too weak to do much about his insolence.

"Father Penda," Wulfheard said, "let us pray that God persuades the Lord Uhtred to cast away his pagan trinkets. God listens to our prayers," he added to me.

"He does?"

"And I prayed for your recovery," he lied.

"So did I," I said, touching Thor's hammer.

Wulfheard gave a vague smile and turned away. His priests followed him like scurrying ducklings, all except for the young Father Penda who stood close and belligerent. "You disgrace God's church," he said loudly.

"Just go away, Father," Finan said.

"That is an abomination!" the priest said, almost shouting as he pointed at the hammer. Men turned to look at us. "An abomination unto God," Penda said, then leaned down to snatch the hammer away. I grasped his black robe and pulled him toward me and the effort sent a stab of pain through my left side. The priest's robe was damp on my face and it stank of dung, but the thick wool hid my agonized grimace as the wound in my side savaged me. I gasped, but then Finan managed to wrestle the priest away from me. "An abomination!" Penda shouted as he was pulled backward. Osferth half rose to help Finan, but I caught his sleeve to stop him. Penda lunged at me again, but then two of his fellow priests managed to grasp him by the shoulders and pull him away.

"A silly man," Osferth said sternly, "but he's right. You shouldn't wear the hammer in a church, lord."

I pressed my spine into the wall, trying to breathe slowly. The pain came in waves, sharp then sullen. Would it ever end? I was tired of it, and perhaps the pain dulled my thoughts.

I was thinking that Æthelred, Lord of Mercia, was dying. That much was obvious. It was a wonder he had survived this long, but it was plain that the Witan had been called to consider what should happen after his death, and I had just learned that the Ealdorman Æthelhelm, King Edward's father-in-law, was in Glea-wecestre. He was not in the church, at least I could not see him, and he was a difficult man to miss because he was big, jovial, and loud. I liked Æthelhelm and trusted him not at all. And he was here for the Witan. How did I know that? Because Father Penda, the spitting priest, was my man. Penda was in my pay and when I had pulled him close he had whispered in my ear, "Æthelhelm's here. He came this morning." He had started to hiss something else, but then he had been pulled away.

I listened to the monks chanting and to the murmur of the priests gathered around the altar where a great golden crucifix reflected the light of the scented candles. The altar was hollow and in its belly lay a massive silver coffin that glinted with crystal inserts. That coffin alone must have cost as much as the church, and if a man bent down and looked through the small crystals he could dimly see a skeleton lying on a bed of costly blue silk. On special days the coffin was opened and the skeleton displayed and I had heard of miracles being performed on folk who paid to touch the yellow bones. Boils were magically healed, warts vanished, and the crippled walked, and all because the bones were said to be those of Saint Oswald, which, if true, would have been a miracle in itself because I had found the bones. They had probably be-longed to some obscure monk, though for all I knew the remains might have come from a swineherd, though when I'd said that to Father Cuthbert he said that more than one swineherd had become a saint. You cannot win with Christians.

Besides the thirty or forty priests there must have been at least a hundred and twenty men in the church, all standing beneath the high beams where sparrows flew. This ceremony in the church was supposed to bring the nailed god's blessing on the Witan's deliberations, so it was no surprise when Bishop Wulfheard delivered a powerful sermon about the wisdom of listening to the advice of sober men, good men, older men, and rulers. "Let the elders be treated with double honor," he harangued us, "because that is the word of God!" Maybe it was, but in Wulfheard's mouth it meant that no one had been summoned to give advice, but rather to agree with whatever had already been decided between the bishop, Æthelred, and, as I had just learned, Æthelhelm of Wessex.

Æthelhelm was the richest man in Wessex after the king, his son-in-law. He owned vast tracts of land and his household warriors formed almost a third of the West Saxon army. He was Edward's chief counselor and his sudden presence in Gleawecestre surely meant that Edward of Wessex had decided what he wanted with Mercia. He must have sent Æthelhelm to announce the decision, but Edward and Æthelhelm both knew that Mercia was proud and prickly. Mercia would not simply accept Edward as king, so he must be offering something in return, but what? True, Edward could just declare himself king on Æthelred's death, but that would provoke unrest, even outright opposition. Edward, I was sure, wanted Mercia to beg, and so he had sent Æthelhelm, genial Æthelhelm, generous Æthelhelm, gregarious Æthelhelm. Everyone liked Æthelhelm. I liked Æthelhelm, but his presence in Gleawecestre suggested mischief.

I managed to sleep through most of Wulfheard's sermon and then, after the choir had chanted an interminable psalm, Osferth and Finan helped me leave the church while my son carried Serpent-Breath and my crutches. I exaggerated my weakness by leaning heavily on Finan's shoulders and shuffling my feet. Most of it was pretense, but not all. I was tired of the pain, and tired of the stinking pus that seeped from the wound. A few men stopped to express their regret at my feeble appearance, and some of that sympathy was genuine, but many men took an obvious pleasure in my downfall. Before I had been wounded they had been frightened of me, now they could safely despise me.

Father Penda's news had hardly been necessary because Æthelhelm was waiting in the great hall, but I supposed the young priest had wanted to give me what small warning he could as well as show that he was earning the gold I gave him. The West Saxon ealdorman was surrounded by lesser men, all of whom understood that the real power in this hall was his because he spoke for Edward of Wessex, and without the West Saxon army there would be no Mercia. I watched him, wondering why he was here. He was a big man, broad faced, with thinning hair, a ready smile, and kindly eyes that looked shocked when he saw me. He shook off the men who spoke with him and hurried to my side. "My dear Lord Uhtred," he said.

"Lord Æthelhelm." I made my voice slow and hoarse.

"My dear Lord Uhtred," he said again, taking one of my hands in both of his. "I cannot express what I feel! Tell me what we can do for you." He pressed my hand. "Tell me!" he urged.

"You can let me die in peace," I said.

"I'm sure you have many years yet," he said, "unlike my dear wife."

That was news to me. I knew Æthelhelm was married to a pale, thin creature who had brought him half of Defnascir as her dowry. She had somehow given birth to a succession of fat, healthy babes. It was a marvel she had lasted this long. "I'm sorry," I said weakly.

"She ails, poor thing. She wastes away and the end can't be long now." He did not sound particularly upset, but I supposed the marriage to the wraith-like wife had only ever been a convenience that brought Æthelhelm land. "I'll marry again," he said, "and I trust you will come to the wedding!"

"If I live," I said.

"Of course you will! I'll pray for you!"

He needed to pray for Æthelred too. The Lord of Mercia had not attended the church service, but was waiting enthroned on the dais at the western end of the great hall. He slumped there, vacant-eyed, his body swathed in a great cloak of beaver fur. His red hair had turned white, though most of it was hidden beneath a woolen cap which, I supposed, hid his wound. I had no love for Æthelred, but I felt sorry for him. He seemed to become aware of my gaze because he stirred, raised his head and looked down the hall to where I had taken a bench at the back. He stared at me for a moment, then he leaned his head against the chair's high back and his mouth fell slackly open.

Bishop Wulfheard climbed the dais. I feared he would deliver another sermon, but instead he rapped on the wooden boards with the base of his staff, and when silence fell over the hall contented himself with a brief blessing. Æthelhelm, I noticed, took a modest place to one side of the assembly, while Eardwulf stood against the other wall and between them the leading men of Mercia sat on uncomfortable benches. Æthelred's household warriors lined the walls, the only men allowed to carry weapons in the hall. My son slipped through the door and crouched beside me. "The swords are safe," he muttered.

"Sihtric's there?"

"He is."

Bishop Wulfheard spoke so softly that I had to lean forward to hear what he said, and leaning forward hurt me. I endured the pain to listen. It was the Lord Æthelred's pleasure, the bishop said, to see the kingdom of Mercia safer and larger than it had been for many years. "We have gained land by the strength of our swords," Wulfheard said, "and by the grace of God we have driven the pagans from the fields our forefathers tilled. We thank God for this!"

"Amen," Lord Æthelhelm interjected loudly.

"We owe this blessing," Wulfheard continued, "to the victory won last year by our Lord Æthelred with the help of his staunch West Saxon allies." He gestured toward Æthelhelm and the hall was filled with the noise of men stamping their feet in approbation. The bastard, I thought. Æthelred had been wounded from behind, and the battle had been gained by my men, not his.

The bishop waited for silence. "We have gained land," he went on, "good farmland, and it is Lord Æthelred's pleasure to grant that land to those who fought for him last year," and the bishop pointed to a table at the side of the hall where two priests sat behind a heap of documents. The bribe was obvious. Support whatever Æthelred proposed and a man could expect a grant of land.

"There'll be none for me," I growled.

Finan chuckled. "He'll give you enough land for a grave, lord."

"And yet," the bishop was speaking a little louder now, which meant I could lean back against the wall, "the pagans still hold towns which were a part of our ancient kingdom. Our land is still fouled by their presence, and if we are to bequeath to our children the fields that our forefathers plowed then we must gird our loins and expel the heathen just as Joshua drove out the sinners of Jericho!" He paused, perhaps expecting to hear foot-stamping again, but the hall was quiet. He was suggesting we had to fight, which we did, but Bishop Wulfheard was no man to inspire others to the bloody business of facing a shield wall of snarling spear-Danes.

"But we shall not fight alone," the bishop continued. "The Lord Æthelhelm has come from Wessex to assure us, indeed to promise us, that the forces of Wessex will fight beside us!"

That provoked applause. Someone else would do the fighting, it seemed, and men stamped their feet as Æthelhelm climbed the wooden steps to the dais. He smiled at the hall, a big man, easy in his authority. A gold chain glinted from his mail-clad breast. "I have no right to speak at this noble gathering," he said modestly, his rich voice filling the hall, "but with Lord Æthelred's permission?" He turned and Æthelred managed to nod.

"My king," Æthelhelm said, "prays daily for the kingdom of Mercia. He prays that the pagans will be defeated. He thanks God for the victory you gained last year and, my lords, let us not forget that it was the Lord Uhtred who led that fight! Who suffered in that fight! Who trapped the heathen and delivered them to our swords!"

That was a surprise. There was not a man in the hall who did not know that I was an enemy to Æthelred, yet here, in Æthelred's own hall, I was being praised? Men turned to look at me, then one or two started to stamp their feet and soon the great hall was filled with noise. Even Æthelred managed to rap the arm of his chair twice. Æthelhelm beamed and I kept a straight face, wondering what serpent was hidden in this unexpected flattery.

"It is the pleasure of my king," Æthelhelm waited for the racket to subside, "to keep a large force in Lundene, which army will be ever ready to oppose the Danes who infest the eastern parts of our land." That was greeted by silence, though it was hardly a surprise. Lundene, the greatest town of Britain, was part of Mercia, but it had been under West Saxon rule for years now. What Æthelhelm meant, and was not quite making plain, was that the city would now formally become a part of Wessex, and the men in the hall understood that. They might not like it, but if that was the price of West Saxon help against the Danes then it was already paid and so was acceptable.

"We shall keep that mighty army in the east," Æthelhelm said, "an army dedicated to the task of bringing East Anglia back to Saxon rule. And you, my lords, will keep an army here, in the west, and together we shall clear the heathen from our land! We shall fight together!" He paused, staring around the hall, then repeated the last word. "Together!"

He stopped there. It was a very abrupt ending. He smiled at the bishop, smiled at the silent men on the benches beneath him, then stepped back down to the floor. "Together," he had said, by which he surely meant a forced marriage between Wessex and Mercia. The serpent, I thought, was about to be let loose.

Bishop Wulfheard had sat through Æthelhelm's words, but now stood again. "It is necessary, lords," he said, "that we keep an army of Mercia that will free the northern part of our land of the last pagans and so spread the rule of Christ to every part of our ancient kingdom." Someone in the hall began to speak, though I could not catch the words, and the bishop interrupted him. "The new lands that we grant will pay for the warriors we need," he said sharply, and his words stilled any protest that might have been made. Doubtless the protest had been about the cost of keeping a permanent army. An army has to be fed, paid, armed, and supplied with horses, weapons, armor, shields, and training, and the Witan had scented new taxes, but the bishop seemed to be suggesting that the captured Danish farmlands would pay for the army. And so they might, I thought, and it was not a bad idea either. We had defeated the Danes, driven them from great swathes of Mercian land, and it made sense to keep them running. That was what Æthelflaed was doing near Ceaster, but she was doing it without the support of her husband's money or men.

"And an army needs a leader," Bishop Wulfheard said.

The serpent was flickering its tongue now.

There was silence in the hall.

"We have thought long about this," Wulfheard said piously, "and we have prayed too! We have laid the problem before Almighty God and he, in his omniscience, has suggested an answer."

The serpent slithered into the light, small eyes glinting.

"There are a dozen men in this hall," the bishop continued, "who could lead an army against the heathen, but to raise one man above the rest is to provoke jealousy. If the Lord Uhtred was well then there would be no other choice!" You lying bastard, I thought. "And we all pray for the Lord Uhtred's recovery," the bishop went on, "but until that happy day we need a man of proven ability, of fearless character, and of godly reputation."

Eardwulf. Every eye in the hall looked at him, and I sensed rebellion stirring among the ealdormen. Eardwulf was not one of them. He was an upstart who owed his command of Æthelred's household warriors to his sister, Eadith, who shared Æthelred's bed. I had half expected to see her at the Witan, perhaps pretending to be Æthelred's nurse, but she had the sense, or someone had the sense, to make sure she had stayed hidden.

And then the bishop sprang his surprise, and the serpent's mouth opened to show the long curved fangs. "It is the Lord Æthelred's pleasure," he said, "that his dear daughter should marry Eardwulf."

There was a gasp in the hall, a murmur, and then silence again. I could see men frowning, more in perplexity than disapproval. Eardwulf, by marrying Ælfwynn, was joining Æthelred's family. He might not be nobly born, but no one could deny his wife's royal lineage. Ælfwynn was King Alfred's granddaughter, King Edward's niece. The open thighs of Eardwulf's sister had given him command of Æthelred's household warriors, but now Ælfwynn could spread her legs to lift him higher still. Clever, I thought. A few men started to speak, their voices a low grumble in the big hall, but then came another surprise: Æthelred himself spoke.

"It is my pleasure," Æthelred said, then paused to gulp in a breath. His voice had been weak and men hushed each other in the hall to hear him. "It is my pleasure," he said again, his words halting and slurred, "that my daughter Ælfwynn should marry my Lord Eardwulf."

Lord, I thought? Lord Eardwulf? I stared in amazement at Æthelred. He seemed to be smiling. I looked at Æthelhelm. What did Wessex gain from the marriage? Maybe, I thought, it was simply that no Mercian ealdorman could marry Ælfwynn and so inherit Æthelred's power, thus leaving the throne open for Edward, but what was to stop Eardwulf himself aspiring to the throne? Yet Æthelhelm was smiling and nodding his approval, then he crossed the hall and held his arms out to embrace Eardwulf. There could be no plainer signal than that. King Edward of Wessex wanted his niece to marry Eardwulf. But why?

Father Penda scuttled past, heading for the door. He glanced at me, and Osferth stiffened, expecting another assault from the young priest, but Penda kept walking. "Go after that priest," I told my son.

"Father?"

"He's gone for a piss. Piss beside him. Go!"

"I don't need a . . ."

"Go and piss!"

Uhtred went and I watched Æthelhelm lead Eardwulf onto the dais. The younger man looked handsome, confident, and strong. He knelt to Æthelred, who reached out a hand. Eardwulf kissed the hand and Æthelred said something, but too low for any of us to hear. Bishop Wulfheard stooped to listen, then straightened and turned to the hall. "It is the pleasure of our dear Lord Æthelred," he announced, "that his daughter be married on the feast of Saint Æthelwold."

Some of the priests began stamping their feet and the rest of the hall followed. "When is Saint Æthelwold's Day?" I asked Osferth.

"There are two Æthelwolds," he said pedantically, "and you should know that, lord, as they both come from near Bebbanburg."

"When?" I snarled.

"The nearest is in three days, lord. But Bishop Æthelwold's feast day was last month."

Three days? Far too soon for Æthelflaed to interfere. Her daughter Ælfwynn would be married to an enemy before she even knew about it. That enemy was still kneeling to Æthelred while the Witan cheered him. Just minutes before they had been scornful of Eardwulf because of his low birth, but they could see which way the wind blew, and it blew strong from the south, from Wessex. Eardwulf was at least a Mercian, and so Mercia would be spared the indignity of begging a West Saxon to lead them.

Then my son came back into the church and bent to my ear. He whispered to me.

And I understood at last why Æthelhelm approved of the marriage and why I had been invited to the Witan.

I should have known, or I should have guessed. This meeting of the Witan was not just about Mercia's future but about the fate of kings.

I told Uhtred what he must do, then I stood. I stood laboriously and slowly, letting the pain show on my face. "My lords," I shouted, and that hurt so much. "My lords!" I shouted again, letting the pain rip at me.

They turned to look at me. Every man in the room knew what was about to happen, indeed Æthelhelm and the bishop had feared this would happen, which is why they had hoped to silence me with flattery. Now they knew the flattery had failed because I was going to protest. I was going to argue that Æthelflaed should have a say in her daughter's fate. I was going to challenge Æthelred and Æthelhelm, and now they waited for that challenge in silence. Æthelred was staring at me, so was Æthelhelm. The bishop's mouth hung open.

But, to their relief, I said nothing.

I just fell to the floor.

There was commotion. I was shaking and moaning. Men ran to kneel at my side and Finan bellowed at them to give me room. He also shouted to my son, telling him to come to me, but Uhtred had gone to do my bidding. Father Penda pushed through the crowd and, seeing me stricken, loudly announced that this was God's righteous judgment on me, and even Bishop Wulfheard frowned at that. "Silence, man!"

"The heathen is struck down," Father Penda said, trying too hard to earn his gold.

"Lord? Lord!" Finan was rubbing my right hand.

"Sword," I said faintly, then louder, "sword!"

"Not in the hall," some fool insisted.

"No swords in the hall," Eardwulf said sternly.

So Finan and four other men carried me outside and laid me on the grass. A thin rain was falling as Sihtric brought me Serpent-Breath and closed my right hand about her hilt. "Paganism!" Father Penda hissed.

"Does he live?" the bishop asked, bending down to peer at me.

"Not for long," Finan said.

"Carry him to shelter," the bishop said.

"Home," I muttered, "take me home. Finan! Take me home!"

"I'll take you home, lord," Finan said.

Æthelhelm arrived, driving the crowd apart like a bull scattering sheep. "Lord Uhtred!" he exclaimed, kneeling beside me. "What happened?"

Osferth made the sign of the cross. "He can't hear you, lord."

"I can," I said. "Take me home."

"Home?" Æthelhelm asked. He sounded anxious.

"Home to the hills," I said, "I want to die on the hills."

"There's a convent nearby." Æthelhelm was holding my right hand, tightening my grip on Serpent-Breath. "They can minister to you there, Lord Uhtred."

"The hills," I said, sounding weak, "just take me to the hills."

"It's pagan nonsense," Father Penda said scornfully.

"If Lord Uhtred wants to go to the hills," Æthelhelm said firmly, "then he must go!" Men muttered as they watched me. My death took away Æthelflaed's strongest supporter, and doubtless they were wondering what would happen to her lands and mine when

Eardwulf became Mercia's lord. It was raining harder and I moaned. It was not all pretense.

"You'll catch cold, lord bishop," Father Penda said.

"And we still have much to discuss," Wulfheard said, straightening. "Send us news," he said to Finan.

"It is God's judgment," Penda insisted as he walked away.

"It is indeed!" Wulfheard said heavily. "And let it be a lesson to all the heathen." He made the sign of the cross, then followed Penda toward the hall.

"You will let us know what happens?" Æthelhelm asked Finan.

"Of course, lord. Pray for him."

"With all my might."

I waited to make certain that everyone from the Witan had retreated from the rain, then looked up at Finan. "Uhtred's bringing a wagon," I said. "Get me in it. Then we go east, all of us. Sihtric?"

"Lord?"

"Find our men. Look in the taverns. Get them ready to travel. Go!"

"Lord?" Finan asked, puzzled by my sudden energy.

"I'm dying," I explained, then winked at him.

"You are?"

"I hope not, but tell people I am."

It took time, but at last my son brought the wagon harnessed with two horses and I was lifted onto the damp bed of straw. I had brought most of my men to Gleawecestre, and they rode in front, behind, and alongside the cart as we threaded the streets. Folk pulled off their hats as we passed. Somehow the news of my imminent death had spread through the city and people spilled out of shops and houses to watch my passing. Priests made the sign of the cross as the wagon rolled by.

I feared I was already too late. My son, going to join Penda for a piss against the church wall, had heard the priest's real news. Æthelhelm had sent men to Cirrenceastre.

And I should have known.

That was why I had been invited to the Witan, not because Æthelred and Æthelhelm wanted to persuade Mercia that somone had spoken in support of Æthelflaed, but to get me out of Cirrenceastre, or rather to get my household warriors out of the town, because there was something Æthelhelm desperately wanted in Cirrenceastre.

He wanted Æthelstan.

Æthelstan was a boy, just ten years old as far as I could remember, and his mother had been a pretty Centish girl who had died giving birth to him. But his father was alive, very much alive, and his father Edward, son of King Alfred, was now the King of Wessex himself. Edward had since married Æthelhelm's daughter and fathered another son, which made Æthelstan an inconvenience. Was he the eldest son? Or was he, as Æthelhelm insisted, a bastard? If he was a bastard then he had no rights, but there was a persistent rumor that Edward had married the Centish girl. And I knew that rumor was true because Father Cuthbert had performed the marriage ceremony. The people of Wessex pretended to believe that Æthelstan was a bastard, but Æthelhelm feared those persistent rumors. He feared that Æthelstan could be a rival to his own grandson for the throne of Wessex, and so Æthelhelm had plainly decided to do something about that. According to Penda he had sent twenty or more men to Cirrenceastre where Æthelstan was living in Æthelflaed's house, but my absence meant that the boy was protected by only six household warriors. Would Æthelhelm dare kill him? I doubted that, but he would certainly dare capture him and have him removed far away so that he could not threaten the ealdorman's ambitions. And if Penda was right then the men sent to take Æthelstan had a day's start on us. But Æthelhelm had plainly been frightened I was going to Cirrenceastre, or perhaps Fagranforda, which suggested his men might still be there, and that was why I had muttered the nonsense about dying on the hills. When I die I want it to be in a girl's warm bed, not on some rainswept Mercian hilltop.

I dared not hurry. People watched us from the walls of Gleawecestre, so we traveled painfully slowly, as if the men did not want to jolt a wagon in which a man lay dying. We could not abandon that pretense until we reached the beech woods on the steep slope that climbed to the hills where sheep would keep the pale grass short all summer, and once among those trees and thus safely hidden from curious eyes, I climbed off the cart and onto my horse's back. I left Godric Grindanson, my son's servant boy, to bring the cart, while the rest of us spurred ahead. "Osferth!" I called.

"Lord?"

"Don't stop in Cirrenceastre," I told him. "Ride on with two men and make sure Father Cuthbert's safe. Get the blind bastard out of bed and bring them both to Cirrenceastre."

"Them? Out of bed?" Osferth could be slow to understand sometimes.

"Where else will they be?" I asked, and Finan laughed.

Father Cuthbert was my priest. I did not want a priest, but he had been sent to me by King Edward and I liked Cuthbert. He had been blinded by Cnut. He was, I was constantly assured, a good priest, meaning he did his work well enough. "What work?" I had asked Osferth once and had been assured that Cuthbert visited the sick and said his prayers and preached his sermons, but every time I visited his small house beside Fagranforda's church I had to wait while he dressed. He would then appear smiling, disheveled and flustered, followed a moment later by Mehrasa, the dark-skinned slave girl he had married. She was a beauty.

And Cuthbert was in danger. I was not certain that Æthelhelm knew that it had been Father Cuthbert who had married Edward to his Centish love. If he did know, then Cuthbert would have to be silenced, though it was possible Edward had never revealed the priest's identity. Edward was fond of his son, and he was fond of Cuthbert too, but how far did that affection reach? Edward was not a weak king, but he was a lazy one, happy to leave most of the kingdom's affairs to Æthelhelm and to a pack of diligent priests who, in truth, ruled Wessex fairly and firmly. That left Edward free to hunt and to whore.

And while the king hunted deer, boars, and women, Æthelhelm gathered power. He used it well enough. There was justice in Wessex, and the burhs were kept in repair, and the fyrd practised with weapons, and the Danes had finally learned that invading Wessex led only to defeat, and Æthelhelm himself was a decent enough man except that he saw a chance to be the grandfather of a king, and a great king at that. He would guide his grandson as he guided Edward, and I did not doubt that Æthelhelm's ambition was the same dream that had haunted Alfred. That dream was to unite the Saxons, to take the four kingdoms and make them one. And that was a good dream, but Æthelhelm wanted to be sure it was his family that made the dream come true.

And I would stop him.

If I could.

I would stop him because I knew Æthelstan was legitimate. He was the ætheling, the king's eldest son and, besides, I loved that boy. Æthelhelm would stop at nothing to destroy him and I would do anything to protect him.

We did not have far to go. Once on the hilltops we could see the smear of smoke that marked Cirrenceastre's hearth fires. We were hurrying and my ribs hurt. The land either side of the Roman road belonged to Æthelflaed, and it was good land. The first lambs were in the fields, guarded by men and dogs. The wealth of the land had been granted to Æthelflaed by her father, but her brother could take it away, and Æthelhelm's unexpected presence in Gleawecestre suggested that Edward was siding with Æthelred, or rather that Æthelhelm was making the decisions that would dictate Mercia's fate.

"What will he do to the boy?" Finan asked, evidently thinking much the same thoughts as those in my head. "Cut his throat?"

"No. He knows Edward likes the twins." Æthelstan had a twin sister, Eadgyth.

"He'll put Æthelstan into a monastery," my son suggested, "and little Eadgyth into a convent."

"Like enough."

"Somewhere far away," my son went on, "with some bastard abbot who beats the shit out of you every two days."

"They'll try to make him into a priest," Finan said.

"Or hope he falls ill and dies," I said, then winced as my horse came down heavily on a rough patch of stone. The roads decayed. Everything decayed.

"You shouldn't be riding, Father," my son said reprovingly.

"I'm in pain all the time," I said, "and if I gave in to it then I'd do nothing."

But that journey was painful and by the time I came to Cirenceastre's western gate I was almost weeping with agony. I tried to hide the pain. I sometimes wonder whether the dead can see the living. Do they sit in Valhalla's great feast-hall and watch those they left behind? I could imagine Cnut sitting there and thinking that I must join him soon, and we would raise a horn of ale together. There is no pain in Valhalla, no sadness, no tears, no broken oaths. I could see Cnut grinning at me, not with any pleasure at my pain, but rather because we had liked each other in life. "Come to me," he was saying, "come to me and live!" It was tempting.

"Father?" My son sounded worried.

I blinked and the shadows that had clouded my eyes drained away and I saw we had reached the gate and one of the town guards was frowning up at me. "Lord?" the man said.

"Did you speak?"

"The king's men are in my lady's house," he said.

"The king's men!" I exclaimed, and the man just stared at me. I turned to Osferth. "Keep going! Find Cuthbert!" His route to Fagranforda lay through the town. "The king's men?" I asked the guard again.

"King Edward's men, lord."

"And they're still there?"

"So far as I know, lord."

I spurred on. Æthelflaed's house had once belonged to the Roman commander, or I assumed it had been the commander's house because it was a lavish building that lay in a corner of the old Roman fort. The fort's walls had been pulled down, except for the northern side, which was part of the town's ramparts, but the house was easily defended. It was built about a large courtyard, and the outer walls were of honey-colored stone and had no windows. There was a pillared entrance facing south, and Æthelflaed had made a new gateway from her stable yard through the town's northern wall. I sent Sihtric with six companions to guard that northern entrance while I rode with thirty men to the small square that faced the southern door. There was a crowd of curious folk in the square, all wondering why King Edward of Wessex had sent armed men to Cirrenceastre. The crowd parted as our horses' hooves sounded loud in the street behind them, then we were in the open space and I saw two spearmen beside Æthelflaed's door. One was sitting on a stone urn that held a small pear tree. He stood and snatched up his shield as we arrived, while the other rapped on the closed door with the butt of his spear. Both men were in mail, they wore helmets, and their round shields were freshly painted with the dragon of Wessex. There was a small hatch in the door and I saw it slide to one side and someone peered out at us. Two boys were guarding horses on the eastern side of the square beside Æthelflaed's tall wooden church. "Count the horses," I told my son.

"Twenty-three," he answered almost at once.

So we outnumbered them. "I don't expect a fight," I said.

Then a scream sounded from inside the house.

A scream to pierce the ears with all the force of a well-made spear striking through the willow boards of a shield.

"Sweet God," Finan said.

And the screaming stopped.

Two

The door to Æthelflaed's house opened.

Brice appeared.

I knew Brice. Not well, but inevitably our paths had crossed in the long years we had struggled to push the Danes farther northward. I had seen him in encampments, had even exchanged a word or two before battle, and he was a veteran of many battles, a man who had stood in the shield wall time after time, and always under Ealdorman Æthelhelm's banner of the leaping stag. He was skilled with weapons, strong as a bull, but slow of wit, which is why he had never risen to command one of Æthelhelm's larger companies. Yet today, it seemed, Brice had been put in charge of the men sent to find Æthelstan. He strode toward us, a warrior in his formidable war-glory, but I had too often dressed in the same way to be impressed by the display.

His mail was good and tight, probably from Frankia, but it had been cut in a half-dozen places where new rings showed against the duller metal. He wore tall boots of dark leather, while his sword belt, buckled tight about the bright mail, was decorated with silver lozenges. His sword was long and heavy, scabbarded in a red sheath criss-crossed with silver bands. A silver chain hung at his neck. A dark-red cloak was spread by his wide shoulders, clasped at his throat by an ornate brooch studded with garnets. He wore no helmet. His red hair was longer than most Saxons liked to wear it, framing a face that had seen many enemies. He had gouged a cross onto his right cheek then rubbed the wound with soot or dirt to leave the dark mark that proclaimed him a

Christian warrior. He was a hard man, but what else would he be? He had stood in the shield wall, he had watched the Danes come to the attack, and he had lived. He was no youngster. His beard was gray and his dark face deep-lined. "My Lord Uhtred," he said. There was no respect in his voice, instead he spoke sourly as though my arrival was a tedious nuisance which, I suppose, it was.

"Brice." I nodded to him from my saddle.

"The king sent me," he said.

"You serve King Edward now?" I asked. "What happened? Did Lord Æthelhelm tire of your stench?"

He ignored the insult. "He sent me to fetch the boy bastard," he said.

I looked up at the wooden tower that crowned Æthelflaed's church. A bell that had cost her a heavy chest of silver hung there. She had been so proud of the bell, which had been made by Frisian craftsmen and brought across the sea. It carried an inscription about its skirt: "Æthelflaed, by the grace of God and by the blessing of Saint Werburgh, had this bell made," and by the grace of God the bell had cracked the very first time it was struck. I had laughed when it happened, and ever since the bell had not rung to summon folk to church, instead it just hurt the sky with its harsh noise.

"Did you hear me?" Brice demanded.

I took my time to turn from the cracked bell, then I looked Brice up and down. "Which boy bastard?" I finally asked.

"You know who," he said.

"I should buy the Lady Æthelflaed another bell," I said to Finan.

"And she'd like that," he said.

"Maybe I'll have 'the gift of Thor' written on the thing."

"And she won't like that at all."

"Lord Uhtred!" Brice interrupted our nonsense.

"You're still here?" I asked, pretending surprise.

"Where is he?"

"Where is who?"

"The bastard Æthelstan," he said.

I shook my head. "I don't know a bastard called Æthelstan. Do you?" I asked Finan.

"Never heard of him, lord."

"The boy Æthelstan," Brice said, struggling to restrain his temper. "King Edward's boy."

"He's not home?" I pretended surprise again. "He should be at home or else at school."

"He's not here," Brice said curtly, "and we looked in the school. So find him."

I took a deep breath, then dismounted. It took an effort to hide the pain and I had to hold onto the horse for a moment as the agony drained from my side. I even wondered whether I could walk without support, but then managed to let go of the saddle. "That sounded like a command," I said to Brice as I took a few slow steps toward him.

"From the king," he said.

"The King of Wessex?" I asked. "But this is Mercia."

"The king wants his son returned to Wessex," Brice said flatly.

"You're a good warrior," I told Brice. "I'd welcome you into any shield wall, but I wouldn't trust you to empty my piss pot. You're not clever enough. That's why you don't command Æthelhelm's household troops. So no, you don't serve the king because the king wouldn't want you. So who did send you? Lord Æthelhelm?"

I had annoyed him, but he managed to bite back his anger. "The king," he said slowly, "wants his son, and you, Lord Uhtred, will find the boy and bring him here."

"You might find it strange," I said, "but I don't take orders from you."

"Oh, you will," he said, "you will." He thought he was hiding his nervousness by belligerence, but I could see he was confused. He had orders to fetch Æthelstan and the boy had gone missing and my warriors now outnumbered his, but Brice did not have the sense to abandon his mission, instead he would tackle it as he did every other problem, by savage directness. He turned his head toward the house. "Bring her!" he called.

The house door opened and a man brought Stiorra into the sunlight. A murmur sounded through the crowd because my daughter's face was smeared with blood and she was clutching her torn robe to her breasts. Finan leaned from his saddle and put a hand on my arm, restraining me, but I had no need of his gesture. I was angry, yes, but I was no fool. I was too weak to attack Brice, and besides, my anger was cold. I was going to win this confrontation, but not by brute force. Not yet. Brice, meanwhile, was certain I had no choice but to obey him. "You bring me the boy," he said with a sneer, "and your daughter is freed."

"And if I don't?"

He shrugged. "You'll find out, won't you?"

I turned and jerked my head at my son. "Come here." I waited till Uhtred had dismounted and joined me. "Where is he?" I asked quietly. If anyone knew where Æthelstan was hiding it would be my son.

He glanced at Brice, then half turned his back on the West Saxon. "He spends time at the smithy," he told me.

"The smithy?"

"Godwulf's smithy. He's got friends there." He spoke too low for Brice to hear what he was saying. "Godwulf's son and daughter. He goes to see her, really."

"He's just ten!"

"Nine, I think. And she's twelve."

"He likes older women, does he?" I asked. "So go and find the little brute and bring him here, but take your time. Don't hurry."

He nodded and left, pushing through the sullen crowd. "Where's he going?" Brice demanded.

"To fetch the boy, of course," I said.

He was suspicious, but not clever enough to think beyond the next step, though he must have thought that step was a good idea. "Tell your men to leave," he demanded.

"Leave?" I pretended to be as stupid as Brice.

"Leave!" he snarled. "I want them out of sight, now!"

He thought he was ridding himself of their threat, though in truth he was demanding just what I wanted him to demand. "Take the men onto the city wall," I told Finan quietly, "and when I give the signal go in through the stable roof."

"What are you telling him?" Brice wanted to know.

"To wait in the Barley inn," I said, "the ale's good there, much better than the stale muck they serve in the Muddy Goose." I nodded to Finan and he led my men away, vanishing into one of the narrow alleys that opened from the church square. I waited till the sound of their hooves had faded, then walked slowly toward my daughter. "What's your name?" I asked the man holding her.

"Hrothard," he said.

"Quiet!" Brice snarled at him.

"If you hurt her, Hrothard," I said, "you will die very slowly."

Brice took two fast paces to stand in my face. "Hrothard will do what I tell him to do," he said and I smelled his rotten breath, but then he could probably smell the filthy pus that was seeping from my wound.

"And you'll tell him to let her go when I bring you Æthelstan," I said, "isn't that what you want?"

He nodded. He was still suspicious, but too stupid to see the trap. May the gods always send me stupid enemies. "You know where the boy is?" he asked.

"We think so," I said, "and, of course, if the king wants his son then who am I to stand in his way?"

He thought about that question for a few heartbeats and must have decided that I had yielded altogether to his demands. "The king asked Lord Æthelhelm to fetch the boy," Brice said, trying to shade his lies into truth.

"You should have told me that from the beginning," I said, "because I've always liked Æthelhelm." Brice half smiled, placated by the words. "But I don't like men who strike my daughter," I added.

"It was an accident, lord," he said too quickly. "The man will be punished."

"Good," I said, "and now we wait." We waited while Finan's men dismounted and then climbed to the city wall by steps hidden beyond the church and far from Brice's sight. The old fort, most of which had been pulled down, had stood in a corner of those walls and so the ramparts formed the northern and western sides of Æthelflaed's house. The servant quarters and stables were on the northern side, and over the years their roofs had decayed to be replaced by thatch held up by rafters and wattles. Tear the thatch aside and break through the wattles and a man could drop into the stables. I could see Finan and his men on the wall now, and Brice would have seen them too had he turned around, but I kept his attention by asking him about Teotanheale and listening as he described his part in that battle. I pretended to be impressed, encouraging him to tell me more while Finan's men ducked down low. Only one stayed upright, leaning lazily against the outer rampart. "What about the boy's twin sister?" I asked Brice.

"The king wants her too," he said.

"Where is she now?"

"In the house. With the kitchen maids."

"She'd better be safe and unharmed," I said.

"She is," Brice said.

I turned away. "You will forgive me," I said, "but my wound still hurts. I need to sit."

"I pray for your recovery," he said, though it took an effort for him to say it.

"The gods will have their will," I said and turned back to my horse, which was being held by Edric, a lad of some eight or nine years who was my new servant. I braced myself against the pain, then climbed into the saddle. Brice had also turned away and walked back to the house door where he waited close to Stiorra.

She was staring at me. I have been a bad father, though I have ever loved my children. Yet small children bore me, and as they grew I was forever away fighting. I trained my son to be a warrior, and I was proud of him, but Stiorra puzzled me. She was my youngest, and it hurt to look at her because she so resembled her dead mother; she was tall and lithe and had her mother's long face, the same black hair, the same dark eyes, and the same grave expression that could light into beauty with a smile. I did not know her well because I had been fighting as she grew, and Æthelflaed had raised her. She had been sent to the nuns in Cracgelad for much of her youth, schooled there in religion and the womanly arts. She was sweet-natured, though there was steel beneath that honey, and she was affectionate, though I never did know what she was thinking. It was time, I knew, that she was married, but I had found no one to whom I wanted to give my daughter, and she had never spoken of wanting to be married. Indeed she never spoke much, guarding her truth-hoard behind silence and stillness.

Her lower lip had been broken. It was swollen and bloody. Someone had hit her hard to do that and I would find that man and kill him. Stiorra was my daughter and no one hit her without my permission, and she was too old to be struck now. Children should be whipped into obedience, but once a child comes of age then the beatings stop. Husbands beat wives, of course, though I had never beaten Gisela, nor any of my lovers. I was not alone in that. Many men do not beat their wives, even though the law allows it and the church encourages it, but a man gains no reputation by beating a weaker person. Æthelred had beaten Æthelflaed, but he was a weak man, and it takes a weak man to prove his strength by striking a woman.

I was thinking these thoughts and watching my daughter, who stood very straight and still. A gust of wind brought a spatter of rain. I looked up, surprised, because most of the day had been fair, but the rain was brief and light.

"Lord," Brice called harshly. He was becoming suspicious again, but before he could voice his fears my son appeared with Æthelstan. "Bring the boy here," Brice called to my son.

"Bring him to me," I ordered, and Uhtred obediently brought Æthelstan to my stirrup. I grinned down at the boy who I loved as though he were another son. He was a good boy, mischievous as a boy should be, but intelligent and tough. He had started his weapon training, learning sword-craft and shield-lore, and the exercises had filled him out. In time, I thought, he would be a good-looking man. He was dark-haired, thin-faced, with green eyes that I supposed had come from his mother. "You get the boy," I called to Brice, "when I get my daughter."

That made him think. He was such a stupid man. His brains, I thought, must be made of barley mush. A good warrior, yes, but men like Brice need to be controlled like dogs. I assumed Æthelhelm had sent him to Cirrenceastre because Brice could be relied on to obey his orders come what may, he was unstoppable like a boar-hound, but when the boar has sunk his tusk into the dog's belly and is ripping the intestines out then the dog should know he's beaten. Brice was still thinking, something he found hard to do, but at last he saw the apparent trap in my words. "We shall make the exchange outside the town," he proposed.

"Outside the town?" I asked, pretending not to understand.

"You think I'm a fool, lord?" he asked.

"I would never think that," I said gently.

"Your men will stay inside the walls," he ordered, "and you will bring the boy outside."

I frowned as if I was considering that proposal, which, of course, made sense for Brice. He had worked out that my men could ambush him in Cirrenceastre's narrow streets, but if the exchange was made in the fields outside the town then there was no danger of such a trap.

"Well?" he demanded.

I stared at the man on the wall and, very slowly, raised my head. I paused, then nodded fast. The man on the wall vanished, but Brice, of course, believed the nod was for him. "We shall do it your way," I said to Brice, "but I want your word of honor."

"My word, lord?"

"That the man who struck my daughter will be punished."

"I said so, didn't I?"

I spurred my horse a little closer. The hooves were loud on the Roman paving. "I want you to give the man to me," I said.

"He will be punished," Brice said stubbornly.

Then the shouts started and the unmistakable sound of swords clashing and I knew Finan and his men were inside the house. They had not bothered to clear the thatch and break the wattles beneath, but simply jumped onto the roof, which instantly gave way. Gerbruht, a Frisian who never seemed to stop eating and who weighed as much as a horse, had evidently jumped first, and the rest of Finan's men followed through the gaping hole he had made. I did not react to the sounds, but just kept looking at Brice. "You will give the man to me," I said, and might have saved my breath because Brice suddenly heard the commotion and realized he had been tricked. I was ready to spur my horse at him, using the stallion's weight to throw him down, but instead he drew his sword and ran at me.

"You bastard!" he shouted. He was quick. No warrior stays alive by being slow, but for a big man he was surprisingly fast. He covered the few paces toward me, sword swinging to take my horse in the face and I wrenched the reins and almost blacked out with the stab of pain that seared from my lower ribs, and I knew I had lost, that he was too fast, that he would drag me from the saddle and either kill me or, if he had a grain of sense, hold me as another hostage.

Yet if he was fast, my son was like lightning.

Brice's sword never struck me or my horse. I was hardly aware what happened, but I learned that Uhtred drew his seax, Attor, and threw it. The short blade struck Brice's legs, tripping him. I heard the clatter as he fell, but I was still trying to calm my breathing. Brice stood immediately, but Uhtred had his long-sword, his precious Raven-Beak, drawn. He had thrust Æthelstan back, away from the fight. "Come on, earsling," he taunted Brice. The crowd that had been so silent suddenly cheered.

"Bastard," Brice said. He kicked Attor away, then went for my son. Brice, remember, was an experienced sword-warrior, a man who had spent his life training with blades, a man who had become wealthy with sword-skill. He had no fear, and Uhtred, my son, had an open face that looked forever cheerful and gave him the appearance of innocence. Brice reckoned he could chop him down with two or three strokes, and the first stroke was a scything blow that would have opened my son's belly like a knife slashing across a sack of eels.

Uhtred skipped back, he laughed. He lowered Raven-Beak and

laughed again, and Brice took the bait and attacked a second time, this time lunging and, as Raven-Beak rose to parry, he twisted the lunge, turning it about my son's blade and dragging his sword back so it would saw across his enemy's neck. That was fast and that was skillful, and Uhtred just leaned back and away, the edge of Brice's blade missing by the breadth of a finger, and Brice was slightly off balance and my son just reached out and pushed him with Raven-Beak's tip. "You're slow," he said reprovingly as the West Saxon staggered.

"Bastard," Brice muttered. It seemed to be his only curse. He had gained his balance and now looked at my son, saw that insolent grin on the innocent face, and the fury surged in him again. "Bastard," he shouted, and drove forward, lunging again, and Uhtred simply deflected the blade and Brice, with his extraordinary speed, kept the sword moving into a savage cut aimed at my son's head, and again Raven-Beak was there, and I heard the crash of the blades and there was a harshness to the sound.

Blades ring together. Not like a bell rings, but there is an echo of that sound in the clash of blades, but Brice's last cut had ended in a crack, like the noise of Æthelflaed's bell. The blade was not broken, but the sound was ominous and he knew it. He stepped back.

Men were coming from the house. They were Brice's men, but pursued by mine and none interfered as my son attacked for the first time. Thus far he had been content to defend and to taunt Brice, but now he went forward with a lunge that was never intended to strike home, but merely to force a parry, and then a waist-high cut that Brice parried again, and the cut did not seem too fast or vicious, yet when Brice's sword met Raven-Beak it broke. It just broke into two pieces, and Uhtred turned his wrist over and held the point of his sword at Brice's neck. "What shall I do with him, Father?"

"Drop what's left of your sword," I ordered Brice. He hesitated, and so I drew Wasp-Sting, my seax, and held the hilt toward Æthelstan who had taken refuge beside my horse. "If he doesn't drop his sword, boy," I told him, "then use that to cut his spine

at the back of his neck. It's time you learned how to kill a man."
Æthelstan hesitated, not sure I was serious. I thrust the seax at
him. "Take it," I said. The boy took hold of the short-sword, then
looked back at me. "You're the son of a king," I told him, "and
one day you might be a king yourself. Life and death will be your
gifts, so learn how to give them, boy."

He walked toward Brice who half turned, then went very still
when my son prodded his neck with Raven-Beak's tip. Then, at
last, some sense leaked into Brice's brain and he dropped the remnant of his sword. "Let him live," I told Æthelstan, who looked
relieved at the command.

Sixteen of Brice's men had fled the house. They had no fight
in them and Finan's men were now taking their weapons. Stiorra
was free and ran to my side. I smiled down at her and held her
hand. "Who hit you?" I asked her.

"The priest," she said.

"The priest?" I asked, surprised, then saw the man among the
West Saxon prisoners. He was scowling, an angry man in a black
robe, with a heavy silver cross hanging at his neck. He was older,
perhaps in his forties, with thick gray eyebrows and thin lips. "Was
he the one who made you scream?"

"I heard the hooves," she said, "and hoped it was you. So I
screamed."

"And that's when he hit you?"

"He hit me before that," she said bitterly, "and tore this." She
showed me the ripped breast of her linen dress.

Finan strolled across the small square. "There's no fight in the
bastards," he said, sounding disappointed.

Brice and his remaining men were standing by the house door,
guarded by my swords. "Take them back inside the house," I ordered, then took a deep, painful breath. "It's over!" I called to the
crowd. "Nothing more to see! So go back to work!"

Father Creoda, the priest who looked after Æthelflaed's church
and who taught in the town's small school, hurried to Æthelstan's
side. He took the boy's face in his hands, closed his eyes, and
seemed to be saying a prayer of thanks for his safety.

"Father Creoda!" I called. "So the little bastard wasn't at school?"

"He was not, lord."

"And he should have been?"

"Yes, lord."

"So thrash him," I said.

"It does no good, lord," the priest said plaintively. Father Creoda was a decent man, earnest and honest. He had come to Mercia from Wessex and believed in King Alfred's dream of an educated community, pious and diligent, and I did not doubt that Æthelstan, who was as clever as a weasel, had long ago decided that Father Creoda's authority was easily defied.

"It doesn't do any good," I agreed, "but it might make you feel better." I leaned down to take the seax from Æthelstan. "And if you don't thrash him, I will. And take the grin off your ugly face," I added to the boy.

But I was grinning too. And wondering what new enemies I had just made.

And knowing I was about to make a lot more.

Æthelflaed's house was built around a courtyard. It was not unlike the house in Lundene where I had lived with Gisela, only this building was larger. The courtyard had a square pool in the center where frogs left thick skeins of spawn. I often tried to imagine the Romans in these houses. They had left pictures of themselves, either painted on the wall plaster or made of small floor tiles, but the paintings were all faded and water-streaked, while the tiles were usually broken. Yet enough could be seen to tell us that Roman men had worn a kind of white sheet wrapped about themselves, or else a skirt sewn with metal panels that was worn beneath a breastplate. They were often naked too, especially the women. In the largest room of Æthelflaed's house there was a picture on the floor that showed naked women running through leafy trees and being pursued by a man with goat horns and hairy goat legs. Father Creoda, when he first arrived in Cirrenceastre, had insisted that the picture be destroyed because, he said, it showed a pagan god, but Æthelflaed had refused. "He never stopped looking at it," she had told me, amused, "so I told him it was a warning about the dangers of paganism."

Father Creoda was staring at the picture now, or rather gazing at one lissome girl who was looking over her shoulder at the pursuing goat-god. "She's pretty, Father," I said, and he immediately looked away, cleared his throat, and found nothing to say. I had not asked him to join us in the house, but he had come anyway, staying protectively close to Æthelstan. "So," I said to the boy, "you weren't at school?"

"I forgot to go, lord," he said.

"You were at the smithy?" I demanded, ignoring his grin.

"I was, lord."

"Because your girlfriend is there?"

"Girlfriend, lord?" he asked innocently, then shook his head. "No, lord, I was there because Godwulf is making me a sword. He's teaching me how to work the metal."

I took the boy's hands in mine and looked at his wrists and saw the small burn marks where sparks had scorched him.

"Doesn't Godwulf know you should be at school?" I asked.

The boy grinned. "He does, lord, but he also thinks I should learn something useful."

"Useful," I growled and tried to look stern, but he must have sensed my pleasure at his answer because he smiled. I looked at Father Creoda. "What are you teaching him, Father?"

"Latin, lord, and the lives of the holy fathers and, of course, his letters."

"Is Latin useful?"

"Of course, lord! It's the language of our holy scripture."

I grunted. I was sitting, which was a relief. Finan had put all our prisoners into a room across the courtyard and I just had my family, Father Creoda, and Æthelstan in the room where the naked girls ran across the floor. The wide chamber was Æthelflaed's favorite. "So you heard there were armed men here?" I asked Æthelstan.

"I did, lord."

"And you had the sense to stay in the smithy?"

"Godwulf told me to stay, lord."

Good for the smith, I thought, then looked at Stiorra. "And you?"

"Me, Father?"

"Brice's men came here, what did you do?"

"I welcomed them, Father," she spoke very softly, "I thought they came from King Edward."

"So why did the priest hit you?"

"He wanted to know where Æthelstan was, and I wouldn't tell him."

"You knew?"

She looked at Æthelstan and smiled. "I knew."

"And you said you didn't know? Why?"

"Because I didn't like them."

"And they didn't believe you?"

She nodded. "And Father Aldwyn became angry," she said.

"They searched the schoolroom and the church," Father Creoda put in.

"And when they couldn't find him," my daughter went on, "Father Aldwyn called me a lying bitch and said he would find the truth."

"A lying bitch?" I asked. She nodded. A servant had repaired her dress with one of Æthelflaed's brooches and wiped the blood from her face, but her lip was swollen and disfigured by a scab. "Did he knock a tooth out?"

"No, Father."

Finan pushed open the door and stood there, lazy and confident. I looked at him. "You taught my son sword-craft," I said.

"I did."

"He's quicker than you," I said.

Finan smiled. "I'm getting slow as I get older, lord."

"You taught him well," I said, "he danced around Brice like a hawk around a crane. How many dead?"

"Just two," he said, "and four wounded. The rest are under guard."

I looked at Father Creoda. "Take Æthelstan into another room and beat some Latin into him. Finan? Bring me the priest."

There was little point in questioning Brice. He was Æthelhelm's dog, but I suspected the priest was really the man who commanded these troops. Æthelhelm would trust Brice to force his way through any obstacle, but would never trust him to be subtle or clever, and Father Aldwyn had doubtless been sent to give advice and to take charge of Æthelstan. I wanted to know what fate that would have meant for the boy.

The priest staggered as he crossed the threshold, evidently pushed hard by Finan, who followed him, then closed the door. "He's protesting," Finan said, amused.

"I am chaplain to Lord Æthelhelm," Father Aldwyn said, "his confessor and father in God."

"You're my prisoner," I said, "and you will tell me what Ealdorman Æthelhelm ordered you to do."

"I will tell you nothing!" he said scornfully.

"Hit him," I told my son, but Uhtred hesitated. The Christian sorcerers have power and my son was frightened of the consequences.

"You see?" Father Aldwyn sneered. "My god protects me." He thrust a finger toward my son. "Touch me, young man, and you will rot in everlasting damnation."

"How do we even know you're a priest?" I asked.

"I am Lord Æthelhelm's chaplain!"

I frowned. "Aldwyn, yes? Is that your name? But I seem to remember meeting Father Aldwyn. An old man with long white hair and a shaking hand. He had the palsy, isn't that right, Finan?"

"That's the fellow, right enough," Finan caught my lie and embroidered it, "a little fellow with a lame leg. He dribbled a bit."

"So this isn't Father Aldwyn?"

"Can't be, he's not dribbling."

"You're an impostor," I told the priest.

"I am not . . ." he began, but I interrupted him.

"Take his frock off," I told Finan. "He's no more a priest than I am."

"You dare not . . ." Father Aldwyn shouted, then stopped

abruptly because Finan had buried a fist in his belly. The Irishman shoved Aldwyn against the wall and drew a knife.

"See?" I said to my son. "He's an impostor. He's just pretending to be a priest like that fat fellow who came to Cirrenceastre last winter." The man had been collecting coins that he said were to feed the poor and hungry, but all they did was add to his belly till we had Father Creoda question him. The fat fellow could not even repeat the creed, so we stripped him down to his shirt and then whipped him out of town.

Aldwyn made a strangled noise as Finan slashed down through his black robe. The Irishman sheathed the knife, then ripped the robe clean down the center and tugged it off the priest's shoulders. Aldwyn was left wearing a dirty shift that hung to his knees. "See?" I said again. "He's no priest."

"You make an enemy of God!" Aldwyn hissed at me. "Of God and his holy saints!"

"I don't give a rat's turd for your god," I said, "and besides, you're not a priest. You're an impostor."

"I . . ." the words were cut off because Finan had hit him in the belly again.

"So tell me, impostor," I said, "what Lord Æthelhelm planned to do with Prince Æthelstan."

"He's no prince," Aldwyn gasped.

"Uhtred," I looked at my son, "hit him." My son paused a heartbeat, then crossed the room and slapped the priest hard around the head. "Good," I said.

"The boy is a bastard," Aldwyn said.

"Again," I told my son, and he backhanded the priest hard.

"King Edward and Æthelstan's mother," I said, "were married in a church and the priest who married them lives." I hoped Father Cuthbert was still alive and, judging by Aldwyn's surprised reaction, he was. Aldwyn was staring at me, trying to judge the truth of what I had said, and I suspected that if he had been told of Father Cuthbert's existence then he would not be gazing at me so fixedly. "He lives," I went on, "and will swear on oath that he married Edward and the Lady Ecgwynn. And that means Æthelstan is the king's eldest son, the ætheling, next in line to the throne."

"You lie," Aldwyn said, though without conviction.

"So now answer my question," I said patiently. "What were you planning to do with the ætheling?"

It took time and threats, but in the end he told us. Æthelstan was to be sent south across the sea to Neustria, which is a great stretch of rocky land that forms the westernmost province of Frankia. "There is a monastery there," Aldwyn said, "and the boy would be entrusted to the monks for his education."

"His imprisonment, you mean."

"His education," Aldwyn insisted.

"In a place racked by warfare," I said. The province of Neustria had been invaded by Northmen, hordes of them, men who reckoned that there were easier pickings in Frankia than in Britain. Any monastery on that wild land beside the ocean was likely to be sacked by vengeful Norsemen, with everyone inside the walls put to the sword. "You want the ætheling dead," I accused him, "without blood on your hands."

"They are holy men in Neustria," he said weakly.

"Holy jailers," I said. "Does King Edward know of this?"

"The king agrees that his bastard son should be educated by the church," Aldwyn said.

"And he thinks it will be in some West Saxon monastery," I guessed, "not in some Neustrian cesspit waiting for the Norsemen to open his guts with a blade."

"Or sell him into slavery," Finan put in quietly.

And that made sense. Æthelstan and his sister? Two young children? They could fetch a high price in Frankia's slave markets. "You bastard," I said to Aldwyn, "and what of his twin sister? You were hoping she'd be enslaved too?" He said nothing, just raised his head and stared defiantly at me. "Did you travel to Neustria?" I asked on an impulse.

Aldwyn hesitated, then shook his head. "No, why would I do that?"

I stood, wincing at the inevitable pain. I drew Wasp-Sting and walked so close to the priest that I could smell his foul breath. "I'll give you another chance," I said. "Did you travel to Neustria?"

He hesitated again, but this time out of fear of the seax's short blade. "Yes," he admitted.

"And who," I asked, "did you see there?"

He grimaced as I twitched Wasp-Sting. "The abbot of Saint Stephen's in Cadum," he said in a panic.

"You lying bastard," I said. If he had simply wanted to place a boy in the monastery's school then a letter would have been sufficient. I raised the blade, lifting the ragged hem of his shift. "Who did you see?"

He shuddered, feeling the tip of the blade at his groin. "Hrolf," he whispered.

"Louder!"

"Hrolf!"

Hrolf was a Norseman, a chieftain who had taken his crews to Frankia where he had ravaged great stretches of countryside. News had come to Britain that Hrolf had captured a large part of Neustria and was intent on staying there. "You planned to sell the twins to Hrolf?" I asked Aldwyn.

"Hrolf is a Christian. He would raise them properly!"

"Hrolf is no more a Christian than I am," I snarled. "He says he is because the Franks demanded that as a price for him staying there. I'd say the same thing if it gave me a new kingdom to rule. You'd have sold Æthelstan and Eadgyth to the bastard, and what would he do? Kill them?"

"No," the priest whispered, but without conviction.

"And that would have left Lord Æthelhelm's grandson as the only heir to the kingdom of Wessex." I raised Wasp-Sting higher till her tip touched Aldwyn's belly. "You're a traitor, Aldwyn. You were planning to murder the king's eldest children."

"No," he whispered again.

"So tell me why I shouldn't kill you."

"I am a priest," he whimpered.

"You're not dressed as a priest," I said, "and you struck my daughter. That's not the act of a priest, is it?"

He had nothing to say. He knew my reputation as a priest-killer. Most men, of course, feared to kill a monk or priest, knowing that the act would condemn them to the nailed god's perpetual torment, but I had no fear of the Christian god's vengeance. "You're a traitor, Aldwyn," I said again, "so why shouldn't I kill you? You deserve it."

"Let me," my daughter said and I turned in astonishment. Stiorra had taken two paces forward and was just looking at me with an expressionless face. She held out her right hand for the seax. "Let me," she said again.

I shook my head. "Killing isn't woman's work," I said.

"Why not?" she asked. "We give life, can't we take it too?"

"No," Aldwyn said, "no!"

I ignored him. "It's harder than you think to kill a man," I said to Stiorra, "and though this bastard deserves to die, he should have a quick end."

"Why?" she asked. "He thought to enjoy me, Father. Would that have been quick?"

"Think of your soul," my son said.

"My soul?" she asked him.

"God will see what you do," he said, "and killing a priest is an unforgivable sin."

"Not to my gods," she said and I just stared at her, scarcely believing what I had heard. I wanted to say something, but nothing came, so I just stared and she turned back to me, smiling now. "My mother was a pagan," she said, "and you are. Why shouldn't I be?"

My son looked horrified, Finan was grinning. "You worship my gods?" I asked.

"I do, Father."

"But you were raised Christian!" her brother said.

"So was father," she said, still gazing at me, "and so were you, brother, but don't tell me you don't pray to our gods too. I know you do." Then she looked past me at Aldwyn, and her face hardened. At that moment she looked so like her mother that it hurt to see her. "Let me, Father," she said, holding out her hand again.

I gave her Wasp-Sting.

"No!" Aldwyn exclaimed.

Stiorra used her left hand to tear the linen dress out of the brooch so that one breast was exposed. "Isn't that what you wanted to see, priest?" she asked. "So look at it!"

"No!" Aldwyn was whimpering. He half crouched, not daring to look.

"Stiorra!" my son whispered.

But my daughter had no pity. I watched her face as she killed the priest and it was hard, merciless, and determined. She cut him first, slashing the short-sword to open his scalp and his neck, then to slice his forearms as he tried to defend himself, and her breast and dress were spattered with his blood as she beat him down with two more cuts to the head, and only then did she use two hands on Wasp-Sting's short hilt to slice hard at his throat. The blade lodged there and she grunted as she hauled it back and across to cut his gullet. She watched as he fell, as his blood spurted to puddle on one of the naked women running from the goat-god. She watched Aldwyn die and I watched her. It was always difficult to read her face, but I did not see any revulsion at the slaughter she had made, only what looked like curiosity. She even smiled slightly as the priest twitched and made a gurgling noise. His fingers clawed at the little tiles, then he gave a great jerk and was still.

Stiorra offered the sword hilt-first to me. "Thank you, Father," she said calmly. "Now I must wash." She held the ruined, blood-soaked dress over her nakedness and walked from the room.

"Christ Jesus," my son said quietly.

"She's your daughter, so she is," Finan said. He walked to the priest's corpse and nudged it with his foot. "And the image of her mother," he added.

"We need six wagons," I said, "at least six."

Finan and my son were still both staring at the dead priest, who, quite suddenly, farted.

"Six wagons," I said again, "harnessed with horses, not oxen. And preferably loaded with hay or straw. Something heavy, anyway. Logs, maybe."

"Six wagons?" Finan asked.

"At least six," I said, "and we need them by tomorrow."

"Why, lord?" he asked.

"Because we're going to a wedding," I said, "of course."

And so we were.

Three

There was a cavernous space beneath Father Creoda's church, a space so big that it stretched beyond the church's walls, which were supported by massive stone pillars and arches. The cellar walls were also of stone, great blocks of roughly trimmed masonry, while the floor was beaten earth. There were some ancient bones piled on a stone shelf against the eastern wall, but otherwise the cellar was empty, dark, and stinking. The Romans must have built it, though in their day I doubted that a nearby cesspit would have been allowed to leak through the stonework. "You can smell it in the church," Father Creoda said sadly, "unless the wind is in the east."

"Shit leaks through the masonry?" I asked. I had no intention of finding out by dropping through the massive trapdoor into the dark space.

"Constantly," he said, "because the mortar has crumbled."

"Then seal it with pitch," I suggested, "like a boat's timbers. Stuff the cracks with horsehair and smother it in pitch."

"Pitch?"

"You can buy it in Gleawecestre." I peered into the darkness. "Whose bones?"

"We don't know. They were here before the Lady Æthelflaed built the church, and we didn't like to disturb them." He made the sign of the cross. "Ghosts, lord," he explained.

"Sell them as relics," I said, "and use the money to buy a new bell."

"But they could be heathens!" He sounded shocked.

"So?" I asked, then straightened, wincing at the inevitable pain.

For now the foul-smelling cellar would be a prison for Brice and his men. They deserved worse. They had ransacked Æthelflaed's house, making a pile of her most precious possessions; her clothes, tapestries, jewels, kitchen pots, and lamps. "It all belongs to her husband," Brice had told me sullenly, "and she won't be needing finery in a nunnery."

So that, too, was part of the bargain Æthelhelm had made with Æthelred, that the powerful West Saxon would somehow force Æthelflaed into a convent. Would her brother approve of that? I wondered. But Edward, I realized, was probably jealous of his sister's reputation. He was constantly being compared with his father and found wanting, and now, even worse, he was reckoned to be a lesser warrior than his sister. Kings, even decent ones like Edward, have pride. He might accept that he could never rival his father, but it must gall him to hear his sister praised. He would gladly see her retired to a convent.

Father Aldwyn's body had been brought into the church. Finan had dressed the corpse in the torn black robe, but there was no hiding the violence of the priest's end. "What happened?" Father Creoda had asked in an appalled whisper.

"He killed himself out of remorse," I had told him.

"He . . ."

"Killed himself," I had growled.

"Yes, lord."

"So as a suicide," I said, "he can't be buried in hallowed ground. I don't know why Finan even brought him into the church!"

"I wasn't thinking," Finan said, grinning.

"So you'd best dig the bastard a deep grave somewhere out of town," I advised.

"At a crossroads," Finan said.

"A crossroads?" Father Creoda asked.

"So his soul gets confused," Finan explained. "He won't know which way to go. You don't want his spirit coming back here, God forbid, so plant him at a crossroads and confuse him."

"Confuse him," Father Creoda repeated, staring in horror at the grimace on the dead priest's savaged face.

Brice and his men were thrust down into the darkness of the

shit-stinking cellar. They had all been stripped of their mail, their boots, their jewelry, and their sword belts. "You can let them out in two days," I told the town's reeve. "Throw down some bread for the bastards, give them some buckets of water, then leave them for two whole days. They'll try to persuade you to let them out sooner, they'll try to bribe you, but don't release them."

"I won't, lord."

"If you do," I said, "you make an enemy of me and of Lady Æthelflaed." There had been a time, I thought, when that threat carried real weight.

"And of me," Finan put in.

The reeve shuddered at Finan's soft words. "They'll stay two days, lord, I promise. I swear it on our Lord's body." He turned and bowed to the altar, where feathers from the geese expelled from the cornfield by Saint Werburgh were encased in silver.

"Let them out sooner," Finan added, "and the ghosts of the bones will come for you."

"I swear it, lord!" the reeve said in desperation.

"I suppose they'll bury me at a crossroads," I said to Finan as we walked back to Æthelflaed's house.

He grinned. "We'll give you a proper funeral. We'll light a fire big enough to dim the sun. Trust me, your gods will know you're coming."

I smiled, but I was thinking of the crossroads, of all the roads that the Romans had made, and which crumbled across Britain. Parts were washed away by floods, sometimes the stones were stolen because the big flat slabs made good field markers or foundations for pilings. As often as not when we traveled across country we rode or walked beside the road because the surface was too pitted and ruined for comfort, and so the road was just a weed-strewn marker for our journeys. Those markers led all across Britain, and they decayed, and I wondered what would happen to them. "Do you think," I asked Finan, "that we can see what happens here after we're dead?"

He looked at me strangely. "The priests say so."

"They do?" I was surprised.

"They say you can look into hell," he said, frowning, "so why not into this life too?"

"I'd like to know what happens," I said. I supposed the roads would disappear, and the fields on either side would be overgrown with hazel saplings, and after them the thorny brambles would shroud the old paths. Is that what I would see from Valhalla? And was some Roman gazing at Cirrenceastre even now and wondering how it had turned from honey-colored stone and white marble to damp thatch and rotted timbers? I knew I was making Finan uncomfortable, but I knew too that the Norns, those grim women who control our lives, were fingering my thread and wondering when to slice it with their sharp shears. I had feared that cut for so long, yet now I almost wanted it. I wanted an end to the pain, to the problems, but I also wanted to know how it would all end. But does it ever end? We had driven the Danes back, but now a new fight loomed, a fight for Mercia.

"Here's Father Cuthbert," Finan announced, and I was startled from my thoughts to see Osferth had brought the priest safely from Fagranforda. That was a relief. Cuthbert's wife, Mehrasa, was with him. "You're going north now," I told Osferth.

"Lord!" Cuthbert called, recognizing my voice. He had been blinded by Cnut, and his face quested around as if trying to find where I was.

"North?" Osferth asked.

"We all are," I said. "Families too. We're going to Ceaster."

"Lord?" Cuthbert said again.

"You're safe," I told him. "You and Mehrasa, you're safe."

"From what, lord?"

"You're the only living witness to Edward's first marriage," I told him, "and there are men in Wessex who want to prove that wedding never happened."

"But it did!" he said plaintively.

"So you're going north to Ceaster," I told him, "both of you." I looked at Osferth. "You'll take all the families north. I want you to leave by tomorrow. You can take two carts from Fagranforda to carry food and belongings, and I want you to travel through

Alencestre." There were two good roads to Ceaster. One went close to the Welsh border and I encouraged my men to use it to prove to the Welsh that we did not fear them, but the road through Alencestre was safer because it lay much farther from the frontier lands. "You can take ten men as guards," I said, "and you wait for us at Alencestre. And you take everything valuable. Money, metal, clothes, harness, everything."

"We're leaving Fagranforda for good?" Osferth asked.

I hesitated. The answer, of course, was yes, but I was not sure how my people would respond to that truth. They had made their homes and were raising their children in Fagranforda, and now I was moving them to Mercia's northernmost frontier. I could have explained that by saying we needed to defend Ceaster against the Norse and Danes, and that was true, but the larger truth was that I wanted Ceaster's stone walls about me if I had to defend myself against Eardwulf's spite and Æthelhelm's ambitions. "We're going north for a time," I said evasively, "and if we're not at Alencestre in two days then assume we're not coming. And if that happens you must take Æthelstan and his sister to Ceaster."

Osferth frowned. "What would stop you arriving?"

"Fate," I said too glibly.

Osferth's face hardened. "You're starting a war," he accused me.

"I am not."

"Æthelhelm wants the boy," Finan explained to Osferth, "and he'll fight to get him."

"Which means he starts the war," I said, "not me."

Osferth's grave eyes flickered between me and Finan. Finally he scowled, looking astonishingly like his father, King Alfred. "But you're provoking him," he said disapprovingly.

"You'd rather Æthelstan was dead?"

"Of course not."

"So what would you have me do?" I demanded.

He had no answer to that. Instead he just grimaced. "It will be Saxon against Saxon," he said unhappily, "Christian against Christian."

"It will," I responded harshly.

"But . . ."

"So we'd better make sure the right Christians win," I said. "Now get ready to leave."

"For Ceaster?" Finan asked.

"Osferth goes to Alencestre," I said, "but you and me are going to Gleawecestre. We have a wedding to stop."

And a war to provoke.

My daughter refused to ride with Osferth and the families. "I'm coming to Gleawecestre," she insisted.

"You'll go with Osferth," I told her.

She was rummaging through Æthelflaed's clothes, which Brice and his men had piled untidily in the courtyard. She pulled out a precious dress made from rare silk the color of thick cream and embroidered with strips of oak leaves. "This is pretty," she said, ignoring my order.

"And it belongs to Æthelflaed," I said.

She held the dress to her shoulders and peered down to see if it fell as far as her feet. "Do you like it?" she asked me.

"It probably cost more than a ship," I said. Silk was one of those rarities that could be found in Lundene where it was sold by traders who claimed it came from some country far to the east, where it was woven by strange people, some with three legs, some with the heads of dogs, and some with no heads at all. The stories differed, but men swore they were all true.

"It's beautiful," Stiorra said wistfully.

"It'll go north with Osferth," I said, "and with you."

She folded the dress over one arm and pulled a white linen cloak from the pile. "This will look well with the dress," she said.

"He's taking all the families north," I explained. "He's taking two wagons, so you can ride in one of them."

"Father," she said patiently, "I can ride a horse. And draw a bow. This one will be better," she pulled another white cloak free, "because it has a hood. Oooh! And a silver brooch, see?"

"Are you listening to me?" I growled.

"Of course, Father. And we can pick some stitchwort, can't we?"

"Stitchwort?" I asked.

"To wear in my hair."

"Are you mad?" I asked. "You're going north with Osferth. Why would you want flowers in your hair?"

"Because it's too early for apple blossom, of course." She turned and gazed at me, and for a moment she looked so like her mother that the breath caught in my throat. "Father," she said in a patient tone, "how do you propose to reach Ælfwynn?"

"Reach her?"

"She'll be in Lord Æthelred's palace. To get married she just has to walk through the gate to Saint Oswald's church next door, and I suppose there will be guards along the path, and in the church as well. You can't just ride in and pick her up. So how will you reach her?"

I stared at her. In truth I had no idea how I was to find Ælfwynn. Sometimes it is impossible to make plans, you just reach the battlefield and snatch whatever chance presents itself. Which, I thought ruefully, was the mistake Brice had made, and now I was planning to do exactly the same.

"She's my friend!" Stiorra said when it was plain I had no answer.

"I've seen you with her," I acknowledged grudgingly.

"I like her. Not everyone does, but I do, and it's the custom for girls to go with the bride to the wedding."

"It is?"

"So you give me two of your young men and we go to Lord Æthelred's palace with a bridal gift."

"And they arrest you," I said flatly.

"If they know who I am, maybe? But I've only spent a few days in Gleawecestre, and I've no wish to go into the great hall, just to the outer courtyard where Ælfwynn's rooms are."

"So you go to the courtyard. What then?"

"I'll say I've come with a gift from Lord Æthelfrith."

That was shrewd. Æthelfrith was the wealthy Mercian ealdorman whose lands lay next to Lundene. He disliked Æthelred and refused to travel to Gleawecestre. He might have been an ally for Æthelflaed, except that his real loyalty was to the West Saxons. "And what gift?" I asked.

"A horse," she said, "a young mare. We groom her and plait ribbons in her mane. I'm sure they'll let Ælfwynn see the gift."

"They?"

"She'll be guarded," Stiorra said patiently.

"And she just mounts the mare and rides away with you?"

"Yes."

"And the guards at the gate don't stop you?" I sneered.

"That's the task for your men," she said.

"Suppose she doesn't want to ride away?"

"Oh, she does," Stiorra said confidently, "she doesn't want to marry Eardwulf! He's a pig!"

"A pig?"

"There isn't a maid in Gleawecestre who's safe from him," Stiorra said. "Lady Æthelflaed tells me that no man can ever be trusted, though some can be trusted more than others, but Eardwulf?" She shuddered. "He likes to beat women too."

"How do you know?"

"Oh, Father!" She smiled at me pityingly. "So you see? I'm riding with you to Gleawecestre."

And so she was, because I could think of no better plan. In my mind I had half thought of waylaying Ælfwynn as she walked to the church, but Stiorra was right, the short walk would be well guarded by Æthelred's men. Or I could have gone into the church itself, but that would have been desperate because the big building would be filled with Æthelred's allies. I did not like putting my daughter in danger, but till I arrived in Gleawecestre I could see no better idea.

I had thought to arrive in Gleawecestre that day, but finding carts took time, and giving men careful instructions took more time, and so we were delayed until shortly after dawn on Saint Æthelwold's feast day. I had also hoped to have six carts, but we had found only three in Cirrenceastre and those three would have to be enough. I had sent them westward the night before. The men driving the carts would have to spend an uncomfortable night waiting for the town gates to open, but by the time we left Cirrenceastre two of those three wagons should be inside the walls. They were all loaded with hay, and the men were instructed to tell the gate guards that it was fodder for Lord Æthelred's stables.

It was a typical March day. The sky was gray as iron and the wind cold off the hills behind us. Osferth had taken his ten men back to Fagranforda, where they would load their two wagons with belongings, and, accompanied by Father Cuthbert, set off northward with my men's families. Æthelstan traveled with them. The wagons would make their journey slow, perhaps too slow, and ten men were hardly enough to protect them if they found trouble, but if all went well I would catch up with them before nightfall.

If we survived the next few hours.

Stiorra rode beside me, swathed in a great brown cloak. Beneath it she wore cream silk and white linen, silver chains and amber brooches. We had chosen a young mare, and brushed the animal, combed her, polished her hooves with wax, and woven blue ribbons in her mane, but the road was staining the hooves, and nasty spits of rain bedraggled the carefully tied ribbons. "So," I asked her as we rode down from the hills, "you're a pagan?"

"Yes, Father."

"Why?"

She smiled from beneath her cloak's thick hood, which hid the stitchwort that made a coronet about her black hair. "Why not?"

"Because you were raised Christian."

"Maybe that's why." I growled at that response and she laughed. "Do you know how cruel the nuns are?" she asked. "They hit me and even burned me because I was your daughter."

"Burned you!"

"With a spit from the kitchen fire," she said, and pulled up her left sleeve to show me the scars.

"Why didn't you tell me?" I demanded.

"I told Lady Æthelflaed instead," she said calmly, ignoring my anger, "so of course it didn't happen again. And then you sent me Hella."

"Hella?"

"My maidservant."

"I sent her to you?"

"Yes, Father, after Beamfleot."

"I did?" There had been so many captives taken at Beamfleot that I had forgotten most of them. "Who is Hella?"

"She's behind you, Father," Stiorra said, twisting in the saddle to nod at her maid, who followed us on a placid gelding. I winced with pain when I turned to see a snub-nosed, round-faced girl who looked nervous when she saw me stare at her. "She's a Dane," Stiorra went on, "and a little younger than I am, and a pagan. She told me stories about Freya and Idunn and Nanna and Hyrokin. Sometimes we sat up all night and talked."

"Good for Hella," I said, then rode in silence for a few paces. I did not know my own daughter. I loved her, but I did not know her, and now I had thirty-three men with me, thirty-three men to wreck a wedding and escape a town full of vengeful warriors, and I was sending my daughter into that wasps' nest? What if she was caught? "Christians don't like pagans," I said, "and if Æthelred's men catch you they'll hurt you, persecute you, hound you. That's why you were raised Christian, so you wouldn't be in danger."

"I might worship your gods," she said, "but I am not noisy about it." She opened the cloak and showed me the silver cross hanging over the pretty silk dress. "See? It doesn't hurt me and it keeps them quiet."

"Does Æthelflaed know?"

She shook her head. "As I said, Father, I am not noisy."

"And I am?"

"Very," she said drily.

And an hour later we were at the gates of Gleawecestre, which had been decorated with leafy boughs in honor of the wedding. Eight men guarded the eastern gate where a crowd was trying to enter the city, but they were being delayed as the guards searched a line of wagons. One of my wagons was there, but those men were not trying to enter. They had parked the big cart with its load of hay just to one side of the road. They ignored us as we pushed through the waiting crowd, which, because we were mounted and armed, made way for us. "What are you searching for?" I asked the guard commander, a big man with a scarred face and a black beard.

"Just taxes, lord," he said. Merchants sometimes hid valuable goods beneath piles of cheap cloth or untreated hides and so cheated towns of the proper payments. "And the city's busy," he grumbled.

"The wedding?"

"And the king being here."

"The king!"

"King Edward!" he said, as if I should have known. "Him and a thousand others."

"When did he come?"

"Yesterday, lord. Make way for Lord Uhtred!" He used his long spear to push people aside. "I'm glad you're alive, lord," he said when the gate arch was unobstructed.

"I am too," I told him.

"I was with you at Teotanheale," he said, "and before that." He touched the scar on his left cheek. "Got that when we fought in East Anglia."

I found a coin in my pouch and handed it to him. "What time is the wedding?"

"They don't tell me, lord. Probably when the king gets his royal arse out of bed." He kissed the shilling I had given him. "Poor girl," he added in a lower voice.

"Poor?"

He shrugged as if his comment needed no explanation. "God bless you, lord," he said, touching the rim of his helmet.

"I'm not here," I said, adding a second coin.

"You're not . . ." he began, then looked at the armed men following me. "No, lord, you're not here. I haven't set eyes on you. God bless you, lord."

I rode on, ducking beneath a great spread hide that was hung above a leather shop. Edward was here? That made me angry. Edward had always expressed a fondness for Æthelstan and his sister. He had put them under Æthelflaed's protection, just as he had placed Father Cuthbert under mine, and I thought he had done that to protect them from those men in Wessex who resented their existence. Yet if Edward had come for this wedding it could only mean that he had given way to Æthelhelm completely.

"He recognized you," Finan said, jerking his head toward the guard at the gate, "suppose he sends warning?"

I shook my head. "He won't," I said, hoping I was right. "He's not loyal to Eardwulf."

"But if Eardwulf knows you're here?" Finan said, still worried.

"He'll set more guards," I suggested, but still pulled the hood of my cloak further over my head to shadow my face. It had begun to rain more persistently, puddling the filth-caked street which had lost most of its old paving stones. The main gate to the palace was straight ahead, not far, and spearmen were sheltering beneath its arch. The church was to the left, hidden by the thatched houses and shops. We splashed over a cross street and I saw one of my big wagons half blocking the road to the right. The third one should be waiting near the palace.

The city was crowded, which was hardly a surprise. Every man who had attended the Witan was still here, and they had brought house-warriors, wives, and servants, while folk from a dozen nearby villages had come to Gleawecestre in hope of sharing the feast offered by the bride's father. There were jugglers and magicians, tumblers and harpists, and a man leading a massive brown bear on a chain. The marketplace had been cleared of stalls, and a heap of firewood showed where an ox was to be roasted. The rain fell harder. A greasy-haired priest harangued the passers-by, shouting that they should repent before Christ returned in glory, but no one seemed to be listening to him except for a mangy dog that barked whenever the priest paused for breath.

"I don't like this," I growled.

"What don't you like?" Stiorra asked.

"You going into the palace. It's too dangerous."

She gave me a patient look from beneath her cloak's hood. "So you'll just ride in yourself, Father? Ride in and start a fight?"

"You sound like your mother," I said, and did not mean it as a compliment. But of course she was right. I could not ride in without being challenged and recognized, and then what? I would fight my way into Æthelred's palace and find his daughter? There were not only Æthelred's warriors in the palace, but Æthelhelm's, and King Edward's men too, and it was probably the presence of the West Saxon king that made the guards on the gate so watchful. They had seen us approaching, and two of them moved to block the archway with massive spears, but stepped back when we sheered away into the street that ran alongside the palace wall, close to where my third wagon was parked. "So what will you do?" I asked Stiorra.

"I shall find Ælfwynn, tell her she's welcome to come away with us, and if she agrees I'll bring her," she said as if it was the simplest task imaginable.

"And if she says no?"

"She won't. She hates Eardwulf."

"Then do it," I said to Stiorra. Hella, the maid, would go with her because no well-born woman would ride without a female companion. They would be escorted by two warriors, Eadric and Cenwulf, who had both served me a long time. There was a chance, a small one, that they might be recognized as my men, but I preferred their experience to sending a pair of youths who might panic if challenged. I could, of course, simply have said that the mare was a present from me, but that generosity might raise suspicion, and it was better to pretend it came from Æthelfrith in far-off Lundene. I doubted that the guards on the gate would realize that there had not been time for the news of the wedding to reach Æthelfrith yet. Those guards were cold, damp, and miserable, and probably would not care whether the mare was a gift from Æthelfrith or from the holy ghost. "Go," I told the four of them, "just go."

I dismounted, and the pain was such that I had to lean against my saddle for a few heartbeats. When I opened my eyes I saw Stiorra had taken off the big dark cloak so she appeared now in white and cream, hung with silver, and with flowers in her hair. She spread the pale cloak over her mare's rump and rode straight-backed and tall in her saddle. Hella led the gift mare by the bridle, while Cenwulf and Eadric rode at either side of my daughter. "She looks like a queen," Finan said quietly.

"A wet queen," I said. It was raining harder.

The guards still blocked the archway, but Stiorra's very appearance made them draw back their spears. They bowed their heads respectfully, recognizing her as a highborn lady. I saw her speak to them, but what she said I could not hear, and then the five horses and four riders vanished through the high stone gateway.

I walked back along the street until I could see into the palace grounds. Beyond the archway was a wide courtyard where grass grew. There were a few saddled horses being led up and down by servants and at least twelve more guards standing by the far buildings. That seemed a large number of guards, but other than that there was little sense of urgency, so little that I wondered if the wedding had already happened. "When is the wedding?" I asked one of the spearmen at the gate.

"Whenever Lord Æthelred decides," was the surly reply. The man could not see my face, which was deeply shadowed by my cloak's hood.

"He might wait for the rain to end?" a younger guard answered more helpfully.

"It's set in for the day," the older one said. "It'll piss till nightfall."

"Then Lord Eardwulf will have to wait, won't he?" the younger man said mischievously.

"Wait for what? He takes what he wants. The poor girl can probably hardly walk this morning."

And that was another worry. Had Eardwulf claimed his bride early? Was she in his rooms, and if she was then Stiorra could never reach her. I paced through spreading puddles. Rain dripped from my hood. I had the cloak fastened with brooches to hide the mail I wore and to hide Serpent-Breath, which hung at my side. Stiorra and Hella had both dismounted and vanished into the palace, not into the great hall, which was made of Roman stone, but through a small door that led into a long, low wooden building. The guards there had questioned them, but let them pass. Cenwulf and Eadric waited close by the door. Both men still had their swords. Weapons were not permitted inside the palace buildings, but the two men would be left alone unless they tried to enter any of the doors. I sent Sihtric to look inside the church. "See if it looks ready for a wedding," I told him.

The rain was sheeting down now, running in the road's central gutter and pouring off the roofs. "The girl won't come out in this rain even to see a unicorn," Finan grumbled, "let alone to look at a horse."

"Father Pyrlig saw a unicorn," I said.

"He did?"

"In the mountains. He said it was white and ran like a hare."

"He likes his ale, does Father Pyrlig."

"There are strange things in Wales," I said. "Snakes with two heads. He said the unicorn's horn was red."

"Red?"

"Red as blood." I watched the far door where the guards clustered. "Ælfwynn will come if Stiorra tells her we're here," I said, hoping I was right.

"And if she's not under guard."

I should never have let Stiorra go inside. This whole wet morning was madness. I was no better than Brice, just charging blindly into a place without any real idea how to achieve what I wanted. I had let Stiorra talk me into this madness because at least she had given it some thought, but now, as I watched the guards across the courtyard, I was regretting my impulsiveness. "We might have to fetch her out," I said.

"Us against all those house-warriors?" Finan asked.

"There's only about twenty of them," I said. There were the two men on the gate and the others in the courtyard.

"Twenty we can see. Most of the bastards will be sheltering from the rain. Still, if that's what you want?"

I shook my head. It was not just Æthelred's men, but all the West Saxon warriors too. Perhaps if I had felt well, if I could have swung Serpent-Breath without doubling over in sudden pain, I would have gone into the palace. Palace! A group of stinking timber houses around the remnants of a Roman hall. I imagined the pleasure Æthelred would take if he could seize Stiorra. He was my cousin and we had hated each other since childhood. I would have to negotiate her release, and that would cost me dear. "I'm a fool," I muttered.

"I wouldn't argue with that," Finan said, "but your daughter's clever. She's like her mother."

Thunder sounded far away. I looked up into the rain and saw only dark clouds, but I knew Thor had sent a storm eagle, maybe Ræsvelg himself, the giant eagle that would bring wind behind his wings and, sure enough, the rain that had been falling straight down suddenly bent and shivered as a gust blew through Gleawecestre's streets. Finan crossed himself. The shop signs creaked as they swung. The spearmen guarding the palace gate had retreated deep under the arch, while the guards in the courtyard huddled beneath the thatched porch of the big hall. Cenwulf and Eadric sat patiently on their horses, waiting.

Sihtric splashed through the puddles. "They're lighting candles in the church, lord," he almost had to shout to be heard above the seething rain. "And the roof leaks."

"So the wedding isn't over?"

"Over? They say they might wait till tomorrow."

"They'll surely wait for this to blow over before they marry the poor girl," Finan said.

Thunder sounded louder, a great crack in the sky, and that time I saw a flash of lightning split the clouds. I touched the cloak hiding the hammer that hung from my neck, and sent a prayer to Thor, begging him for my daughter's safety. The rain beat on my cloak's hood. It was a malevolent rain, drenching and vicious.

And Stiorra appeared.

She came into the courtyard and gazed up at the clouds as though reveling in the pelting rain. She spread her arms, and I could see she was laughing, and just then a half-dozen other girls followed her. They were all laughing, squealing in delight at the heavy rain. They splashed through puddles and danced in crazy joy, watched by two guards who had followed them through the door. Then Stiorra ran to the horses and I saw Ælfwynn was following her, and I wondered how she could be a friend to my daughter. Stiorra was so grave and solemn, so controlled and thoughtful, while Ælfwynn was frivolous and silly. Like Stiorra she was dressed in white, and the rain had soaked her dress so it clung to her thin body. The guards watched as she stroked the gray mare's nose. The other girls clustered behind her. Ælfwynn's bright fair hair hung flat, rain-soaked. She turned to Stiorra and jumped for joy, squealing again as the water splashed up from her bare feet. Then, quite suddenly, she, Stiorra, and Hella climbed into their saddles. The guards took no apparent notice. This was a wedding gift, after all, and if the girl was mad enough to come into this rainstorm then she was mad enough to ride the horse around the courtyard.

They rode toward the great hall. Cenwulf and Eadric followed them. My men were mounting. I beckoned to my servant, and the boy brought me my stallion and I took a deep breath, knowing I was about to be hit by a stab of pain as I climbed into the saddle. The pain came, making me wince. I managed to stifle a moan, then I pushed my foot into the stirrup and leaned forward to see through the gate arch, but the pain hit again and I straightened. Finan, still dismounted, could see into the palace's courtyard. "Are you ready?" he called to the men with the hay wagon. "They're coming," he added to me, and pulled himself onto his horse.

Stiorra had led Ælfwynn toward the hall, then swerved toward the gate. I heard them before I saw them, heard the sudden clatter of hooves on the stone paving just beyond the arch, and then the three girls and my two men appeared through the gateway. "Now!" Finan shouted, and the men whipped the cart forward to block the palace arch. One carried an ax to splinter a wheel, and once the cart was crippled they would use the big draft horses to follow us. I had riding horses waiting for them, and for the men on the wagon that would block the cross street halfway to the gate.

The rain had emptied the streets. We trotted over the crossroads and I shouted at those men to block the street. Æthelred's men would have to use one of the city's other two gates to join us. The carts were just there to hamper the pursuit I was sure would follow. Even a few minutes would gain us precious time.

We trotted beneath the city's gate. I paused to look down at the black-bearded man who had fought at Teotanheale. "I'm sorry for what's about to happen," I told him.

"Lord?" he asked, puzzled.

"Your gate's about to be blocked," I said, "and just trust me that I know what I'm doing."

"You always did know, lord," he said, grinning.

We overturned the third wagon at the gate, spilling the hay under the archway. Our pursuers could use the other gates, of course, but it would take time for them to discover this direct path was blocked. The rain would delay them, as would the need to saddle horses, and I guessed we had at least an hour before they followed us. The men who had manned the carts rode north, using the road that ran closest to the Welsh frontier and that led directly toward Ceaster. They would take the news of what I had just done to Æthelflaed, and should arrive in Ceaster in two or three days.

"Uncle!" Ælfwynn rode alongside me. She had always called me that.

"Aren't you cold?"

"Freezing!" She was grinning. She liked mischief, and this exploit was mischievous enough. "Where are we going?"

"To your mother."

That took the smile from her face. Æthelflaed had never approved of her daughter, finding Ælfwynn flippant and irresponsible. "A head full of feathers," she had said often enough. "To mother?" Ælfwynn asked anxiously.

"I can take you back to Gleawecestre instead?" I suggested.

"No, no!" She grinned again. "She's always nicer when you're with her."

"I'll be with you," I said.

"They said you were dying!"

"I am."

"Oh, I hope not."

Finan rode alongside her and handed her a cloak. My men probably regretted that because she was wearing nothing but a light linen shift which, soaked through, clung to her skin. "You ride well!" I told her.

"So does Stiorra!"

I let my horse slow so I could ride beside my daughter. "I was worried," I told her.

She gave me a quick smile. "She wasn't even out of bed when I arrived. I had to wait."

"And no trouble?"

She shook her head. "The guards suspected nothing. I told them I had the horse as a gift and they let her go outside to see it. They thought she was mad to go into the rain, but they're used to her whims."

I twisted in the saddle, instantly regretting it, but there was no sign of any pursuit. The city lay gray under its own smoke and beneath the wind-thrashed rain. "They'll be coming after us," I said grimly.

Ælfwynn had slowed to join us. "Is mother in Cirrenceastre?" she asked.

"She's in Ceaster."

"Isn't Ceaster that way?" she asked, pointing north.

"I want your father to think we're riding to Cirrenceastre," I said.

"Oh, he won't think anything," she said happily.

"He'll be angry!" I warned her.

"No, he won't."

"He'll send men to catch us," I told her, "and to take you back."

"Eardwulf might send men," she said, "and Uncle Edward might, but not Father."

"And why not?" I asked.

"Because he died yesterday," she said. Stiorra and I just stared at her.

"He died . . ." I began.

"No one's supposed to know," she went on airily, "it's a secret, but you can't keep secrets in a palace. The servants told me, and of course they know! They know everything."

"Servants' gossip?" I asked. "It might not be true."

"Oh, there were priests all over the palace!" Ælfwynn said. "It was commotion all night and doors slamming and lots of mumbled prayers. I think it's true." She did not sound in the least upset.

"I'm sorry," I said.

"Sorry?"

"That your father's dead," I said awkwardly.

"I suppose I ought to be sorry," she said, "but he didn't like me and I didn't like him." She looked at Stiorra and grinned, and I wondered whether that was what the two girls had in common: bad fathers. "And he was evil-tempered," Ælfwynn went on, "even more than Mother! And I didn't want to marry Eardwulf so I know I ought to be sorry, but I'm not."

"That's why they're keeping his death a secret," I said. "So they can marry you to Eardwulf before they announce it."

"Well they can't do that now, uncle, can they?" she said happily.

But they could and they would, because without her Eardwulf was nothing, but with her he inherited his father-in-law's power and became Æthelhelm's deputy in Mercia.

So he had to find his bride. I looked behind and saw an empty road, but that meant nothing.

We would be pursued.

PART TWO

The Lady of Mercia

Four

The rain settled into a steady downpour. The thunder had faded and with it the gusting winds, but the rain persisted. It seemed impossible that the sky could hold so much water. It was as though the oceans of the gods were being emptied on us, relentlessly, endlessly, a drenching rainstorm that soaked us as we climbed the steep hills and, once at their summit, turned north to follow sheep paths across the gently rolling slopes. The men on Gleawecestre's walls would have seen us going east toward Cirrenceastre, and I hoped Eardwulf assumed that was our destination, but now we left the Roman road to cross the hills and join the road that led to Alencestre.

The paths were slippery, but there was little mud until we dropped down into the wide valley of Eveshomme, and there the tracks became deep and difficult. I had once heard a Christian priest proclaim that Adam and Eve had lived in this wide, fertile valley, and that it was in this Eden that sin had entered the world. The man had preached like a crazy person, waving his arms, spitting his words, and glaring at the church. "Woman!" he had snarled. "It is woman who brought sin into this world! It is woman who spoiled God's paradise! It is woman who brought evil!" I had been young then, too young to realize what rubbish he spewed. Besides, Father Beocca had told me that the real Eden lay far off beyond the rising sun in a land that was guarded by angels and hidden by golden mists, while Eveshomme, he claimed, was named for a swineherd who had chatted with the Virgin Mary while his pigs rooted about in the beech woods. "What did they talk about?" I had asked him.

"God's grace, I'm sure!"

"That sounds thrilling."

"It is, Uhtred, it is!" he had insisted. "And men and women go to Eveshomme in hope of meeting our Lady."

"And do they meet her?"

"I pray so." He had sounded dubious.

"Have you been?" I had asked him, and he nodded, rather reluctantly. "And did you see her?"

"Alas, no."

"Maybe you'd have had better luck if you'd taken some pigs with you."

"Pigs?" He had been puzzled.

"Perhaps she likes bacon?"

"That is not amusing," he had said. Poor Father Beocca, dead now.

There was no sign of any pursuit, but I knew it would come. Eardwulf needed to find Ælfwynn fast, he needed to drag her back to the church and marry her, only then could he claim some legitimacy as the heir to her father's power. The thegns of Mercia, I thought, would not accept that power readily. They would think him an upstart, but if he had Æthelred's daughter in his bed and the strength of Wessex behind him, then they would sullenly accept his new authority. But without Ælfwynn? Without Ælfwynn he would be nothing but a usurper. It was her virginity, if that still existed, which would tie him to Æthelred's family and status. I thought of finding a priest somewhere in this rainswept valley and have him marry Ælfwynn to my son, then wait while Uhtred took her into a hovel and did the necessary. I thought hard about doing that, but the absence of any pursuit persuaded me to keep traveling instead.

The streams we crossed were swollen by rain, their water overflowing the banks and swirling deep across the fords. There were frequent homesteads, for this was fertile, rich land. The villages were plump and growing. Our defeat of the Danes at Teotanheale had made these folk feel safe; they built without palisades now and they built large. The new barns were as big as churches, and the churches were high-roofed with bright thatch. There were rich orchards and lush meadows, a good land, but low lying so that already floods were reaching across the pastures, the spreading waters thrashed by the stubborn rain. We were cold, we were tired, we were sodden. The temptation was to stop at any of the great halls we passed and let the fire in the hearth dry and warm us, but I dared not halt till we reached Alencestre.

We arrived at dusk, not long after Osferth and his crowd of families had reached the village, though it flattered Alencestre to call the place a village. It was built where two rivers and two roads met, and where the Romans had made two forts. The older fort, its earth walls now overgrown with brambles, lay on a hill south of the rivers, while the newer fort had been built where the rivers met and it was there that Osferth waited. There were a few hovels just outside the fort's decrepit walls, and a hall, a barn, and a half-dozen cattle byres inside. The hall had belonged to a Dane who had died at Teotanheale, and his confiscated land had been granted to the church by Æthelred. "Bishop Wulfheard prays there will be a monastery here," the steward told me.

"Another monastery? There aren't enough?"

Alencestre must have been important to the Romans because the ruins of their buildings lay all about the fort. Now those ruins were covered in ivy and thick with nettles, though the steward had cleared one roofless house. "The bishop said we must make it into a church," he explained.

"You'd do better to repair the fort walls," I said.

"You think the Danes will come again, lord?" he asked nervously.

"The Danes always come again." I snarled that answer, partly because I was in a bad mood and partly because he was a sniveling little man who had tried to deny us his stores of food and ale, claiming they belonged to Bishop Wulfheard. I had been prepared to pay silver for whatever we took, but decided now we would just take the supplies, and the bishop could piss into the wind for all I cared.

I posted sentries on the remnants of the fort wall. The rain was at last slackening as dusk darkened the wet land. A great fire burned in the hall, and we lit another in the barn. I stayed on the ramparts, watching the floodwaters in the fading light. Floating debris had piled itself against the piers of the Roman bridge so that the water foamed there, rippling out to seethe on either side of the bridge's stone roadway. If Eardwulf was following us, I thought, he must cross that bridge, and so I guarded it with six men and a crude barricade made from rafters torn from the cattle byres. Six men would be enough because I doubted our pursuers would come this night. They would be as tired, as wet, and as cold as we were, and the night promised to be black as pitch, too dark for men to travel safely.

"Is Æthelred really dead?" Osferth had joined me on the rampart.

"So Ælfwynn says."

"We've heard that rumor before."

"I think it's true," I said. "But they'll keep it a secret for as long as they can."

"So Eardwulf can marry Ælfwynn?"

I nodded. Ingulfrid, Osferth's woman, had followed him, and I beckoned for her to join us. Life was so complicated, I thought. Ingulfrid was married to a cousin of mine, another Uhtred, the son of my uncle who had usurped Bebbanburg. She had chosen to stay with us when I failed to capture that fortress. Her son had been with her, but Osferth had sent the boy back to his father. I would have cut the little bastard's throat, but I had given the gift of his life to Osferth and he had been generous.

"Eardwulf must find us soon," Osferth said, "he can't keep Æthelred's body long. Not before it starts to stink."

"He has a week," I guessed.

Osferth gazed south. The light had almost gone and the hill beyond the river was nothing but a black shape in the darkness. "How many men will they send?"

"All they have."

"How many is that?" Ingulfrid asked.

"Two hundred? Three hundred?"

"And we're how many?"

"Forty-three," I said bleakly.

"Not enough to hold the fort," Osferth put in.

"We can stop them at the bridge," I said, "but as soon as the river level drops they'll ford it upstream."

"So we keep going tomorrow?"

I did not answer because I had suddenly realized my own stupidity. I had thought Brice a dull-witted enemy, but I had now joined him in the ranks of fools, and granted Eardwulf all the advantage he needed. He was no fool, nor was Æthelhelm, and they must know where I was traveling. I could pretend to head for Cirrenceastre, but they would know I was riding to join Æthelflaed, and they had no need to follow me on the road to Alencestre, they only needed to take the quicker route to Ceaster, the road that followed the Welsh borderlands, and so position their forces ahead of me while I, obligingly, used the longer and slower route through the heart of Mercia. The six sentries on the bridge were guarding nothing because Eardwulf was not pursuing us, instead he would be hurrying northward on the road to our west. His scouts would be looking for us and doubtless they would find us, and then Eardwulf would lead his men eastward to block our path. "Lord?" Osferth asked anxiously.

"He won't come from the south," I said, "but from there." I pointed.

"From the west?" he asked, puzzled.

I did not explain my stupidity. I could blame it on my pain, but that was a feeble excuse. I had sent Osferth, the families, Æthelstan, and his sister on this road because it kept them from the danger of any marauding Welshmen, but all I had achieved was to trap them. "They'll come from the west," I said bitterly, "unless the floods slow them."

"They'll slow us," Osferth said uncertainly, gazing into the wet darkness.

"You should go into the hall, lord," Ingulfrid said to me, "you're cold and wet."

And probably defeated, I thought. Of course Eardwulf was not following me, he had no need to! He was ahead of me, and soon he would block my path and take Ælfwynn as his bride. And then I wondered if I was even on the right side of this argument, because Eardwulf, even married to Ælfwynn, would never be named Lord of Mercia. Edward would surely take the throne, and Eardwulf would be his instrument, his reeve, and perhaps Æthelflaed would approve of her brother taking Mercia's crown, for that would bring their father's dream closer to reality.

Alfred had dreamed of uniting the Saxons. That meant driving the Danes out of northern Mercia, from East Anglia, and, eventually, from Northumbria. Then the four kingdoms would become just one, Englaland. For years now Mercia had depended on Wessex for its survival, so why shouldn't the King of Wessex assume the crown? Three kingdoms were better than four, and three kingdoms were more likely to become one, so was I being stubborn and foolish? Æthelflaed might not approve of Eardwulf, who had ever been her enemy, but perhaps his ennoblement was a price worth paying to bring the dream of Englaland closer?

Then I rejected the idea. Because, I thought, this was not Edward's idea. Edward would doubtless like to be King of Mercia, but at the expense of his eldest son's life? Did Edward want Æthelstan killed? I doubted it. This was Lord Æthelhelm's doing, he wanted Æthelstan removed to ensure that his own grandson would become the King of Wessex and of Mercia and, if the gods of war allowed it, the King of Englaland too. And Æthelstan was as dear to me as my own son and daughter, and now I had led him to this muddy fort in the center of Mercia, and his enemies were already farther north, cutting him off from Æthelflaed's men, who were his only hope of survival.

"Lord?" Osferth said.

"To the hall," I said, "and pray."

Because I had been a fool.

Thunder disturbed the night. Sometime around midnight the rain, which had lessened at dusk, became torrential again and then fell for the rest of the dark hours. It was a seething, soaking, and hard rain.

"We shall have to build an ark, lord," Father Cuthbert spoke to me just before the dawn. I was standing at the hall door, listening to the rain beat on the thatch.

"How did you know it was me?" I asked him.

"You all smell differently," he said. He groped with his hands and found the doorjamb. "And besides," he went on as he leaned against the pillar, "you were muttering."

"I was?"

"Calling yourself a damned fool," he sounded amused, "which is what you usually call me."

"You are," I said.

He turned his eyeless face toward me. "What have I done now?"

"Marrying Edward to his Centish girl," I said, "that was a damn fool thing to do."

"It kept him from sin, lord."

"Sin! You mean swiving a girl is a sin?"

"No one said life is fair."

"Your god makes strange rules."

He turned his face to the rain. I could just see the first faint light touching the east with a damp gray line. "Rain," he said, as if I hadn't noticed.

"Floods," I growled.

"You see? We need an ark. Polecats."

"Polecats?"

"Sheep I can understand," he said. "Noah wouldn't have found it difficult to find a pair of sheep or a couple of cows. But how on earth did he persuade two polecats to enter the ark?"

I had to smile. "You think it really happened," I asked him, "your story of a flood?"

"Oh yes, lord. It was God's judgment on a wicked world."

I stared into the downpour. "Then someone must have been very wicked to bring this rain," I said lightly.

"It wasn't you, lord," he said loyally.

"For a change," I said, still smiling. And Father Cuthbert was right. We needed an ark. What I should have done was have Osferth take the families and all their baggage to the Temes and find a boat, then we should have followed him. The voyage to Ceaster would have taken time, a long time, but once at sea we would have been safe from pursuit. Better still would have been to keep a boat on the Sæfern, south of Gleawecestre, but since my fight with Cnut I had been too feeble to even think about such things.

"So we just keep going now, lord?" Cuthbert asked in a tone suggesting that the last thing he wanted was another day's difficult travel through a rainstorm.

"I'm not sure we can," I said, and a few moments later I splashed through the wet grass and climbed the low rampart to see that the fort was now almost an island. In the half-light of the gray dawn all I could see was water. The rivers had flooded and still the rain fell. I stared as the light slowly grew, then heard a mewing sound and turned to see that Father Cuthbert had followed me and was now lost, standing in ankle-deep water and casting about with the long staff he carried to guide his steps. "What are you doing?" I asked him. "You can't see, so why come out here?"

"I don't know," he said plaintively.

I fetched him to the rampart's weatherworn top. "There's nothing to see," I said, "just floods."

He leaned on the staff, his empty eye sockets staring north. "Have you ever heard of Saint Loginos?" he asked me.

"Never," I said.

"Sometimes he's called Longinus," he added as if that might spur my memory.

"What did he do? Preach to polecats?"

"Not so far as I know, lord, though perhaps he did. He was a blind soldier, the man who thrust his spear into the side of our lord when he hung on the cross."

I turned on Cuthbert. "Why would you give a blind soldier a spear?"

"I don't know. It just happened."

"Go on," I said. I was bored with the stories of saints, how they hung their cloaks on sunbeams or revived the dead or turned chalk into cheese. I would believe the nonsense if I saw even one of those miracles, but I indulged Father Cuthbert. I liked him.

"He wasn't a Christian," the priest said, "but when he thrust the spear some of our Lord's blood fell on his face and he could see again! He was cured! And so he became a Christian too."

I smiled, said nothing. The rain was coming straight down, not a breath of wind.

"Loginos was cured," Father Cuthbert went on, "but he was cursed too. He had wounded our savior and the curse meant that he would never die!"

"That is a curse," I said feelingly.

"He still lives, lord, and every day he takes a mortal wound. Maybe you have fought him! Maybe you gave him that day's mortal wound, and every night he lies down to die and the spear he used against our Lord lies at his side and it cures him."

I realized he was telling me the story because he wanted to help me. I kept quiet, staring at the few hummocks of land showing above the spreading water. Cattle crowded on one such hillock. A drowned lamb had fetched up at the foot of the ramparts and the first crows were already tearing at the fleece. Father Cuthbert's ravaged face was turned to me. I knew what he was saying, but I asked anyway. "What are you suggesting?"

"The weapon that gave the wound can cure it, lord," he said.

"But Loginos's spear did not wound Loginos," I pointed out.

"Loginos wounded himself when his spear pierced Christ's side, lord. He wounded all of us. He wounded mankind."

"It's a muddled story," I said. "He becomes a Christian, but he's cursed? He dies every day and yet he lives? His spear cures him even though it didn't wound him?"

"Lord," Father Cuthbert was entreating me, "find the sword that wounded you. It can cure you."

"Ice-Spite," I said.

"It must exist!"

"Oh, she exists," I said. I assumed the sword had been carried from the battlefield by one of Cnut's men. "But how do I find it?"

"I don't know," Cuthbert said, "I only know you must." He spoke so earnestly, and I knew his words sprang from loyalty. He was not the first person to suggest that the blade that had wounded me could cure me, and I believed it, but how did I find that one blade in all Britain? Cnut's sword, I thought, was in the hands of an enemy, and that enemy was using it to give me pain. There were spells and incantations that would do that. It was an ancient magic, older than Cuthbert's Christian sorcery, a magic that went back to the beginnings of time.

"I will look for it, my friend," I told him. "Now come, you don't need to stand in the rain."

I took him back to the hall.

And the rain did not stop.

Nor did the enemy.

The floods trapped us. The wagons that Osferth had brought from Fagranforda could not go farther, at least not till the waters receded, nor did I want to abandon them. Everything we possessed of any value was on those wagons. Besides, even if we struggled through the floodwaters to the higher ground we could be caught in open country by the horsemen I knew were searching for us. It was better to stay in the Roman fort where, for the moment, we were safe. The flood meant that we could only be approached from the north. We could not be outflanked.

Yet to stay was to invite an enemy to find us, and once the floodwaters drained away we could be assaulted from east, west, and north, and so I sent three of my younger men eastward. They had to ride north first, following the Roman road that was raised on a slight embankment, but even so the water rose well above their stirrups before they reached the low hills and could turn east. They were riding to find men who supported Æthelflaed. "Tell them Æthelred is dead," I told them, "and that Eardwulf is trying to become Lord of Mercia. And ask them to send men here."

"You're starting a rebellion," Osferth accused me.

"Against who?" I challenged him.

He hesitated. "Æthelred?" he finally suggested.

"He's dead."

"We don't know that."

"So what would you have me do?" I asked, posing the same question with which I had challenged him in Cirrenceastre and, once again, he had no answer. He was not opposed to me, but rather, like his father, Osferth was a man who cared about the law. God, he believed, would support the right cause and Osferth suffered agonies of conscience as he tried to discover what was right and what was wrong, and in his mind the right was usually whatever cause the church supported. "Supposing Æthelred still lives," I pressed him, "does that give him the right to help Æthelhelm destroy Æthelstan?"

"No," he admitted.

"Or marry Ælfwynn to Eardwulf?"

"She's his daughter. He can dispose of her as he wishes."

"And her mother has no say?"

"Æthelred is the Lord of Mercia," he said, "and even if he wasn't, then the husband is the head of the family."

"Then why are you tupping another man's wife?" I asked him. He looked desperately unhappy, poor man, and I wondered at the struggle he had to feel between his love for Ingulfrid and the nailed god's disapproval. "And if Æthelred's dead," I asked another question so he would not have to answer the first, "where does that leave Æthelflaed?"

He still looked miserable. Æthelflaed was his half-sister, and he was fond of her, but he was also hounded by his god's ridiculous demands. "The custom," he said quietly, "is for the ruler's widow to enter a nunnery."

"And you want that for her?" I asked angrily.

He flinched at the question. "What else can she do?" he demanded.

"She could take her husband's place," I said.

He stared at me. "She could rule Mercia?"

"Can you think of anyone better?"

"But women don't rule!"

"Æthelflaed can," I said.

"But . . ." he began and fell silent.

"Who better?" I demanded.

"Her brother?"

"Edward! And what if Mercia doesn't want to be ruled by Wessex?"

"They already are," he said, which was true enough though everyone pretended it was not.

"And who'd be the better ruler?" I demanded. "Your half-brother or your half-sister?"

He said nothing for a while, but Osferth was always truthful. "Æthelflaed," he finally admitted.

"She should rule Mercia," I said firmly, though that would only happen if I could keep her daughter from Eardwulf's marriage-bed and so prevent Wessex from swallowing Mercia.

And that looked unlikely because in the middle of the morning as the rain at last showed signs of lessening, the horsemen came from the west. Just one man at first, riding a small horse that he checked on a hilltop across the flooded valley. He gazed at us, then spurred out of sight, but a few moments later there were six riders on the skyline. More men came, perhaps ten or eleven, but it was hard to tell because they scattered from the crest to explore the river valley, looking for a place to cross. "What happens now?" my daughter asked.

"They can't hurt us so long as the floods stay," I said. The floods meant there was only one narrow way to approach the old fort, and I had more than enough men to hold that path.

"And when the floods go?"

I grimaced. "Then it becomes difficult."

Stiorra was holding a lambskin pouch that she now held toward me. I looked at the pouch, but did not take it. "Where did you find that?" I asked her.

"In Fagranforda."

"I thought it burned with everything else." I had lost so much when the Christians burned my buildings.

"I found it years ago," she said, "before Wulfheard burned the hall. And I want to learn how to use them."

"I don't know how," I said. I took the pouch and untied the drawstring. Inside were two dozen alder sticks, slender and polished, none longer than a man's forearm. They were runesticks, and they had belonged to Stiorra's mother. Runesticks could tell the future, and Gisela had known how to read them, but I had never learned the secret. "Does Hella know?"

"She never learned," Stiorra said.

I turned the slender sticks, remembering Gisela casting them. "Sigunn will teach you," I said. Sigunn was my woman and, like Stiorra's maid, she had been captured at Beamfleot. She had been among the women and children who had been brought this far by Osferth.

"Sigunn can read the sticks?" Stiorra asked, sounding dubious.

"A little. She says you have to practice. Practice and dream." I slid the runesticks back into their pouch and smiled ruefully. "The sticks once said you would be the mother of kings."

"Was that mother's prophecy?"

"Yes."

"And the sticks don't lie?"

"They never did for your mother."

"Then those people can't hurt us," Stiorra said, nodding across the valley at the horsemen.

But they could and they would as soon as the floods subsided, and there was little I could do to stop them. I had sent men to find ale in the flooded village, and others had pulled down another cattle byre so our fires would have fuel, but I sensed the enemy tightening a ring about us. By afternoon the rain was slight, gusting now on a cold east wind, and I watched from the ramparts and saw horsemen on every side, and then, as dusk darkened the floodwaters, I saw a line of horses and riders on the high ground to the north. One carried a banner, but the cloth was so waterlogged that it hung limp by the staff and was impossible to decipher.

That night the glow of campfires lit the northern sky. The rain had stopped though every now and then a bitter shower swept spitefully through the darkness. I had sentries watching the lone path to the north, but no one tried to approach us in the darkness. They were content to wait, knowing that the floods would drain and we would be vulnerable. Folk stared at me in the hall's firelight. They expected a miracle.

Sigunn, my woman, was showing Stiorra the runesticks, but Sigunn, I knew, did not wholly understand them. She had dropped the sticks, and she and Stiorra were staring at their pattern, but what it meant neither could tell. Nothing good, I suspected, but I did not need the sticks to see the future. In the morning the enemy would demand two things: Æthelstan and Ælfwynn. Hand them over and we would be left in peace, but if I refused?

Finan knew it too. He squatted beside me. "So?"

"I wish I knew."

"They'll not want to fight us."

"But they will if they must."

He nodded. "And there'll be plenty of them."

"What I'll do," I said, "is marry Uhtred to Ælfwynn. Father Cuthbert can do that."

"You can do that," Finan said, "and that just invites Eardwulf to kill him and make Ælfwynn a widow. Eardwulf won't mind marrying a widow if she brings him Mercia."

He was right. "So you'll take six men," I said, "and carry Æthelstan away."

"They're all around us," he said.

"Tomorrow night," I said, "in the dark."

He nodded again, but he knew as well as I did that we were pissing into a gale. I had tried and I had failed. I had led my men, their women, their families, and everything we possessed to this waterlogged fort in the middle of Mercia, and my enemies were all around me. If I had been well, if I had been the Uhtred who had led men to battle against Cnut, then those enemies would be nervous, but they knew I was weakened. I had frightened men once, now I was the one who was frightened. "If we live through this," I told Finan, "I want to find Ice-Spite."

"Because she'll cure you?"

"Yes."

"And so she will," he said.

"But how?" I asked gloomily. "Some bastard Dane will have her, and who knows where?"

He stared at me, then shook his head. "A Dane?"

"Who else?"

"It can't be a Dane," he said, frowning. "You went down the hill to meet Cnut and he came up the slope."

"I remember that much."

"The two of you fought in the open. There were no Danes near you. And once you'd killed him the Danes ran. I was the first to reach you."

I did not remember that, but then I remembered little of that fight except for the sudden surprise of Cnut's blade in my side and the scream I gave as I cut his throat.

"And the Danes can't have taken his sword," Finan went on, "because they never went near his body."

"Then who did?"

"We did," Finan was frowning. "Cnut was on the ground and you were on top of him with his blade in you. I pulled you off and tugged the sword free, but I didn't keep it. I was more worried about you. I looked for it later, but it was gone. Then I forgot about it."

"So it's here," I said softly, meaning the sword was somewhere in Saxon Britain. "Who else was with you?"

"Christ! They all came down the hill. Our men, the Welsh, Father Pyrlig, Father . . ." he stopped abruptly.

"Father Judas," I finished for him.

"Of course he came!" Finan said robustly. "He was worried for you." Father Judas. The man who had been my son. He called himself something else these days. "He wouldn't hurt you, lord," Finan added earnestly.

"He already has," I said savagely.

"It's not him," Finan said firmly.

But whoever it was, they had won. Because I was trapped, and the dawn showed that the floods were already shrinking. Water foamed at the Roman bridge where trees and branches were trapped against the arches, while the roadways on either bank were still flooded, and those waters were keeping the men on the southern and western hills away from the fort. But the largest number of men were to our north. Those were the warriors who could attack straight down the Roman road and there were at least a hundred and fifty of them on the low rise of ground swelling from the water meadows. A few had spurred their horses into the floods, but abandoned their attempts to reach us when the water rose above their stirrups. Now they were content to wait, walking up and down on the skyline or just sitting on the nearer slope and staring toward us. I could see black-robed priests there, but most of the men were warriors, their mail and helmets gray in the clouded day.

By mid-afternoon the water had drained from much of the road, which was raised a few hand breadths above the fields. A dozen riders spurred from the hill. There were two priests, two standard-bearers, and the rest were warriors. The larger flag showed Æthelred's white horse, while the smaller depicted a saint holding a cross. "Mercia and the church," Finan said.

"No West Saxons," I noted.

"They sent Eardwulf to do their dirty work?"

"He has the most to gain," I said, "and the most to lose." I took a breath, bracing myself for the pain, and hauled myself into the saddle. Osferth, Finan, and my son were already mounted. The four of us were dressed for war, though, like the men who approached from the north, we carried no shields.

"Do we take a banner?" my son asked.

"Don't flatter them," I growled, and kicked my horse forward.

The fort's gateway was above water, but after a few yards the horses were splashing fetlock deep. I rode some eighty or ninety paces from the fort and there reined in and waited.

Eardwulf led the Mercians. His dark face was grim, framed by a helmet decorated with silver serpents that writhed about the metal skull. He wore a white cloak over his polished mail, the linen edged with ermine, while his sword scabbard was bleached leather trimmed with silver strips. There was a heavy gold chain about his neck from which hung a golden cross studded with amethysts. There was a priest either side of him, both men riding smaller horses. Their black robes had dragged in the floods and hung dripping by their stirrups. They were the twins Ceolnoth and Ceolberht who, some thirty years before, had been captured with me by the Danes, a fate I had embraced, while the twins had become vehement haters of all pagans. They hated me too, especially Ceolberht, whose teeth I had kicked out, but at least that meant I could now tell them apart. Most of the horsemen stopped fifty paces away, but Eardwulf and the twins rode on until their horses confronted ours on the flooded road. "I bring a message from King Edward," Ceolnoth spoke without any greeting, "he says you are . . ."

"Brought your puppies to do your yapping?" I asked Eardwulf.

"He says you are to return to Gleawecestre," Ceolnoth raised his voice, "with the boy Æthelstan and the king's niece, Ælfwynn."

I stared at the three of them for a few heartbeats. A gust of wind brought a few drops of rain, sharp and fast, but the rain was gone almost as soon as it started. I looked up at the sky, hoping the rain would start again because the longer the floods lasted the more time I had, but if anything the clouds were lightening. Finan, Osferth, and my son were gazing at me, waiting for my response to Ceolnoth, but I just turned my horse. "Let's go," I said.

"Lord Uhtred!" Eardwulf called.

I spurred on. I would have laughed if it had not hurt so much. Eardwulf called again, but then we were out of earshot and cantering through the fort's entrance. "Let them pick the bones out of that," I said. He would be confused. He had been hoping to test my resolve, perhaps even hoping that I would obey a summons from the West Saxon king, but my refusal to even talk to him suggested he would have to fight, and I knew Eardwulf would be reluctant to attack. He might outnumber me by at least three to one, but he would take grievous casualties in any fight, and no man wanted to face warriors like Finan in battle. Eardwulf could not even be sure that all his men would fight; plenty of them had served under me over the years and they would be reluctant to attack my shields. I remembered the black-bearded man in Gleawecestre's gateway; he was a Mercian, sworn to Æthelred and Eardwulf, but he had grinned at me, been pleased to see me, and it would be difficult to persuade such men to fight me. And though Eardwulf was a warrior, and had a reputation, he did not inspire loyalty in his men. No one spoke of Eardwulf's conquests, of the men he had cut down in single combat. He was a clever enough leader of men, but he let others do the grim work of slaughter, and that was why he did not inspire loyalty. Æthelflaed did, and I dare say that I did too.

Eardwulf was still watching us when I dismounted. He stared for a while longer, then turned his horse and rode back to the dry ground. That ground was spreading as the waters fell, and there was further bad news as the afternoon wore on. More men came to join Eardwulf. They came from the north, and I guessed they were patrols that had been searching for us, but had been recalled so that by dusk there were over two hundred men on the low hill, and the floods were almost gone. "They'll come at dawn," Finan said.

"Probably," I agreed. Some of Eardwulf's men might be reluctant, but the more warriors he gathered, the more likely they were to attack. The reluctant fighters would be in the second rank, hoping others would bear the brunt of the fight, and meanwhile the priests would be whipping them into a holy fervor, and Eardwulf would be promising them plunder. And Eardwulf had to attack. It was plain to me that Edward and Æthelhelm had wanted no part in this fighting. They could take Mercia whenever they wanted, but Eardwulf stood to lose his inheritance from Æthelred. If he failed, then the West Saxons would cut him adrift, and so he had to win. He would come in the dawn.

"Suppose he attacks at night?" my son asked.

"He won't," I said. "It's going to be black as pitch, they'll be floundering in water, they'll get lost. He might send men to harass us, but we'll put sentries on the road."

We also lit fires on the rampart, pulling down the last two cattle byres to find the fuel. Eardwulf could see my sentries coming and going in the light of those fires, though I doubted he knew I had men posted closer to him, but none of them was disturbed. He did not need to make a risky attack in the dark of night, not when he had the men to overwhelm me in the dawn.

A star showed in the sky just before dawn. The clouds were clearing at last, blown away by a cold east wind. I had thought to send Osferth and forty horsemen across the bridge because there were fewer enemy on the south bank of the river. I planned to send Æthelstan, his sister, and Ælfwynn with them, and let them hurry eastward to Lundene while I stayed behind to defy Eardwulf, but he had anticipated me and, as the first light spilled over the world's edge, I saw forty horsemen waiting just beyond the bridge. The flooding there was almost gone. The sun rose to show a damp world. The fields were half green and half shallow pools. Gulls had come from the faraway sea and flocked across the watery land.

"That's a pity," I said to Finan, pointing to the horsemen who blocked the bridge. The two of us were on horseback in the entrance gate of the old fort.

"That's a pity," he agreed.

It was fate, I thought. Just fate. We think we control our own lives, but the gods play with us like children playing with straw dolls. I thought how often I had maneuvered enemies into traps, of the joy of imposing my will on a foeman. The enemy believes he has choices, then discovers he has none, and now I was the one in the trap. Eardwulf had surrounded me, he outnumbered me, and he had foreseen my one desperate move, to escape across the bridge.

"There's still time to marry Ælfwynn to your son," Finan said.

"And as you said that just invites Eardwulf to kill him," I said, "so he can marry the widow."

The sun was casting long shadows across the wet fields. I could see Eardwulf's men mounting their horses on the northern crest. They carried shields now, shields and weapons.

"It's Æthelstan I care for," I said. I turned to look at the boy, who looked back at me with a brave face. He was doomed, I thought. Æthelhelm would have his throat cut in an eyeblink. I beckoned to him.

"Lord?" He looked up at me.

"I've failed you," I said.

"No, lord, never."

"Quiet, boy," I told him, "and listen to me. You are the son of a king. You are the eldest son. Nothing in our laws says the eldest son must be the next king, but the ætheling has more claim on the throne than anyone else. You should be the King of Wessex after your father, but Æthelhelm wants your half-brother on the throne. Do you understand?"

"Of course, lord."

"I swore an oath to protect you," I said, "and I've failed. For that, Lord Prince, I am sorry."

He blinked when I called him "prince." I had never addressed him as royalty before. He opened his mouth as if to speak, then found nothing to say.

"I have a choice now," I told him. "I can fight, but we're out-numbered and this is a battle we can't win. By mid-morning there'll be a hundred dead men here and you'll be a captive. They plan to send you across the sea to a monastery, and in two or three years, when you've been forgotten in Wessex, they'll kill you."

"Yes, lord," he said in a whisper.

"My other choice is to surrender," I said, and the word was like gall in my mouth. "If I do that," I went on, "then I live to fight another day. I live to take ship to Neustria. I will find you and rescue you." And that, I thought, was a promise with about as much substance as breath on a winter's morning, but what else could I say? The truth, I thought sadly, was that Eardwulf would probably slit the boy's throat and blame me. That would be his gift to Æthelhelm.

Æthelstan looked past me. He was watching the horsemen on the far hill. "Will they let you live, lord?" he asked.

"If you were Eardwulf," I asked him, "would you?"

He shook his head. "No," he said seriously.

"You'll make a good king," I said. "They'll want to kill me, but they don't really want to fight me either. Eardwulf doesn't want to lose half his men, so he'll probably let me live. He'll humiliate me, but I'll live."

Yet I would not surrender too easily. At the least I could per-suade him that to fight me was to lose men, and maybe that would make his surrender terms easier. Just outside the fort, to the south, the river made a bend, and I sent all our women and children to wait in the water meadow encircled by the river's loop. The warriors made a shield wall in front of them, a shield wall that just stretched from river bank to river bank. That way, at least, Eardwulf could only attack from the front. It would even the fight somewhat, but he had such a predominance in numbers that I could not imagine winning. I just needed to delay him. I had sent those three young men to find help and maybe it was coming? Or maybe Thor would come from Asgard and use his hammer on my enemies?

Finan and I waited on horseback in front of the shield wall. The men behind us, like their families, were ankle deep in floodwater.

Our horses and our baggage were still in the fort. All I brought to the river bend was my hoard, the leather bags of silver and gold. Almost all I possessed and almost everyone I loved was now trapped in the noose made by the river's loop.

The fates were laughing at me, those three hags at the foot of the tree who decide our lives. I touched the hammer at my neck. A small mist was drifting off the soaked fields as the sun rose higher. Somewhere beyond the river a lamb bleated.

And Eardwulf led his forces off the hill.

Five

Eardwulf came in the full panoply of war, armed and armored, the snake-wreathed helmet bright-polished, his horse dressed with a scarlet saddle-cloth tasseled with gold that skimmed the remaining floodwaters. His shield showed Æthelred's prancing horse, and I wondered how long that symbol would stay painted on the willow boards. Once he had married Ælfwynn and was confirmed as the heir to Æthelred's lands and fortune he would doubtless find his own badge. What would that be? If I were him I would take my banner of the wolf's head, daub it with blood, and put a cross above it to show he had beaten me. He would be Eardwulf the Conqueror, and I had a sudden vision of his rise, not just to dominate Mercia, but perhaps all Britain. Did Edward and Æthelhelm know what a viper they suckled?

Wyrd bið ful āræd. Fate is inexorable. We are given power and we lose it. I was wounded and growing old, and my strength was slipping away, and I was seeing the new man, the new lord, and he looked formidable as his men advanced across the half-flooded fields to scatter the gulls. He had formed his warriors into a battle line, spread wide across the waterlogged meadows, over two hundred horsemen on big horses. They were all in their war gear, helmeted, carrying shields, their bright-bladed spear-points stark against the faint mist that was fading as the sun rose higher. The priests followed Eardwulf, clustering around the two standard-bearers who carried Æthelred's prancing horse banner and a flag of Saint Oswald, which showed a one-armed skeleton holding up a bright red cross.

"There's a woman there," Finan said.

"It must be his sister," I said.

Eadith had been Æthelred's mistress. I had been told she was as ambitious and as cunning as her brother, and doubtless she was here to enjoy his victory which would be all the sweeter for being at my expense. I was hated, and I knew it. Part of it was my fault, I am arrogant. Just as Eardwulf was about to relish his victory, so I had relished victories all my life. We live in a world where the strongest win, and the strongest must expect to be disliked. Then I am a pagan, and though Christians teach that they must love their enemies, few do.

"If you had your life over again," I asked Finan, "what would you do differently?"

He gave me a curious look. "That's a strange question."

"But what would you do?"

He shrugged. "Kill my younger brother," he growled.

"In Ireland?"

"Where else?"

He never spoke of what had driven him from Ireland, but there was a bitterness to his words. "Why?" I asked, but he said nothing. "Maybe we should go there," I said.

He gave me a swift unamused smile. "You have a death wish now, do you?" he asked, then looked back toward the approaching horsemen. "It looks as if you'll get your wish. Will you fight them?"

"It's the only threat I have."

"Aye, but will you?"

"You can't make an empty threat," I said, "you know that."

He nodded. "True." He watched Eardwulf's men, his right hand caressing the hilt of his sword. "And what would you do differently?" he asked after a while.

"Take better care of my children."

He smiled at that. "You have good children. And you'd better stay alive to look after them now, which means you don't fight in the front rank."

"I will not . . ." I began.

"You're not strong enough!" he insisted. "You stand in the second rank and I'll kill that whore-begotten bastard before they kill me."

"Unless I kill him first," my son said. I did not realize he had joined us, and I felt embarrassed for what I had just said. "But there's one thing I know about Eardwulf," Uhtred said, "he never fights in the front rank." He loosened Raven-Beak in its scabbard, then touched the cross hanging about his neck to his lips. "We'll have to hack our way through to him."

"You and me," Finan said.

"We'll do it too," Uhtred said wolfishly. He looked happy. He was outnumbered, facing death or disgrace, and looked happy.

We watched Eardwulf, his sister, and the priests leave the road and slant across the soaking fields toward the loop of the river where we waited. Eardwulf raised a hand to stop his men a hundred paces away, but he and his companions walked their horses through the shallow floods, finally stopping just ten paces away.

"Lord Uhtred," Eardwulf greeted me. His voice was muffled by the wide cheek-pieces of his silver helmet that almost closed over his mouth. I said nothing.

"You will give . . ." Father Ceolnoth began.

"Quiet!" Eardwulf snapped with a surprising authority. The priest looked at him with astonishment, but went silent.

Eardwulf pushed the cheek-pieces away from his face. "We've come to take the boy Æthelstan and the Lady Ælfwynn back to Gleawecestre," he said. He spoke quietly and reasonably.

"Prince Æthelstan," I said, "was placed under the Lady Æthelflaed's care. I am taking him to her, and taking her daughter too."

"Lady Æthelflaed's husband has decided otherwise," Eardwulf said.

"Lady Æthelflaed has no husband."

He looked startled at that, but recovered swiftly enough. "You listen to rumor, Lord Uhtred."

"Lord Æthelred is dead," I said.

"He lives," Eardwulf said harshly, but I was looking at his sister and I could see the truth of my words on her face.

She was lovely. I was prepared to hate her, but who could hate a woman so beautiful? No wonder she had found wealth and power. I knew she was the daughter of a thegn from southern Mercia, a man of no great wealth or position, but she had become

Æthelred's lover and so she and her brother had risen in status and influence. I had expected someone harsh to match the rumors of her cunning ambition, but Eadith's pale-skinned face was intelligent, and her green eyes were glistening with tears. She had very red hair, mostly hidden beneath a cap of ermine that matched the white cape she wore over a dress of pale green linen. "Shouldn't you be dressed in mourning, lady?" I asked her.

She did not reply, just looked away from me to gaze eastward where the sun was shimmering on what remained of the floods. The reflected sunlight made ripples on her face.

"Lord Æthelred's health is no concern of yours," Eardwulf said. "He wishes his daughter returned, and the boy too."

"And my wish is to take them to the Lady Æthelflaed," I answered.

Eardwulf smiled. He was a handsome brute and very confident of himself. He looked past me to where my men were standing in their shield wall. "At this moment, Lord Uhtred," he said, "my wishes will prevail."

He was right, of course. "You want to test that?" I asked.

"No," he said, and his honesty surprised me. "I don't want twenty or thirty of my men dead and as many others wounded. And I don't want all your men dead either. I just want the boy, his sister, and the Lady Ælfwynn."

"And if I let you take them?" I asked.

"They will be safe," he lied.

"And you just leave?"

"Not quite." He smiled again. The twins Ceolnoth and Ceolberht were glaring at me. I could see they wanted to intervene, presumably to spit threats at me, but Eardwulf was calmly in control. His sister was still gazing eastward, but turned suddenly and looked at me and I saw the sadness on her face. So she had been fond of my cousin? Or was she mourning the destruction of her power? Æthelred's favor had made her rich and influential, but now? Only her brother's ambitions could save her future.

"Not quite," Eardwulf said again, forcing me to look back to him.

"Not quite?" I asked.

Eardwulf's horse tossed its head and he calmed it with a gloved hand on its muscled neck. "No one," he said, "underestimates you, Lord Uhtred. You are the greatest warrior of our time. I salute you." He paused, as if expecting a response, but I just stared at him. "If I merely leave you," he said, "then I would expect you to attempt a rescue of the boy Æthelstan. Maybe of the Lady Ælfwynn too?" He inflected it as a question, but again I said nothing. "So you will yield me all your weapons and all your horses, and you will give me your son and daughter as hostages for your good conduct."

"You will be exiled too!" Father Ceolnoth could no longer contain himself. "You've polluted Christian land too long!"

Eardwulf held up a hand to check the priest's spite. "As Father Ceolnoth says," he still spoke in a reasonable tone, "you must leave Wessex and Mercia."

My heart was sinking. "Anything else?" I snarled.

"Nothing more, lord," Eardwulf said.

"You expect me to give you my sword?" I asked angrily.

"It will be returned to you," he said, "in time."

"You want Prince Æthelstan," I said, "the Princess Eadgyth, Lady Ælfwynn, my son and my daughter?"

"And I swear on the cross that your son and daughter will not be harmed so long as you stay far from Mercia and Wessex."

"And you want our weapons and horses," I went on.

"Which will all be returned to you," Eardwulf said.

"In time," I spat.

"Jesus," Finan said quietly.

"And if I don't give you what you wish?" I asked.

"Then your life story ends here, Lord Uhtred."

I pretended to consider his terms. I waited a long time. Father Ceolnoth became impatient and twice began to speak, but both times Eardwulf quietened him. He waited, sure that he knew my answer and equally sure that I was just loath to say it. Finally I nodded. "Then you may have what you want," I said.

"A wise decision, Lord Uhtred," Eardwulf said. His sister looked at me with a frown as if I had just done something unexpected.

"But to get what you want," I added, "you must take them." And with those words I turned my stallion and spurred toward the shield wall. Eardwulf shouted something as I went, but I did not catch the words. The shields parted and Finan, my son, and I went through. The pain stabbed at me as I dismounted and I felt the pus seeping from the bloody wound. It hurt. I leaned my helmeted head against my horse, waiting for the agony to go. I must have looked as though I was praying, and so I was. Odin, Thor, help us! I even touched the silver cross in the pommel of Serpent-Breath, a keepsake from an old lover, and said a prayer to the Christian god. They all have power, all the gods, and I needed their help. I straightened and saw that Finan and my son had gone to the center of the front rank. If they could kill Eardwulf then we might snatch victory from this disaster.

Eardwulf was still watching us, then he said something to his sister and turned back to his men. I watched them dismount and heft their shields. I watched as boys came to take the horses and as the warriors formed a shield wall, touching the shields together, overlapping them, shuffling to make the wall tight.

And I stood in the second rank and knew I must surrender. We would lose anyway, so why make widows and orphans? I suppose I had thought that Eardwulf might choose not to fight, or that his men would be reluctant to attack me, but I was wrong and, worse, Eardwulf knew exactly what to do. He would not bring his shield wall to oppose mine, instead he took time to change his formation, turning the wall into a swine-head, a wedge, that was aimed at my right flank. He would charge at us, driving his force at one end of our wall, and when he broke through he would surround the survivors and there would be a slaughter in the river's loop.

"We'll turn into him as he comes," Finan said, tacitly taking command of my men. "As soon as they come we attack the side of their wedge."

"And go for Eardwulf," my son added. Eardwulf had stayed mounted at the back of the wedge, so if by some miracle we broke his men he could flee out of danger.

"I've broken swine-heads before," Finan said, trying to give my men confidence. "Attack the side and they crumble!"

"No," I said quietly.

"Lord?" he asked.

"I can't kill my men," I told Finan. "Whether I fight or not, he gets his way."

"So you'll surrender?"

"What choice do I have?" I asked bitterly. I was tempted to let Finan swing our shield wall to attack the right side of Eardwulf's wedge. It would be a rare fight and we would kill a good number of Mercians, but sheer weight of numbers must win in the end. I had no choice. It was bitter and shameful, but I would be throwing away the lives of my men, my good and loyal men.

"It seems you might have a choice," Finan said, and I saw he was staring past Eardwulf toward the northern hill. "See?" he asked.

There were more horsemen on the hill.

A horn sounded. It was a melancholy call, fading away before the horn was blown a second time. Eardwulf, still on horseback, turned.

Twenty horsemen had appeared on the far hill. It was one of them who had sounded the horn. The horsemen were clustered beneath a banner, though the lack of wind meant the banner hung limp, but as we watched I saw three more banners appear. Four standards held by four horsemen arrayed along the hill's long crest. Each of the three new standard-bearers was accompanied by a group of armed riders, but whatever other horsemen followed the banners stayed on the far slope so we could not see them. What we could see was the gray of mail and the glint of sun reflecting from spearheads and helmets.

Eardwulf looked toward me, then back to the hilltop. He could count. There was no rule about it, but one standard suggested a hundred men, and there were four flags behind him. The horsemen who had first appeared had ridden back now, hidden like the others on the far slope, but the standards stayed, and then the horn called a third time and four horsemen appeared at the center of the ridge and, accompanied by just one of the standard-bearers, spurred down the slope toward us.

"Who are they?" Finan asked.

"Who knows?" I said. Eardwulf seemed similarly puzzled because he looked at me again before turning his horse and kicking it back toward the road.

"Æthelhelm's men?" I suggested, though if Æthelhelm had sent men then why had they not stayed with Eardwulf? My suspicion was that Æthelhelm and Edward had decided to let Eardwulf untangle the mess I had caused. They did not want West Saxons fighting Mercians, it was better to let the Mercians fight each other.

And the approaching horsemen were Mercians. The standard-bearer waved his flag as he rode and my heart sank because it showed Æthelred's prancing horse. "That's a pity," I said bleakly.

But Finan was laughing. I frowned at him, then looked back as the five horsemen galloped past Eardwulf. Their horses' hooves threw up great splashes of water, the splashes as white as the leading rider's cloak, and then I saw why Finan was laughing.

The rider in white was Æthelflaed.

She had ignored Eardwulf, riding past him as if he was a nobody. She wore her mail coat, though no helmet, and she did not slow as she approached the rear of Eardwulf's men. She rode Gast, her gray mare, and the horse's legs, belly, and chest were thick with mud to show how hard she had been ridden these last two or three days. Once past the shield wedge, Æthelflaed turned the mare in a flurry of splashing water. Her standard-bearer and three men reined in beside her. She did not look at me, nor did I move to join her.

"You will go home," she spoke to Eardwulf's men. She pointed south past the fort to where his men guarded the bridge. "You go that way and you go now."

None of them moved. They stood watching her, waiting for Eardwulf, who pushed his horse forward. "Your husband has decided . . ." he began in a harsh tone.

"Her husband is dead!" I shouted over him.

"Your husband . . ." Eardwulf began again.

"Is dead!" I shouted even louder, and winced as the pain seared from my lower ribs.

Æthelflaed turned and looked at me. I could see from her face that she had not known about Æthelred's death. Nor was I completely certain of it myself, I only had Ælfwynn's word for it, but I suspected the girl had spoken truthfully. Æthelflaed was still frowning at me, waiting for a sign, and I nodded. "He's dead, my lady," I said.

Æthelflaed made the sign of the cross as she turned back to Eardwulf's shield wall. "Your lord is dead," she said to them, "Lord Æthelred is dead. We mourn him and we shall have masses said for his soul, which God preserve. And your duty now is to go home. So go!"

"My lady . . ." Eardwulf began again.

"Who rules here?" she interrupted him savagely. "You or I?"

It was a good question and one Eardwulf could not answer. To say that Æthelflaed ruled was to bow to her authority, while to claim that he ruled was to usurp the lordship of all Mercia. His slender claim to power depended on marrying Ælfwynn and on the support of the West Saxons, and both were slipping away. And Æthelflaed was sister to the King of Wessex. Attacking or defying her were both risks that could tip Edward's support against him. Eardwulf had lost, and he knew it.

"My husband prized your obedience," Æthelflaed spoke again to the shield wedge, "and he would want that obedience to continue. I will carry on his work until the Witan decides who should assume his responsibilities. Until then I look for your obedience and support." I noticed some men were gazing at her while others looked away, and I reckoned the latter were men sworn to Eardwulf rather than to Æthelred. Maybe a third looked uncomfortable, but the rest, like me, seemed relieved. "You," Æthelflaed looked at Eardwulf, "will stay in command of my household warriors and lead them back to Gleawecestre. I shall follow you. Go now, go!"

He hesitated. I could read his thoughts at that moment. He was thinking, daring to think, of drawing his sword and attacking Æthelflaed. He was so close to her! Her men were still on the far hill, too far away to offer immediate help, and he had all his men facing my few, and she was destroying his hopes. He was calculating the future. Was Æthelhelm's support enough to deflect Edward's rage if he killed Æthelflaed? His mouth was suddenly grim, his eyes narrow. He stared at her, and she at him, and I saw his right hand move toward his sword hilt, but Ceolnoth saw it too and the priest reached out and grasped Eardwulf's forearm. "No, lord," I heard Father Ceolnoth say. "No!"

"I will meet you in Gleawecestre," Æthelflaed said, her voice steady.

And Eardwulf turned away. His whole future had trembled in that instant and he had lost. And so he and his men went. I remember watching in disbelief and feeling a wave of relief as Eardwulf's warriors retrieved their horses and, without a word, filed over the bridge and disappeared to the south.

"Sweet Jesus Christ," Finan breathed.

"Help me up," I told my son, and he heaved me into the saddle where I held my breath until the pain passed.

Æthelflaed signaled my men to make a gap so she could join us. "Is it true?" she demanded. She offered no greeting, just the curt question.

"I think so," I said.

"You think!"

"Your daughter heard the news," I said, "though Eardwulf denied it."

"Not his sister, though," Finan said, "she was weeping. She was mourning."

"He died on the eve of Æthelwold's Day," I said, "the night before the wedding."

"It's true, Mother." Ælfwynn, looking nervous, had joined us.

Æthelflaed looked from her daughter to Finan, then to me. I nodded. "He's dead. They want to keep it secret, but he died."

"God give him rest," Æthelflaed said, and crossed herself, "and God forgive me." There were tears in her eyes, though whether those tears were for Æthelred or for her own sinfulness I could not tell, nor would I ask. She shook her head abruptly then stared at me. Her face was stern, almost hurt, so her next words surprised me. "How are you?" she asked softly.

"In pain, of course. And glad you came. Thank you."

"Of course I came." There was anger in her voice now. "Marrying Ælfwynn to Eardwulf! His own daughter!" That was why she had been riding south. Like me she kept her own people in

Æthelred's court, and one of those had sent a message to Ceaster as soon as the wedding was announced. "I knew I couldn't reach Gleawecestre in time," she said, "but I had to try. Then we met your people coming north." Those were the men who had manned the carts blocking Gleawecestre's streets. Those carts had probably not been needed because Eardwulf's pursuit had been slow in starting, but the men had given Æthelflaed the news that I had snatched her daughter out of Æthelred's palace and was coming north on the roads that led through Alencestre. "After that," she said, "it was just a question of finding you."

"How many men did you bring?"

"Thirty-two. I had to leave the rest to defend Ceaster."

"Thirty-two?" I sounded astonished, and was. I looked north and saw the horsemen coming from the hill. I had expected hundreds, but there were just the few. "And the four flags?"

"Three of them were cloaks hanging from ash branches," she said.

I almost laughed, except it would have hurt too much. "So where now?" I asked instead. "Back to Ceaster?"

"Ceaster!" She almost spat the name. "Mercia is not ruled from Ceaster. We ride to Gleawecestre."

"And Eardwulf," I said, "is ahead of us."

"So?"

"Will you keep him as your commander of the household troops?"

"Of course not."

I looked south to where Eardwulf had gone. "Maybe we should have made him a prisoner?"

"By what right? So far as I knew he still commanded my husband's troops. And his men might have fought for him."

"Might," I said. "But he's still got one chance left. He knows that if he marries Ælfwynn and kills you then he will be Lord of Mercia. And within an hour he'll also know we have fewer than half as many men as he does."

"He'll be watching us?"

"Of course he is," I said. Eardwulf was bound to have scouts watching us.

Æthelflaed gazed southward as if looking for Eardwulf's men. "Then why didn't he kill me just now?" she asked.

"Because not all his men would have obeyed him, and because he thought you had two or three hundred men on the hill. And if you had brought two hundred men he would have died himself. But now? Now he knows he has nothing to lose."

She frowned at me. "You really think he'll attack us?" She sounded incredulous.

"He has no choice," I said. "He has one day left to achieve his ambitions. One day and one night."

"Then you'll have to stop him," she said simply.

And we rode south.

We did not all travel south. I left our baggage and our families in the fort with twenty-five men to guard them and with Osferth once again in command. "When the roads are fit for the wagons," I told him, "keep going to Ceaster."

"To Ceaster?" He sounded surprised.

"Where else?"

"It's safe to go back to Fagranforda surely?"

I shook my head. "We're going north."

I was abandoning the south. My country is Northumbria, a northern land where the harpists play loud in the halls to lift their songs above the sound of the wild wind scouring from a cold sea, a northern land of long winter nights and of raw hills and high cliffs, a land of hard people and shallow soil. The Danes had spread southward through Britain, driving out the Saxon rulers from Northumbria, Mercia, and East Anglia, and now we were thrusting back. Mercia was almost free, and if I lived I would see our Saxon armies march still farther north, ever north until every man, woman, and child who spoke the Saxon tongue would be ruled by one of their own. That was Alfred's dream, and it had become mine even though I loved the Danes and worshipped their gods and spoke their language. So why did I fight them? Because of the oaths I had taken to Æthelflaed.

We live by oaths, and, as we rode south into the evening, I wondered about the men who followed Eardwulf. How many had given him their oath? And how many had sworn allegiance to Æthelred rather than to Eardwulf? And how many would draw a sword against Æthelflaed? And would Eardwulf dare kill her? He was a man who had risen high, but his hold on power was precarious. It had depended on Æthelred's favor, and now it depended on his marrying Æthelred's daughter. If he could do that and so inherit Æthelred's wealth, then, with West Saxon backing, he would be the gold-giver in Mercia, the lord of the land, but without Ælfwynn he was nothing, and when a man must choose between nothing and everything he has small choice.

"Perhaps he won't kill you," I told Æthelflaed as we rode south.

"And why not?"

"Too many Mercians love you. He'd lose sympathy."

She laughed grimly. "So what will he do? Take me to wife instead of my daughter?"

"He could," I said. I had not thought of that. "But my guess is that you'd be forced into a convent. Edward and Æthelhelm would approve of that."

She rode in silence for a few moments. "Maybe they're right," she said bleakly, "maybe I should retire to a convent."

"Why?"

"I am a sinner."

"And your enemies are not?" I snarled.

She did not answer. We were riding through beech woods. The ground had risen, and there was no flooding here. I had scouts well ahead, and though I knew Eardwulf would also have scouts looking for us, I was sure my men were better. We had been fighting the Danes for so long, and we had become skilled at such work. I had told my men to let Eardwulf's horsemen see us, but not to allow them to know they were themselves being watched, because I was crafting a trap for him. So far he had out-thought me, but tonight he would be my victim. I turned in the saddle, wincing at the sudden pain. "Boy!" I shouted at Æthelstan, "come here!"

I had made Æthelstan ride with us. My daughter and Ælfwynn

also came. I had thought of sending the girls with Osferth, but I wanted them under my eye. Besides, with warriors like Finan, they were well protected, and, more vitally, I needed Ælfwynn to bait the trap I planned. Even so there was a danger in bringing Æthelstan because we were far more likely than Osferth's men to be attacked, but this fight was also about him and he needed to know it, see it, smell it, and survive it. I was training the boy not just to be a warrior, but to be a king.

"I'm here, lord," he said, curbing his horse to match pace with ours.

"I can smell you, so there's no need to tell me you're here."

"Yes, lord." He rode just the other side of Æthelflaed's mare.

"What is this country called, boy?" I asked.

He hesitated, looking for the catch in the question. "Mercia, lord."

"And Mercia is part of?"

"Britain, lord."

"So tell me of Britain," I said.

He glanced at his aunt, but Æthelflaed offered him no help. "Britain, lord," he said, "is a land of four peoples."

I waited. "That's it?" I asked. "That's all you know? A land of four peoples?" I imitated his voice, making it pathetic. "You un-wiped earsling. Try harder."

"To the north are the Scots," he went on hurriedly, "and they hate us. To the west are the Welsh, and they hate us, and the rest is divided between ourselves and the Danes, who also hate us."

"And do we hate the Welsh, Scots, and Danes?"

"They are all our enemies, lord, and the church says we must love them."

Æthelflaed laughed. I scowled. "Do you love them?" I asked.

"I hate them, lord."

"All of them?"

"Perhaps not the Welsh, lord, because they are Christians and so long as they stay in their mountains then we can ignore them. I don't know the Scots, lord, but I hate them because you tell me they are bare-arsed thieves and liars, and I believe every word you say, and yes, lord, I hate the Danes."

"Why?"

"Because they would take our land."

"Didn't we take the land from the Welsh?"

"Yes, lord, but they allowed us to do that. They should have prayed more and fought harder."

"So if the Danes take our land it's our fault?"

"Yes, lord."

"So how do we stop them? By praying?"

"By praying, lord, and by fighting them."

"How do we fight them?" I asked. One of the scouts had ridden back and turned his horse to ride beside me. "Think about your answer," I told Æthelstan, "while I talk to Beadwulf."

Beadwulf was a small, wiry man who was one of my best scouts. He was a Saxon, but he had marked his face with inked lines as the Danes liked to do. A lot of my men had adopted the fashion, using a comb with sharpened teeth to etch oak-gall ink into their cheeks and foreheads. They thought it made them look frightening, though I thought they looked frightening enough without the ink. "So did you find a place?" I asked Beadwulf.

He nodded. "There's a place that might suit you, lord."

"Tell me."

"A steading. Small hall and a big barn. There are a dozen folk there, but no palisade."

"And around the hall?"

"Mostly pasture, lord, and some plowland."

"And Eardwulf's men are watching us?"

He grinned. "Three of them, lord, clumsy as bullocks. My five-year-old could do it better."

"How far is the woodland from the hall?"

"A long bowshot?" he suggested. "Maybe two?"

It was earlier in the day than I might have chosen to make a halt, but Beadwulf's description sounded ideal for what I had in mind. "How far is it from here?"

"An hour's riding, lord."

"Take us there," I said.

"Yes, lord." He spurred to the front where Finan was leading.

"So, boy," I looked back to Æthelstan, "tell me how we fight the Danes?"

"By building burhs, lords."

"Burhs keep the surrounding land and its people safe," I said, "but what captures land?"

"Warriors, lord."

"And warriors are led by?"

"Lords," he said confidently.

"And what lords, boy, have been leading their warriors against the Danes?"

"My father, lord?" He made it a question because he knew it was not the right answer, though it was the politic reply.

I nodded. "Where has he fought them?"

"In East Anglia, lord."

And that was true, to a point. West Saxon forces were concentrated in Lundene, which bordered on Danish East Anglia, and there were constant skirmishes in the lands north and east of the city. "So," I said, "your father fights the Danes in the east. Who fights them to the north?"

"You do, lord," he said confidently.

"I'm old and a cripple, you feather-brained piece of stinking toad shit. Who fights the Danes in the north of Mercia?"

"The Lady Æthelflaed does," he said.

"Good. That's the right answer. Now," I said, "imagine that a great tragedy has struck Mercia and Wessex because you have just become the king of those lands. King Æthelstan, wet behind the ears and still pissing in his breeches, is on the throne. You have two wars to fight. One against East Anglia and the other in northern Mercia, and even a king can't be in two places at once. So who would you rely on to fight them in the north?"

"The Lady Æthelflaed," he said without hesitation.

"Good!" I said. "So, as the King of Wessex and perhaps of Mercia too, would you suggest that the Lady Æthelflaed should go to a nunnery because she's a widow?" He frowned, embarrassed to be asked such a question. "Answer!" I snapped. "You're the king! You have to make these decisions!"

"No, lord!"

"Why not?"

"Because she fights, lord. You and she are the only ones who do fight the Danes."

"Here ends your catechism," I said, "now piss off."

"Yes, lord." He grinned and spurred ahead.

I smiled at Æthelflaed. "You're not going to a nunnery. The next King of Wessex just made the decision."

She laughed. "If he lives," she said.

"If any of us lives."

The land was climbing gently. The woods were thick, broken by farms, but in the late afternoon we came to the hall and barn that Beadwulf had described. The farmstead lay just a hundred or so paces from the Roman road, and it would do. It would do very well.

It was the place to lay my trap.

The old man was called Lidulf. I call him old, though he was probably younger than I was, but a lifetime of digging ditches, cutting back woodland, grubbing weeds, plowing fields, chopping wood, and raising livestock had left him white-haired, bent, and half blind. Half deaf too. "You want what, lord?" he shouted.

"Your home," I shouted back.

"Thirty years," he said.

"Thirty years?"

"Been here thirty years, lord!"

"And you'll be here another thirty!" I showed him gold. "All yours."

He understood eventually. He was not happy, but nor did I expect him to be happy. He would probably lose his hall and barn and a good deal else besides, but in return I would give him more than enough gold to rebuild twice over. Lidulf, a shrill-tongued wife, an elderly son with a crippled leg, and eight slaves all lived in the small hall that they shared with three milk cows, two goats, four pigs, and a mangy hound that growled whenever any of us went near the hearth. The barn was half collapsed, its timbers rotted and its thatch riddled with weeds, but it was shelter for the horses and enough of the barn survived to hide the animals from Eardwulf's scouts, who saw them being led through the big door, and probably assumed they were being unsaddled. We strolled between the two buildings. I told my men to talk loudly, to laugh, to take off their mail and helmets. Some of the younger men started wrestling to loud cheers and jeers, the losers being thrown into a duck pond. "We get eggs from that!" Lidulf shouted at me.

"Eggs?"

"Duck eggs!" He was very proud of his duck eggs. "I like a duck egg. No teeth left, you see? I can't eat meat so I eats duck eggs and pottage."

I made sure Stiorra, Ælfwynn, and Æthelstan watched the wrestling. Beadwulf, who could slide through woodland like a ghost, told me that two of Eardwulf's men peered at them from the trees. "I could have lifted the swords from their scabbards and they wouldn't have known about it, lord."

Three more of my scouts reported that Eardwulf himself was two miles or so to the north. He had stopped once his own scouts told him that we had found shelter for the night. "You were right, lord," Eadric, one of my Danes and a man as skilled as Beadwulf in concealing himself, came back to the hall at dusk. "They're in two groups, one large, one smaller."

"How many?"

"Thirty-four are with Eardwulf, lord."

"The others are reluctant?"

"They look miserable, lord."

"Thirty-four is enough," I said.

"Enough for what?" my daughter asked.

We were in the hall. The men who had been soaked in the duck pond had their clothes drying by the fire, which we had fed with fresh wood so that it blazed bright. "Enough," I said, "for a hall burning."

It had been years since I saw a hall burning, but a few men can kill a large number if they do it right and I was certain that was what Eardwulf planned. He would wait for the heart of the night, for the darkest hour, and then he would bring embers in a clay pot. Most of his men would wait outside the hall door, while a few went to the southern side and blew life into the embers. Then they would fire the thatch. Even damp straw will burn if fed with enough fire, and once the flames catch they spread fast, filling the hall with smoke and panic. Folk run for the door and so flee into the waiting swords and spears. Those that stay inside are burned to death as the great hall collapses and the huge rafters fall in. His risk, of course, was that Ælfwynn would die in the blaze, but he must have reckoned we would hurry the girls out of danger first and so deliver them into his arms. It was a risk he had to take because this dark night was his only chance. Like a man losing at dice, he would risk everything on one throw.

"Pray," I told Æthelflaed.

"I always pray," she said tartly.

"Pray for darkness," I said fervently, "for thick darkness. For utter darkness. Pray for clouds over the moon."

I made the men sing, shout, and laugh. Except for three scouts hidden at the edge of the woodland they were all in the hall and all dressed in mail, with helmets and shields, the bright fire glinting off the metal of spearheads and shield bosses. They still sang as night fell, the mangy hound howling along with the bellowed songs, and as the clouds I had prayed for did come, as the moon was shrouded, and as the night grew as dark as Eardwulf's ambitions, I had the men leave in small groups. They went to the barn, found a horse, any horse, and led the beasts southward. I had told them to be silent, but it seemed to me that each group made as much noise as drunken men staggering through a street at midnight, though doubtless the sounds made little sense to Eardwulf's men, who my scouts told me were gathering in the northern trees. I went with Æthelflaed and the girls, protected by Finan and four men, and we found some saddled horses and led them by the bridles till we could mount and ride south into the black shelter of the beech woods. Sihtric and a half-dozen men led Lidulf, his wife, and household out into the night. The old woman complained shrilly, but her noise was drowned by the raucous singing of the men left in the hall.

Finally there were just a dozen men singing, led by my son. They left at last, shutting the hall's big doors and crossing to the barn where they found the remaining horses. They still sang. It was deep in the night's dark heart when the last song faded. I had hoped to give Eardwulf's listening men the impression of a drunken night in the hall, a night of shouting and singing, of ale and laughter. A night for a killing.

And we waited in the trees.

And we waited. An owl called. Somewhere a vixen cried.

And we waited.

Six

Time passes slower at night. Years ago, when I was a child, my father asked our priest why that was so, and Father Beocca, dear Father Beocca, preached a sermon about it the next Sunday. The sun, he said, was the light of the Christian god and is quick, while the moon is the lamp that travels through the darkness of sin. All of us, he explained, tread more slowly at night because we cannot see, so therefore, he declared, the night moves more slowly than the day because the sun moves in Christian brilliance, while the moon stumbles around in the devil's darkness. The sermon made little sense to me, but when I asked Father Beocca to explain it he clipped me around the ear with his maimed hand and told me to concentrate on reading how Saint Cuthbert baptized a flock of puffins. But whatever the reason, time does slow at night, and puffins do go to heaven, or at least those puffins do who were lucky enough to have met Saint Cuthbert.

"Are there herrings in heaven?" I remember asking Father Beocca.

"I can't think so."

"Then what do the puffins eat if there aren't any fish?"

"None of us eat in heaven. We sing God's glories instead."

"We don't eat? We just sing forever?"

"And ever, amen."

It sounded boring then, it still sounds boring now, almost as boring as waiting in the darkness for an attack I was sure was coming, but which never seemed to happen. It was quiet except for the sigh of wind in the treetops and, every now and then, the

138

splash of men pissing or horses staling. An owl called for a time, then was silent.

And in the silence the doubts came. Suppose Eardwulf had anticipated the trap? Was he even now leading horsemen through the dark woods to attack us among the trees? I told myself that was impossible. The clouds had thickened, no one could travel these woods without blundering. I persuaded myself it was more likely that he had abandoned his ambition, that he had accepted defeat, and that I was imposing this discomfort and fear on my men for no reason.

We shivered. Not just because it was cold, but because the night is when the ghosts and sprites and elves and dwarves come to Midgard. They prowl silently through the dark. You might not see them, and will never hear them unless they choose to be heard, but they are there; malevolent things of darkness. My men were silent, fearful, not of Eardwulf or his warriors, but of the things we cannot see. And with the fears came memories, the recollection of Ragnar's death in a fearful hall burning. I had been a child, shivering with Brida on the hill, watching the great hall flame and collapse, and listening to the screams of men, women, and children dying. Kjartan and his men had surrounded the hall and massacred those who fled the fire, all but the young women who could be taken and used just as Ragnar's lovely daughter, Thyra, had been raped and shamed. She had found happiness in the end by marrying Beocca, and she still lived, a nun now, and I had never spoken to her of that night of fire when her mother and father had died. I had loved Ragnar. He had been my true father, the Dane who had taught me to be a man, and he had died in those flames, and I always hoped he had seized his sword before he was killed so that he was in Valhalla to see when I took revenge for him by slaughtering Kjartan on a northern hilltop. Ealdwulf had died in that fire, his name so similar to my newest enemy. Ealdwulf had been the blacksmith at Bebbanburg, the fortress stolen from me by my uncle, but he had fled Bebbanburg to be my man, and it had been Ealdwulf who had hammered Serpent-Breath into life on his massive anvil.

So many dead. So many lives twisted by fate, and now we

began the dance again. Æthelred's death had woken ambitions, Æthelhelm's greed was threatening the peace, or perhaps it was my stubbornness that tried to thwart West Saxon hopes.

"What are you thinking?" Æthelflaed asked me in a voice scarcely above a whisper.

"That I must find the man who took Ice-Spite from Teotanheale," I answered just as quietly.

She sighed, though perhaps that was the wind in the leaves. "You should submit to God," she finally said.

I smiled. "You don't mean that. You just have to say it. Besides, it isn't pagan magic. Father Cuthbert told me to find the sword."

"I sometimes wonder if Father Cuthbert is a good Christian," she said.

"He's a good man."

"He is, yes."

"So a good man can be a bad Christian?"

"I suppose so."

"Then a bad man," I said, "can be a good Christian?" She did not answer. "That explains half the bishops," I went on, "Wulfheard for one."

"He's a very able man," she said.

"But greedy."

"Yes," she admitted.

"For power," I said, "for money. And for women."

She was silent for a while. "We live in a world of temptation," she finally spoke, "and few of us aren't tainted by the devil's fingers. And the devil works hardest on men of God. Wulfheard is a sinner, but which of us isn't? You think he doesn't know his failures? That he doesn't pray to be redeemed? He's been a good servant to Mercia. He's administered the law, he's kept the treasury filled, he's given sage advice."

"He burned down my home too," I said vengefully, "and for all we know he conspired with Eardwulf to have you killed."

She ignored that accusation. "There are so many good priests," she said instead, "so many decent men who feed the hungry, tend the sick, and comfort the sad. Nuns too! So many good ones!"

"I know," I said, and thought of Beocca and of Pyrlig, of Willibald and Cuthbert, of Abbess Hild, but such men and women rarely achieved power in the church. It was the sly and ambitious ones like Wulfheard who gained preferment. "Bishop Wulfheard," I said, "wants you gone. He wants your brother as King of Mercia."

"And is that such a bad thing?" she asked.

"It is if they put you in a nunnery."

She thought for a short while. "It's thirty years since Mercia had a king," she said. "Æthelred ruled for most of that time, but only because my father let him. Now you say he's dead. So who succeeds him? We had no son. Who better than my brother?"

"You."

She said nothing for a long while. "Can you see any ealdorman supporting a woman's right to rule?" she finally asked. "Any bishop? Any abbot? Wessex has a king, and Wessex has kept Mercia alive these thirty years, so why not unite the countries?"

"Because Mercians don't want that."

"Some don't. Most don't. They'd like a Mercian to rule here, but will they want a woman on the throne?"

"If it's you, yes. They love you."

"Some do, many don't. And all of them would think a woman as ruler to be unnatural."

"It is unnatural," I said, "it's ridiculous! You're supposed to spin wool and have babies, not rule a country. But you're still the best choice."

"Or my brother Edward."

"He's not the warrior you are," I said.

"He's the king," she said simply.

"So," I asked, "you'll just hand the kingdom to Edward? Here you are, brother, here's Mercia."

"No," she said quietly.

"No?"

"Why do you think we go to Gleawecestre? There's going to be a meeting of the Witan, there has to be, so we'll let them choose."

"And you think they'll choose you?"

She paused a long time and I sensed that she smiled. "Yes," she finally said.

I laughed. "Why? You just said no man will support a woman's right to rule, so why will they choose you?"

"Because you might be old and crippled and headstrong and infuriating," she said, "but they're still frightened of you, and you're going to persuade them."

"I am?"

"Yes," she said, "you are."

I smiled in the darkness. "Then we'd better make sure we live through this night," I said, and just then heard the unmistakable sound of a hoof striking a stone in the plowland to our north.

The waiting was over.

Eardwulf was being careful. The hall door faced north, which meant the hall's southern side was a great blank timber wall, and so he had brought his men to the southern fields where they could not be seen by any sentry I might have placed at the hall door. We heard that first hoof, then more hooves, then the soft chink of bridles, and we held our breath. We could see nothing, just hear the men and horses who were between us and the hall and then, quite suddenly, there was light.

There was a flare of light, a sudden burst of flame that appeared much closer than I had expected, and I realized Eardwulf was lighting the brands well away from the hall. His men were not far beyond the trees, and the sudden light made me think they must see us, but none of them was looking back into the tangled shadows of the woodland. The first brand flamed high, then six more were lit, one bundle of straw lighting another. They waited till all seven were burning fiercely, then the torches' long handles were given to seven horsemen. "Go," I distinctly heard the command given, then watched all seven flamebearers gallop across the pasture. They held the torches wide, the sparks trailing behind. Eardwulf's men followed.

I kicked my horse to the wood's edge and paused there. My men waited with me as the bright torches were hurled up onto the hall's roof and as Eardwulf's men dismounted and drew their swords. "One of my ancestors crossed the sea," I said, "and captured the rock on which Bebbanburg is built."

"Bebbanburg?" Æthelflaed asked.

I did not answer. I was gazing at the seven fires, which looked dull now. For a moment it seemed the hall roof would not burn, but then the flames spread as they found the drier straw beneath the wet outer layer of tightly woven thatch, and once that drier straw caught the fire it spread with a vicious speed. Most of Eardwulf's men had gone to make a cordon around the closed hall door, which meant they were hidden from us, though some stayed on horseback and a half-dozen others remained on the southern side of the building in case anyone tried to break through the wall and so escape.

"What has Bebbanburg to do with this?" Æthelflaed asked.

"My ancestor's name was Ida the Flamebearer," I said, looking at the lurid flames, then took a deep breath. "Now," I shouted, and drew Serpent-Breath. The pain stabbed at me, but I shouted again. "Now!"

Eadric had been right. There were no more than thirty men with Eardwulf, the rest must have refused to join the murder of Æthelflaed. And thirty men would have been enough if we had been inside the hall. The morning would have revealed smoldering embers and thick smoke and would have left Eardwulf as Æthelred's heir, but instead he was my victim, and I spurred my horse as my men streamed from the trees and galloped through the flame-lit darkness.

And Eardwulf's hopes died. It was sudden and it was slaughter. Men expecting to see half-woken panic come from the hall door were instead overwhelmed by mounted spearmen erupting from the night. My men attacked from both sides of the hall, converging on the warriors waiting at the hall door, and there was nowhere for them to run. We hacked down with swords or lunged with spears. I saw my son split a helmet with Raven-Beak, saw the blood fly in the firelight, saw Finan spear a man through the belly and leave the spear buried in the dying man's gut before drawing his sword to find the next victim. Gerbruht used an ax to crush and split a man's helmeted skull, all the time bellowing in his native Frisian.

I was looking for Eardwulf. Æthelflaed galloped in front of me and I shouted at her to get out of the fight. Pain filled me. I turned my horse to follow her and to push her away, and it was then I saw

Eardwulf. He was still mounted. He too had seen Æthelflaed, and he spurred toward her, followed by a group of his men who had also stayed on horseback. I headed him off. Æthelflaed vanished to my left, Eardwulf was to my right, and I swung Serpent-Breath in a wide cut that slammed into his ribs but did not break his mail. More of my men arrived, and Eardwulf wrenched his reins and dug his spurs back. "Follow him!" I shouted.

There was chaos. Horsemen wheeling, men shouting, some trying to surrender, and all in a whirl of sparks and smoke. It was hard to tell which horsemen were enemies in the flickering light. Then I saw Eardwulf and his companions galloping clear and I spurred after him. The fire was bright enough to light the pastureland, casting long black shadows from the grass tussocks. Some of my men were following, whooping as though they were on a hunt. One of the fugitives' horses stumbled. The rider had long dark hair hanging beneath his helmet. He glanced back and saw me catching him and kicked desperately as I lunged with Serpent-Breath, aiming the blade's tip at the base of his spine, but instead the sword caught in the high cantle of his saddle just as the horse twisted hard aside. The horse stumbled again and the man fell. I heard a scream. My own horse sheered away from the tumbling stallion, and I almost lost my grip on Serpent-Breath. My horsemen pounded past me, hooves throwing up gobbets of damp soil, but Eardwulf and his remaining companions were far ahead of us now, vanishing into the northern woods. I swore and reined in.

"Enough! Stop!" I heard Æthelflaed shout, and I turned back to the burning hall. I had thought she was in trouble, but instead she was halting the slaughter. "I will kill no more Mercians!" she shouted. "Stop!" The survivors were being herded together and stripped of their weapons.

I sat motionless, pain filling my chest, my sword held low. The fire was roaring now, the whole hall roof ablaze and filling the night with smoke, sparks, and blood-colored light. Finan came to my side. "Lord?" he asked anxiously.

"I'm not hurt. It's just the wound."

He led my horse back to where Æthelflaed had gathered the prisoners. "Eardwulf escaped," I told her.

"There's nowhere he can go," she said. "He's an outlaw now."

A roof beam collapsed, surging new flames higher and showering the sky with bright sparks. Æthelflaed kicked her horse toward the prisoners, fourteen of them, who stood beside the barn. There were six corpses between the barn and the hall. "Take them away," Æthelflaed ordered, "and bury them." She looked at the fourteen men. "How many of you," she asked, "swore oaths of loyalty to Eardwulf?"

All but one raised their hands. "Just kill them," I growled.

She ignored me. "Your lord," she said, "is now an outlaw. If he lives he will flee to a far country, to heathen lands. How many of you wish to accompany your oath-lord?"

Not one of them raised a hand. They stood silent and fearful. Some were wounded, their scalps or shoulders bleeding from sword cuts made by the horsemen who had ambushed them.

"You can't trust them," I said, "so kill them."

"Are you all Mercians?" Æthelflaed asked, and all nodded except for the one man who had not admitted his loyalty to Eardwulf. The Mercians looked at that man and he flinched. "What are you?" Æthelflaed asked him. He hesitated. "Tell me!" she commanded.

"Grindwyn, my lady. I'm from Wintanceaster."

"A West Saxon?"

"Yes, my lady."

I kicked my horse closer to Grindwyn. He was an older man of maybe thirty or forty summers with a neatly trimmed beard, expensive mail, and a finely crafted cross hanging at his neck. The mail and the cross suggested he was a man who had earned silver across the years, not some adventurer driven by poverty to seek service with Eardwulf. "Who do you serve?" I asked him.

Again he hesitated. "Answer!" Æthelflaed called.

Still he hesitated. I could see he was tempted to lie, but all the Mercians knew the truth and so he grudgingly spoke it. "The Lord Æthelhelm, my lady," he said.

I laughed sourly. "He sent you to make certain Eardwulf did his bidding?"

He nodded for answer and I jerked my head to Finan, indicating he should take Grindwyn aside. "Keep him safe," I told Finan.

Æthelflaed looked down at the remaining prisoners. "My husband," she said, "gave high privileges to Eardwulf, yet Eardwulf had no right to make you swear loyalty to him instead of to my husband. He was my husband's servant and had sworn an oath to him. But my husband is dead, God rest his soul, and the loyalty you should have offered him is now mine. Is there any one of you who refuses to give me that loyalty?"

They shook their heads. "Of course they'll offer you loyalty," I snarled, "the bastards want to live. Just kill them."

She ignored me again, looking instead at Sihtric who stood over a pile of captured weapons. "Give them their swords," she commanded.

Sihtric glanced at me, but I just shrugged and so he obeyed. He carried a bundle of swords and let the men choose their own. They stood holding their weapons, still uncertain, wondering if they were about to be attacked, but instead Æthelflaed dismounted. She gave the reins of her horse to Sihtric and walked toward the fourteen men. "Did Eardwulf give you orders to kill me?" she asked.

They hesitated. "Yes, my lady." It was one of the older men who answered.

She laughed. "Then now is your chance." She spread her arms wide.

"My lady . . ." I began.

"Be silent!" she snapped at me without turning her head. She gazed at the prisoners. "You either kill me," she said, "or you kneel to me and give me your oaths."

"Guard her!" I snapped at my son.

"Stand back!" she told Uhtred, who had drawn Raven-Beak and moved to her side. "Further back! These are Mercians. I need no protection from Mercians." She smiled at the captives. "Which of you commands?" she asked and, when none answered, "Then who is the best leader among you?" They shuffled their feet, but finally two or three of them pushed the oldest man forward. He was the man who had confirmed that Eardwulf's ambition had been to kill Æthelflaed. He had a scarred face, a short beard, and a wall eye. He had lost half an ear in the fight and the blood was black on his hair and neck. "Your name?" Æthelflaed asked.

146

"Hoggar, my lady."

"Then for the moment you command these men," she said, indicating the prisoners. "Now send them to me one by one to take their oaths."

So she stood alone in the flamelight, and one after another her enemies came to her, each holding a sword, and each knelt to her and swore to be her man. And, of course, none raised their sword to kill her. I could see their faces, see how they had been seduced by her, how the oath they swore was heartfelt. She could do that to men. Hoggar was the last to swear his oath, and I could see tears in his eyes as he felt her hands clasp his about the hilt of his sword and as he said the words that tied his life to hers. Æthelflaed smiled at him, then touched his gray hair as if she was blessing him. "Thank you," she said to him, then turned to my men. "These warriors are no longer prisoners! They are my men now, they are your comrades, and they will share in our fortune, for good or for ill."

"But not that one!" I called, indicating Æthelhelm's man, Grindwyn.

"Not that one," Æthelflaed agreed, then touched Hoggar's head again. "Treat your wounds, Hoggar," she said gently.

And then the fifteenth prisoner was brought into the flamelight, the long dark-haired rider whose horse had stumbled just in front of me. The rider wore a long mail coat and a finely chased helmet that Eadric hauled off.

It was Eardwulf's sister, Eadith.

We rode to Eardwulf's camp in the dawn. I did not expect to find him there, nor was he. Instead the rest of his men, those who had refused to accompany him in the night, were either sitting about campfires or else saddling horses. They panicked when we appeared, some clambering into saddles, but Finan led a half-dozen men to head them off and the show of swords was enough to drive the fleeing men back to their comrades. Few were wearing mail, and none looked ready for a fight, while our men were mounted, armored, and carrying weapons. I saw some of Eardwulf's men cross themselves as if they expected sudden slaughter.

"Hoggar!" Æthelflaed called sharply.

"My lady?"

"You and your men will escort me. The rest of you," she turned and pointedly looked at me, "will wait here." She was insisting that she needed no protection from Mercians and, just as she had seduced Hoggar and his men in the night, so she would work her sorcery on the rest of Eardwulf's troops.

She had ordered me to stay behind, but I nevertheless rode close enough to hear her words. The twin priests, Ceolberht and Ceolnoth, met her, bowing their heads respectfully, then claimed that they had restrained the rest of Eardwulf's men from joining the night-time attack. "We told them, my lady, that what he planned was a sin and would be punished by God," Father Ceolnoth said. His toothless twin nodded vigorous agreement.

"And did you tell them," I asked loudly, "that a failure to warn us was also a sin?"

"We wanted to warn you, my lady," Father Ceolnoth said, "but he set guards on us."

I laughed. "Two hundred of you and forty of them?"

Both priests ignored the question. "We thank God for your life, lady," Ceolberht lisped instead.

"As you'd have thanked your god for Eardwulf's success if he'd killed Lady Æthelflaed," I said.

"Enough!" Æthelflaed motioned me to silence. She looked back to the twin priests. "Tell me of my husband," she demanded.

They both hesitated, glancing at each other, then Ceolnoth made the sign of the cross. "Your husband died, my lady."

"So I hear," she said, but I sensed her relief that what had been mere rumor so far was now confirmed. "I will pray for his soul," she said.

"As do we all," Ceolberht said.

"It was a peaceful death," the other twin said, "and he received the sacraments with grace and calmness."

"Then my Lord Æthelred has gone to his heavenly reward,"

Æthelflaed said, and I snorted with laughter. She gave me a warning look, and then, escorted only by the men who just hours before had tried to kill her, she rode among the other Mercian troops. They had been her husband's household warriors, supposedly the best in Mercia and for years her sworn enemies and, though I could not hear what she said to them, I watched them kneel to her. Finan joined me, leaning on his saddle's pommel. "They love her."

"They do."

"So what now?"

"So now we make her Mercia's ruler," I said.

"How?"

"How do you think? By killing any bastard who opposes her."

Finan smiled. "Oh," he said, "by persuasion!"

"Exactly," I agreed.

But first we had to go to Gleawecestre, and we rode there over three hundred men strong, a band of warriors who, not hours before, had been fighting each other. Æthelflaed ordered her standard raised alongside her husband's flag. She was telling the places we passed that her family still ruled in Mercia, though we still did not know whether the men waiting in Gleawecestre would agree with that claim. I wondered too how Edward of Wessex would take his sister's ambition. He, of all people, could thwart her, and she would obey him because he was a king.

The answers to those questions must wait, but as we rode I sought out the twin priests because I had other questions for them. They bridled when I spurred my horse between their two geldings, and Ceolberht, whose mouth I had ruined, tried to kick his horse ahead, but I leaned down and seized the bridle. "You two," I said, "were at Teotanheale."

"We were," Ceolnoth said guardedly.

"A great victory," his brother added, "thanks to God."

"Granted by Almighty God to Lord Æthelred," Ceolnoth finished, trying to irritate me.

"Not to King Edward?" I asked.

"To him too, yes," Ceolnoth said hurriedly, "God be praised."

Eadith was riding alongside Ceolnoth, guarded by two of my men. She still wore the mail coat over which hung a bright silver cross. She must have thought of the two priests as allies because they had been such stalwart supporters of Æthelred. She looked at me sullenly, wondering no doubt what I planned to do with her, though in truth I had no plans. "Where do you think your brother went?" I asked her.

"How would I know, lord?" she asked in a cold voice.

"You know he's outlawed?"

"I assumed so," she said distantly.

"You want to join him?" I asked. "You want to fester away in a Welsh valley, perhaps? Or shiver in some Scottish hovel?"

She grimaced, but said nothing. "The Lady Eadith," Father Ceolnoth said, "can find refuge in a holy nunnery."

I saw her shudder and I smiled. "She can join the Lady Æthelflaed, perhaps?" I asked Ceolnoth.

"If her brother desires it," he said stiffly.

"It is customary," Ceolberht said, "for a widow to seek God's shelter."

"But the Lady Eadith," I heaped scorn on the word "lady," "is not a widow. She's an adulterer like the Lady Æthelflaed." Ceolnoth looked at me with shock. What I had said was common knowledge, but he had hardly expected me to say it aloud. "As am I," I added.

"God offers his protection to sinners," Ceolnoth said unctuously.

"Especially to sinners," Ceolberht said.

"I'll remember that," I said, "when I've finished sinning. But for now," I looked at Ceolnoth, "tell me what happened at the end of the battle of Teotanheale?"

He was puzzled by the question, but seemed to do his best to answer it. "King Edward's forces pursued the Danes," he said, "but we were more concerned for the Lord Æthelred's wound. We helped carry him from the field and so saw little of the pursuit."

"But before that," I said, "you saw me fight Cnut?"

"Of course," he said.

"Of course, lord," I reminded him of his absent courtesy.

He grimaced. "Of course, lord," he said reluctantly.

"I was carried from the field too?"

"You were, and we thank God you lived."

Lying bastard. "And Cnut? What happened to his corpse?"

"It was stripped," Father Ceolberht said, his lack of teeth making a thickly sibilant sound of the words. "He was burned with the other Danes," he paused, then forced himself to add, "lord."

"And his sword?"

There was a moment's hesitation, a moment so short that it was hardly noticeable, but I noticed it, just as I noted that neither priest looked at me as Ceolnoth answered. "I did not see his sword, lord."

"Cnut," I said, "was the most feared warrior in Britain. His sword had killed hundreds of Saxons. It was a famous weapon. Who took it?"

"How would we know, lord?" Ceolnoth retorted.

"It was probably a West Saxon," Ceolberht said vaguely.

The bastards were lying, but short of thumping the truth from them there was little I could do, and Æthelflaed, who was riding not twenty paces behind me, disapproved of me thumping priests. "If I discover that you're lying to me," I said, "I'll cut your damned tongues out."

"We do not know," Ceolnoth said firmly.

"Then tell me what you do know," I said.

"We told you, lord, nothing!"

"About the next person to rule in Mercia," I finished my question. "Who should it be?"

"Not you!" Ceolberht spat.

"Listen, you spavined piece of serpent shit," I said, "I don't want to rule in Mercia, nor in Wessex, nor anywhere except my home in Bebbanburg. But you two supported her brother." I nodded toward Eadith who had been listening closely to the conversation. "Why?"

Ceolnoth hesitated, then shrugged. "The Lord Æthelred," he said, "left no heir. Nor was there any ealdorman who was a natural successor. We discussed the problem with the Lord Æthelhelm, who convinced us Mercia needed a strong man to defend its northern frontiers, and Eardwulf is a good warrior."

"Not good enough last night," I said.

Both twins ignored that. "And it was decided he could rule as King Edward's reeve," Ceolnoth said.

"So Edward would rule in Mercia?"

"Who else, lord?" Ceolberht said.

"The lords of Mercia would have retained their lands and privileges," Ceolnoth explained, "but Eardwulf would have commanded the royal household troops as an army to face the Danes."

"And with Eardwulf gone?" I asked.

The twins paused, thinking. "King Edward must rule directly," Ceolnoth said, "and appoint someone else to command Mercia's troops."

"Why not his sister?"

Ceolnoth gave a bitter laugh. "A woman! Commanding warriors? The idea is absurd! A woman's task is to obey her husband."

"Saint Paul gave us explicit instructions!" Ceolberht agreed vigorously. "He wrote to Timothy saying that no woman could have authority over a man. The scripture is plain to understand."

"Did Saint Paul have brown eyes?" I asked.

Ceolnoth frowned, puzzled by the question. "We don't know, lord, why do you ask?"

"Because he's full of shit," I said vengefully.

Eadith laughed, suppressing it almost immediately, while both twins made the sign of the cross. "The Lady Æthelflaed must retire to a nunnery," Ceolberht said angrily, "and reflect on her sins."

I looked at Eadith. "What a future you have!"

She shuddered again. I touched a spur to my horse and turned away. Someone, I thought, knew where Ice-Spite was hidden. And I would find her.

It was raining again when we reached Gleawecestre. Water was puddling in the fields, pouring down the road's stone-choked gutters, and turning the stone of the Roman walls dark. We rode toward the eastern gate in mail, helmeted, with shields on our arms and spears held high. The gate guards stepped back without a challenge and watched in silence as we rode under the arch, spears momentarily lowered, and then clattered down the long street. The town seemed sullen, but perhaps that was just because of the low dark clouds and the rain that spilled from the thatched roofs and washed the roadway's shit toward the Sæfern. We lowered spears and banners again to ride under the palace archway, which was guarded by three men carrying shields that were painted with Æthelred's prancing horse. I curbed my stallion and looked at the oldest of the three. "Is the king still here?"

He shook his head. "No, lord. He left yesterday." I nodded and spurred on. "But the queen stayed, lord," he added.

I stopped and turned in the saddle. "Queen?"

He looked confused. "Queen Ælflæd, lord."

"West Saxons don't have queens," I told him. Edward was king, but Ælflæd, his wife, was denied the title of queen. It had ever been thus in Wessex. "You mean the Lady Ælflæd?"

"She's here, lord." He jerked his head toward the largest hall, a Roman building, and I rode on. So Æthelhelm's daughter was here? That suggested Æthelhelm himself had stayed in Gleawecestre and, sure enough, when I rode into the wide grassy courtyard there were men carrying his badge of the leaping stag on their shields. Other shields showed the West Saxon dragon.

"Ælflæd's here," I told Æthelflaed, "and probably occupying your quarters."

"My husband's chambers," she corrected me.

I looked at the West Saxon guards, who watched us silently. "They're telling us they've moved in," I said, "and won't move out."

"But Edward left?"

"Seems so."

"He doesn't want to be involved in the argument."

"Which we have to win," I said, "and that means you move into the royal quarters."

"Without you," she said tartly.

"I know that! I'll sleep in a stable, but you can't." I turned in the saddle and summoned Rædwald, a nervous warrior who had served Æthelflaed for years. He was a cautious man, but he was also loyal and reliable. "The Lady Æthelflaed will be using her husband's quarters," I told him, "and your men will guard her."

"Yes, lord."

"And if anyone tries to stop her using those rooms you have my permission to slaughter them."

Rædwald looked worried, but was saved by Æthelflaed. "I will share the rooms with the Lady Ælflæd," she said sharply, "and there will be no slaughter!"

I turned back to the gate and beckoned the guard who had told me about Edward leaving. "Did Eardwulf return here?" I asked him.

He nodded. "Yesterday morning, lord."

"What did he do?"

"He came in a hurry, lord, and was gone again in an hour."

"He had men?"

"Eight or nine, lord. They left with him."

I dismissed him and went to Eadith's side. "Your brother came here yesterday," I said, "stayed a short while, and left."

She made the sign of the cross. "I pray he lives," she said.

There would have been no time for news of Eardwulf's failed attempt to kill Æthelflaed to reach Gleawecestre before he arrived in the city, so no one would have suspected his treachery, though doubtless they had wondered why he had fled so quickly. "Why did he come here?" I asked Eadith.

"Why do you think?"

"So where was the money kept?"

"It was hidden in Lord Æthelred's private chapel."

"You'll go there," I said, "and tell me if it's gone."

"Of course it's gone!"

"I know that," I said, "and you know that, but I still want to be sure."

"And afterward?" she asked.

"Afterward?"

"What happens to me?"

I looked at her and was envious of Æthelred. "You're not an enemy," I said, "if you want to join your brother then you can."

"In Wales?"

"Is that where he went?"

She shrugged. "I don't know where he's gone, but Wales is closest."

"Just tell me if the money is gone," I said, "and after that you can go."

Her eyes glistened, but whether that was tears or the rain I could not tell. I slid from my horse, wincing at the pain in my ribs, and went to discover who ruled in Gleawecestre's palace.

I was not reduced to sleeping in the stable, but instead found rooms in one of the smaller Roman buildings. It was a house built around a courtyard with just a single entrance, above which was nailed a wooden cross. A nervous steward told me the rooms were used by Æthelred's chaplains. "How many chaplains did he have?" I asked.

"Five, lord."

"Five in this house! It could sleep twenty!"

"And their servants, lord."

"Where are the chaplains?"

"Standing vigil in the church, lord. The Lord Æthelred is buried tomorrow."

"Lord Æthelred doesn't need chaplains now," I said, "so the bastards can move out. They can sleep in his stables."

"His stables, lord?" the steward asked nervously.

"Wasn't your nailed god born in a stable?" I asked, and he just looked at me dumbly. "If a stable was good enough for Jesus," I said, "it's good enough for his damned priests. But not for me."

We moved the priests' belongings into the courtyard, then my men took over the empty rooms. Stiorra and Ælfwynn shared a room with their maids, while Æthelstan would sleep under the same roof as Finan and a half-dozen other men. I called the lad into the room I had taken, a room furnished with a low bed on which I was lying because the pain in my lower ribs was throbbing. I could feel pus and muck oozing from the wound.

"Lord?" Æthelstan said nervously.

"The Lord Æthelhelm is here," I said.

"I know, lord."

"So tell me what he wants with you?"

"My death?"

"Probably," I agreed, "but your father wouldn't like that. So what else?"

"He wants to take me away from you, lord."

"Why?"

"So his grandson can be king."

I nodded. Of course he knew the answers to my questions, but I wanted him to be alive to those answers. "Good boy," I said, "and what will he do with you?"

"Send me to Neustria, lord."

"And what happens in Neustria?"

"Either they kill me or sell me into slavery, lord."

I closed my eyes as the pain sharpened. The stuff oozing from the wound stank like a cesspit. "So what must you do?" I asked, opening my eyes to look at him.

"Stay close to Finan, lord."

"You do not run off," I said savagely. "You do not look for adventure in the city. You do not find a girlfriend! You stay by Finan's side! You understand me?"

"Of course, lord."

"You might be the next King of Wessex," I told him, "but you won't be anything if you're dead or if you're snatched away to some damn monastery to be arse-fodder for a pack of monks, so you stay here!"

"Yes, lord."

"And if Lord Æthelhelm sends for you, you don't obey him. You tell me instead. Now go."

I closed my eyes. The damn pain, the damn pain, the damned pain. I needed Ice-Spite.

She came to me after dark. I had slept, and Finan or perhaps my servant, had brought a tall church candle into the room. It burned smokily, casting a small light on the cracked and peeling plaster of the walls and dancing strange shadows on the ceiling.

I woke to hear the voices outside, one pleading and the other gruff. "Let her in," I called, and the door opened so that the candle flame shuddered and the shadows leaped. "Close the door," I said.

"Lord . . ." the man standing guard started to speak.

"Close the door," I said, "she's not going to kill me." Though the pain was such that I might have welcomed it if she had.

Eadith came hesitantly. She had changed into a long dress of dark green wool, belted with a rope of gold and hemmed with thick strips embroidered with yellow and blue flowers. "Aren't you supposed to be in mourning?" I asked cruelly.

"I am in mourning."

"So?"

"You think I'll be welcome at the funeral?" she asked bitterly.

"You think I will?" I asked, then laughed and wished I had not.

She watched me nervously. "The money," she finally spoke, "has gone."

"Of course it has." I winced as pain throbbed. "How much?"

"I don't know. A lot."

"My cousin was generous," I said sourly.

"He was, lord."

"So where has the bastard gone?"

"He took a ship, lord."

I looked at her in surprise. "A ship? He didn't have enough men to crew a ship."

She shook her head. "Maybe he didn't. But Sella gave him bread and hams to take, and he told her he would find a fishing boat."

"Sella?"

"She's a kitchen maid, lord."

"A pretty one?"

She nodded. "Pretty enough."

"And your brother didn't take her with him?"

"He asked her to go, lord, but she said no."

So Eardwulf was gone, but gone where? He had a handful of followers and a lot of money, and he would need refuge some-where. A fishing boat made sense. Eardwulf's few men could row it, the wind would carry it, but to where? Would Æthelhelm have offered him refuge in Wessex? I doubted it. Eardwulf was only useful to Æthelhelm if he could rid the ealdorman of Æthelstan, and he had failed in that, so he would not be in Wessex and certainly not in Mercia. "Is your brother a seaman?" I asked her.

"No, lord."

"What about his men?"

"I doubt it, lord."

So he could hardly sail from the Sæfern to Neustria in a small boat, so it had to be either Wales or Ireland. And with any luck a Danish or Norse ship would see his ship and that would be the end of Eardwulf. "If he's no sailor," I said, "and if you love him, then you'd better pray for good weather." I had spoken sourly and decided I had been boorish. "Thank you for telling me."

"Thank you for not killing me," she responded.

"Or for not sending you to join Sella in the kitchen?"

"For that too, lord," she said humbly, then wrinkled her nose at the stench pervading the room. "Is that your wound?" she asked, and I nodded. "I smelled the same when my father died," she went on, then paused, but I said nothing. "When was the wound last dressed?" she asked.

"A week ago, more. Can't remember."

She turned abruptly and went from the room. I closed my eyes. Why had King Edward gone? He had not been close to Æthelred, but it still seemed strange that he had left Gleawecestre before the funeral. Yet he had left Æthelhelm, his father-in-law, chief adviser, and the power behind the throne of Wessex, and my best guess was that Edward wanted to distance himself from the dirty work that Æthelhelm planned. That work was to ensure that the nobles of Mercia appointed Edward as Mercia's ruler and encouraged Æthelflaed to retire to a convent. Well damn him. I was not dead yet, and so long as I lived I would fight for Æthelflaed.

Some time passed. It was the slow passing of time in a pain-filled night, but then the door opened again and Eadith returned. She was carrying a bowl and some cloths. "I don't want you to clean the wound," I growled.

"I did it for my father," she said, then knelt beside the bed and pulled back the pelts. She grimaced at the smell.

"When did your father die?" I asked.

"After the battle at Fearnhamme, lord."

"After?"

"He took a wound in the stomach, lord, and lingered for five weeks."

"That was almost twenty years ago."

"I was seven, lord, but he wouldn't allow anyone else to tend him."

"Not your mother?"

"She was dead, lord." I felt her fingers unbuckle the belt at my waist. She was gentle. She pulled up my tunic, unsticking it from the pus. "It should be cleaned every day, lord," she said reprovingly.

"I've been busy," I said, and almost added that my business had been thwarting her damned brother's ambitions. "What was your father called?" I asked instead.

"Godwin Godwinson, lord."

"I remember him," I said. I did too, a lean man with long mustaches.

"He always said you were the greatest warrior of Britain, lord."

"That opinion must have sat well with Lord Æthelred."

She pushed a cloth against the wound. She had warmed the water and the touch of it was strangely comforting. She held the cloth there, just soaking the crusted mess beneath. "Lord Æthelred was jealous of you," she said.

"He hated me."

"That, too."

"Jealous?"

"He knew you were a warrior. He called you a brute. He said you were like a dog that attacks a bull. You had no fear because you had no sense."

I smiled at that. "Perhaps he was right."

"He wasn't a bad man."

"I thought he was."

"Because you were his wife's lover. We pick sides, lord, and sometimes loyalty gives us no choice in our opinions." She dropped the first cloth on the floor, then placed another on my ribs. The warmth seemed to dissolve the pain.

"You loved him," I said.

"He loved me," she said.

"And he raised your brother high."

She nodded. In the candlelight her face was stern, only the lips soft. "He raised my brother high," she said, "and Eardwulf is a clever warrior."

"Clever?"

"He knows when to fight and when not to fight. He knows how to trick an enemy."

"But he doesn't fight in the front rank," I said scornfully.

"Not every man can do that, lord," she said, "but would you call the men in your second rank cowards?"

I ignored that question. "And your brother would have killed me and the Lady Æthelflaed."

"Yes," she said, "he would."

I smiled at that honesty. "So did Lord Æthelred leave you money?"

She looked at me, taking her eyes from my wound for the first time. "The will, I am told, depended on my brother marrying the Lady Ælfwynn."

"So you're penniless."

"I have the jewels Lord Æthelred gave me."

"How long will they last?"

"A year, perhaps two," she said bleakly.

"But you'll get nothing from the will," I said.

"Unless the Lady Æthelflaed is generous."

"Why should she be generous?" I asked. "Why should she give money to a woman who slept with her husband?"

"She won't," Eadith said calmly, "but you will."

"I will?"

"Yes, lord."

I winced slightly as she began wiping the wound clean. "Why would I give you money?" I asked harshly. "Because you're a whore?"

"Men call me that."

"And are you?"

"I hope not," she answered evenly, "but I think you will give me money, lord, for another reason."

"And what reason is that?"

"Because I know what happened to Cnut's sword, lord."

I could have kissed her and, when she had cleaned the wound, I did.

Seven

I was woken by the harsh sound of a church bell tolling. I opened my eyes and for a moment had no idea where I was. The candle had long guttered out and the only light came from a small gap above the door. It was daylight, which meant I had slept long, then I smelled the woman and turned my face into a tangle of red hair. Eadith stirred, made a mewing noise in her sleep, and snaked an arm across my chest. She stirred again, coming awake, and rested her head on my shoulder, and after a few heartbeats began to weep.

I let her cry as I counted the bell tolling twenty-two times. "Regret?" I finally asked her.

She sniffed and shook her head. "No," she said, "no, no, no. It's the bell."

"The funeral, then?" I asked, and she nodded. "You loved him," I said, almost accusingly.

She must have thought about her response because she did not answer until the bell had rung another sixteen times. "He was kind to me."

It was strange to think of my cousin Æthelred being kind, but I believed her. I kissed her forehead and held her close. Æthelflaed, I thought, would kill me for this, but I found myself strangely unworried by the thought. "You must go to the funeral," I said.

"Bishop Wulfheard said I can't."

"Because of adultery?" I asked and she nodded. "If no adulterers go," I said, "the church will be empty. Wulfheard himself couldn't go!"

She sniffed again. "Wulfheard hates me." I began to laugh. The pain in my rib was still there, but duller now. "What's funny?" she asked.

"He hates me too."

"He once . . ." she began, then stopped.

"He once what?"

"You know."

"He did?"

She nodded. "He demanded to hear my confession, then said he'd only shrive me if I showed him what I did with Æthelred."

"And did you?"

"Of course not." She sounded offended.

"Sorry."

She raised her head and looked into my eyes. Her eyes were green. She looked for a long time, then put her head down again. "Ælfwynn told me you were a good man."

"And you said?"

"I told her you were a brute."

I laughed at that. "You'd never met me!"

"That's what she said."

"But you were right," I said, "and she was wrong."

She laughed softly. It was better than crying.

And we lay listening to the cocks crow.

The bell still tolled as I dressed. Eadith lay under the bed pelts, watching me. I dressed in the clothes I had traveled in, damp, stained, and smelly, then bent to kiss her, and the pain stabbed at me. It was less severe, but it had not vanished. "Come and have some breakfast," I told her, then went into the central courtyard. A mist seeped from the river, mingling with a drizzle from low gray clouds.

Finan was waiting in the courtyard and grinned at me. "Sleep well, lord?" he asked.

"Go and jump in a lake, you Irish bastard," I said. "Where's the boy?"

"He's awake. Eadric's watching him." He looked up at the sky. "Not a good day to bury a soul."

"Any day they bury Æthelred is a good day."

"I'll take another sniff outside," he said, nodding toward the arched gate. "See what's happening. It was all quiet an hour ago."

I went with him, but the palace grounds looked asleep. A few guards were visible by the great hall, some geese cropped the wet grass, and a lone priest hurried toward the private chapel by the main gate. "Did you look into the hall?" I asked Finan.

"All's well. Her ladyship's in the upper chamber and our two Frisians are blocking the stairway like a pair of bullocks. No one can get past those two." I had sent Gerbruht and Folcbald to reinforce Æthelflaed's own warriors. "And no one tried," Finan added.

"And Æthelhelm?"

"He's in the main hall with his daughter and Bishop Wulfheard. He said to say a good morning to you." Finan grinned. "You've no need to worry, lord."

"I should have slept in the hall," I said.

"Aye, that would have been wise. Lady Æthelflaed's lover giving her a good swiving on the night before her husband's funeral? Why didn't I think of that?"

I smiled ruefully, then went to the kitchen where my son and daughter were eating breakfast. Both looked at me reproachfully, presumably because gossip had told them who had shared my bed. "Welcome to one of the best days of my life," I greeted them.

"Best?" my son asked.

"We're burying Æthelred," I said, then sat and tore a lump from the loaf and cut some cheese. "You remember Father Penda?" I asked my son.

"I remember pissing with him."

"When you've finished stuffing your belly," I said, "I want you to find him. He's probably in the great hall, so find him and tell him I need to see him. But tell him privately. Make sure the bishop doesn't know!"

"Father Penda?" Stiorra asked.

"He's one of Bishop Wulfheard's priests," I said.

"A priest!" She sounded surprised.

"I'm turning Christian," I said, and my son choked on his ale just as Æthelstan came into the room and bowed his head in greeting to me. "You're going to the funeral," I told the boy, "and you'll pretend to be sad."

"Yes, lord, I will."

"And you'll stay by Finan's side."

"Of course, lord."

I pointed the knife at him. "I mean it! There are bastards out there who want you dead." I paused, letting the knife drop point first into the table. "Come to think of it, though, that might make my life easier."

"Sit down," Stiorra told the grinning boy.

The bell still tolled. I supposed it would ring till the funeral began, and that could not happen until the lords of Mercia decided to go to the church. "What they'll do," I said, "is hold a meeting of the Witan right after they've buried the bastard. Maybe today, but for sure tomorrow."

"Without issuing a summons?" my son asked.

"They don't need to. Everyone who matters is here."

"Except King Edward."

"He's not a member of the Mercian Witan, you numbskull," I told him. "He's a West Saxon."

"He wants to be invited," Stiorra said.

"To the Witan?" my son asked.

"To take the crown," she said patiently. "If he's here it will look as if he just took it. It's better to be invited."

"And he will be invited," I added. "That's why Bishop Wulfheard and Lord Æthelhelm are here. To make sure he is."

"And Æthelflaed?" Stiorra asked. "What happens to . . ." She abruptly fell silent as Eadith came nervously into the room, pausing at the door. Her hair was piled on her head and held by ivory combs, but strands had escaped to fall raggedly about her face. The green dress looked crumpled.

"Make room for Lady Eadith," I told Æthelstan who was sitting beside Stiorra. "You can sit beside Prince Æthelstan," I told Eadith. "It's all right," I looked back to the boy, "she's decided not to kill you after all."

"I'm not hungry, lord," Eadith said.

"Yes you are. Sit down. Stiorra will pour you ale. You were asking," I had turned to my daughter, "what will happen to the Lady Æthelflaed? They'll try to put her in a nunnery."

"And you'll stop them," my son said.

"No, you and the Lady Eadith will."

"I will?" Uhtred asked.

"By finding me that priest. Now! Go! Bring him here."

My son left. As he opened the door I could see it was raining harder. "And what will I do, lord?" Eadith asked quietly.

"Whatever I tell you," I said brusquely, "and you'll go to the funeral with Stiorra. Not in that dress, though. Find her a black cloak," I added the last words to my daughter, "with a hood."

"A hood?"

"A big one," I said, "so no one can see her face and tell her to leave the church." I turned as Finan barged through the door.

He swore, took off a piece of sacking he was wearing as a cape, and flung it onto a stool. "There'll be more floods if this goes on," he grumbled. "Raining like the devil's piss, it is."

"What's happening out there?"

"Nothing. Bastards are all in bed. Best place to be."

The great bell tolled on. Rain hammered the thatched roof and dripped through to puddle on the stone floor. The house had been roofed with tiles once, now the old rafters were covered by straw thatch in need of repair, but at least the fire in the hearth burned bright and there was a plentiful supply of wood.

Father Penda arrived after an hour or so. He looked miserable and indignant, forced to walk through the downpour that had soaked through his long black robe, but he nodded to me guardedly. "Lord," he said. He was puzzled that so many people were in the room, and even more puzzled when he saw Eadith. His loyalty to me was supposed to be a secret, and he did not understand why I had fetched him into company.

So I explained it to him. "Father," I said respectfully, "I want you to baptize me."

He just stared at me. They all did. My son, who had returned with the priest, opened his mouth to speak, but found nothing to say and so closed it again.

"Baptize you?" Father Penda managed to ask.

"I have seen the wickedness of my ways," I said humbly, "and I wish to return to God's church."

Father Penda shook his head, not in refusal, but because his wits were rain-soaked and scattered. "You are sincere, lord?" he asked.

"I am a sinner, Father, and seek forgiveness."

"If you are sincere . . ." he began.

"I am."

"You will have to confess your sins," he said.

"I shall."

"And a gift to the church will show your sincerity."

"Consider it given," I said, still speaking with humility. Stiorra was gazing at me in shock, the rest were just as astonished.

"You truly desire this?" Father Penda asked. He was suspicious. I was, after all, the most prominent pagan in Saxon Britain, a man who had been forthright in my opposition to the church, a killer of priests, and a notorious heathen. Yet the priest was also hopeful. My conversion and baptism would make Penda famous.

"I desire it with all my heart," I said.

"Might I ask why?"

"Why?"

"It is sudden, lord. Did God speak to you? Did his blessed Son appear to you?"

"No, Father, but he did send an angel."

"An angel!"

"She came in the night," I said, "and she had hair like flames of fire and eyes that glowed like emeralds and she took away my pain and replaced it with joy."

Stiorra choked. Father Penda looked at her and she quickly lowered her head into her hands. "I'm crying for happiness," she said in a strangled voice. Eadith was blushing deeply, but Father Penda did not notice her. "Praise God," Stiorra managed to say.

"Praise him indeed," Father Penda said faintly.

"I believe," I said, "that you baptize converts in the river here?"

He nodded. "But in this rain, lord . . ." he began.

"God's rain," I said, "has been sent to cleanse me."

"Hallelujah," he said. What else could he say?

So we took Penda to the river and there he ducked me, and that was the third time I had been baptized. I was too young to remember the first time, but later, when my elder brother died and my father gave me the name Uhtred, my stepmother insisted I was washed again in case Saint Peter did not recognize me at heaven's gate, and so I had been dunked in a barrel of North Sea water, but this third baptism was in the chill waters of the Sæfern, though before Father Penda could perform the rite he insisted that I kneel and confess all of my sins. I asked whether he really meant all, and he nodded enthusiastically, so I began with childhood, though it seemed stealing freshly churned butter was not what he wanted to hear. "Lord Uhtred," he said carefully, "did you not tell me you were raised a Christian? So did you not confess your sins as a child?"

"I did, Father," I said humbly.

"Then we don't need to hear them again."

"But I never confessed about the holy water, Father," I said ruefully.

"Holy water? You didn't drink it, surely?"

"I peed in it, Father."

"You . . ." He seemed incapable of further speech.

"My brother and I had a peeing contest," I said, "to see who could piss the highest. You must have done the same as a boy, father?"

"Never into holy water!"

"I regret that sin, Father."

"It is dire, but go on!"

So I confessed to the women I had slept with, or at least those to whom I was not married, and despite the rain Father Penda demanded more details. He whimpered once or twice, especially when I talked of rutting a nun, though I took care not to name Hild. "Who was she?" he demanded.

"I never knew her name, Father," I lied.

"You must have done! Tell me!"

"I only wanted to . . ."

"I know what sin you committed!" he said sternly, and then, rather hopefully, "is she still alive?"

"I wouldn't know, Father," I said innocently. In truth Hild was alive and well and feeding the poor and healing the sick and clothing the naked. "I think she was called Winfred," I said, "but she moaned so much it was hard to hear her properly."

He whimpered again, then gasped as I confessed to the churchmen I had killed. "I know now how wrong that was, Father," I said, "and worse, Father, I took pleasure from their deaths."

"No!"

"When Brother Jænberht died," I said humbly, "I enjoyed it." And I had enjoyed it too. The bastard had conspired to send me into slavery, and killing him had been a pleasure, just as it was a pleasure to kick Father Ceolberht's teeth into his throat. "And I have attacked priests, Father, like Ceolberht."

"You must apologize to him."

"Oh, I will, Father. And I have wished to kill other priests, like Bishop Asser."

Father Penda paused. "He could be difficult."

I almost laughed at that. "But there is one sin that lies most heavily on my conscience, Father."

"Another woman?" he asked eagerly.

"No, Father. It was I, Father, who discovered the bones of Saint Oswald."

He frowned. "That is no sin!"

So I told him how I had faked the discovery by concealing the bones where I knew they would be found. "He was just a body in a graveyard, Father. I ripped off an arm to make it look like Saint Oswald."

Penda paused. "The bishop's wife," he said, obviously referring to Wulfheard's grim woman, "suffered from a plague of slugs in her garden. She sent Wulfheard a gift of fine linen for the saint and the slugs went! This was a miracle!"

"Do you mean . . ." I began.

"You thought you deceived the church," Penda said enthusiastically, "but miracles have happened at the shrine! Slugs were banished! I think God guided you to the true bones of the saint!"

169

"But the saint only had one arm," I pointed out.

"Another miracle! Praise God! You were his instrument, Lord Uhtred! It is a sign!"

He gave me absolution, extracted another promise of gold, then led me into the river. The water was cold, stabbing into my wound like a dagger of ice, but I endured the prayers and praised the nailed god after Father Penda had thrust my head down into the duckweed. He did it three times, once for the father, again for the son, then for the holy ghost.

Penda was happy. He had made his famous convert, and he had Finan and my son as his witnesses and as my godfathers. I took Finan's big silver cross and hung it about my neck, giving him my pagan hammer in exchange, and after that I put my arm about Father Penda's narrow shoulders and, still dressed in nothing but a sopping wet shirt, led him up the river bank to the shelter of a willow where we had a quiet discussion. We talked for a few minutes. At first he was reluctant to tell me what I wanted, but he yielded to persuasion. "You want a knife between your ribs, Father?" I asked him.

"But, lord . . ." he began, then his voice faded away.

"Who frightens you more," I asked him, "me or Bishop Wulf-heard?" He had no answer to that, but just looked up at me with a miserable expression. He was frightened of my violence, I knew, but he was equally scared that Wulfheard could condemn him to a lifetime of being a priest in some miserable village where there was no chance of enrichment or advancement. "You want to be a bishop yourself?" I asked.

"If God wills it, lord," he said unhappily, meaning that he would sacrifice his own mother for the chance of a diocese.

"I'll make it happen," I said, "if you tell me what I want to know."

So he told me, then I dressed, made sure the cross was hidden beneath my cloak, and went to a funeral.

Someone had paid mourners to screech and wail, the noise as cacophonous as blades on shields in battle. The hired women stood at the sides of the church, beating their fists on their heads as they shrieked their pretend misery, and meanwhile a choir of monks tried to be heard above the clamor, and every now and then a priest shouted something, though no one seemed to take any notice.

The church was full, with maybe four hundred men and a few women standing between the high wooden pillars. They talked among themselves, ignoring mourners, choir, and clerics, and it was not till Bishop Wulfheard climbed onto a wooden platform beside the high altar and began to hammer his lectern with a shepherd's staff that the sound died into silence, though not before the silver crook had fallen from the staff and clattered across the flagstones to come to rest beneath Æthelred's coffin, which stood on a pair of trestles and was draped with his flag of the prancing white horse. A few of the paid mourners went on moaning, but a pair of priests scurried along the walls and told them to end their damned noise. One of the women gasped for air and I thought she was half choking to death, but then she fell to her knees and vomited. A brace of hounds rushed to gobble up the unexpected treat.

"We are in God's house!" Bishop Wulfheard bellowed.

The sermon that followed must have lasted the best part of two hours, though it seemed like four or five. Wulfheard extolled Æthelred's character, his bravery and wisdom, and even managed to sound convincing. "We lay a good man to his eternal rest this day," the bishop proclaimed, and I thought the sermon must be ending, but then he demanded that one of his priests hand him a gospel book and he flipped the heavy pages to find the passage he wanted and read it in a forbidding tone. "If a kingdom be divided that kingdom cannot endure!" he read, then slammed the heavy book shut. What followed was a thinly disguised plea to unite the crowns of Mercia and Wessex, a plea we were told was the nailed god's will.

I ignored most of it. I watched Stiorra who stood with Eadith. I had seen Eadith bow her head and hold a hand to her shadowed face, and I assumed she was crying. Æthelstan was near me at the back of the church, surrounded by my warriors. No man could carry a sword into the church, but I was certain that all the men guarding Æthelstan had seaxes hidden beneath their cloaks, just as I was certain that Æthelhelm had men looking for a chance to seize the boy. Æthelhelm himself was at the front of the church, nodding vigorously at Wulfheard's rant. With him was his daughter Ælflæd, King Edward's wife. She was a little thing, her fair hair plaited and wrapped around her head on which she wore a small black cap with a long trail of black ribbons hanging past her plump rump. She had a small sulky mouth and looked thoroughly un-happy, but that was hardly surprising, as she was forced to endure two hours of Wulfheard's nonsense. Her father kept a hand on her shoulder. He and I were both taller than most men and he caught my eye during one of the bishop's more impassioned passages, and we exchanged wry smiles. He knew a fight was coming, but he was confident of winning it. His daughter would soon be Queen Ælflæd of Mercia, and that meant she could be called a queen in Wessex too, and I had no doubt Æthelhelm wanted his daughter to be called Queen Ælflæd. I had never understood why Wessex did not extend that courtesy to the king's wife, but they could hardly withhold it from Ælflæd if she was Mercia's queen. And if Æthelhelm could just rid himself of the nuisance of Æthelstan, he would be the father of a queen and the grandfather of kings. Wulfheard was still expounding his text about a divided kingdom, shouting now, and Æthelhelm caught my gaze again, jerked his head almost imperceptibly toward Wulfheard and rolled his eyes in exasperation, and I had to laugh.

I had always liked Æthelhelm, but till now we had always been on the same side and his ambitions and energy had been devoted to causes I fought for. Now, however, we were enemies, and he knew it, and he would use his wealth and position to crush me. I would use guile, and hoped that Sihtric had succeeded in the task I had given him.

The bishop finally ran out of words. The choir began chanting again, and six of Æthelred's warriors picked up the coffin and carried it to the tomb that had been opened beside the altar. They were struggling, probably because there was a lead coffin inside the wooden casket that was sumptuously carved with saints and warriors. My cousin was to be buried as close as possible to the bones of Saint Oswald, or rather close to the bones of whoever really was encased in the silver reliquary. On the day of judgment, the bishop had preached, Saint Oswald would miraculously leap from his silver prison and be whisked to heaven, and Æthelred, being close by, would be swept up by the saint. No one doubted that the bones were the real relics. The priests and monks all claimed that miracles occurred in the church, that the cripples walked, and the blind saw, and all because of the bones.

The bishop watched the coffin being lowered into the tomb. Æthelhelm and his daughter stood beside him, while on the far side of the gaping hole Æthelflaed stood in a dress of black silk that shimmered when she moved. Her daughter Ælfwynn was beside her, and managed to look sad. When the heavy coffin was at last settled in the crypt I saw Æthelhelm stare at Æthelflaed, and the two locked their eyes. They stood thus for a long time, then Æthelhelm turned away and led his daughter out of the church. A maidservant handed Æthelflaed a heavy cloak, which she draped over her shoulders and walked into the rain.

And so my cousin Æthelred passed from my life.

The Witan was held the next day. It began not long after dawn, an early hour, but I reckoned that was because Æthelhelm wanted the business over so he could start for home. Or, perhaps more likely, so that Edward could be summoned from wherever he was waiting to make a formal entry into the chief city of his new kingdom. And it all should be done swiftly, or so they thought. The men who had attended Æthelred's funeral were, as expected, those nobles who had supported him, and very few of Æthelflaed's men were in Gleawecestre. The Witan would hear what Æthelhelm wanted, they would vote it by acclamation, and Wulfheard and Æthelhelm would earn the gratitude of the new King of Mercia.

Or so they thought.

The Witan began, of course, with a prayer from Bishop Wulfheard.

I thought, after his endless sermon of the previous day, he would keep the prayer short, but no, he had to harangue his god endlessly. He begged the nailed god to give the Witan wisdom, which was not a bad idea, then instructed his god to approve whatever the bishop was about to propose. The prayer dragged on for so long that the ealdormen, thegns, and high churchmen began shuffling their feet or scraping the benches on the tiled floor until finally Æthelhelm cleared his throat noisily and the bishop hurried to his prayer's end.

Æthelred's throne stood on the wooden platform. It had been draped with a black cloth on which sat an ornate helmet. In times past kings were never crowned, they were given a royal helmet instead, and I did not doubt that everyone in the hall knew what the helmet signified. To the left of the throne, as we looked at it, there was a lectern probably carried from the church, while on the right was a simple deal table and two chairs. The twin priests, Ceolberht and Ceolnoth, sat at the table with quills ready. They would record the Witan's proceedings, which began with a statement from the bishop.

Mercia, he said, had been without a king for a generation. It was God's will, he claimed, that a kingdom should have a king, a statement that brought a murmur of agreement from the assembled lords. "A kingdom without a king," the bishop said, "is like a diocese without a bishop, or a ship without a master. And no one here," he glanced toward me as he said this, "would deny that Mercia is one of the ancient kingdoms of Britain." Another and louder murmur of agreement filled the hall, and the bishop, heartened by the support, plowed on. "Our Lord Æthelred," he raised his voice, "was too modest to claim the kingship!" I almost laughed out loud when he said that. Æthelred would have given an eye, an arm, and both his balls to have worn the crown of Mercia, but knew only too well that his West Saxon paymasters would have punished him because Wessex wanted no king in Mercia except their own West Saxon king. "Yet he was a king in all but name!" Wulfheard was shouting now, probably because he knew his argument was weak. "And on his deathbed our Lord of Mercia, our dear departed Lord Æthelred, announced that it was his wish that his brother-in-law, King Edward of Wessex, should be invited to assume the ancient crown of our beloved country!" The bishop paused, presumably to allow a bellow of acclamation, but the hall remained silent except for Æthelhelm and his men, who stamped their feet in agreement.

And that silence, I thought, was interesting. The vast majority of the nobles in the hall was ready to do whatever Wulfheard and Æthelhelm wanted, yet they were not enthusiastic about that fate. There was still a good deal of pride in Mercia. They would accept a West Saxon king, but it would be a loveless marriage, and so they remained quiet, all except one, Ealdorman Aidyn. "This Witan has the power to choose a king," he growled. He was a noble from the eastern part of Mercia, a man whose troops had long been allied with the West Saxons in their forays against the East Anglian Danes, and a man I would have expected to be an enthusiastic supporter of Edward's claim, but even he had sounded skeptical.

"It has ever been the prerogative of the Witan to choose their king," Bishop Wulfheard allowed somewhat grudgingly, "do you have a proposal?"

Aidyn shrugged. Did he hope to be chosen himself, I wondered. "Mercia should be ruled by a Mercian," he said.

"But who?" Bishop Wulfheard barked, and it was a good question. Aidyn sensed that few men in the hall would support his claim, if indeed he had any claim, and so he said nothing more.

"The crown," another man spoke up, but I could not see who it was, "should go to the king's son."

"Lord Æthelred had no son," the bishop snapped.

"Then to the nearest kin," the man said.

"The nearest kin is his widow's brother, King Edward," Wulfheard said, and that, interestingly, was not true, though I did not say so. "And let me remind this Witan," the bishop went on, "that King Edward's mother was a Mercian." That was true, and some men in the hall nodded. Wulfheard waited for another comment, but none came. "I therefore propose . . ." he began, but then stopped because I had stood.

"I have a question, lord bishop," I said respectfully.

"Lord Uhtred?" he responded cautiously.

"Can Mercia's ruler," I asked, "appoint a successor if he has no heir?"

Wulfheard frowned, looking for the trap in the question, then decided to lay a trap of his own. "Are you saying, Lord Uhtred," he asked in a silky voice, "that Lord Æthelred was the ruler of this realm?"

"Of course he was," I said, giving Wulfheard the answer he wanted, "but I am not expert in Mercian law as you are, so I just wished to know if the Lord Æthelred's last wishes have any legal validity."

"They do!" Wulfheard answered triumphantly. "The ruler's wishes carry great force, and only need this noble assembly's support to be enacted."

Silence again. Men turned and looked at me. They knew I wanted Æthelflaed to rule Mercia, but my question and humble answer suggested I was ready to support her brother. Wulfheard, smiling because he believed he had just scored a great triumph over me, spoke again. "We would be remiss," he said unctuously, "if we were not to give great weight to Lord Æthelred's dying wish, and that wish was for his brother-in-law, King Edward of Wessex, to become Mercia's king." He paused, but again there was silence. The Witan might recognize the inevitability of the choice, but that did not mean they liked it. These men were witnessing the death of a proud country, a country once led by the great King Offa who had dominated all Britain. Wulfheard gestured to Æthelhelm. "The Lord Æthelhelm of Wessex," he said, "is not a member of this Witan . . ."

"Yet," a man interrupted and was rewarded with laughter.

"Yet," the bishop agreed, "but with your permission he will tell us how King Edward will rule this land."

Æthelhelm stood. He had always been a good-looking and affable man, and his demeanor now was friendly, humble, and earnest. He declared what an honour the Witan would do to Edward and how Edward would be forever grateful, and how Edward would labor "night and day" to nurture Mercia, to protect her frontiers, and to expel those Danes who still remained in the northern part of the country. "He will do nothing," Æthelhelm said fervently, "without the guidance of this Witan. Advisers from Mercia will be the king's constant companions! And the king's eldest son, my grandson Ælfweard, the ætheling, will spend half his time in Gleawecestre so that he will learn to love this country as much as his father does, indeed, as much as all West Saxons do!"

He had spoken well, but his words were still met with the same sullen silence. I saw Wulfheard was about to speak again, so it was time, I thought, to toss a turd into the pottage. "And what of King Edward's sister?" I asked before the bishop could draw breath. "The Lady Æthelflaed?"

She was listening, I knew. She had not been allowed into the Witan because women had no voice in the council, but she was waiting just beyond the door that was closest to the dais. Æthel-helm knew she was listening too. "The Lady Æthelflaed," he said carefully, "is now a widow. She will doubtless wish to retire to her estates, or else join a nunnery where she can pray for the soul of her departed husband."

"And will she be safe in any nunnery?" I asked.

"Safe?" Bishop Wulfheard bridled at the question. "She will be in God's hands, Lord Uhtred. Of course she will be safe!"

"Yet just two days ago," I said, raising my voice and speaking slowly so that the oldest and deafest members of the Witan could hear my words, "Ealdorman Æthelhelm allied his men with the traitor Eardwulf's troops in an attempt to kill her. Why should we believe that he won't try again?"

"That's outrageous!" Wulfheard sputtered.

"You dream dreams," Æthelhelm said, though his voice had lost its friendly tone.

"You deny it?" I asked.

"I deny it absolutely," he said, angry now.

"Then I call witnesses to testify before this Witan," I said, and beckoned to the hall's main door. Hoggar appeared there, leading the men who had accompanied Eardwulf, and with them came Finan who had Grindwyn as his prisoner. Grindwyn's hands were bound. Finan came and stood beside me. "Sihtric's back," he whispered, "and he has what you want."

"Good," I said, then raised my voice. "That man," I pointed

at Grindwyn, "is sworn to Lord Æthelhelm's service. He is Lord Æthelhelm's oath-man, and I will bring further witnesses who will swear before this Witan that he was doing Lord Æthelhelm's bidding when he accompanied the traitor Eardwulf in his attempt to kill the Lady Æthelflaed." I clapped my hands, and the sound brought Eadith into the hall. She stood, pale-faced and straight-backed, beside Grindwyn. "This woman needs no introduction," I said, "but she will testify to her brother's treachery and to Lord Æthelhelm's approval of that treachery. I demand that a priest administer the oath of truthfulness to my witnesses."

"This is unseemly," Bishop Wulfheard snarled.

"The killing of Lady Æthelflaed would have been unseemly," I snarled back.

"The word of an adulteress can carry no truth!" Wulfheard bellowed. "I demand that you remove that woman from this assembly and that you withdraw your foul lies and that you . . ."

Whatever else he was going to demand went unsaid because again I had clapped my hands, and this time Sihtric appeared with three more women. One, like Eadith, was tall, red-haired and slender, the second was fair-haired and plump, the third was black-haired and tiny. All three looked scared, though all three were earning more silver in five minutes than they made on their backs in a week. Some men in the hall laughed when the women appeared, and a few men looked angry, but almost every man present knew who the three were. They were whores from the Wheatsheaf, and Father Penda had somewhat reluctantly given me their names. He told me he had frequently escorted one, two, or even all three from the tavern to the bishop's house inside Æthelred's palace.

"Who are those creatures?" Æthelhelm demanded.

"Let me introduce you," I said, "the tall lady is called . . ."

"Lord Uhtred!" The bishop was shouting now. I noticed that Ceolnoth and Ceolberht had stopped writing.

"Bishop?" I asked innocently.

"Do you have something to propose?" He knew why the whores were there, knew too that given the chance I would have all three squawking like geese. And Wulfheard, of course, was a married man. "Do you insist, bishop," I asked, "that adulterers cannot speak in this council?"

"I asked what you proposed!" he insisted. He was red-faced.

"I propose that the arrangements between Mercia and Wessex continue as before," I said, "and that the Lady Æthelflaed assumes her husband's responsibilities."

"A woman?" someone snarled.

"A woman cannot rule!" Aidyn said, and maybe a third of the men in the room growled agreement.

I walked to the platform, trying not to limp because of the pain in my rib. No one disputed my right to climb up beside Æthelhelm and the bishop, though for a moment Wulfheard looked as if he was going to protest, then glanced at the whores and abruptly shut his mouth. "It is not unusual," I said, "for the ruler's closest relative to take the throne. May I remind this Witan that my mother was a Mercian and that I am first cousin to Æthelred?"

There was a moment of stunned silence, then a sudden protest erupted from a group of priests sitting to one side of the hall. I heard the word "pagan" being shouted, most loudly by two abbots who were on their feet shaking fists, so I simply pulled aside my cloak to show them the big cross hanging at my breast. The sight of the silver brought a moment of utter silence, then an outburst of more protests. "Are you trying to convince us you're a Christian now?" the fat abbot, Ricseg, bellowed.

"I was baptized this morning," I said.

"You mock Christ!" Abbot Ricseg shouted. He was not wrong.

"Father Penda?" I said.

So Father Penda defended my conversion, struggling to convince a skeptical Witan that my baptism was genuine. Did he believe that? I doubt it, but on the other hand I was a notable convert for him and he fiercely defended my integrity. Æthelhelm half listened to the wrangling clerics, then took me aside. "What are you doing, Uhtred?" he asked.

"You know what I'm doing."

He grunted. "And those three women?"

"Wulfheard's favorite whores."

He laughed. "You clever bastard," he said. "Where are they from?"

"The Wheatsheaf."

"I must try them."

"I recommend the redhead," I said.

"And Eadith?"

"What of her?"

"A week ago she was saying how much she hated you."

"I have a golden tongue."

"I thought that was her asset." He looked at the rows of men on the benches, who were listening to the furious argument raging between the priests. "So Wulfheard won't speak against you now," he said, "and I run the risk of having you depict me as a tyrant who'd kill women, so what do you want?"

"That," I said, nodding at the throne.

He frowned, not in disapproval but because I had surprised him. "You want to be Lord of Mercia?"

"Yes."

"And suppose we allow it," he said, "what will you do?"

I shrugged. "Wessex already has Lundene, and you can keep it. You're fighting into East Anglia, so go on doing that with Lundene as your base. I want Mercia to be fighting on our northern frontier, out of Ceaster."

He nodded. "And the boy Æthelstan? Where is he?"

"Safe," I said curtly.

"He's not legitimate."

"He is."

"I have evidence that his mother was already married when she rutted Edward."

I laughed. "You're rich enough to buy witnesses who'll say that."

"I am."

"But it isn't true."

"The Witan of Wessex will believe it, that's all that matters."

"Then your grandson will probably be the next King of Wessex," I said.

"That's all I want." He paused to look at the Witan again. "I don't want to make an enemy of you," he said, "so swear an oath to me."

"What oath?"

"That when the time comes," he said, "you will use all your strength to ensure Ælfweard succeeds to his father's throne."

"I'll die long before Edward," I said.

"No one knows when any of us will die. Swear it."

"I . . ."

"And swear that the throne of Wessex will be united with Mercia's throne," he growled.

I hesitated. An oath is a serious promise. We break oaths at the risk of fate, at the risk of the revenge of the Norns, those vicious goddesses who spin our life's thread and can cut it on a whim. I had broken other oaths and survived, but for how long would the gods allow me to do that?

"Well?" Æthelhelm prompted me.

"If I'm ruler of Mercia when your son-in-law dies," I said, touching the silver cross around my neck, "then I shall . . ."

He roughly swatted my hand away. "Swear it, Lord Uhtred," he said, "on whatever god you truly worship."

"As the lord and ruler of Mercia," I said, picking my words with care, "then I shall use all my strength to ensure Ælfweard succeeds to his father's throne. And that the kingdoms of Wessex and Mercia will be united to the throne of Wessex. I swear it by Thor and by Woden."

"And swear that you will be a true and loyal ally to Wessex," he demanded.

"I swear that too," I said, and meant it.

"And Æthelflaed," he said.

"What of her?"

"She must go to the nunnery her mother founded. Make sure she does."

I wondered why he was so insistent. Was it because Æthelflaed protected Æthelstan? "I can't command a king's daughter," I said. "Edward must tell his sister what she must do."

"He'll insist she goes to a nunnery."

"Why?"

He shrugged. "She shines brighter than he does. Kings don't like that."

"She fights Danes," I said.

"Not if she's in a nunnery, she won't," he said caustically. "Tell me you won't oppose Edward's wishes."

"It's nothing to do with me," I said, "it's a matter for you and him."

"And you'll leave it to us? You won't interfere?"

"I'll leave it to you," I said.

He frowned at me for a few heartbeats, then decided I had offered him enough reassurance. "The Lord Uhtred," Æthelhelm turned from me and raised his voice to still the clamor in the hall, "agrees with me that the thrones of Wessex and Mercia should be united! That one king should rule us all, that we become one country!" At least half the men in the hall were frowning. Mercia had its ancient pride, and it was being trampled by the more powerful Wessex. "But the Lord Uhtred," Æthelhelm continued, "convinces me that the time is not yet ripe. King Edward's forces are concentrated in the east to drive the foreigners from East Anglia, while Mercia's business is in the north, to whip the pagans from your land. Only when those pagan foreigners are gone can we call ourselves one blessed country. For that reason I support the Lord Uhtred's claim to the overlordship of Mercia."

And so it happened. I was made Lord of Mercia, heir to all Æthelred's fortune, to his troops and all his land. Bishop Wulfheard looked disgusted, but the three whores left him helpless, and so he pretended to approve the choice. Indeed it was Wulfheard who beckoned me toward the empty throne.

The men in the hall were stamping their feet. I was not their first choice, maybe not the choice of even one tenth of the assembled lords. These men had mostly supported Æthelred, and knew of the hatred he bore me, but to their minds there was no obvious candidate to succeed him, and I was better than a foreign king whose loyalty would surely be to Wessex first. And, more, I was the son of a Mercian and Æthelred's closest male relative. By choosing me they salved their pride and many, surely, believed I could not live long. Soon, perhaps, they would be given the chance to elect another ruler.

I walked to the throne and picked up the helmet. A few men cheered. Even more cheered when I swept up the black cloth that draped the seat and tossed it aside.

"Sit, Lord Uhtred," Æthelhelm said.

"Lord Bishop!" I called.

Wulfheard forced a smile. He even managed a hint of a bow as he turned to me. "Lord Uhtred?" he asked.

"You persuaded us earlier that the ruler's wishes for his successor possess great weight."

"They do," he said, frowning in puzzlement.

"And you said that those wishes need only the Witan's support to be enacted?"

"I did," he said stiffly.

"Then let me remind this Witan," I said, "that the new lands we have gained have been through the efforts of the Lady Æthelflaed." I crossed to the table and lifted the parchments, the land-grants, the riches that these men wanted. "It is the Lady Æthelflaed who has garrisoned Ceaster and defended its territory from the Northmen." I dropped the parchments. "It is therefore my wish that I relinquish the throne of Mercia in favor of Lord Æthelred's widow, the Lady Æthelflaed."

They could have defeated me at that moment. If the Witan had risen in protest, if they had shouted me down, then the whole pretense would have been in vain, but I had shocked them into silence and it was during that silence that Æthelflaed entered from the side door. She still wore funeral black, though over the silk dress she had draped a white cloak embroidered with blue crosses entwined with pale green withies. The long cloak trailed on the floor. She looked beautiful. Her hair was plaited and wrapped around her skull, a necklace of emeralds hung at her neck, and in her right hand was her dead husband's sword. No one spoke as she crossed the dais. I sensed the Witan was holding its breath as I gave her the helmet. She handed me the sword so that she could use both hands to pull the helmet over her golden hair, then, without a word, she sat on the empty throne and I gave her back the sword.

And the hall cheered. The Witan was suddenly loud with acclamation. Men stood and stamped their feet, they shouted at her, and Æthelflaed's face did not stir. She looked stern, she looked like a queen. And why did the hall suddenly acclaim her? Maybe it was the relief that I was not to be their lord, but I like to think that they had secretly wanted Æthelflaed all along, but none had dared fly in the face of custom by proposing her name. Yet all the Witan knew that she had proven herself as a warrior, as a ruler, and as a Mercian. She was the Lady of Mercia.

"You bastard," Æthelhelm said to me.

Oaths were sworn. It took the best part of an hour as, one by one, the ealdormen and chief thegns of Mercia went to Æthelflaed, knelt before her, and swore their loyalty. Her husband's household warriors and her own troops stood at the hall's edges, and they were the only men permitted to carry swords. If any man there was reluctant to swear fealty then those blades persuaded him to sense, and, by midday, all of the Witan had clasped hands with their new ruler and promised her loyal service.

She spoke briefly. She praised Mercia and promised that those lands to the north still infested by pagans would be freed. "To which end," she said, her voice clear and strong, "I shall require troops from you all. We are a nation at war, and we shall win that war." And that was the difference between her and her dead husband. Æthelred had done just enough to fend off Danish incursions, but he had never wanted to attack the Danish lands. Æthelflaed would scourge them from the kingdom. "Lord Uhtred?" she looked at me.

"My lady?"

"Your oath."

And so I knelt to her. The sword's tip was resting on the floor between her feet, her hands clasped about the heavy hilt, and I put my hands around hers. "I swear loyalty to you, my lady," I said, "to be your man and to support you with all my might."

"Look at me." She had dropped her voice so only I could hear. I looked into her face and saw she had forced a smile. "Eadith?" she hissed, bending toward me and still forcing the smile.

I wondered who had told her. "You want her oath too?" I asked.

"You bastard," she said. I felt her hands twitch beneath mine. "Get rid of her." She still spoke in a hiss, then raised her voice. "Take your troops north to Ceaster, Lord Uhtred. You have work to do."

"I will, my lady," I answered.

"Fifty of my men will go with you," she announced, "and the Prince Æthelstan will accompany you."

"Yes, my lady," I said. It was sensible, I thought, to remove Æthelstan as far as possible from Æthelhelm's ambitions.

"I will follow as soon as I am able," Æthelflaed said, "but there is work to do first." She was speaking to the whole Witan now. "There are lands to distribute and responsibilities to be given. Bishop Wulfheard?"

"My lady?" He sounded nervous.

"You were my husband's most valued adviser. I trust you will stay as head of my council?"

"With God's help, my lady, I hope to serve you as I served him." You could hear the relief in the bastard's voice. Æthelflaed had seduced Eardwulf's men into loyalty, now she would start on her dead husband's supporters, and by so publicly appointing Wulfheard she was giving notice that those supporters had no reason to fear her enmity. Yet she had cause to fear Æthelhelm's anger. I watched him as I moved to the side of the dais, and I could see he was angry, his usually genial face tight with fury. He would be waiting for her to make a mistake or to lose land to the pagans, and then he would use his money and influence to have her replaced.

And if land was to be lost it would be in the north, so I would go to Ceaster, because that city was not yet entirely safe from our enemies. There was work to do there and Norsemen to fight.

But first I had to find a sword.

PART THREE

The God of War

Eight

The oars dipped, pulled slow, and rose. The long blades dripped water, swung forward, then dipped again. The boat surged with each long stroke, then slowed as the oars trailed their drips in the gray-green Sæfern. We were not hurrying because the tide and the river's current were carrying us to the sea, and the oar strokes just held the Ðrines steady and let the steering-oar bite. Finan was chanting a slow, sad-sounding song in his native Irish, the rhythm driving the thirty-six men who pulled on the Ðrines's oars. More men sat in the bows, idly watching the reeds bend to the Ðrines's wake. Ðrines! Why name a ship after the trinity? I have yet to meet a single priest, monk, nun, or scholar who can explain the trinity to me. Three gods in one? And one of those a ghost?

It had been three days since Æthelflaed was acclaimed as Mercia's ruler. I had sworn loyalty to her, then taken the cross from about my neck and tossed it to Finan, replacing the bauble with my usual hammer. That done I had taken Father Ceolberht by the scruff of his gown and dragged him through the side door of the great hall. Æthelflaed had called a sharp reprimand, but I ignored her, dragging the squealing priest into the passageway, where I slammed him against the wall. Pulling him and pushing him had made the ache in my rib sudden agony, and the smell of the leaking pus was vile, but my anger was far greater than the pain. "You lied to me, you toothless bastard," I told him.

"I . . . ," he began, but I slammed him again, hammering his balding head against the stones of the Roman wall.

"You told me you didn't know what happened to Ice-Spite," I said.

"I . . . ," he tried a second time, but again I gave him no chance to speak, just thrust him hard into the wall, and he whimpered.

"You carried the sword from the battle," I said, "and you brought it here." That was what Eadith had told me. She had seen the priest carrying the sword. Her brother Eardwulf had even offered to buy the blade, but Ceolberht had refused, saying it had been promised to another. "So where is it?" I asked, but Ceolberht said nothing, just looked at me in terror. Finan came through the door from the hall and raised an eyebrow. "We're going to disembowel this lying priest," I told the Irishman, "but slowly. Give me a knife."

"Lord!" Ceolberht gasped.

"Tell me, you turd-slime, what you did with Cnut's sword."

He just whimpered again, so I took the knife Finan offered me. The edges were so sharp they looked feathered. A man could have shaved with that blade. I smiled at Ceolberht and slid the knife through his black robe till the tip touched the skin of his belly. "I will gut you slowly," I said, "so very slowly." I felt the needle-sharp tip puncture his skin, provoking a mewing sound. "So where is it?" I asked.

"Lord!" he gasped. I would not have gutted him, but he thought I would. His mouth opened and closed fast, his remaining teeth chattered, then at last he managed to speak. "It went to Scire-burnan, lord."

"Say that again!"

"It went to Scireburnan!" he said in a desperate tone.

I held the knife still. Scireburnan was a town in Thornsæta, one of the richer shires of Wessex, and the land all about Scireburnan belonged to Æthelhelm. "You gave Ice-Spite to Æthelhelm?" I asked.

"No, lord!"

"Then who, you bastard, who?"

"To the bishop," he whispered.

"To Wulfheard?"

"He means Bishop Asser," Finan said drily.

190

"Bishop Asser?" I asked Ceolberht, who just nodded. I took the knife away from his belly and placed the bloodied tip a finger's breadth from his right eye. "Maybe I'll blind you," I said. "I've already taken your teeth, why not your eyes too? Then your tongue."

"Lord!" It was scarcely a whisper. He dared not move.

"Bishop Asser is dead," I said.

"He wanted the sword, lord."

"So it's at Scireburnan?"

He just moaned. I think he had wanted to shake his head, but he dared not.

"Then," I let the blade's tip touch the skin just beneath his lower eyelid, "where is it?"

"Tyddewi," he whispered.

"Tyddewi?" I had never heard of the place.

"Bishop Asser went there to die, lord," Ceolberht hardly dared to speak, and his voice was lower than a whisper, while his eyes were crossed as he stared at the knife's wicked-looking blade. "He wanted to die at home, lord, so he went to Wales."

I let go of Ceolberht, who fell to his knees in relief. I gave the knife back to Finan. "So it's in Wales," I said.

"Seems so." Finan wiped the blade clean.

Bishop Asser! That made sense. He was a man I hated, and he had hated me. He had been a vengeful little Welshman, a rabid priest, who had wormed his way into King Alfred's affections and then licked the royal arse like a demented dog lapping up blood after the autumn livestock slaughter. I had fallen out with Asser long before he met Alfred, and he was never a man to abandon a grudge, and so he had ever struggled to create ill-feeling between the king and myself. If no Danes threatened, then Alfred would treat me like an outcast, egged on by Asser's viperous hatred, but as soon as Wessex was under siege I would suddenly be back in favor, and that meant Asser had never managed to wreak his revenge on me. Until now.

His reward for licking Alfred's arse was to be given monasteries and a bishopric with all their fat incomes. He had been made bishop of Scireburnan, an especially rich reward in a plump shire.

I had heard that he had left the town just before he died, and had thought nothing of that news except to say a word of thanks to Thor and Woden for killing the cunning little bastard. But the bastard truly had been cunning because my wound was still hurting. Which meant someone else now possessed Cnut's sword, and that someone must still be working Christian sorcery on the blade.

And that was why the *Ðrines* was heading west into a rising wind. The river was widening into the sea now. The Sæfern's tide was still falling, the wind was growing, and whenever the wind opposes the tide the sea shortens, and so the *Ðrines* buffeted into sharp, steep waves. She had been one of Æthelred's small fleet, which had patrolled the southern coast of Wales to deter the pirates who came out of the bays and inlets to harass Mercian traders. It had taken me two days to provision her, two days in which I constantly expected to be summoned and reprimanded by Æthelflaed for not obeying her. I should have been riding north to Ceaster, instead I had spent those days a few miles south of Gleawecestre where I had loaded the *Ðrines* with dried fish, bread, and ale. My daughter had wanted to come with me, but I had insisted she go with Æthelflaed's fifty men who had been sent to reinforce Ceaster. A man who loves his daughter does not let her go into Wales. Æthelflaed had also insisted that her nephew, Æthelstan, go to Ceaster. He would be safe behind those tough Roman walls, a long way from Æthelhelm's malice. His twin sister, Eadgyth, who offered no threat to Æthelhelm's ambitions, had stayed with Æthelflaed in Gleawecestre.

The *Ðrines* was a good ship, except for her name. She was tightly made with a sail that had hardly been used, nor could we use it now for we were heading straight into the spiteful wind. I was letting my son be the helmsman and master and I saw him frown as a bigger wave threw the cross-decorated prow of the *Ðrines* sharply upward, and I waited to see what decision he made, then watched as he thrust the steering-oar to take us on a more southerly course. Our destination lay on the northern shore, but he was right to go southerly. When the tide changed we would want the wind's help, and he was making sea room so we could hoist the big sail and let it drive us. If the wind stayed as it was then I doubted we could make enough room, but it was more than likely that it would swing southerly too. Besides, I suspected we would shelter for a night on the Wessex coast, perhaps near the place where I had killed Ubba so many years before.

We numbered forty-six men, a considerable war-band, and Eadith had come too. Some of my men had wondered at that. Most folk consider that a woman aboard a ship brings nothing but bad luck because it provokes the jealousy of Ran, the goddess of the sea who will abide no rivals, but I dared not leave Eadith in Gleawecestre to suffer Æthelflaed's jealousy. "She'll kill the poor girl," I had told Finan.

"She'll send her to a nunnery, maybe?"

"It's the same thing. Besides," I lied, "Eadith knows Wales."

"She does, does she?"

"Intimately," I said, "that's why she's going with us."

"Of course," he said and said no more.

Eadith, of course, knew nothing of Wales, but who did? Luckily Gerbruht had been to Tyddewi. He was a friend of my son's and noted among my warriors for his appetite, which had made him fat, though much of that ox-like bulk was solid muscle. I summoned him to the stern of the boat where we sat just beside the steering platform and I made Eadith listen. "How do you know Wales?" I asked Gerbruht.

"I went on pilgrimage, lord."

"You did?" I sounded surprised. Gerbruht struck me as a most unlikely pilgrim.

"My father was a priest, lord," he explained.

"He came from Frisia to visit Wales?"

"King Alfred fetched him to Wintanceaster, lord, because my father knew Greek." That made sense. Alfred had brought dozens of foreign churchmen to Wessex, but only if they were learned. "So my father and mother liked to visit shrines," Gerbruht went on.

"And they took you to Tyddewi?" I asked.

He nodded. "I was just a child, lord," he said.

"Don't tell me," I said, "there's a dead saint there."

"There is, lord!" He sounded awed and made the sign of the cross. "Saint Dewi."

"Never heard of him. What did he do?"

"He preached, lord."

"They all do that!"

"Well the folk at the back of the crowd couldn't see him, lord."

"Why not?" I asked. "Was he a dwarf?"

Gerbruht frowned, plainly trying to help me, but could find no answer. "I don't know if he was a dwarf, lord, but they couldn't see him so Dewi prayed to God and God made a hill under his feet."

I stared at Gerbruht. "Dewi made a hill in Wales?"

"Yes, lord."

"And they call that a miracle?"

"Oh yes, lord!"

Gerbruht did not have the quickest mind in my shield wall, but he was staunch and strong. He could pull an oar all day or wield a war ax with savage skill. "So tell me about Tyddewi," I ordered him.

He frowned again as he tried to remember. "It's not far from the sea, lord."

"That's good."

"There are monks there. Good men, lord."

"I'm sure they are."

"And hills, lord."

"Dewi was there," I said, "so perhaps he made them?"

"Yes, lord!" He liked that idea. "And they have little fields, lord, with lots of sheep."

"I like mutton."

"I do too, lord," he said enthusiastically.

"Did you see any warriors at Tyddewi?"

He nodded, but he could not tell me if a lord lived anywhere near the monastery, nor whether the warriors had their home near the settlement. There was evidently a church where the hill-making saint was buried, and stone cells where the monks lived, but Gerbruht could not remember much about the nearby village. "The church is in a hollow, lord."

"A hollow?"

"In low ground, lord."

"You'd have thought they'd make the church on a hill," I said.

"On a hill, lord?"

"The one Dewi made."

"No, lord," he frowned, perplexed, "it's in low ground. And the monks fed us fish."

"Fish."

"And honey, lord."

"Together?"

He thought that was funny and laughed. "No, lord, not together. That wouldn't taste nice." He looked at Eadith, expecting her to share the joke. "Fish and honey!" he said, and she giggled, which pleased Gerbruht. "Fish and honey!" he said again. "They were herrings."

"Herrings?" Eadith asked, trying not to laugh.

"And cockles, winkles, and eels. Mackerel too!"

"So tell me about the warriors you saw."

"But the bread was strange, lord," he said earnestly, "it tasted of seaweed."

"Warriors?" I prompted him.

"There were some at Dewi's shrine, lord."

"They could have been visiting? Like you?"

"Yes, lord."

"Seaweed?" Eadith asked.

"The bread was knobbly, my lady, and sour. But I quite liked it."

"How did you get there?" I asked him.

"They led us down a path to the food hut, lord, and we ate with the monks."

"No! To Tyddewi!"

He frowned. "We rode, lord."

Gerbruht could tell me little more. It was plain that Tyddewi was a place of Christian pilgrimage, and, if Gerbruht's memory was correct, strangers could travel the rough tracks of the southern Welsh kingdoms in some safety, and that thought was encouraging. Christians do like pilgrims, those pious folk who gaze at pig bones that pretend to be dead saints and then give money, lots of money, and there's hardly a church, monastery, or nunnery that does not have the eyelid of Saint John or the bellybutton of Saint Agatha or the pickled trotters of the Gadarene swine. Many such pilgrims are poor, yet the fools will give their last bent coin to receive the blessing of a thimbleful of dirt scraped from beneath a dead saint's toenail, but the fact that Tyddewi welcomed such gullible fools was good because it meant we could arrive there in the guise of pilgrims.

We sheltered that first night somewhere on the north coast of Defnascir. We found a cove and dropped the anchor stone and let the night fall on our tired ship. Some time that day we had passed the mouth of the river where I had killed Ubba. That fight on the sand had made my reputation, but it had happened so long ago now, and some day, I thought, a young man would cut me down as I had cut Ubba down and he would take Serpent-Breath and he would strut his fame. Wyrd bið ful āræd.

The next morning brought a hard day's rowing, for the wind was still in our face and at times the tide tried to drive us back, and it was already dusk when we came to Lundi, an island I had visited many years before. It had hardly changed, though some folk must have tried settling there, which was a foolish thing to do because marauding Northmen would have seen their farmstead and rowed ashore. There were two piles of decayed ashes marking where the buildings had stood and a skeleton on the shingle where we grounded the *Ðrines*. Goats watched us from the heights where puffins had their burrows. We killed and butchered two goats and cooked an evening meal over a driftwood fire. The sky had cleared, the stars were a smear of light, the air cool but not cold, and we slept on the thin turf guarded by sentries.

Next day we rowed westward through a limpid sea that heaved slowly to ripple misted light. Puffins whirred past us on their short wings, and seals lifted their whiskered faces to watch us pass. The wind rose in mid-morning and, after swerving north and south, it settled into a steady southwesterly, and we hoisted the sail and let the *Ðrines* run free. I took the steering-oar for a time, not because my son could not manage the ship, but just for the joy of feeling the sea's tremor through the long loom. Then the effort of handling the long oar began to make my rib hurt and so I gave him back the oar and just lay on the steering platform and watched the glittering sea pass. I wondered if there were ships in Valhalla. Imagine eternity with a good ship and a shining sea and the wind in your face and a crew of good men and a woman beside you.

"*Skidbladnir*," I said.

"Skid?" Eadith asked.

"It's a ship of the gods," I explained, "and it fits into a warrior's pouch, and when you need her you just throw the ship into the sea and she grows to her full size."

She smiled. "And you mock Christian miracles."

"I've yet to see a dead man raised or a blind man given sight."

"But you have seen a ship grow on the sea?"

"I hate clever women," I growled.

She laughed. She had never been on a ship before, except to row decorously up and down the Sæfern beside Gleawecestre, and she had been nervous when our hull first met the wider sea and the short waves had buffeted us. She had seen the hull bend to the steeper waves and thought the planks must break, until I told her that if the hull did not bend then the ship would surely sink. "The planks bend," I explained, "and the frame just stops them bending too much. It's like a sword. Make it too brittle and it breaks, too soft and it won't hold an edge."

"And the stones?" She had nodded at the bilge.

"They keep us upright," I said, and laughed because I remembered a ridiculous sermon Father Beocca had once preached in which he had likened ballast stones to a Christian's faith, and he had kept adding more stones to his imaginary ship until my father growled that he had just sunk the damned boat, and poor Beocca just stood by the altar with his mouth open.

"You're happy," Eadith said, sounding happy herself.

And I was happy too. The pain in my side was bearable, the ship was riding smoothly, and the only thing that worried me was Wales. I knew little of the Welsh except that they were Christian, spoke a barbarous tongue and, if Gerbruht was right, ate seaweed. Their country was divided into little kingdoms that seemed to change names with the weather, though Tyddewi, I knew, was part of a realm called Dyfed, though I had no idea who ruled that land. Some petty king, no doubt, all beard and bellyache. Yet the men of Wales were great warriors, and it had become a rule among Saxons that only fools went into their hills to be slaughtered, though that did not stop fools trying. And the Welsh, who claimed we had stolen their land, liked to raid into Mercia to steal livestock and slaves, and that constant warfare was useful training for young warriors. Indeed I had fought against Welshmen in my very first shield wall. I often wondered why the Welsh did not worship the gods who were enemies of the Saxons, for surely those gods would have helped them regain their land, but they insisted on being Christian, and a good thing too because it had been Welsh Christian warriors who had come to Teotanheale and helped defeat Cnut.

Now Cnut's sword was in Dyfed and the *Ðrines* ran toward it with a bellied sail and a spreading wake. I saw a few other ships, all far off. The small dark sails were probably fishermen, but two larger pale sails were cargo ships heading toward the Sæfern's mouth. I doubted they were fighting ships because, though they sailed close together, they headed sharply away from us and were soon lost in the sea's haze.

By late afternoon we were off the Welsh coast, rowing now, for the wind was heading us again. In the two days we had spent filling the *Ðrines*'s belly with casks of ale and barrels of smoked fish and sacks of double-baked bread I had talked to a shipmaster who knew the coast. He had been a big man, full-bearded, his face darkened and lined by weather. He had assured me that finding Tyddewi would be easy. "Go west to the land's end, lord," he had said, "and you pass a big inlet and come to a rocky headland with islands just off it, and you turn north there and cross a great bay, and the headland on the bay's far side is Tyddewi. A blind man could find it on a dark night."

"Come with us," I invited him.

"You want me to set foot in that land?" he had asked. "In thirty-eight years at sea, lord, I've never landed in Wales and never will."

"We'll be pilgrims."

"With swords?" he had laughed. "You can't miss it, lord. Go west till there's no land left and then cross the bay to the north. Go east a little till you see an island with a great rock arch, and you'll find good anchorage at the inlet there. The man who taught me the coast called it the dragon's mouth. Sharp rocks like teeth, lord, but you can walk to Tyddewi from there."

"You anchored in the dragon's mouth?"

"Three times. One anchor stone off the bow, another off the stern, and good sentries to stay awake through the night."

"And didn't go ashore? Not even to get water?"

He grimaced. "There were hairy bastards with axes waiting. I sheltered there, lord, from gales. And I prayed that the dragon kept his mouth open. Just cross the bay, look for the arch, and God preserve you."

And perhaps the Christian god would preserve us. Wales was, after all, a place of Christians, but I still touched the hammer at my neck and prayed to Odin. Once upon a time he had come to this middle world, and he had made love to a girl and she had given him a mortal son, and the son had a son, and that son had another, and so it went on until I was born. I have the blood of gods, and I stroked the hammer and begged Odin to preserve me in the land of our enemies.

And that evening, as the wind lulled and the sea settled into a long swell, we crossed the wide bay and came to the arched rock and beyond it, high in the darkening sky, a great pall of smoke hung above the rocky land. Finan stood beside me and stared at the dark smear. He knew what it marked. Our whole lives had been spent seeing such smoke of destruction. "Danes?" he suggested.

"More likely Norsemen," I said, "or a Welsh quarrel? They squabble enough."

We rowed slowly eastward, searching for the dragon's mouth, and there it was, a dark shadowed cleft in the coast, and I touched my hammer again as the long oars pulled us into the land's embrace. There were sheep on the high slopes, and a huddle of thatched hovels deeper in the narrow valley, but I saw no men with or without axes. We saw no one. If folk lived in the inlet's valley then they were hiding from whoever had smirched the sky with smoke.

"Someone will be watching us," Finan said, gazing up at the high slopes. "We can't see them, but they're watching us."

"Probably."

"And they'll send news of our coming."

"We have a cross on our bows," I said, meaning that we appeared to be a Christian-manned ship and, in a Christian land, that might protect us.

"God help us," Finan said, and made the sign of the cross.

We set sentries, then tried to sleep.

But sleep came hard that night. We were in the dragon's mouth.

Seven of us slipped ashore before dawn. I took Finan, of course, my son, Gerbruht because he had been to the shrine before, and two other warriors. Eadith insisted she come too. "You're safer on the ship," I told her, but she shook her head stubbornly and, persuading myself that the presence of a woman made the pretense of being pilgrims more convincing, I let her come. We all wore cloaks, and I had changed my hammer for a cross. The cloaks hid short-swords.

Once ashore we scrambled up the western side of the dragon's mouth, and, by the time we had reached the stony crest and my rib was feeling as though every devil in Christendom was stabbing it with red-hot forks, Sihtric had taken the *Ðrines* back to sea. If the unseen watcher of the dragon's mouth had sent word to his lord, then warriors would come to the inlet and find it empty. They would assume we had sheltered for the night and voyaged on, or rather I hoped they would believe that, and I had told Sihtric to keep the ship offshore until twilight and then slip back into the inlet.

And we walked.

It was not far, not far at all.

By the time the rising sun was slanting across the world we had found Tyddewi and, just like the hovels at the dragon's mouth, it was empty. I had expected to hear the usual cacophony of howling dogs and crowing cocks, but there was silence beneath the sifting smoke, which still rose to besmirch the morning sky. There had been a settlement here, but now it was ashes and smoldering timbers, all except a gaunt stone church that lay in a hollow. I had seen this so often, indeed I had caused it myself. Raiders had come, they had burned and plundered, but as we went closer I saw no bodies. The attackers would have taken the young and the nubile for slaves and for pleasure, such raiders usually killed the old and the sick, but there were no bodies being ripped by crows, no blood splashed on stone, no shrunken black corpses stinking in the embers. The village smoked and lay empty.

"If Cnut's sword was ever here," Finan said grimly, "it's gone now."

I said nothing, not wanting to think about what he had just said, though of course he was right. Someone, either sea-raiders or men from another Welsh kingdom, had come to Tyddewi and left it a wilderness of ash. A cat arched its back and hissed at us, but nothing else lived. We walked toward the church that was built of dark, stark stone. Beyond it was a mess of burned buildings that smoked more heavily than the rest and I guessed that had been the monastery where Asser had gone to die. At the far side of the ruins, built against the northern hill's lower slope, were small stone cabins shaped like beehives. A couple had been pulled apart, but a dozen others looked whole. "Stone huts," Gerbruht told us, "where the monks live."

"I wouldn't put a dog in one of those," I said.

"You like dogs," Finan pointed out, "so of course you wouldn't. But you'd put a monk in one of them. Jesus! What was that?" He was startled because a lump of charred timber had just been hurled from the church's western door. "Christ," Finan said, "someone's here."

"Sing," my son said.

"Sing?" I looked at him.

"We're pilgrims," he said, "so we should be singing."

"He's right," Finan growled.

"A psalm," my son said.

"Then sing," I snarled. And so they sang, though it was hardly impressive, and only Gerbruht knew more than a few words. My son had supposedly been educated by monks, but he just roared nonsense as we walked between the burned-out cottages. The place stank of smoke.

A flight of stone steps led down into the hollow, and just as we reached the steps a monk appeared at the church door. He stared at us for a frightened moment, threw down more charred timber, then fled back into the shadows. The psalm faltered as we went down the slope, then I was at the church door and went inside.

Three monks faced me. One, a brave fool, carried a baulk of half-burned wood like a club. His face was white, tense, and determined, and he did not lower the makeshift weapon even as my men came through the door. Behind him was the blackened remains of an altar, above which hung a painted wooden crucifix that had caught the flames, but not the fire. The feet of the nailed god were scorched, and the paint of his naked body smeared smoke-black, but the crucifix had survived the blaze. The monk holding the charred club spoke to us, but in his own language, which none of us understood.

"We're pilgrims," I said, feeling foolish.

The monk spoke again, still hefting the length of wood, but then the youngest of the three, a pale-faced, skimpy-bearded youth, spoke to us in our own tongue. "Who are you?"

"I told you, pilgrims. Who are you?"

"Have you come to harm us?" he asked.

"If I wanted to harm you," I said, "you'd be dead by now. We come in peace. So who are you?" The young monk made the sign of the cross, then gently pushed his companion's baulk of wood down and spoke to him in Welsh. I heard the word *season*, which is their name for the Saxons, and I saw the relief on all their faces when they realized we had not come to kill them. The oldest monk, a white-bearded man, fell to his knees and wept. "So who are you?" I asked the young monk again.

"My name is Brother Edwyn," the young monk said.

"A Saxon?"

"From Scireburnan."

"From Scireburnan, lord," I told him harshly.

"Yes, lord, from Scireburnan."

"You came here with Bishop Asser?" I asked. It seemed an obvious explanation for why a Saxon monk should be in this smoke-stinking corner of Wales.

"I did, lord."

"Why?"

He frowned, apparently puzzled by my question. "To learn from him, lord. He was a most holy man and a great teacher. He asked me to accompany him, to take down his words, lord."

"And what happened here? Who burned the place?"

Norsemen had happened. Somewhere to the north of Tyddewi was a river mouth, Brother Edwyn called it Abergwaun, though the name meant nothing to me, and Norsemen from Ireland had settled there. "They had permission, lord," Edwyn said.

"Permission?"

"From the king, lord, and they promised to pay him tribute."

I laughed at that. Other kings in Britain had invited the North-men to settle and had believed their promises to live in peace and to pay land-rent, and gradually more ships had arrived, and the settlers' war-band had grown in strength, and suddenly instead of tenants the king discovered he has a marauding band of savage warriors, cuckoos with claws, who wanted his fields, his women, his treasury, and his throne. "So who leads these Norsemen?" I asked.

"His name is Rognvald, lord."

I looked at Finan, who shrugged to show the name meant nothing to him. "He came from Ireland?" I asked the monk.

"Many Norsemen have fled Ireland these last few years, lord."

"I wonder why," Finan said, amused.

"And how many men does Rognvald lead?"

"At least a hundred, lord, but we knew he was coming! We were watching from the hills and received warning, so we had time to flee. But the treasures." His voice trailed away and he looked in despair around the gaunt church.

"Treasures?"

"We took the small reliquaries and the altar goods, but the rest? The great gold chest of Saint Dewi, the silver crucifix, they were too heavy, and we had no time to rescue them, lord. We only had moments. They came on horses."

"They took the saint?"

"We rescued his bones, lord, but his coffins? There was no time to take them."

"When was this?"

"Two days ago, lord. We three came back yesterday." He hesitated. The monk who had held the great baulk of wood like a club was speaking urgently and Brother Edwyn looked nervous. He summoned his courage and turned back to us. "And you, lord? May I ask where you're from?"

"We come from King Edward," I said. It was sensible to claim we had come from Wessex rather than Mercia. Wessex was further away and its warriors rarely fought against the Welsh, while Mercia was a neighbor and perpetually fighting raiders from the hills.

"King Edward! God be praised," Edwyn said, "a good Christian."

"As are we all," I said piously.

"And the king, lord, he sent you?"

"To see the grave of Bishop Asser," I said.

"Of course!" Brother Edwyn exclaimed, smiling. "The bishop was a great friend to Wessex! And such a holy man! What a servant of God he was! A soul of such kindness and generosity."

Such a piece of slug-shit, I thought, but managed a sickly smile. "He is missed in Wessex," I said.

"He was bishop here," Brother Edwyn said, "and we may never see his equal again, but now he is joined to the saints in heaven where he deserves to be!"

"He does indeed," I said fervently, thinking just what dull company the saints must be.

"His tomb is here." He crossed to the far side of the burned altar and pointed to a great slab of stone that had been lifted and slid aside. "The Norsemen, dear God, would not even let the dead rest in peace!"

I crossed to the grave and stared into the stone-lined tomb where Bishop Asser's simple wooden coffin had been splintered open. The bastard was still there, wrapped in gray cloth that was stained black. His whole body was wrapped so I could not see his pinched face, but I could smell his decay. I was tempted to spit into the tomb, but managed to resist the urge and at that moment I had an inspiration, an idea so brilliant that I wondered why I had not thought of it earlier. "King Edward," I turned back to Brother Edwyn and adopted my most earnest voice, "has asked us to bring back a remembrance of Asser."

"I understand, lord! He was so beloved in Wessex."

"He was indeed," I said, "and the king gave Bishop Asser a sword, a Danish sword, and asked that we might take it to place on the high altar of Wintanceaster's new church."

"Ah! The sword," Edwyn said. He sounded nervous again.

"We would pay for it, of course," I said.

Edwyn looked close to tears. "The bishop was very fond of that sword," he said, "and yet he was not a warlike man."

"He would value it," I said, "as a king's gift."

"Oh, he valued it! He did indeed, but alas, we cannot give it to King Edward."

"Cannot?"

"Bishop Asser's final wishes were to be buried with the sword. It was in the grave. The Norsemen must have known, for they took it."

"How would they know?"

"It was no secret," Brother Edwyn said, "and the missionaries might have mentioned it."

"Missionaries?"

"Rognvald was given permission to settle, lord, on condition that he gave a home to two of our missionaries and listen to their message. It was Father Elidell who sent us warning of Rognvald's coming."

And the bastard missionaries, I thought, must also have boasted of the sword. "King Edward desired the blade," I said helplessly.

"Perhaps King Edward would like another relic of the bishop?" Edwyn suggested helpfully. "We have some shoes the bishop wore? At least I think we do. Oh, I know! We still have some of the cloths we used to wipe up the vomit of his final illness, the king would like one of those?"

"A vomit cloth?" I asked.

"The vomit has dried, lord! It's nothing but a crust now and somewhat delicate, but if he becomes a saint, as well he might, then the crust will surely work miracles!"

"And the king will surely treasure it," I said, "but he had set his heart on the sword."

"No wonder," Edwyn said, "for he killed the pagan who carried it! We heard the story often!"

"King Edward killed him?" I asked.

"Oh, indeed! Bishop Asser was quite sure of that. And Bishop Asser said he would use the blade to fight valiantly against the devil even from the grave. Such a holy man!" Such a mean-spirited, tight-fisted, cunning piece of lying weasel-shit, I thought. "He was a great fighter against evil," Edwyn continued enthusiastically, "why, he even begged that the sword be wrapped in nettle leaves so it would sting the demons who taunt the Christian dead!" He made the sign of the cross. "Even in death the bishop fights for Christ."

Even in death he went on torturing me, except now the sword was in the hands of some Norseman, but I did not doubt that whatever Christian sorcery Asser had used on the blade would still be potent. But it was gone, and to find it I would have to treat with Rognvald. "This Norseman," I asked Edwyn, "he's still at Abergwin?"

"Abergwaun, lord, yes, as far as we know."

"And how far . . ." I began to ask, but was interrupted by my son.

"Father!" Uhtred's voice was urgent. He was standing at the church door, gazing into the day's new sunlight, and as I turned to him I heard the voices. Men's voices, and then the sound of footsteps. A lot of footsteps. I walked to the door, and there, not twenty paces away, were warriors.

A horde of warriors. Men in mail and helmets, some men in leather armor, and a few with nothing but padded jackets that will stop a sword slash, but not a lunge. Most had shields, almost all had swords, though a few were armed only with heavy, wide-bladed spears. They were bearded, dark-faced, hostile, but they had crosses hanging at their necks and some had the cross painted on their shields, which meant they were not Rognvald's men, but Welshmen. I started to count them, but there were too many.

"Thank Christ!" Brother Edwyn had come to the door. "The king is here."

"King?"

"King Hywel!" he said reprovingly, as though I should have known what savage ruled this corner of Wales. "He will be pleased to meet you, lord."

"The honor will be mine," I said, and I thought of all the men who had gone into Wales and never returned. There were stories of great caves into which the souls of Saxons were trapped by Welsh magicians. "What we should call our land," Father Pyrlig had once told me with a most unchristian relish, "is the graveyard of the Saxons! We do love them to visit! It gives the boys sword practice."

And the leader of the Welsh warriors, a grim beast with a red scarf wrapped about his helmet and a beard that hung to his waist and a shield on which a dragon breathed fire, drew his long-sword.

Wyrd bið ful āræd.

The grim man with the red scarf about his helmet stepped aside, and a much smaller man walked toward us. He too was in mail and wore a helmet, but he carried no shield. He had a pale green cloak of very fine linen, its edges hemmed with golden crosses. I might have thought him a priest, except for the splendor of his helmet and the richness of the scabbard fittings that hung from a belt plated with small gold panels. A chain of gold held a golden crucifix, which he touched as he stopped to stare at us. Something about him reminded me of Alfred. His face had none of the drawn lines of constant sickness and unending worry that had etched Alfred, but he did have a look of keen intelligence.

This man was no fool. He took another pace toward us and I saw his calm confidence. He called out in his own language, and Brother Edwyn stepped two paces forward and bowed. "The king," he hissed at us.

"Bow," I ordered my companions, then offered a bow myself.

So this was King Hywel. I guessed he was about thirty years of age, a head shorter than me, but strongly built. I had heard of him, though taken small notice because kings come and go in Wales like mice in thatch, but there was something about this man that suggested he was far more formidable than most of his kind. He seemed to be amused as he asked Brother Edwyn questions and listened to the translation of our answers. We had come as pilgrims, I said. From King Edward? I hesitated, not wanting to claim to be an official embassy because we had brought neither gifts nor letters, but then I said the king had known we were coming and had instructed us to offer Christian greetings. Hywel smiled at that. He knew a lie when he heard one. He looked along my men, recognizing them for what they were. His eyes lingered appreciatively on Eadith for a moment, then came back to me. He spoke to Brother Edwyn, who turned to me. "The king wishes to know your name, lord," he said.

"Osbert," I answered.

"Osbert," Brother Edwyn told the king.

"Osbert," Hywel repeated the name thoughtfully, then turned and listened as the brute with the red scarf about his helmet whispered in his ear. Whatever was said made Hywel smile again. He spoke to Brother Edwyn, who looked at me nervously. "The creed," the monk translated, "the king wishes you to recite the creed."

"The creed," I said, and for the life of me could not remember those words that had been hammered into my childhood mind by Father Beocca.

"We believe in one god," my son said, "the Father Almighty, maker of heaven and earth, and of all things visible and invisible. And in one Lord Jesus Christ," Finan and the others joined in, "the only-begotten Son of God," they all made the sign of the cross as they chanted the last three words, and I hurriedly copied the gesture, "begotten of the Father before all worlds, Light of Light, very God of very God, begotten, not made . . ."

King Hywel held up a hand to check the recitation. He spoke to Edwyn again, though keeping his shrewd eyes on me. "The king wants to know," Brother Edwyn interpreted, "why you don't speak the words?"

"Being of one substance with the Father," I said as the words suddenly came back to me from the mists of childhood, "by whom all things were made and who for us men and for our salvation came down from heaven and was incarnate by the holy ghost of the Virgin Mary, and was made man."

Again the king held up his hand and I dutifully stopped as Hywel looked at Brother Edwyn. The monk nodded, presumably confirming I had repeated the words correctly. Hywel was still smiling as he spoke to Edwyn, who suddenly looked terrified. "The king says," he began, hesitated, then found the courage to continue, "the king says that he is impressed that the infamous Lord Uhtred knows the creed." I said nothing, but just stared at the king, who spoke again. "He wishes to know," Brother Edwyn said, "why you lied about your name."

"Tell him I have a bad memory," I said.

Hywel laughed, and I noted he did not wait for Brother Edwyn's translation. He had laughed as soon as I spoke, and then he smiled at me. "A bad memory," he said, using our language.

"It seems, lord," I said, "that your memory has just remembered that you speak the English tongue."

"The church," he said, "teaches us to love our enemies. My father believed you should know them too." I realized he had pretended to need a translator so he could listen, watch, and make up his mind about us. He seemed to like us well enough. He pointed to the man who had whispered in his ear. "Idwal was one of the men who followed Father Pyrlig to your battle with Cnut. He recognized you. So, Lord Uhtred with the bad memory, you're no pilgrim, so why are you here?"

And there was no choice but to tell the truth, or as little of the truth as I wanted to reveal. We had come, I said, because Jarl

Cnut's sword had been stolen from me, that the sword belonged to the man who had cut him down, and that man was me. I had come to find Ice-Spite.

"Which is now in Rognvald's possession," Hywel said, "so you are fortunate."

"Fortunate, lord?" I asked.

"Because we have come to kill him. And you can join us."

So we would go to war.

Nine

King Hywel's chief adviser was a shrewd priest called Anwyn who spoke our tongue and who questioned me closely as we rode north. He wanted to know who ruled in Mercia and was surprised at, and even dubious of, my answer. "The Lady Æthelflaed?" he asked. "Truly?"

"I was there when the Witan chose her."

"You astonish me," he said, "you astonish me indeed." He frowned, thinking. He was bald as an egg with a long, bony face and thin, unfriendly lips, though his dark eyes could light with amusement or understanding. He was one of those clever priests who rise high in royal service, and I suspected Anwyn was an honest, loyal servant to the equally shrewd Hywel. "I understood Wessex was determined the Lady Æthelflaed should not assume her husband's burden," he continued, still frowning, "so what happened?"

"Mercians are proud of their country," I said, "and they're not ready to lie back and open their legs to a foreign king quite yet."

He smiled at my crudity. "I understand that, lord, but to appoint a woman! The last news we heard was that Eardwulf was to marry Æthelflaed's daughter and then administer the country in Edward's name!"

"Eardwulf is an outlaw," I said, surprising Anwyn. It was plain that King Hywel had his sources in the Saxon kingdoms and those sources were good, but any news those spies might have sent about Eardwulf's bid for power and Æthelflaed's success had still not reached western Wales. I told him of Eardwulf's attack on

Æthelflaed and of its failure, though I did not mention my part in it, nor did I tell him how I had influenced the Witan.

"I can't say I feel any sorrow for Eardwulf," Father Anwyn said with evident relish, "he was always an enemy to the Welsh."

"He was a Mercian," I said drily, and the priest smiled.

"So Æthelflaed will rule!" he said, amused. "A woman! On the throne!"

"A very capable woman," I said, "and she's more of a warrior than her brother."

He shook his head, still trying to comprehend the idea of a woman on a throne. "We live in strange times, lord."

"We do," I agreed. We had been given ponies to ride, while the rest of Hywel's force were on war horses that followed a stony track which led north through small fields and rocky outcrops. The king had brought over three hundred men, and Father Anwyn believed that would be sufficient. "Rognvald doesn't lead more than a hundred and thirty warriors. Scarce enough to man his palisade!"

I watched a falcon spiral high above a hill, and followed as it slid away to the east. "How long has Rognvald lived here?"

"Six years."

"Your king," I said, nodding at Hywel, who rode just ahead of his two standard-bearers, "strikes me as a very clever man. Why did he allow Rognvald to settle?"

"Oh, he didn't! That was the last king, a fool called Rhodri."

"So Rognvald," I said, "has been here six years, and in all that time he's never made trouble?"

"Some cattle raids," Anwyn said dismissively, "but nothing more."

"You say he leads only a hundred and thirty men, and he must know how many warriors you can bring against him. So is he a fool? Why attack Tyddewi? He must know you'll want revenge."

"Opportunity!" Anwyn said brusquely. "Idwal," he paused to nod toward the big man with the red scarf, "usually has a score of men at Tyddewi, but the king needed him elsewhere."

"Elsewhere?"

Anwyn ignored that question. Whatever squabble Hywel had just settled was evidently none of my business. "We thought it safe to leave the shrine unguarded for a few days," Anwyn admitted ruefully, "and we were wrong, but we headed back as soon as we heard of the fleet."

"Fleet?" I repeated the word dourly. With Sihtric at sea, waiting for us, fleet was not a word I wanted to hear.

"Some days ago," Anwyn explained, "twenty or more ships appeared off the coast. At least one of them put into Abergwaun, but she didn't stay. They all sailed northward a day later, and we just received word that they're coming south again."

"Norse ships?"

He nodded. "Ivar Imerson sent the fleet, led by his son. It seems they're looking for land."

"Ivar Imerson?"

Anwyn seemed surprised that I had not heard of Ivar. "He's a formidable man, but so are his Irish enemies."

I knew Mercia and Wessex, Northumbria and East Anglia, but now I was in a different world, a place where warlords with strange names fought to make petty kingdoms at the sea's edge. Hywel, I realized, had enemies on three sides. He had Saxons to his east, rival Welsh kingdoms to the north, while to his west the Norse and the Irish struggled with each other, both ever ready to raid his coasts, and, if what Anwyn had heard was true, ready to take more land from Dyfed.

The horsemen ahead of us had halted, and a group of men had gathered around Hywel and his standard-bearers. I assumed one of the Welsh scouts had brought back news, and now the king held a hasty council of war, which Anwyn hurried to join. We had climbed to a wide plateau with small, stone-walled fields interrupted by shallow valleys, which Hywel's scouts diligently explored. Rognvald would surely be expecting trouble and must have his own scouts on the plateau, but if Anwyn was right then the Norseman was severely outnumbered. I suspected he would be cautious, preferring to retreat to some easily defended high ground rather than seek a running fight with Hywel's warriors on this bare upland.

"So there's a fleet nearby," Finan said. He had been listening to my conversation with the priest.

"Let's hope it's nowhere near Sihtric," I said.

"Sihtric's canny," Finan said, "and he'll keep out of their way. But something's got them worried," the Irishman nodded at the horsemen bunched about the king, "and Ivar Imerson is a man that should worry you."

"You know of him?"

"Of course! He's a big bad man. But the Irish are just as big and bad and they're pushing on him. Pushing hard."

"So he's looking for land over here?"

"And sent his son to find it. I wonder which son." I was always surprised how much Finan knew of what happened in Ireland. He pretended to take no interest, insisting he had abandoned his native land forever, but for somebody who claimed no interest he knew a lot. Someone there must send him news. "Now what's happening?" he asked, nodding toward the war council.

Two of Hywel's scouts had come galloping from the north to push their way into the knot of horsemen around the king. They had only been there a moment before all the Welshmen began whooping and hurrying north. Whatever news the scouts had brought was being shouted back along the column, each repetition provoking more and louder cheers. Some men had drawn swords. Father Anwyn waited with the king's two standard-bearers. "The pagans are fleeing!" he called to me. "They're running away!" He kicked his horse to follow Hywel's warriors, who were now racing toward the plateau's northern crest where smoke was just appearing. At first I thought the smoke to be mist, but it was thickening too quickly. A village or a hall was burning.

"Someone got there before us?" Finan called to me, kicking his pony to ride beside me.

"Looks that way," I said. I twisted in the saddle, wincing at the inevitable pain. "Stay together!" I called to my men. If there was about to be a fight I did not want my men separated because it would be too easy to mistake one of them for an enemy. The Welshmen all knew each other, but if they saw a stranger they might attack without thinking. "And you," I called to Eadith, "stay away from the fighting!"

"You too," Finan said to me. "You're not well enough to fight."

I made no answer, but felt a surge of anger. He was right, of course, but that did not make the truth any easier to accept, and then we crossed the skyline and I slowed the pony. The Welsh were still galloping, already halfway down the slope that led into a deep river valley. This, I realized, was Abergwaun.

To my right the river flowed through thick woods that filled much of the valley's bed, while to the left it widened to meet the open ocean. Rognvald's settlement was on the far bank, just where the river met the sea-reach, and that sea-reach, sheltered by hills, was filled with ships.

There had to be thirty or more ships, far more than Rognvald would possess if, as Anwyn said, he could only muster a little over a hundred warriors. So the mysterious fleet from Ireland must have returned to Abergwaun and was now leaving again. The ships were heading to sea, their oars biting the water and their sails filling and falling as the gusts of a light east wind rose and stilled. And behind them, on the river's northern shore, the settlement was ablaze.

No enemy had set the fires. There was no evidence of any fighting, no corpses, and the men who were still running from hall to house, from house to barn, and hurling firebrands up onto the thatch were not dressed in mail. Rognvald was leaving and he was plainly determined to leave nothing useful behind. Fires had been set against the palisade, and the nearest gateway was already burning fiercely. Father Anwyn had been right, the Norsemen were running away, but not because King Hywel's men were coming. Rognvald must have decided to join forces with the fleet from Ireland in its search for another place to settle.

The fleet was moving seaward, but there were still two fighting ships by the beach. Those had to be the rearguard, the boats belonging to the men who were carrying fire from house to house. Both boats were manned by half a dozen men who hauled on stern lines to keep the bows from grounding in the falling tide.

The Welsh were already in the valley bottom, hidden there by trees. We followed, plunging into the woods and hearing the shouts of Hywel's men drawing ever further ahead of us. The track led to a ford. The river was tidal and, helped by the ebb tide, the shallow water was running fast. We splashed through and turned west on the river's far bank, following an earthen road that led beside the hurrying river, then we were out of the trees and Rognvald's burning settlement was ahead of us. Some of Hywel's men were already inside the walls, their horses abandoned in the fields that surrounded the palisade. A whole section of that palisade had been pushed over, the timbers presumably weakened by fire, and more Welshmen were scrambling over the still smoldering trunks, shields on their arms and weapons in their hands. They vanished into smoke-wreathed alleys. I heard shouts, the clash of swords, and then I slid from the saddle and called to my men to stay together. The sensible thing would have been to stay outside the burning walls. We had no shields, no swords, no spears, only seaxes, and, being strangers, we could easily be mistaken for enemies, but I was as eager as Finan or any of the others to see what happened inside. "Stay with me," I told Eadith. An osprey flew through the smoke, wings fast, a pale streak of feathered glory flying north, and I wondered what omen that was. I touched the hilt of Wasp-Sting, my seax, then splashed through the shallow ditch that surrounded the settlement, climbed the bank, and followed Finan and my son over the smoldering timbers.

Two men lay dead in the first alley. Neither wore mail and both had faces deeply marked with ink. They were dead Norsemen, presumably men who had been setting the fires and had been surprised by the speed of the Welsh attack. We walked cautiously through the alley. The houses on either side were blazing, the heat hammering us until we reached an open space where Hywel's two standard-bearers were guarded by a dozen warriors. Father Anwyn was there and he called sharply to the men who had turned toward us and hefted their weapons. One flag showed a Christian cross, the other was blazoned with a scarlet dragon. "The king has gone to attack the boats!" Father Anwyn shouted at me.

A half-dozen prisoners were under guard. The open space was evidently where Hywel was sending captives, and not just captives but weapons too. There was a pile of swords, spears, and shields. "Help yourselves," I told my men.

"God go with you!" Father Anwyn called.

Finan pulled swords from the heap, selected two and offered

one to me. My son had found a long blade, while Gerbruht picked up a double-bladed ax and an ironbound shield. "Drop the shield," I told him.

"No shield, lord?"

"You want the Welsh to kill you?"

He frowned, then realized there was a crude painting of an eagle on the shield's willow boards. "Ah!" he said, and threw the thing down.

"Keep your crosses visible," I ordered my men before going into another alley which led between unburned houses onto a long beach, all green slippery stones, mud, and broken shells. Driftwood fires smoldered beneath empty fish-smoking frames. A single small fishing craft was stranded at the beach's end, well above the high-water mark, while most of Hywel's men seemed to be down at the water's edge. I guessed they had scoured the settlement and driven the surviving Norsemen back to their two ships, which were now trapped. Welshmen were clambering aboard, outnumbering the enemy, who had retreated to the ships' sterns where swords, axes and spears took them down in bloody slaughter. Some of the Norsemen leaped into the water, trying to wade or even swim out to the fleet that was in a chaotic tangle halfway down the sea-reach.

It was chaos because some of the ships were trying to return, hampered by their sails, which drove them away from the shore, while other vessels still headed seaward. Three ships had managed to escape the chaos. None of the three had been under sail, all were driven only by oars, and now those three headed back toward the settlement. All three were crammed with helmeted warriors who were gathered beneath the high carvings of the prows. The oarsmen drove the ships fast, heading for the wide gap between the two beached vessels, then there was the scrape of a keel on stone and the first Norsemen leaped screaming from the ship's dragon prow.

Hywel had seen the ships coming and his men had made a shield wall on the beach that was more than strong enough to stop the Norsemen who came with anger, but no order, and the first men died in the shallow water at the river's edge where blood swirled sudden. The Welsh on the boat nearest us had killed the last of its crew and they now scrambled back across the rowers' benches to jump down onto the beach just as the second vessel arrived, its prow riding up the mud and its mast bending forward as the long hull shuddered to a halt. Men leaped from the bows, bellowing their war cries, joining the shorter Norse wall and driving their heavy spears hard into Welsh willow. The Norsemen had not expected a fight this day and few wore mail, though all had helmets and shields. The newly arrived boats were trying to rescue their comrades, but even after the third boat slammed into the beach there were not enough Norsemen to push back Hywel's furious warriors. Both sides were screaming their war cries, but the Welsh shouts were louder, and Hywel's men were wading into the small waves as they drove the Norsemen relentlessly back. Most battles of the shield walls begin slowly as men summon the nerve to go within lover's reach of the enemy trying to kill them, but this battle had erupted in a moment.

My son started toward the left flank of the Welshmen, but I called him back. "You don't have a shield," I snarled, "and you don't have mail. We were supposed to be pilgrims, remember?"

"We can't do nothing," he snarled back at me.

"Wait!"

The Welsh hardly needed our help. There were more than enough of them to stem the furious counterattack of the three ships, and if that was all it was, a counterattack that was doomed to be beaten down to bloody ruin in the shallows of the sea-reach, I would simply have sat and watched. But the rest of the Norse ships were now trying to return, and they would bring an overwhelming force that would butcher Hywel's men, and all that was keeping the Welsh from disaster was the chaos in that larger fleet. They had turned too soon, too eager to help, and in the haste their hulls had fallen foul of each other. Long oars were clashing, sails were backing and filling, hulls blocking other hulls, and the whole tangle was being carried seaward by the tide. But the Norse were good seamen and I knew it would take but a moment for the chaos to be resolved, and then Hywel's men would be facing a horde of angry warriors eager for revenge. In short the slaughter would go the other way.

"Fetch me fire," I told my son.

He frowned at me. "Fire?"

"Fetch fire, lots of fire! Kindling! Wood, fire! Now! All of you." The ship nearest to us had been stranded by the falling tide, but it had also been cleared of its crew. "Gerbruht! Folcbald!" I called the two Frisians back.

"Lord?"

"Get that ship off the beach!"

They lumbered through the mud, both strong as oxen. The nearest ship was well grounded now, but it was our only chance of preventing a massacre. The closest Norsemen were twenty paces beyond, defending themselves from the Welsh shield wall, which was threatening to overlap them and drive them back into the river, but the Norse wall had found some security by anchoring the right-hand end of their line against the prow of another beached ship. Three men had climbed aboard and were using spears to stop the Welsh from clambering over the ship's bows. The beleaguered wall was holding firm and it only had to survive a few more minutes before reinforcements poured in from the rest of their fleet.

Folcbald and Gerbruht were heaving on the prow of the nearest ship and achieving nothing. The hull seemed stuck fast in the thick mud. Finan ran down the beach with a rusty iron pan filled with embers and burning wood. I assumed the shallow pan had been used to make salt, and Finan now reached up and tipped the contents over the ship's side. More kindling and burning wood followed. "Help Gerbruht," I shouted to my son.

Hywel was still on horseback, the only mounted man on the beach. He had been using his height to thrust a spear at the Norse line, but he saw what we were doing and understood immediately. He could see the approaching fleet. The tide had drifted them some way seaward, but the first ships were free of the tangle now and their oars were biting the small waves. I saw Hywel shouting, and then a dozen Welsh warriors came to help us, and the grounded ship began to move at last. "More fire!" I shouted. Smoke was thickening from inside the hull, but I could see no flames yet. Eadith brought an armful of driftwood and threw it on board, then Finan added another pan of embers before clambering over the bows just as the ship slid off the mud and floated. Fire was showing at last, and Finan was wading through the blaze as he headed for the ship's stern. "Finan!" I shouted, fearing for him, and almost moaned aloud from the pain in my rib.

Finan was engulfed in flame and smoke. The ship, when it caught the fire, did so with sudden hunger. It was dry wood, well cured, caulked with pitch that also coated the lines that held the mast, and the flames leaped up the rigging to the furled sail that had been hoisted out of the crew's way. Then I saw why Finan had leaped aboard. The stern of the ship was held by a line that had to be connected to an anchor stone, and the tide was swinging the boat, but the ship would not leave her makeshift mooring so long as that anchor line held. Then Finan appeared on the high steering platform and I saw his sword slash down once, twice, and the anchor line parted with a sudden jolt. Finan jumped.

"Now that ship!" I pointed to the next along the beach, the one defended by the three Norse spearmen. "Hurry!" I shouted again, and this time the pain was so severe that I bent over, and that made the pain worse. I gasped, then fell backward so that I was sitting on the green-slimed rocks. My borrowed sword slid onto the mud, but the pain was such that I could not reach for it.

"What is it?" Eadith crouched beside me.

"You shouldn't be here," I said.

"But I am here," she said, putting an arm around my shoulder and looking out at the river. Finan was wading ashore, sword in hand, and beyond him, turning on the current and carried by the tide, the burning boat was drifting seaward. I guessed the ebbing tide was halfway between high and low water because the current was running fast, swirling and streaming, hurrying the blazing boat and slowing the approaching ships, who saw their danger, which was made worse because the sea-reach had one narrow place that crowded the Norsemen's ships. One boat, its high prow showing an eagle's beak, backed water, and was immediately rammed by another, and the blazing craft, its furled sail now a fury of flames and smoke, drifted ever closer.

Finan had hauled himself onto the second boat. One of the spearmen saw him and leaped down the rowers' benches, but a spear is no weapon to carry against a man skilled in sword-craft, and few were more skilled than Finan. It took him less time than a man needs to blink. He feinted to his right, let the spear slide past his waist, and rammed his blade into the Norseman's belly, and then my son hurled fire into the boat and a dozen men followed him, and the two remaining spearmen leaped for safety as a pack of burly Welshmen thrust the boat back into the river. It was not yet burning like the first, but the smoke was thickening from the hull, and Finan cut the stern line and then jumped down into the shallows as the Welsh charged into the exposed flank of the Norse shield wall.

The first fire ship had reached the fleet. Two of the enemy boats had gone ashore on the river's farther bank, the rest were desperately trying to escape, and meanwhile the second fire ship was drifting seaward. Those Norsemen left on the shore were dying, being hacked and sliced and cut by angry Welshmen who had flanked their line and now attacked from front and rear. The second ship burst into flames, the fire flickering up the rigging and the smoke churning from the benches. The Norse fleet, at least twenty ships, was fleeing. Sailors fear fire more than they fear rocks, even more than they fear the anger of Ran, that jealous bitch of a goddess. I sat panting, the pain stabbing like a blade, and watched the boats flee and listened to the shouts of those enemy who survived on the beach pleading to be spared. The battle was over.

The Norse fleet could still have returned. They could have rowed from the river, let the two fiery ships drift harmlessly out to sea, and then come back for their vengeance, but they chose to abandon Abergwaun. They knew the Welsh would retreat to high ground and taunt them, inviting them to attack up some harsh slope where they would die on Welsh blades already slick with northern blood.

My son came back along the beach. His clothes were scorched and his hands burned, but he was grinning till he saw my face. He ran then and stooped in front of me. "Father?"

"It's just the wound," I said. "Help me up."

He hauled me to my feet. The pain was almost crippling. There were tears in my eyes, blurring my view of the exultant Welsh, who jeered the retreating enemy. Three of the Norse ships were left on the beach and Hywel's men had invaded one of those and whatever they discovered aboard provoked more cheering. Others of Hywel's men were guarding prisoners, at least fifty or sixty of them, who were being stripped of helmets and weapons. Rognvald himself had been captured, bellowing defiance until he had been driven so far back into the water that he had almost drowned. Now the prisoners were gathered into a pathetic huddle, and I limped toward them. I had thought the pain was going away, that my injury mended day by day, but it now felt worse than ever. I did not limp because my legs were wounded, but because the agony in my side made every move torture. Finan ran to help me, but I waved him away. There was a big boulder above the high-tide line, and I sat on its flat surface, flinching from the pain. I remember wondering if this was the end, wondering if the Norns had cut my thread at last.

"Give me your sword," I said to Finan. If I died I would at least die with a sword in my hand.

"Lord." Finan crouched beside me, sounding worried.

"The pain will pass," I said, suspecting it would pass with death. It hurt to breathe. Father Anwyn and the king's standard-bearers passed close to us, going to join the king. "He looks grim," I said, nodding at the priest. Not that I really cared, but I did not want Finan, Eadith, or my son to make a fuss over my weakness.

"Grim as death," Finan agreed, and Father Anwyn, far from showing happiness at the victory the Welsh had just gained, looked like a man consumed by anger. He talked to Hywel for some time, then the king spurred his horse past us, going back into the burning settlement.

I tried to breathe more deeply, tried to convince myself the pain was passing. "We need to look for Ice-Spite," I said, and knew I wasted my breath. The sword was probably going out to sea, pursued by the burning boats that smeared the ocean's sky with smoke.

Father Anwyn, still looking stern, crossed to us. "The king instructed me to thank you," he said stiffly.

I forced a smile. "The king is generous."

"He is," Anwyn said, then frowned. "And God is generous too." He made the sign of the cross. "The treasures of Saint Dewi were in Rognvald's ship." He nodded toward the boat where the Welsh were celebrating, then looked back to me with a frown. "You were wounded, lord?"

"An old injury which still hurts," I explained, "it will pass. You recovered the treasure?"

"The gold reliquary of the saint, the silver crucifix, both there."

"And the sword?" I asked.

"And Rognvald is a prisoner," Anwyn said, apparently ignoring my question. "It was his boats that returned to the beach. The rest," he stared out to sea where the Norse fleet was disappearing behind a headland, "are commanded by Sigtryggr Ivarson." He said the name as though it tasted sour on his tongue. "He's the more dangerous of Ivar's sons. Young, ambitious, and able."

"And looking for land," I managed to say as another stab of pain lanced into me.

"But not here, thank God," Anwyn said. "And Rognvald agreed to join his search."

What choice had Rognvald had, I wondered. His settlement on the edge of Wales had hardly thrived. It had clung to its rocky shore for six years, but Rognvald had failed to attract more followers or conquer more land, and Sigtryggr had evidently persuaded Rognvald to join his larger forces. That agreement must have been reached a week or so before, when Sigtryggr's fleet had first reached Wales, and Rognvald, knowing he would be abandoning his settlement, had tried to enrich himself at Saint Dewi's expense before he left.

Now Rognvald and his surviving men would die, not because they had attacked the saint's shrine, but because of what they had done to the two Welsh missionaries and their handful of converts. It was that cruelty that had provoked Welsh anger. "It is the work of the devil," Anwyn said in rage. "Satan's doing!" He stared at me with disdain. "Pagan atrocity!" With that he turned back toward the settlement and we followed. The pain was still bad, but it hurt no more to hobble slowly than to be sitting and so I limped behind Anwyn along the narrow path. Ahead of us the settlement still burned furiously, though much of the western side had yet to catch fire, and it was in that part of the village that the Norsemen had killed the Christians.

We went through a gateway that pierced the palisade, and Eadith, who was walking beside me, gasped, then turned away.

"Jesus," Finan murmured and crossed himself.

"You see what they do?" Father Anwyn shouted at me. "They will burn in the everlasting fires of hell. They will suffer the torments of the damned. They will be cursed for all time."

Hywel's warriors were arriving now, their elation turning to rage because the two missionaries and their handful of converts had been slaughtered like animals, though not before they had been tortured. All nine bodies were naked, though all were so lacerated and sliced that blood and guts disguised their nudity. The women's heads had been shaved, a mark of shame, and their breasts had been cut off. The two priests had been gelded. All nine had been eviscerated, blinded, and had their tongues sliced out. They had been tied to posts, and I shuddered to think how long it had taken for death to release them from their pain.

"Why?" Anwyn demanded of me. He knew I was a pagan, just as he must have known I had no answer for him.

"Spite," Finan answered for me, "just spite."

"Pagan evil," Anwyn retorted angrily. "You see the devil at work! This is Satan's doing!"

Rognvald had attacked Tyddewi and found it empty. He had found rich plunder, but not nearly as much as he expected and there had been no young women and children to capture and enslave. He must have decided that the missionaries had betrayed him and so he had avenged himself. Now he would die.

There would be no mercy. Every prisoner would die, and Hywel made them look at the nine dead Christians so they knew why they were dying. And the Norsemen were lucky. Despite the anger of the Welsh, they died quickly, usually from a sword cut to the neck. The settlement stank of smoke and blood, so much blood. Some of the prisoners, very few, begged for their lives, but most went to their execution with resignation. None was allowed to hold a sword, and that was a punishment in itself. Rognvald was made to watch. He was a big man, big-bellied, big-bearded, with hard eyes in a lined face that was decorated with inked designs. An eagle spread its wings on one cheek, a serpent writhed across his forehead, while a raven flew on the other cheek. His hair was turning gray, but it was oiled and combed. He watched his men die and his face showed nothing, but he must have known that his death would be the last, and would not be swift.

I limped along the line of men shuffling toward their end. A boy caught my eye. I say "boy," but I suppose he was sixteen or seventeen. He had fair hair, blue eyes, and a long face that betrayed the struggle in his head. He knew he was about to die and he wanted to cry, but he also wanted to show bravery, and he was trying so hard. "What's your name?" I asked him.

"Berg," he said.

"Berg what?"

"Berg Skallagrimmrson, lord."

"You served Rognvald?"

"Yes, lord."

"Come here," I beckoned him to me. One of the Welsh guards tried to stop him leaving the line of captives, but Finan growled and the man stepped back. "Tell me," I said to Berg, speaking Danish and speaking very slowly so he would understand me, "did you help kill the Christians?"

"No, lord!"

"If you lie to me," I said, "I'll find out. I'll ask your comrades."

"I did not, lord. I swear it."

I believed him. He was shaking with fear, gazing at me with an extraordinary intensity as if he sensed that I was his salvation. "When you raided the monastery," I asked him, "did they find a sword?"

"Yes, lord."

"Tell me about it."

"It was in a tomb, lord."

"You saw it?"

"It has a white hilt, lord. I saw it."

"And what happened to it?"

"Rognvald took it, lord."

"Wait," I said and walked back into the settlement where the bodies were being hauled to one side, to where the soil was stained black and stank of blood, where the smoke of burning houses swirled in the freshening breeze. I went to Anwyn. "I ask a favor," I said to him.

The priest was watching the Norsemen die. He was watching as they were forced to their knees and made to stare at the nine corpses still tied to the poles. Watching as the swords or axes touched their necks, watching as they flinched when the blades were taken away and they knew the killing blow was imminent. Watching as the heads were severed and the blood spurted and the bodies twitched. "Tell me," he said coldly, still watching.

"Spare me one life," I pleaded.

Anwyn glanced along the line of men and saw Berg standing beside Finan. "You want us to spare that lad?"

"That's the favor I ask."

"Why?"

"He reminds me of my son," I said, and that was true, though it was not why I had pleaded, "and he took no part in this slaughter." I nodded toward the tortured Christians.

"He says," Anwyn remarked sourly.

"He says," I said, "and I believe him."

Anwyn stared at me for a few heartbeats, then grimaced as though the favor I asked was too extravagant. Still, he went to the king and I saw them speak. Hywel glanced at me from his saddle, then at the boy. He frowned and I supposed he was going to refuse my request. And why had I made it? At the time I was not sure. I liked the look of the boy because there was an honesty in Berg's face and he did resemble Uhtred, but that was hardly reason enough. Years before I had spared the life of a young man called Haesten and he had seemed open and truthful too, yet he had turned out to be a cunning and deceitful enemy. I was not sure why I wanted Berg's life, though now, so many years later, I know it was fate.

King Hywel beckoned me. I stood by his stirrup and bowed my

head respectfully. "I am minded," he said, "to grant your request because of your assistance on the beach, but there is one condition."

"Lord?" I asked, looking up at him.

"That you promise to make the boy a Christian."

I shrugged. "I can't force him to believe in your god," I said, "but I promise that I'll have him taught by a good priest and do nothing to stop his conversion."

The king considered that promise for a moment, then nodded. "He's yours."

And thus Berg Skallagrimmrson entered my service.

Fate is inexorable. I was not to know it, but I had just made Alfred's dream of Englaland come true.

"Come with me," I told Berg, and walked him back to the beach. Finan, my son, Eadith, and the others all came with me.

Wyrd bið ful āræd.

I did not see Rognvald die, though I heard him. It was not quick. He was a warrior, determined to die defiantly, but before the Welsh had finished he was screaming like a child. The gulls screamed too, the sound forlorn, and over it came the cries of a man wishing he were dead.

Sigtryggr's fleet was gone. The burning ships had sunk, leaving only two fading clouds of smoke being blown westward by the wind. I heard the Welsh singing a dirge and guessed they were burying their dead; the nine martyrs and the half-dozen warriors who had died in the fighting on the beach. The Norse dead were still there, their bodies stranded at the low tide, while, higher up the beach, where a rill of driftwood and weed marked the limit of the last flood tide, there was a heap of clothing, helmets, swords, shields, axes, and spears. A cloak had been spread on the stones and was piled with coins and hacksilver taken from the prisoners and from the dead, while near it, and guarded by two young men, was the great golden chest that had encased Saint Dewi's body, and the huge silver crucifix that had stood on the altar. "Find your helmet and sword," I told Berg.

He looked at me with disbelief. "I can carry a sword?"

"Of course," I said, "you're my man now. You'll swear loyalty to me and if I die, to my son."

"Yes, lord."

And while Berg hunted for his own sword I looked through the heaped weapons, and there she was. As simple as could be. The ivory hilt of Ice-Spite was unmistakable. I bent down, wincing from the sudden pain, and pulled the blade free. I shivered, though it was a warm day.

I drew her from the scabbard. I was accustomed to the weight of Serpent-Breath, but this sword was much lighter. Cnut had always claimed that the blade had been forged in a sorcerer's fire that burned colder than ice in the frost caverns of Hel. He said she was a sword of the gods, but all I knew was that she was the sword that had pierced me, and that Bishop Asser had charmed with Christian sorcery to torment me. The sunlight reflected silver from the blade, which had no patterns, indeed no decoration except for one word at the base of the hilt:

$$\dagger \text{VLFBERH} \dagger \text{T}$$

I showed it to Finan, who made the sign of the cross. "It's one of his swords," he said in a hushed tone. My son came to look, and drew Raven-Beak, and there was the same word inscribed on the plain blade. "It's a magic sword, sure enough," Finan said. "Christ, but you were lucky to survive it!"

I turned the Vlfberht blade, seeing the light reflect from the smooth steel. She was beautiful, a tool for killing, her only extravagance the ivory hand grips of her hilt. For a moment I thought of replacing Serpent-Breath with this sleek killer, but I rejected the notion. Serpent-Breath had served me well, and to discard her would be to tempt the gods, yet I was tempted. I stroked Ice-Spite's edge, feeling the nicks made in the fight, then I touched the point, and it was needle sharp.

"Is that the sword?" Eadith asked me.

"Yes."

"Give it to me," she said.

"Why?"

She looked at me with cold eyes as if she suddenly disliked me. "The sword will cure you, lord."

"You know that?"

"Why did we come here?" she demanded. I said nothing, and she held out her hand. "Give me the sword," she insisted, and when I still hesitated, "I know what to do, lord."

"What?" I asked. "What do you do?"

"I cure you."

I looked down at Ice-Spite. I had wanted her so badly, I had traveled to the end of Britain to find her, yet I had no idea how the possession of her would help me. I had thought that the sword must be laid against the wound, but that was just imagination. I did not know what to do, and I was in pain, and I was tired of the pain, tired of feeling weak, tired of death's close company, and so I reversed the blade and held the hilt to Eadith.

She half smiled. My men were watching us. Berg had stopped looking for his own sword and was gazing at us, wondering what strange things happened at the sea's bloodstained edge. "Lean against the ship," Eadith ordered me and I obeyed her. I stood with my back against the bows of Rognvald's ship and leaned on the timbers. "Now show me the wound, lord," Eadith said.

I unclasped my belt and lifted my tunic. My son grimaced when he saw the wound that was again crusted with bloody pus. I could smell it, despite the smoke and the sea and the slaughter and the freshening wind.

Eadith closed her eyes. "This sword almost killed you," she said in a slow, singsong voice, "and now this blade will heal you."

And she opened her eyes, and her face was suddenly a grimace of hate, and before Finan or any of my men could stop her, she stabbed me.

Ten

The pain was like lightning; sudden, bright, overwhelming, and jagged. I gasped, staggered against the ship's bows, and saw Finan moving to snatch at Eadith's arm, but she had already pulled the sword back. Now she was staring at my wound with a look of horror.

And as the blade left me so the stench came. A foul stench, and I felt liquid pouring from my rib. "It's the evil," Eadith said, "coming out of him."

Finan was holding her arm, but staring at me. "Christ," he murmured. I had bent forward when she stabbed me and saw a mixture of blood and pus pulsing from the new wound, so much blood and pus. It was bubbling, swelling, trickling away, and as I watched the filth erupt so the pain subsided. I looked up at Eadith in disbelief because the pain was flowing out of me, it was vanishing.

"We need honey and cobwebs," she said. She frowned at the sword as if she did not know what to do with it.

"Berg," I said, "take the sword."

"Her sword, lord?"

"You need a sword and that's a good one, I'm told." I straightened up and no pain came, so I bent down again and still there was no pain. "Cobwebs and honey?"

"I should have thought to bring some," Eadith said.

There was a dull ache in my side, but that was all. I pressed a rib just above the wound and, miraculously, there was no agony. "What did you do?"

She half frowned, as if she was not quite sure of her answer. "There was evil inside you, lord," she said slowly, "and it had to be let out."

"Then why didn't we use any sword?"

"Because this was the sword that caused the evil, of course." She looked down at Ice-Spite. "My mother wanted to find the blade that wounded my father, but she couldn't." She shuddered and handed the sword to Berg.

There was honey aboard Rognvald's ship. He had stocked it with food, with salted fish, with bread, ale, cheeses, and barrels of horse-flesh. He had even killed his horses rather than leave them behind. There were also two jars of honey. Cobwebs were harder to find, but my son looked at the single grounded fishing craft at the beach's end. "It looks abandoned," he said, "so it might be crawling with spiders." He wandered off to look while Gerbruht and Folcbald went to search the unburned houses. "Bring lots," Eadith called after them, "I want a whole handful of cobweb!"

"I hate spiders," Gerbruht grumbled.

"Don't they taste good?"

He shook his head. "Crunchy and bitter, lord."

I laughed and there was no pain. I stamped my foot and there was no pain. I stretched high and there was no pain, just the dull ache and the smell. I grinned at Finan. "It's a miracle. There's no pain."

He was smiling. "I pray it stays that way, lord."

"It's gone!" I said, and I drew Serpent-Breath and swept her in a wide cut that thumped her blade hard into the ship's hull. There was still no pain. I did it again, and again there was no rip of agony. I slid the blade into its scabbard and untied the laces that held a pouch to my belt. I gave the whole pouch to Eadith. "Yours," I said.

"Lord!" She was staring at the gold in the heavy pouch. "No, lord . . ."

"Keep it," I said.

"I didn't do it because . . ."

"Keep it!"

231

I grinned at my son who was hurrying back from the abandoned boat. "You found any cobwebs?"

"No, but I found this," he said and held out a crucifix. It was a shabby thing, the cross and its victim both carved from beech wood and so eroded by weather and time that the body was smoothed and bleached. One arm of the cross was missing so that Christ's arm stuck into empty air. There were two rusted nail holes through the cross's upright, one at each end. "It was nailed to the mast," he said, "and the boat isn't abandoned. Or it wasn't. It's been used within the last few days."

A Christian boat on a pagan shore. I tossed the crucifix back to my son. "So Rognvald's men captured a Welsh fishing boat?"

"Called *Godspellere*?" he asked, then jerked his head at the small craft. "It's scratched on the bows, Father. *Godspellere*."

Preacher, a man who preaches the gospel. A typical name for a Christian boat. "Maybe the Welsh use the same word?"

"Maybe." He sounded dubious.

Preacher. It seemed unlikely that the Welsh would use the same word, in which case the boat was Saxon, and I remembered that Eardwulf had stolen a fishing boat from the Sæfern. I looked at Eadith. "Your brother?" I suggested.

"It could be," she said uncertainly, yet the more I thought about it, the more likely it seemed. Eardwulf would have sailed from the Sæfern and would surely seek refuge as soon as he could, because a small boat on a wide sea was prey to enemies. So why not go ashore in Hywel's territory? Because Eardwulf had a reputation as a man who fought the Welsh. If he had landed on Hywel's shore he could have ended screaming as loudly as Rognvald, but the Norsemen might welcome him because he had become an enemy of their enemies. "See if he's among the dead," I ordered my son, and he dutifully walked among the bodies, turning a couple with his foot, but there was no sign of him. Nor was Eardwulf among the men killed in the settlement, which meant that if he had come here then he had sailed away on one of Sigtryggr's boats. "Berg!" I summoned the boy and asked him about the fishing boat, but all he knew was that it had arrived with the rest of Sigtryggr's fleet. "Yet they abandoned it," I said.

"It's too slow, lord," Berg said, and that was true.

I stared at the fishing craft, frowning. "Sigtryggr," I said the unfamiliar name carefully, "first came here a week ago?"

"Yes, lord."

"Then went away? Why?"

"The first rumor, lord, said that Sigtryggr would stay here. That he'd help us take more land."

"And then he changed his mind?"

"Yes, lord."

"So where is his fleet going?"

"They said north, lord," Berg said vaguely, though he was trying to be helpful. "They said we'd all be sailing north."

Sigtryggr had been sent to find a place where his father's forces could safely retreat if their Irish enemies became too strong. He had looked at Rognvald's miserable settlement and thought of using his forces to carve it into a larger kingdom, but he had also explored northward, and then suddenly returned and persuaded Rognvald to abandon Abergwaun and help him conquer some other place. Some other place to the north. A better place, a richer prize.

Ceaster.

And we later learned that the Welsh word for preacher was nothing like *godspellere*. "We might say *efengylydd*," Father Anwyn told me, "but certainly not *godspellere*. That's your barbarous tongue."

I gazed at the boat and wondered about Eardwulf, as his sister made a pad of honey and cobwebs and strapped it to the wound she had opened.

And there was no pain.

Next day I could bend, swing a sword, twist my body, even heave on a steering-oar, and there was no pain. I moved slowly, cautiously, always expecting the agony to return, but it was gone.

"It was an evil trapped in your body," Eadith explained again.

"A spirit," Finan reckoned.

"And the sword was charmed," Eadith said.

"She did a good job, lord," Finan said earnestly, and Eadith smiled at the compliment.

"But if the sword had a spell on it," I asked, frowning, "why didn't it just add to the evil when you stabbed me?"

"I didn't stab you, lord," she said, "I stabbed the evil spirit."

We were aboard the *Ðrines* again. Sihtric had brought her back to the dragon's mouth and Hywel had sent men to greet her. Gerbruht had ridden with them, and he gave Sihtric my orders to wait overnight while Hywel feasted us, which he did with the supplies captured from Rognvald's ships, though the feast had been far from festive. The memory of those tortured bodies hung over the settlement like the smell of burning.

Hywel had been eager to talk, and asked a lot about Æthelflaed. Was her reputation of being a good Christian true?

"It depends," I had said, "what Christian you ask. Many call her a sinner."

"We are all sinners," Hywel had answered.

"But she is a good woman."

He had wanted to know her thoughts about the Welsh. "If you leave her alone," I answered, "she will leave you alone."

"Because she hates the Danes more?"

"She hates pagans."

"Except one, I hear," he had said drily. I ignored that. He smiled, listening to the harpist for a moment, then, "and Æthelstan?"

"What of him, lord?"

"You want him to be king, Lord Æthelhelm doesn't."

"He's a boy," I said dismissively.

"But one you judge worthy to be a king. Why?"

"He's a good, strong lad," I said, "and I like him. And he's legitimate."

"He is?"

"The priest who married his parents is in my service."

"How very inconvenient for Lord Æthelhelm," Hywel said, amused. "And what about the boy's father? You like him too?"

"Well enough."

"But Æthelhelm rules in Wessex, so what Æthelhelm wants will happen."

"You must have good spies in the West Saxon court, lord," I said, amused.

Hywel had laughed at that. "I don't need spies. You forget the church, Lord Uhtred. Churchmen write endless letters. They send news to each other, so much news! Gossip too."

"Then you know what Æthelflaed wants," I said, turning the conversation back to her. "She'll ignore Æthelhelm and his ambitions, because all she cares about is driving the Danes from Mercia. And when she has done that, to drive them out of Northumbria."

"Ah," the king had said, "she wants Englaland!" We had eaten outside, under the smoke-smeared stars. "Englaland," Hywel had said again, savoring the unfamiliar name as he stared into one of the big fires around which we sat. A bard was singing, and for a time the king listened to the words, then began to talk. He had spoken softly, ruefully, gazing into the flames. "I hear the name Englaland," he had said, "but our name for it is Lloegyr. The lost lands. They were once our lands. Those hills and valleys, those rivers and pastures, they were ours and they carried our names and the names were the stories of our people. Every hill had a tale, every valley a story. The Romans came and the Romans went, but the names remained, and then you came, the Saxons, and the names vanished like this smoke. And the stories went with the names, and now there are only your names. Saxon names. Listen to him!" He had gestured toward the bard who was chanting his song, hard-striking the rhythm of his words on a small harp. "He sings the song of Caddwych and how he slaughtered our enemies."

"Our enemies?" I asked.

"How we slaughtered you, the Saxons," Hywel admitted, then laughed. "I told him not to sing of dead Saxons, but even a king can't command poets, it seems."

"We sing songs too," I said.

"And your songs," the king said, "will tell of Englaland, of slaughtered Danes, and what happens then, my friend?"

"Then, lord?"

"When you have your Englaland? When the pagans are gone? When Christ rules all Britain from the south to the north? What then?"

I had shrugged. "I doubt I'll live to see it."

"Will the Saxons be content with their Englaland?" he had asked, then shaken his head. "They will look at these hills, these valleys."

"Perhaps."

"So we must be strong. Tell your Æthelflaed that I will not fight her. I've no doubt some of my folk will steal your cattle, but young men must be kept busy. But tell her that I have a dream like her father's dream. A dream of one country."

I had been surprised, but why? This was a clever man, as clever as Alfred, and he knew that weakness invited war. So just as Alfred dreamed of uniting the Saxon kingdoms into one strong country, so Hywel was dreaming of uniting the Welsh kingdoms. He ruled the south, but to the north was a patchwork of little states, and little states are weak.

"So," he continued, "your Æthelflaed will hear of war in our land, but assure her it is not her business. It is ours. Leave us alone and we will leave you alone."

"Until you don't, lord," I said.

Again he smiled. "Until we don't? Yes, one day we must fight, but you will make your Englaland and we will make our Cymru first. And we will probably both be long dead, my friend, before those shield walls meet."

"Cymru?" I had asked, stumbling over the strange word.

"You call it Wales."

And now we left Cymru, blown by a south-westerly wind, the sea seething at the *Ðrines*'s bow and the wake spreading white and fretful behind us. I had liked Hywel. I knew him for such a short while and met him on only a few occasions, yet of all the kings I have met in my long life he and Alfred impressed me the most. Hywel still lives and now he rules over much of Wales and grows stronger every year, and one day, no doubt, the men of Cymru will come to take back the stories that we

Saxons stole from them. Or we shall march to destroy them. One day. Not now.

And we sailed northward to save Æthelflaed's kingdom.

I could have been wrong. Perhaps Sigtryggr was looking for new land in Scotland, or on the rugged coast of Cumbraland, or perhaps in Gwynedd, which was the northernmost of all the Welsh kingdoms, but I somehow doubted it.

I had sailed Britain's western shore and it is a cruel coast, rock-bound, wave-battered, and tide-swirled, yet north of the Sæfern there is one soft place, one spread of land where the rivers invite a ship to go deep inland, where the soil is not steep and rock-strewn, where cattle can graze and barley grow, and that place was Wirhealum, the land between the River Mærse and the River Dee. Ceaster was there, and it had been at Ceaster that Æthelflaed had led her men against the Norse. The capture of that city and of the rich lands around it had been because of Æthelflaed's insistence, the achievement that had persuaded men to trust her with Mercia, but now, if my suspicions were correct, more Norsemen were going to Wirhealum. A new fleet was sailing with new warriors, hundreds of warriors, and if Æthelflaed was to begin her rule by losing Ceaster, if that great swath of newly conquered land was to be lost, then men would say it was the Christian god's revenge for appointing a mere woman to rule over them.

The safe thing was to return to Gleawecestre. We could have made the voyage quickly enough, helped by the wind, which blew from the southwest two days out of three, but once there we would still be a week's hard march from Ceaster. I reckoned Æthelflaed would have stayed in Gleawecestre, where she was appointing clerks and scribes and priests to administer the lands she now ruled, but I knew she had already sent at least fifty men north to reinforce the garrison at Ceaster. Those were the men Sigtryggr would fight, if indeed he was heading for the land between the rivers.

So I set my course northward. Ahead of us were Sigtryggr's ships, which meant over twenty crews to make an army of at least five hundred men. Five hundred hungry men seeking land. And how many men did Æthelflaed have at Ceaster? I called my son back to the steering-oar and asked him.

"There were just over three hundred when I was there," he said.

"Including your men?"

"Including thirty-eight of us," he said.

"So you left, and Æthelflaed also took thirty-two men south. So Ceaster was garrisoned by what? Two hundred and fifty men?"

"Maybe a few more."

"Or a few less. Men get sick." I stared at the distant shore and saw unfriendly hills beneath heaping clouds. The wind was fretting the waves, shivering them with whitecaps, but also driving our ship hard north. "We know she's just sent fifty men north, so there should still be around three hundred men there. And Merewalh commands."

My son nodded. "He's a good man."

"He's a good man," I agreed.

My son heard the hesitation in my voice. "But not good enough?"

"He'll fight like a bull," I said, "and he's honest. But does he think like a wildcat?" I liked Merewalh, and trusted him. I had no doubt that Æthelflaed would raise him, maybe make him an ealdorman, and I had even thought of Merewalh as a husband for Stiorra. That might still happen, I supposed, but for now Merewalh had to defend Ceaster, and his three hundred men should be more than enough for that task. The burh's walls were made of stone, and its ditch was deep. The Romans had built well, but I assumed Sigtryggr knew of Ceaster's strength and my fear was that the young Norseman had a wildcat's cunning. "So what was the Lady Æthelflaed doing when you left Ceaster?" I asked Uhtred.

"Making a new burh."

"Where?"

"On the bank of the Mærse."

That made sense. Ceaster was a fortress that guarded the Dee, the southernmost river, but the Mærse was an open path. Put a burh there, and enemies could not use the river to pierce deep into the heartland. "So Merewalh needs men to finish the new burh," I said, "and to garrison it, and he needs more men to protect Ceaster. He can't do all that with three hundred men."

"And Osferth is going there with the families," my son said grimly.

"With Stiorra too," I said, and felt a pang of guilt. I have been a careless father. My eldest son was an outlaw to me because of his damned religion, Uhtred had turned out well, but none of that was my doing, while Stiorra was a mystery to me. I loved her, but now I had sent her into danger.

"The families," my son said, "and your money."

Fate is a bitch. I'd sent Osferth north because Ceaster had seemed a safer destination than Gleawecestre, but unless I was wrong about the Norsemen, then I had sent Osferth, my daughter, our families, and all our fortune straight toward a horde of enemies. And worse. Eardwulf might have joined Sigtryggr, and I was certain that Eardwulf was as sly as a spinney of wildcats.

"Suppose Eardwulf goes to Ceaster," I suggested. My son looked at me in puzzlement. "Do they know he's a traitor?" I asked.

He understood my fear. "If they don't know yet . . ." he said slowly.

"They'll open the gates to him," I interrupted.

"But they will know by now," my son insisted.

"They'll know about Eardwulf," I agreed. The reinforcements Æthelflaed had sent from Gleawecestre would have carried that news. "But do they know all his followers?"

"Oh God," he said, thinking about what I had said and realizing the danger. "Jesus!"

"Much help he is," I snarled.

The *Ðrines* slammed into a steeper wave, drenching the deck with cold spray. The wind had been freshening all day and the waves were now fierce and quick, but as night fell the wind died and the sea settled. We had lost sight of the land because we were crossing the vast bay that is the west coast of Wales, though I feared the northern side of that bay, which juts like a rocky arm to trap unwary ships. We lowered the sail, took to the oars, and steered by the infrequent glimpses of the stars. I took the oar and headed the ship slightly west of north. We rowed slowly, and I watched the water sparkle from the strange glowing lights that sometimes twinkle in the sea at night. We call them Ran's jewels, the eerie glitter of the precious stones that are draped around that jealous goddess's neck.

"Where are we going?" Finan asked me some time in the jeweled darkness.

"Wirhealum."

"North or south?"

It was a good question and I did not know the answer. If we used the Dee, the southern river, we could row almost to Ceaster's gates, but if Sigtryggr had made the same choice then we would simply find ourselves facing his men. If we chose the northern river, we would beach the ship a fair way from Ceaster and in all likelihood avoid Sigtryggr's fleet, but it would take us much longer to reach the burh. "I'll guess Sigtryggr wants to capture Ceaster," I said.

"If he's gone to Wirhealum, yes."

"If," I said sourly. Instinct is a strange thing. You cannot touch it, feel it, smell it, or hear it, but you must trust it, and that night, as we listened to the slap of the waves and the creak of the oars, I was as certain as I could be that my fears were justified. Somewhere ahead of us was a fleet of Norsemen intent on capturing Æthelflaed's city of Ceaster. But how would he do it? My instinct was not giving me an answer. "He'll want to capture the city quickly," I suggested.

"He will," Finan agreed. "If he delays, then the garrison only gets stronger."

"So he'll take the faster route."

"The Dee."

"So we'll go north," I decided, "to the Mærse. And in the dawn we take that damned cross off the prow."

The cross on the *Ðrines*'s high bow proclaimed us to be a Christian ship and invited any Dane or Norseman to attack us. A Danish ship would have a proud figure at the bows, a dragon or a serpent or an eagle, but such carvings could always be lifted off the prow timber. The carved and painted beasts were never displayed in home waters, for those waters were friendly and did not need the threat of the beast to tame the unfriendly spirits, but the threat was always needed off enemy coasts. But the cross on the *Đrines*'s bow was fixed. The upright was simply the prow timber extended a few feet above the deck which meant my men would have to use axes to cut the thing down, but once it was gone we would no longer be inviting attack. I was sure there were no Christian ships ahead of us, only enemies.

The axes did their work in the gray light of a limpid dawn. Some of the Christians flinched when the big cross finally splashed overboard, bumped hard against the hull, and was left behind. A flutter of wind rippled the sea and our sail was hoisted again, the oars shipped, and we let the small wind carry us northward. Far off to the east I saw a scatter of dark sails, and guessed they were Welsh fishing craft. A cloud of gulls whirled about the ships, which, seeing us, hurried back toward the land, and that land showed an hour or so after dawn.

And so we sailed. But to what? I did not know. I touched the hammer hanging about my neck and prayed to Thor that my instincts were wrong, that we would reach the Mærse and find nothing but peace.

But my instincts were not wrong. We sailed toward trouble.

Next night we sheltered against the northern Welsh coast, anchored in a cove while the wind howled above us. Rain pelted down. Lightning struck ashore, each flash showing gaunt hills and sleeting rain. The storm came fast and passed quickly. Long before dawn it had gone, a sudden anger of the gods. What it meant I did not know and could only fear, yet by dawn the wind was calm again, the clouds had scattered, and the rising sun was flickering from the settling waves as we hauled the stone and thrust oars into tholes.

I took one of the oars. There was no pain, though after an hour my body ached from the exertion. We chanted the song of

Beowulf, an ancient song telling how that hero swam for a whole day to reach the bottom of a great lake, there to fight Grendel's dam, the monstrous hag. "Wearp ðā wunden-mæl," we bellowed as the oar blades bit, "wrættum gebunden," as we hauled on the looms, "yrre oretta, þæt hit on eorðan læg," as we dragged the hull through the glittering sea, "stið ond styl-ecg," as we recovered the oars and swung them back. The words told how Beowulf, realizing his sword could not bite through the monster's thick hide, had hurled the blade away, had hurled away his blade which had smoke-like curling patterns traced through its steel, just as Serpent-Breath did, and instead he had wrestled with the hag, forcing her to the floor. He took her blows and returned them, and finally snatched one of her own swords, a brutal blade from the days when giants strode the earth, a sword so heavy that only a hero could wield it, and Beowulf chopped the blade into the monster's neck and the shrieks of her dying echoed to the roof of the sky. It is a good tale, taught to me by Ealdwulf the smith when I was a child, though he chanted the old version, not the new one that my men bellowed as the *Ðrines* clove the morning sea. They shouted that "Hālig God" gave Beowulf the victory, but in Ealdwulf's telling it had been Thor, not holy God, who gave the hero the strength to overcome the vile creature.

And I prayed to Thor to give me strength, which is why I hauled on that oar's loom. A man needs strength to wield a sword, to hold a shield, to thrust at the enemy. I was going to battle and I was weak, so weak that after an hour of rowing I gave up the oar to Eadric and joined my son on the steering boards at the stern. My arms ached, but there was no pain in my side.

All day we rowed, and as the sun sank behind us we came to the great mud flats that stretch out from Wirhealum, to the place where the rivers and the land and the sea all mingle, and where the tides race across the rippled flats and the seabirds flock thick as snow. To our south was the mouth of the Dee, wider than the Mærse, and I wondered if I was making the wrong choice and that we should be rowing into the Dee to take our ship straight to Ceaster, but instead we pulled into the enclosing banks of the Mærse. I feared that Sigtryggr, if he had come at all, would already have used the Dee to storm ashore and capture Ceaster. I touched the hammer about my neck and prayed.

The mud gave way to grass and reeds, then to pastureland and heath, to low woods and gentle hills covered in the bright yellow blaze of broom. To our south, on Wirhealum, an occasional trace of smoke showed where a hall or steading stood among the trees but no great smear of fire smirched the evening sky. It looked peaceful. Cows grazed a meadow, and there were sheep on the higher land. I was looking for Æthelflaed's new burh, but saw no sign of it. I knew she was building it to guard this river, which meant it must be close to the bank, and she was no fool, which meant it had to be on the southern bank so that men could easily reach it from Ceaster, but as our shadow grew longer on the water, I saw no wall, no palisade.

The Ðrines drifted on. We were using the oars only to keep her headed upriver, letting the strong tide carry us. We went slowly because the river was treacherous with shallows. Mudbanks showed on either side, but the swirl of the darkening water hinted where the channel lay, and so we crept inland. A small boy was digging in the mud of the northern bank and he paused to wave to us. I waved back and wondered whether he was Dane or Norse. I doubted he was Saxon. This land had been ruled by the Northmen for years, but our capture of Ceaster meant we could now take the surrounding land back and fill it with Saxons.

"There," Finan said, and I looked away from the boy to gaze upriver and saw a thicket of masts showing above a copse. At first I took the masts to be trees, then saw how straight and bare they stood, stark lines against the darkening sky, and the tide was carrying us and I dared not turn for fear of grounding the Ðrines on some unseen shallow. It would have been prudent to turn because those masts showed that Sigtryggr had come here, to the Mærse, and that all his ships were beached on Wirhealum, not at Ceaster, and that an army of Norsemen waited for us, but the tide was like fate. It carried us. And just inland of the masts was smoke, not a great smear of destruction, but the mist of cooking fires sifting the twilight above the low trees, and I guessed we had found Æthelflaed's new burh.

And so, for the first but not for the last time in my life, I came to Brunanburh.

We rounded a gentle curve and saw the Norsemen's ships. They were mostly beached, but a few were still afloat, moored close to the muddy shore. I began counting. "Twenty-six," Finan said. Some of the beached ships had been dismasted, evidence that Sigtryggr planned a long stay.

It was almost low water. The river looked wide enough, but that was deceptive because there were shallows all around us. "What do we do?" my son asked.

"I'll tell you when I know," I grunted, then leaned on the steering-oar so that we went closer to Sigtryggr's fleet. The sun had almost gone and twilight was melding the shadows that stretched dark across the land.

"There's enough of the bastards," Finan said quietly. He was gazing ashore.

I kept glancing ashore, but mostly I watched the river, intent on keeping the *Ðrines* from grounding. My men were gazing southward, forgetting their oars, and I shouted at them to row, and, when the boat was gently moving again, I gave my son the steering-oar and stared at Æthelflaed's new burh. So far her builders had made an earthen wall on a rise of land close to the river. That wall was little more than a mound, perhaps the height of a man and over two hundred paces long. A hall had been built alongside two smaller buildings, perhaps stables, but there was no palisade yet. That wooden wall would need hundreds of stout trunks, oak or elm, and there were no large trees close to the new earthen wall to provide such massive trunks. "She'll have to bring the timbers here," I said.

"If she ever finishes it," Finan remarked.

I assumed the burh was square in shape, but from the deck of the *Ðrines* it was impossible to tell. The hall was not large, and its new timbers showed bright in the fading light. I guessed it was there to shelter Æthelflaed's builders and, once the burh was finished, a larger hall would be made. Then I saw the cross on the hall's gable and almost laughed aloud. "That's a church," I said, "not a hall!"

"She wants God on her side," Finan said.

"She should have built a palisade first," I growled. The moored and beached ships hid most of the river's bank, but I thought I could see the raw sides of a newly dug channel, presumably made to carry the Mærse's water to a ditch surrounding the new work, which was now in the hands of the Norse.

"Jesus," Finan breathed, "there are hundreds of the bastards!" Men were coming from the church to gaze at us and, as he had said, there were hundreds of them. Other men had been sitting around campfires. There were women and children there too, all now walking to the river's edge to watch us.

"Keep rowing!" I called to my men, taking the steering-oar from my son.

Sigtryggr had captured the half-built burh, that was obvious, but the presence of so many men suggested he had not yet assaulted Ceaster. There had not been time for that, but I did not doubt he would make the attack as soon as he could. The riskiest course would have been to take his ships and men up the Dee and attack Ceaster immediately, because once inside those Roman walls he would have been immovable. That is what I would have done, but he had been more prudent. He had taken the lesser fortress, and his men would be busy making a palisade from whatever timber they could cut and from thorn bushes, they would deepen the ditch and, once the burh was finished, once he was enclosed in earth and timber and thorns, he would be almost as secure inside Brunanburh as he would have been inside Ceaster.

A man scrambled over the beached ships that were huddled together as if for protection, then leaped onto one of the moored boats, always making his way toward us. "Who are you?" he shouted.

"Keep rowing!" It was getting darker by the minute and I feared going aground, but I dared not stop.

"Who are you?" the man called again.

"Sigulf Haraldson!" I shouted the invented name.

"What are you doing here?"

"Who is asking?" I called in Danish, speaking slowly.

"Sigtryggr Olafson!"

"Tell him we live here!" I wondered if the man shouting at us was Sigtryggr himself, but it seemed unlikely. He was most likely one of Sigtryggr's men, sent to challenge us.

"You're Danish?" he shouted, but I ignored that question. "My lord invites you ashore!"

"Tell your lord we want to be home before dark!"

"What do you know of the Saxons in the city?"

"Nothing! We ignore them, they ignore us!"

We had passed the ship from which the man shouted and he nimbly leaped onto another to stay near us. "Come ashore!" he shouted.

"Tomorrow!"

"Where do you live?" he called.

"Upriver," I called back, "an hour's journey." I snarled at my men to row harder, and Thor was with us because the *Ðrines* stayed in the channel, though more than once the oars bumped on mud and the hull twice scraped softly over a bank before finding deeper water. The man shouted more questions through the dusk, but we were gone. We had become a shadow ship in the twilight, a ghost ship vanishing into the night.

"Pray God they didn't recognize your voice," Finan said.

"They couldn't hear me ashore," I said, hoping that was true. I had not shouted as loudly as I could, hoping that only the one man on the ship would hear me. "And who would have recognized it?"

"My brother?" Eadith put in.

"Did you see him?" She shook her head. I turned to look astern, but the new burh was now nothing but a shadow within a shadow, a shadow flickering with firelight, while the masts of Sigtryggr's ships were dark streaks against the western sky. The tide had ebbed and it was slack water as the *Ðrines* ghosted upriver. I did not know how far Brunanburh was from Ceaster, but reckoned it must be some miles, maybe ten? Twenty? I had no idea and none of my men had visited Æthelflaed's new burh so could not tell me. I had visited the Mærse before, I had ridden its banks close to Ceaster, but in the gathering darkness it was impossible to recognize any landmark. I watched behind us, seeing the smudge of Brunanburh's smoke get farther and farther away, watching until the western horizon was edged with the flame red of the dying sun and the sky above was blackness pricked with stars. I did not fear any pursuit. It was too dark for a ship to follow us, and men on foot or on horseback would be stumbling through unfamiliar country.

"What do we do?" Finan asked.

"Go to Ceaster," I said.

And keep Æthelflaed's throne safe.

There was a glimmer of moonlight, often hidden by clouds, but just enough to betray the river. We rowed silently until at last the hull slid onto mud and the *Ðrines* shuddered and was still. The southern bank was only some twenty paces away and the first of my men dropped overboard and waded ashore.

"Weapons and mail," I ordered.

"What about the ship?" Finan asked.

"We leave her," I said. Sigtryggr's men would doubtless find her. The *Ðrines* would float off on the rising tide and eventually drift back downstream, but I did not have time to burn her and if I moored her then she would betray where we had gone ashore. Better to let her go wherever she wanted to drift. Wyrd bið ful āræd.

And so we went ashore, forty-seven men and one woman, and we wore our mail and carried shields and weapons. We were dressed for war, and war was coming. The presence of so many men at Brunanburh had told me that Ceaster was still in Saxon hands, but Sigtryggr would surely move against the larger fortress soon.

"Maybe he's decided just to stay at Brunanburh," Finan suggested.

"And leave us in Ceaster?"

"If he finishes Brunanburh's palisade? If he makes a nuisance of himself? Perhaps he hopes we'll pay him to leave?"

"Then he's a fool, because we won't."

"But only a fool would attack Ceaster's stone walls."

"We did," I said, and Finan laughed. I shook my head. "He

won't want to be penned up in Brunanburh. His father sent him to take land, and he'll try. Besides, he's young. He has a reputation to make. And Berg says he's headstrong."

I had talked with Berg. He had been one of Rognvald's men, so had not seen much of Sigtryggr, but what he had seen had impressed him. "He's tall, lord," he had told me, "and golden-haired like your son, and with a face like an eagle, lord, and he laughs and shouts. Men like him."

"You liked him?"

Berg had paused, and then, with the eagerness of the young, had blurted out, "He's like a god come to earth, lord!"

I had smiled at that. "A god?"

"Like a god, lord," he had mumbled, ashamed of the words almost as soon as he had said them.

But the god come to earth still had to make his reputation, and how better to do that than by recapturing Ceaster for the Northmen? Which was why we hurried there, and in the end it was easier to find than I had feared. We followed the river eastward until we saw the Roman road slanting across our front and then we followed that road south. It went through a Roman cemetery, which both Northmen and Saxons had left alone because it would be so full of ghosts. We walked through it in silence, and I saw the Christians make the sign of the cross and I touched my hammer amulet. It was night, the time when the dead walk, and as we passed through the sullen dwellings of the dead, the only sound was that of our feet on the stones of the road.

And there, ahead, was Ceaster.

We reached the town just before dawn. There was a gray sword's edge to the eastern sky, a hint of light, nothing more. The first birds sang. The pale walls of the burh were night-dark, the northern gate a shadowed blackness. If any flag flew above the gate I could not see it. There was firelight inside the walls, but it did not show any men on the parapets, and so I took just Finan and my son, and the three of us walked toward the gate. I knew we could be seen.

"You opened this gate last time," Finan said to my son, "you might have to do it again."

"I had a horse that time," Uhtred said. He had stood on his saddle and leaped over the gate, and so we had captured the burh from the Danes. I hoped we still held it.

"Who are you?" a man shouted from the wall.

"Friends," I called, "is Merewahl still in command?"

"He is," the reply was grudging.

"Fetch him."

"He's asleep."

"I said fetch him!" I snarled the order.

"Who are you?" the man asked again.

"The man who wants to speak with Merewalh! Go!"

I heard the sentry speak to his companions, then there was silence. We waited as the sword's edge of gray in the east widened to a blade of dull light. Cockerels crowed and a dog howled somewhere inside the town, and then at last I saw shadows on the wall. "I'm Merewalh!" the familiar voice called. "And who are you?"

"Uhtred," I said.

There was a moment's silence. "Who?" he asked again.

"Uhtred!" I shouted. "Uhtred of Bebbanburg!"

"Lord?" He sounded disbelieving.

"Did Osferth reach you?"

"Yes! And your daughter."

"Æthelflaed?"

"Lord Uhtred?" He still sounded incredulous.

"Open the damned gate, Merewalh," I demanded, "I want breakfast."

The gate was pushed open and we passed through. There were torches in the arch and I saw the relief on Merewalh's face as he recognized me. A dozen men waited behind him, all with spears or drawn swords. "Lord!" Merewalh strode toward me. "You're healed, lord!"

"I'm healed," I said. It was good to see Merewalh. He was a staunch warrior, an honest man, and a friend. He was guileless, with a round open face that beamed with pleasure at our arrival. He had been one of Æthelred's men, though he had always protected Æthelflaed, and had suffered for that loyalty. "Is Æthelflaed here?" I asked.

He shook his head. "She said she'd bring more men when she could, but we've heard nothing for a week now."

I glanced at his escort who were grinning as they sheathed their swords. "So how many men do you have?"

"Two hundred and ninety-two fit to fight."

"Does that include the fifty men Æthelflaed sent?"

"It does, lord."

"So Prince Æthelstan's here?"

"He's here, lord, yes."

I turned and watched as the heavy gates were pulled shut and as the massive locking bar was dropped into its brackets. "And you know there are five hundred Norsemen at Brunanburh?"

"I was told six hundred," he said grimly.

"You were told?"

"Five Saxons came yesterday. Five Mercians. They watched the Norsemen come ashore and fled here."

"Five Mercians?" I asked, but did not give him time to answer. "Tell me, did you have men at Brunanburh?"

He shook his head. "The Lady Æthelflaed said to abandon it till she returned. She reckoned we couldn't defend both Ceaster and the new burh. Once she's here we'll start the work there again."

"Five Mercians?" I asked again. "Did they say who they were?"

"Oh, I know them!" Merewalh said confidently. "They were Lord Æthelred's men."

"So now they serve the Lady Æthelflaed?" I asked, and Merewalh nodded. "So why did she send them?"

"She wanted them to look at Brunanburh."

"Look at?"

"There are Danes on Wirhealum," he explained. "There aren't many, and they claim to be Christians." He shrugged as if to suggest that claim was dubious. "They graze sheep mostly and we don't trouble them if they don't trouble us, but I suppose she thought they might have done some damage?"

"So the five came here on Æthelflaed's orders," I said, "and they rode straight past your south gate and didn't ask to see you? They came to Brunanburh?" I waited for an answer, but Merewalh said nothing. "Five men come here to make sure some sheep farmers hadn't damaged an earthen wall?" Still he said nothing. "You must have sent your own men to look at the new burh?"

"I did, yes."

"Yet Æthelflaed didn't trust you? She had to send five men to do a job she must have known you were doing already?"

Poor Merewalh frowned, worried by the questions. "I know the men, lord," he said, though he sounded uncertain.

"You know them well?"

"We all served Lord Æthelred. No, I don't know them well."

"And these five," I suggested, "served Eardwulf."

"We all served him. He was Lord Æthelred's household commander."

"But these five were close to him," I stated flatly, and Merewalh gave a reluctant nod. "And Eardwulf," I said, "is probably with Sigtryggr."

"Sigtryggr, lord?"

"The man who has just brought five or six hundred Norsemen to Brunanburh."

"Eardwulf is with . . ." he began, then turned and stared down Ceaster's main street as if expecting to see Norsemen suddenly invading the town.

"Eardwulf is probably with Sigtryggr," I repeated, "and Eardwulf is a traitor and an outlaw. And he's probably coming here right now. But he's not coming alone."

"Dear God," Merewalh said, and made the sign of the cross.

"Say thank you to your god," I said. Because the killing was about to start, and we had arrived in time.

Eleven

Sigtryggr came at noon.

We knew he was coming.

We knew where he would attack.

We were outnumbered, but we had the high stone walls of Ceaster and they were worth a thousand men. Sigtryggr knew that too and, like all the Northmen, he had no patience for a siege. He had no time to make ladders, no tools to dig beneath our ramparts, he had only the courage of his men and the know-ledge that he had tricked us.

Except we knew what the trick was.

Welcome to Ceaster.

The sun had risen, but it was dark in the Great Hall, the gaunt Roman building at Ceaster's center. A fire smoldered in the central hearth, the smoke curling under the roof before finding the hole hacked through the tiles. Men slept at the hall's edges, their snores loud in the vast space. There were tables and benches, and some men slept on the tables. Two maidservants were placing oatcakes on the stones of the hearth, while a third was bringing timber to revive the fire.

There were huge stacks of timber outside the hall. It was not firewood, but trunks of oak and elm that had been rudely trimmed. I had stopped to look at them. "That's the palisade for Brunan-burh?" I asked Merewalh.

He nodded. "There's no large timber left on Wirhealum," he explained, "so we had to cut it here."

"You'll take it by cart?"

"Probably by ship," he said. The timbers were vast, each as thick as a big man's waist and each about twice the height of a man. A trench would be dug along the summit of Brunanburh's earthen mound and the trunks would be sunk upside down so that the tops of the trunks would be in the earth. Timber lasted longer that way. Smaller timbers would be used to make the fighting platforms and the steps. Merewalh looked gloomily at the huge piles. "She wants it all finished by advent."

"You'll be busy!"

Men were stirring as we entered the hall. The sky was lightening, the cocks crowing, it was time to meet the day. Osferth arrived a few minutes later, yawning and scratching, and stopped to stare at me. "Lord!"

"You came here safely."

"I did, lord."

"And my daughter?"

"All safe, lord." He looked me up and down. "You're not flinching!"

"The pain has gone."

"Praise be to God," he said, then embraced me. "Finan! Sihtric! Uhtred!" There was no hiding his pleasure at being back with his own war-band, then he saw Eadith and his eyes widened, and he looked to me for an explanation.

"The Lady Eadith," I said, "is to be treated with honor."

"Of course, lord." He bridled at the suggestion he would treat any woman discourteously, then Finan winked at him and he looked back to her, then to me. "Of course, lord," he said again, but stiffly this time.

"And Æthelstan?" I asked.

"Oh, he's here, lord."

The fire blazed anew and I took my men to a shadowed corner of the hall and hid there while Merewalh summoned the five Saxons who had arrived the previous day. They came smiling. The hall was crowded by then as other men woke and came to find food and ale. Most arrived without weapons or shields, though the five men all had swords at their waists. "Sit!" Merewalh told them, gesturing at a table. "There's ale, and the food won't be long."

"They're my brother's men," Eadith whispered to me.

"You just killed them by saying that," I whispered back.

She hesitated. "I know."

"Their names?"

She told me, and I watched them. They were nervous, though all but one of the five were trying to hide it. The youngest, scarcely more than a boy, looked terrified. The others were speaking too loudly and teasing each other, and one slapped the rump of the girl who brought them ale, but despite the pretended carelessness I could see their eyes were watchful. The oldest, a man called Hanulf Eralson, looked all around the hall and stared into the dark corner where we were half hidden by shadows and tables. He probably thought we were still sleeping. "Are you expecting a fight today, Merewalh?" he called.

"It must come soon."

"Pray God it does," Hanulf said heartily, "because they'll never get past these walls."

"Lord Uhtred did," Merewalh pointed out.

"Lord Uhtred always had the luck of the devil," Hanulf said sourly, "and the devil looks after his own. You have news of him?"

"Of the devil?"

"Of Uhtred," Hanulf said.

I had told Merewalh what to say if that question was asked. He crossed himself. "Men tell us the Lord Uhtred is dying."

"One pagan less," Hanulf said dismissively, then paused as bread and cheese were put on his table. Hanulf fondled the girl who brought the cheese and said something to make the girl blush and pull away. His men laughed, though the youngster just looked even more scared.

"The devil looks after his own, eh?" Finan murmured.

"Let's see if he looks after those five," I said, then turned as Æthelstan entered the hall followed by three other boys and two girls, none older than eleven or twelve. They were laughing and chasing each other, then Æthelstan saw two hounds by the hearth and dropped beside them, stroking their long backs and gray muzzles. The other children copied him, and it was interesting, I thought, that he was the indisputable leader of the small gang. He had that gift, and I did not doubt it would follow him into manhood. I watched as he stole two oatcakes from the hearth stones and split them between himself, the dogs, and the two girls.

"So we can help you on the walls today?" Hanulf asked Merewalh.

"We would expect nothing less of you," Merewalh said.

"Where will they attack?"

"I wish we knew."

"Probably a gate?" Hanulf suggested.

"I would think so."

Men were listening to the conversation. Most of Merewalh's men knew I was in the hall and those men had been told to keep my presence secret. Most were also convinced that Hanulf simply wanted to help defend the walls. So far as they knew he and his companions were simply five Mercians who had fortuitously arrived to help defend the burh.

"What about the land gate?" Hanulf asked.

"The land gate?"

"The one we used yesterday."

"Oh, the North Gate!"

"We'll fight there," Hanulf offered, "with your permission?"

Thus I learned that Sigtryggr was not coming by sea. I had not expected it. He would have been forced to row his fleet out of the Mærse, turn south, and row up the Dee, and it would have taken him all day, bringing him at last to the South Gate. Instead he was coming overland, and the closest gate to Brunanburh would be the North Gate, the same one by which we had just entered.

"Can I fight at the North Gate?" Æthelstan asked Merewalh.

"You, Lord Prince," Merewalh said sternly, "will stay a long way from any fighting!"

"Let the boy come with us!" Hanulf suggested cheerfully.

"You will stay in the church," Merewalh ordered Æthelstan, "and pray for our success."

The hall was becoming lighter as the sun climbed. "It's time," I told Finan. "Take the bastards."

I had drawn Serpent-Breath, but I still did not fully trust my strength, and so I let Finan and my son lead a dozen men toward the table. I followed with Eadith.

Hanulf sensed our approach. He could hardly not sense it because every man in the hall was suddenly still, and their voices hushed. He twisted on the bench, saw the approaching swords, and saw Eadith too. He gaped at her, astonished, then tried to stand, but the bench half trapped him as he wrenched the sword from his scabbard.

"Do you really want to fight us?" I asked. A score of Merewalh's men had also drawn swords. Most of those men were still not sure what was happening, but they took their lead from Finan and that meant Hanulf was surrounded. Æthelstan had stood and was staring at me in surprise.

Hanulf kicked over the bench and looked to the door. There was no escape there. I thought for a heartbeat that he intended to attack us, to die in a sudden welter of one-sided battle, but instead he let the sword drop. It clattered on the floor. He said nothing.

"All of you, drop your swords," I ordered. "And you," I pointed to Æthelstan, "come here."

And then it was just the business of questioning them and their answers came easily. Did they hope to live if they told the truth? They confessed they were Eardwulf's men, that they had fled Gleawecestre with him and sailed westward in *Godspellere* until they encountered Sigtryggr's fleet. Now they had come to Ceaster to open the North Gate to Sigtryggr's men. "And that will be today?" I asked.

"Yes, lord."

"What signal does he give you?"

"Signal, lord?"

"To tell you to open the gate."

"He'll lower his standard, lord."

"And then you would kill whatever men were in your way?" I asked. "And open the gate to our enemies?"

Hanulf had nothing to say to that, but the youngest, the boy, blurted out a plea. "Lord!" he began.

"Silence!" I snarled.

"My son didn't . . ." another of the men began, then fell quiet when I glared at him. The boy was crying now. He could not have been much over fourteen, perhaps fifteen, and he knew what grisly fate now awaited him, but I was in no mood to hear pleas for mercy. The five men deserved none. If Hanulf had succeeded, then Sigtryggr would be inside Ceaster and almost all my men and all Merewalh's men would be slaughtered. "Prince Æthelstan!" I called. "Come here!"

Æthelstan hurried across the hall to stand beside me. "Lord?"

"These men were among those sent to capture you at Alencestre, Lord Prince," I told him, "and now they've come to give Ceaster to our enemies. You will decide their punishment. Osferth? Bring your nephew a chair." Osferth found a chair. "Not that one," I said and pointed to the largest chair in the hall, presumably the one that Æthelflaed used when she came to the burh. It had armrests and a high back, and was the chair that most resembled a throne, and I made Æthelstan sit on it. "One day," I told him, "you might be king of this realm and you must practice kingship just as you practice sword-skill. So now you will dispense justice."

He looked at me. He was just a boy. "Justice," he said nervously.

"Justice," I said, staring at the five men. "You award gold or silver for a deed well done, and you decree punishment for a crime. So dispense justice now." The boy frowned at me, as if to determine whether I was serious. "They're waiting," I said harshly. "We're all waiting!"

Æthelstan looked at the five men. He drew his breath. "You're Christians?" he finally asked.

"Louder," I said.

"You're Christians?" His voice had not yet broken.

Hanulf looked at me as if appealing to me to spare him this silliness. "Talk to the prince," I told him.

"We're Christians," he said defiantly.

"Yet you would have allowed the pagans to capture this place?" Æthelstan asked.

"We were obeying our lord," Hanulf said.

"Your lord is an outlaw," Æthelstan said, and Hanulf had nothing to say.

"Your judgment, Lord Prince," I demanded.

Æthelstan licked his lips nervously. "They must die," he said.

"Louder!"

"They must die!"

"Louder still," I said, "and talk to them, not to me. Look them in the eye and tell them your judgment."

The boy's hands were gripping the armrests now, his knuckles white. "You must die," he said to the five men, "because you would have betrayed your country and your god."

"We . . ." Hanulf began.

"Quiet!" I snarled at him, then looked to Æthelstan. "Quickly or slowly, Lord Prince, and by what method?"

"Method?"

"We can hang them quickly, Lord Prince," I explained, "or hang them slowly. Or we can give them the blade."

The boy bit his lip, then turned back to the five. "You will die by the blade," he said firmly.

The four oldest men tried to snatch up their swords, but they were far too slow. All five were seized and dragged outside to the gray early light where Merewalh's men stripped them of their mail and their clothes, leaving them in nothing but dirty shirts that hung to their knees. "Give us a priest," Hanulf pleaded. "At least a priest?"

Merewalh's priest, a man called Wissian, prayed with them. "Not too long, Father," I warned him, "we have work to do!"

Æthelstan watched the men, who had all been forced to their knees. "I made the right choice, lord?" he asked me.

"When you begin training with a sword," I asked him, "what do you learn first?"

"To block."

"To block," I agreed, "and what else?"

"To block, to swing, and to lunge."

"You begin with those easy things," I said, "and it's the same with justice. That decision was an easy one, which is why I let you make it."

He frowned up at me. "It's easy? To take a man's life? To take five men's lives?"

"They're traitors and outlaws. They were going to die whatever you decided." I watched the priest touch the men's foreheads. "Father Wissian!" I shouted. "The devil doesn't want to be kept waiting while you waste time, hurry!"

"You always say," Æthelstan spoke softly, "that one should be kept alive."

"I do?"

"You do, lord," he said, then strode confidently to the kneeling men and pointed to the youngest. "What's your name?"

"Cengar, lord," the boy said.

"Come," Æthelstan said, and when Cengar hesitated he tugged on his shoulder. "I said come." He brought Cengar to me. "Kneel," he commanded. "May I borrow your sword, Lord Uhtred?"

I gave him Serpent-Breath and watched as he clasped his small hands around the hilt. "Swear loyalty to me," he instructed Cengar.

"You're a mushroom-brained idiot, Lord Prince," I said.

"Swear," Æthelstan told Cengar, and Cengar clasped his hands around Æthelstan's hands and swore loyalty. He stared up at Æthelstan as he said the words and I saw the tears running down his face.

"You have the brains of a stunted toad," I told Æthelstan.

"Finan!" Æthelstan called, ignoring me.

"Lord Prince?"

"Give Cengar his clothes and weapons."

Finan looked at me. I shrugged. "Do as the sparrow-brained idiot tells you."

We killed the remaining four. It was quick enough. I made Æthelstan watch. I was tempted to let him kill Hanulf himself, but I was in haste and did not want to spend time watching a boy try to hack a man to death, and so my son killed Hanulf, spattering the Roman street with yet more blood. Æthelstan looked pale as he watched the slaughter, while Cengar still wept, perhaps because he had been forced to watch his father die. I took the boy aside. "Listen," I said, "if you break that oath to the prince I will break you. I will let weasels gnaw your balls, I'll cut your prick off slice by slice, I'll blind you, I'll tear your tongue out, I'll peel the skin from your back, and I'll break your ankles and your wrists. And after that I'll let you live. Do you understand me, boy?"

He nodded, too scared to speak.

"Then stop sniveling," I said, "and get busy, we have work to do."

Then we became busy.

I did not see my own father die, though I was close by when it happened. I had been about Æthelstan's age when the Danes invaded Northumbria and captured Eoferwic, the chief city of that country. My father took his men to join the army that attempted to recapture the city, and it had looked simple because the Danes had allowed a whole stretch of Eoferwic's palisade to collapse, offering a path into the streets and alleys beyond. I still remember how we mocked the Danes for being so careless and stupid.

I watched our army form three wedges. Father Beocca, who had been told to look after me and keep me from trouble, said the wedge was really called a *porcinum capet*, or a swine-head, and for some strange reason I have never forgotten those Latin words. Beocca had been excited, certain he was about to witness a Christian victory over pagan invaders. I shared his excitement and I remember seeing the banners raised and hearing the cheers as our Northumbrian army swarmed over the low earthen mound, clambered across the wreckage of the palisade, and charged into the city.

Where they died.

The Danes had been neither careless nor stupid. They had wanted our men to enter the city because, once inside, they found the Danes had built a new wall to cordon off a killing ground, and so our army had been trapped, and Eoferwic was renamed

Jorvik, and the Danes became lords of Northumbria, all except for the fortress of Bebbanburg, which was too strong even for an army of spear-Danes.

And in Ceaster, thanks to Æthelflaed, we had dozens of heavy tree trunks, all ready to be carried to Brunanburh to make the palisade.

So we used them to make a wall.

When a man enters through Ceaster's North Gate he finds himself on a long street that runs straight southward. There are buildings either side, Roman buildings made of stone or brick. On the right side of the street is one long building which I have always supposed to be a barracks. It had windows, but only one door, and it was easy to block those openings. On the left side were houses with alleys between, and we stopped up the alleys with tree trunks and nailed up the doors and windows of the houses. The alleys were narrow, so the trunks were laid lengthwise in them, making a fighting platform some five feet above the street, while the long street itself was blocked by more trunks, a great heap of heavy timber. Sigtryggr's men could enter the city, but would find themselves in a street that led nowhere, a street blocked by vast timbers, a street made into a trap fashioned from wood and stone and made deadly by fire and by steel.

Fire. The weakest part of the trap was the long building on the western side of the street. We did not have time to break down the roof and make a fighting platform above the wall, and the trapped Norsemen would find it easy enough to splinter open the building's blocked door and wide windows with their war axes, and so I had men fill the long room with kindling and straw, with baulks of wood, with anything that would burn. If they broke into the old barracks, Sigtryggr's warriors would be greeted with an inferno.

And on the fighting platform above the gate we heaped more tree trunks. I ordered two Roman houses pulled down, and men carried their blocks of masonry to the barricades and to the gate. Throwing spears were gathered to hurl down at Sigtryggr's men. The sun climbed, and we worked, adding timber, stone, steel, and fire to the trap. Then we closed the gate, put men on the walls, raised our bright flags, and waited.

Welcome to Ceaster.

"Æthelflaed knew you weren't coming straight here," my daughter told me. "She knew you were provisioning a ship."

"But she didn't stop me?"

Stiorra smiled. "Shall I tell you what she said?"

"You'd better."

"Your father, she told me, is at his best when he is disobedient."

I grunted. Stiorra and I were standing on the fighting platform above the North Gate, from where I gazed toward the distant woods out of which I expected Sigtryggr to appear. The sun had been shining all morning, but now clouds came from the north and west. Far to the north, somewhere over the wild lands of Cumbraland, the rain was already falling in shadowy veils, but Ceaster was dry.

"More stones?" Gerbruht asked. There must have been two hundred blocks of masonry stacked on the high platform, none of them smaller than a man's head.

"More stones," I said. I waited till he had gone. "What use would I have been here," I asked Stiorra, "if I couldn't fight?"

"I think the Lady Æthelflaed knew that."

"She's a clever bitch."

"Father!" she protested.

"So are you," I said.

"And she thinks it's high time I was married," Stiorra said.

I growled slightly. My daughter's marriage was not Æthelflaed's concern, though she was right in thinking that it was well beyond time that Stiorra found a husband. "Does she have a victim in mind?" I asked.

"A West Saxon, she says."

"A West Saxon! What? Just any West Saxon?"

"She tells me that Ealdorman Æthelhelm has three sons."

I laughed at that. "You don't bring him enough advantages. No land, no great fortune. He might marry you to his steward, but not to one of his sons."

"Lady Æthelflaed says that any son of a West Saxon ealdorman would make a good match," Stiorra said.

"She would."

"Why?"

I shrugged. "Æthelflaed wants to bind me to her brother's kingdom," I explained, "she worries that if she dies I'll go back to join the pagans, so she thinks your marriage to a West Saxon would help."

"And would it?" she asked.

I shrugged again. "I can hardly see myself fighting against the father of your children. Not if you liked him. So yes, it would help."

"Do I have any choice?" she asked.

"Of course not."

She grimaced. "So you and the Lady Æthelflaed choose for me?"

I saw birds flying above the distant wood. Something had disturbed them. "It's not Æthelflaed's business," I said. "I'll choose for you."

Stiorra had also noticed the birds rising from the trees and was gazing at them. "Did mother have a choice?"

"No choice at all. She saw me and was stricken." I had spoken lightly, but it was true, or at least it had been true for me. "I saw her," I went on, "and I was stricken too."

"But you'll marry me for advantage? For land or money?"

"What other use are you?" I asked sternly. She looked up at me and I tried to keep a straight face, but she made me laugh. "I won't marry you to a bad man," I promised, "and I'll provide you with a rich dowry, but you know and I know that we marry for advantage." I stared at the far woods and saw nothing untoward, but I was certain the Norsemen were there.

"You didn't marry for advantage," Stiorra said accusingly.

"But you will," I said, "for my advantage." I turned as Gerbruht carried another chunk of masonry to the fighting platform. "There must be cess pots in the town," I suggested to him.

"Shit pots, lord?"

"Bring as many as you can."

He grinned. "Yes, lord!"

A shaft of sunlight lit the Roman cemetery, glinting off the white stones. "Is there a man you want to marry?" I asked Stiorra.

"No," she shook her head, "no."

"But you're thinking about marriage?"

"I want to make you a grandfather," she said.

"Maybe I'll send you to a nunnery," I growled.

"No," she said, "you won't."

And I remembered Gisela's prophecy, drawn from the runesticks so long ago. One son would break my heart, one would make me proud, and Stiorra would be the mother of kings, and so far the runesticks had been proven right. One son had become a priest, the other was proving to be a warrior, and there was only Stiorra's fate to determine. And thinking of the runesticks made me remember Ælfadell, the old woman who had prophesied a future of dead kings, and I thought of her granddaughter, the girl who could not speak, but who enraptured men with her beauty. Her grandmother had called her Erce, but afterward, when she married Cnut Longsword, she was given the name Frigg. He had not married her for land or for advantage, but simply because she was so lovely. We had captured her before Teotanheale, her and her son, but I had been in such pain ever since that I had half forgotten her. "I wonder what happened to Frigg?" I said to my daughter.

"You don't know?" she asked, surprised.

Her surprise surprised me. "You know?" I asked.

She half smiled. "Your son keeps her."

I stared at her in shock. "Uhtred keeps her?"

"In the farm close to Cirrenceastre. The farm you gave him."

I still stared at her. I had thought my son had taken an admirable interest in farming, an interest I had encouraged. Now I knew why he was so enthusiastic about the farm. "Why didn't he tell me?"

"I assume because he doesn't want you visiting her, Father." She smiled sweetly. "I like her."

"He hasn't married her, has he?" I asked, alarmed.

"No, Father. But it's time he was married. He's older than I am." She stepped back, grimacing, because Gerbruht was carrying a vast metal pot full of shit and piss. "Don't spill it!" she called to him.

"It's just shit from the guardhouse, lady," he said, "it never hurt anyone. Just smells a bit. Where do you want it, lord?"

"Is there more?"

"Lots more, lord. Buckets of the lovely stuff."

"Put it where you can tip it over the Norsemen," I said.

Welcome to Ceaster.

Sigtryggr came at noon. The sun was behind cloud again, yet its light glinted from the blades of his men. He had only brought a dozen horses from Ireland, presumably because horses are difficult to tend aboard ship, so almost all his men were on foot. I assumed Sigtryggr himself was one of the small group of horsemen who rode beneath a great white banner on which was painted a red ax.

I had been wrong about at least one thing. Sigtryggr had brought ladders. They looked clumsy until I realized they were the masts from his beached ships on which crosspieces had been nailed or lashed. There were twelve of them, all long enough to reach across our ditch and up to the ramparts.

The army threaded the graves of the Roman cemetery and stopped a hundred paces from the walls. They were jeering at us, though I could not hear the insults, just the roar of men's voices and the sound of blades being beaten against heavy shields. The horsemen came up the road, their own shields discarded. One man carried a leafy bough, a sign that they wished to talk. I looked for Eardwulf, but could not see him. The horsemen stopped, all except a single rider, who spurred his big stallion closer to the gate.

"You talk to him," I told Merewalh, "he mustn't know I'm here." I stepped back and closed the face-plates of my helmet.

My daughter stayed beside Merewalh and gazed down at the lone rider. "That has to be Sigtryggr," she said, stepping back to join me.

And so it was, and so I saw Sigtryggr Ivarson for the first time. He was a young man, a very young man. I doubted he had even seen twenty years, yet he led an army. He wore no helmet, so that his long bright hair hung down his back. He was clean-shaven and thin-faced, with sharp features softened by a smile. He gave the impression of being very sure of himself, very confident, and, I suspected, very vain. His mail shone, a chain of gold was looped three times around his neck, his arms glowed with rings, his scabbard and bridle were paneled with silver, while his horse was groomed like its master to impress. I thought of Berg's awed words that Sigtryggr was a god come to earth. His gray horse pranced on the road, full of vigor as Sigtryggr curbed him just ten paces short of the ditch. "My name," he called, "is Sigtryggr Ivarson. I bid you all good day."

Merewalh said nothing. One of his men was muttering a translation.

"You are silent," Sigtryggr called, "is that from fear? Then you are right to fear us, for we shall slaughter you. We shall take your women and enslave your children. Unless, of course, you withdraw from the city."

"Say nothing," I muttered to Merewalh.

"If you leave I shall not pursue you. Hounds don't pursue field-mice." Sigtryggr touched heels to his horse and came a couple of paces closer. He glanced down into the flooded ditch, seeing the sharpened stakes showing just above the water, then looked back to us. Now that he was closer I could understand why Berg had been so awed. Sigtryggr was undeniably handsome; golden-haired, blue-eyed, and apparently fearless. He seemed to be amused by our silence. "Do you have dogs and pigs in the city?"

"Let him talk," I muttered.

"You must have both," he went on after pausing for the answer that did not come. "I ask only for practical reasons. Burying your bodies will take time, and burning your corpses will take days and burning corpses do smell so bad! But dogs and pigs will eat your flesh quickly. Unless you leave now." He paused, staring up at Merewalh. "You choose to be silent?" he asked. "Then I must tell you my gods have foretold victory for me this day. The runesticks have spoken, and they do not lie! I will win, you will lose, but I console you with the thought that your dogs and pigs will not go hungry." He turned his horse away. "Farewell!" he shouted, and spurred away.

"Arrogant bastard," Merewalh muttered.

We knew he planned to attack through the North Gate, but if Sigtryggr had massed his men ready for that assault we would have gathered a force to resist him and, even if Hanulf and his companions had lived to betray us by opening the gates, there would have been enough of our men to make a bloody fight in the entrance arch. So Sigtryggr set out to deceive us. He divided his forces, sending half toward the city's northeast corner, and half to the northwest. That northwestern bastion was the weakest because it had been partially undermined by floodwaters early in the spring, yet even the half collapsed bastion was a formidable obstacle. The wall had been reinforced with timbers and the ditch was deep and wide. We had good men there too, just as we did at the northeastern ramparts, though most of our men waited where we had made the trap. They were hidden. All Sigtryggr could see at the North Gate was a group of a dozen men on the high rampart.

Sigtryggr had kept just over a hundred men on the road. They were sitting, either on the road or in the fields on either side. I assumed we were supposed to think they were a force he was holding in reserve, but of course they were waiting for the gate to open. Other men were scattered in groups along the whole northern wall, hurling spears and insults, presumably to keep our defenders looking outward while the five men unbarred the gate. Sigtryggr, still mounted, was just sixty or seventy paces from the wall, surrounded by his other horsemen and by a score of warriors on foot. He was taking care to gaze toward the northwest bastion, pretending no interest in the gate. He drew his sword and held it high for a heartbeat, then dropped it as a signal for the attack on that corner of the city. His men there bellowed their war cries, charged toward the ditch and thrust their cumbersome great ladders up to the wall's top. They threw axes and spears, they made a deafening noise as they clashed their swords on shields, but not one man actually attempted to clamber up the awkward ladders. Instead Sigtryggr's standard-bearer suddenly waved the great flag from side to side, and then, in a deliberate and flamboyant gesture, lowered the banner so that the red ax lay flat on the roadway.

"Now," I called down.

And the men waiting under the arch pushed open the heavy gate.

And so the Norsemen came. They were quick, so quick that the four of my men who unbarred and pushed open the heavy gates were almost caught by Sigtryggr's horsemen who were first through the arch. Those horsemen must have thought themselves lucky, for no spears were hurled down from the gate's top. I did not want to check the charge, I wanted as many Norsemen in the blocked street as possible, and so the horses charged through un-impeded, their hooves suddenly loud on the old stone, and behind them came a swarm of warriors on foot. The men pretending to attack the corner bastions now abandoned their feint and streamed toward the open gateway.

And Sigtryggr was now inside the city, and for a heartbeat or two he must have thought he had the great victory, but then he saw the high barrier in front of him and he saw the men waiting on the barricades to the east of the street, and he turned his horse fast, knowing his attack was already doomed, and the horsemen following collided with his stallion. "Now," I shouted, "now! Kill them!" And the first spears flew.

The horses had almost reached the high barricade that barred the street, and they stood no chance. They screamed as they fell, screamed as the heavy spears came and the throwing axes whirled from three sides. There was blood on the paving stones, thrashing hooves, and riders trying to extricate themselves, and behind them a rush of Norsemen crowding through the gate, still oblivious of the trap beyond.

And this, I thought, is how my father died. How Northumbria fell. How the Danes had started their conquest of Saxon Britain, which had so nearly come to success. Like a flood they had spread south, and their victories brought the Norse in their wake, and now we had to fight back, shire by shire, village by village, taking back our land from south to north.

"Lord?" Gerbruht asked eagerly.

"Yes," I said, and Gerbruht and his companions hurled down the thick tree trunks to make an obstacle in the gate, and then, with glee, hurled the shit pots into the milling Norsemen. More Norsemen were crowding outside the gate now, not understanding what delayed them, not comprehending the horror that we had readied for them, and four of my men began hurling down the big stones, each one capable of crushing a helmeted skull.

It was a pitiless, one-sided slaughter. Some of Sigtryggr's men tried to climb the barricades, but our men were above them, and a climbing man cannot protect himself from a spear thrust, let alone an ax blow. I was watching from the top of the gate, content to let the young men fight this battle. The Norsemen tried to fight back, but only added dead men to the barricades. A dozen warriors tried to break into the long house, hoping to escape through its rear doors. They shattered the street door with axes, but Osferth had already ordered the flaming torches hurled into the room and the thickening smoke and sudden fiery heat drove the men back from the new opening.

Some of Sigtryggr's men wanted to flee through the open gate, but others were still trying to enter, and Gerbruht and his four companions were hurling down the big stones. Men shouted to clear the gate, others tried to escape the masonry blocks, and then Finan struck from the big barricade that blocked the street.

He had refused to let me fight. "You're not strong enough yet, lord," he had insisted.

"He's right," my son had added.

So I had stayed on the fighting platform above the gate and from there I watched as Finan and my son led fifty men across that high barricade. They jumped down into the street, into a space cleared by spears and stones, a space littered with the bodies of men and horses, a space where they made a shield wall, and the Norsemen, infuriated, wounded, frightened, and confused, turned on them like maniacs. But the furious Norsemen did not form their own shield wall, they just saw an enemy and attacked, and Finan's overlapping shields and leveled spears met them. "Forward!" Finan shouted. "Slow and calm! Forward!"

There was a clash of shield on shield, but the Norsemen, still in panic, were assailed by more missiles coming from the edge of the street, and as soon as Finan's men had advanced a few paces so more men came from the barricade to support them. From the gate's top all I could see was that line of overlapping shields with helmets above, and the long spears reaching forward and the whole line advancing slowly, very slowly. It had to be slow. There were too many dead or dying men in their path, and dying horses were still kicking where they lay on the street. To keep the shield wall tight Finan's men had to step over those obstacles. They were chanting as they came. "Kill, kill, kill, kill, kill!" And whenever the Norsemen tried to make a wall to oppose them, so a stone would thump into them from the street's eastern side. The heat of the burning house was driving them from the west and Finan and my son were leading a killing band from the south.

Then I saw Sigtryggr. I thought he must have died in the first moments of our ambush, or at least been wounded as his horse went down, but there he was, still without a helmet, his long hair darkened by blood. He was in the center of the enemy, and he bellowed at men to follow him. He shouted at others to clear the gate. He knew that Finan's grinding shield wall would turn slaughter into butchery, and so he ran, I thought to the gate, but at the last moment he swerved and leaped at the barricade, which blocked the narrow alley running between the north wall and the closest house.

He leaped like a deer. He had lost his shield, but he was still clothed in heavy mail and leather, yet he leaped to the barricade's top. The swerve had been so sudden, so unexpected, and the leap so fast that the three men guarding that barricade were taken by surprise, and Sigtryggr's sword took one in the throat and his speed carried him past that man to crash into another. That man went down, and now Norsemen were following Sigtryggr. I saw the third man hack at him with a sword, but his mail stopped the cut, and then that third man screamed as a Norseman chopped with an ax. There were a half-dozen Norsemen on the barricade now, and Gerbruht and his companions hurled stones to stop more men joining them, but Sigtryggr had jumped from the tree trunks onto the steps that led to the ramparts. He was grinning. He was enjoying himself. His men were being crushed, killed, burned, and beaten, but he was a warlord at war, and his eyes were bright with battle-joy as he turned and saw us at the very top of the long steps.

He saw me.

What he saw was another lord of war. He saw a man enriched by battle, a man with a fine helmet and glittering mail, a man whose arms were thick with the rings that come from victory, a man whose face was hidden behind armor plates chased with silver, a man with gold about his neck, a man who had doubtless planned this ambush, and Sigtryggr saw he could snatch one triumph from this disaster and so he came up the steps, still grinning, and Gerbruht, quick-thinking, threw a stone, but Sigtryggr was also quick, so very quick, and almost seemed to dance out of the missile's way as he came to me. He was young, he was in love with war, he was a warrior. "Who are you?" he shouted as he climbed the last steps.

"I am Uhtred of Bebbanburg," I told him.

He shouted for joy. Reputation would be his.

And so he came to kill me.

Twelve

We have known peace. There are times when we sow our fields and know we will live till harvest, times when all that our children know of war is what the poets sing to them. Those times are rare, yet I have tried to explain to my grandchildren what war is. I am dutiful. I tell them it is bad, that it leads to sorrow and grief, yet they do not believe me. I tell them to walk into the village and see the crippled men, to stand by the graves and hear the widows weep, but they do not believe me. Instead they hear the poets, they hear the pounding rhythm of the songs that quickens like a heart in battle, they hear the stories of heroes, of men, and of women too, who carried blades against an enemy who would kill and enslave us, they hear of the glory of war, and in the courtyards they play at war, striking with wooden swords against wicker shields, and they do not believe that war is an abomination.

And perhaps those children are right. Some priests rant against war, but those same priests are quick to shelter behind our shields when an enemy threatens, and there are always enemies. The dragon-headed ships still come to our coasts, the Scots send their war-bands south, and the Welsh love nothing more than a dead Saxon. If we did as the priests want, if we beat our swords into plowshares, we would all be dead or enslaved, and so the children must learn the strokes of the sword and grow into the strength needed to hold a shield of iron-rimmed willow against the fury of a savage enemy. And some will learn the joy of battle, the song of the sword, the thrill of danger.

Sigtryggr knew it. He reveled in war. I can still see him coming up those stone stairs, his face alive with joy and his long-sword reaching. Had I looked like that when I killed Ubba? Had Ubba seen my youth and eagerness, my ambition, and in those things seen his death? We leave nothing in this world but bones and reputation, and Sigtryggr, his sword already reaching for me, saw his reputation shining like a bright star in the darkness.

Then he saw Stiorra.

She was behind me, just to one side, her hands held to her mouth. How do I know that? I was not looking at her, but all that happened was told to me later, and she was there, and I was told she clasped her hands to stifle a scream. I had pushed Gerbruht back, not willing to let the Frisian fight my battle, and Stiorra was now closest to me. She uttered a small cry, more of shock than fear, though she should have been terrified, seeing how eagerly death leaped up the steps toward us. Then Sigtryggr saw my daughter and for an instant, for the blink of an eye, he kept his gaze on her. We expect to see men on a battlefield, but a woman? The sight of her distracted him.

It was only a heartbeat's hesitation, but it was enough. He had been watching my eyes, but seeing Stiorra he kept looking at her for that instant, and in that instant I moved. I was not as fast as I had been, I was not as strong as I once was, but I had been in battle all my life, and I smashed my shield arm to the left, catching the tip of his blade to sweep his sword aside, and he looked back at me, bellowed a challenge and tried to bring the sword back over the top of my shield, but Serpent-Breath was moving, rising, and I moved too, going down a step and still lifting the shield to keep his sword high and he saw my blade coming for his belly and he twisted desperately to avoid the lunge and missed his footing on the steps, and the shout of battle-rage became a cry of alarm as he stumbled. I flicked Serpent-Breath back just as he recovered to thrust his blade beneath my shield. It was a good lunge, a fast move made by a man who had still not regained his balance, and that stroke deserved to rip the flesh from my left thigh, but my shield dropped on the blade and took the force from it as I swept Serpent-Breath, meaning to cut his throat open, and he jerked his head away.

He jerked his head an instant too late. He was still trying to find his balance and his head came back down as his foot slipped on the step, and Serpent-Breath's sharp tip took his right eye. She took just the eye and the skin on the bridge of his nose. There was a small spurt of blood, a gush of colorless liquid, and Sigtryggr reeled away as Gerbruht pushed me aside to finish the job with his ax. That was when Sigtryggr leaped again, but this time he jumped clean off the rampart steps and down to the ditch, a long fall. Gerbruht shouted in anger at his escape, and thrust the ax at the next man, who took the blow on his shield and staggered back, and then the six Norsemen who had followed their lord fled like him. They jumped from the ramparts. One was impaled on a stake, the others, including Sigtryggr, scrambled up the ditch's far side.

And thus I defeated Sigtryggr and took one of his eyeballs.

"I am Odin!" Sigtryggr roared from the ditch's edge. He had tipped his ravaged face to look at me with his one eye, and he was smiling! "I am Odin," he called to me, "I have gained wisdom!" Odin had sacrificed an eye to learn wisdom and Sigtryggr was laughing in his defeat. His men dragged him away from the spears that were being hurled down from the wall, but he turned again when he was just a dozen paces away and saluted me with his sword.

"I could have killed him if he hadn't jumped," Gerbruht said.

"He would have gutted you," I said, "he would have gutted both of us." He was a god come to earth, a god of war, but the god had lost, and now he went back out of range of our spears.

Finan had reached the gate. The surviving Norse ran, going back to where they had started their charge, and where they formed a shield wall about their wounded lord. The feint attack on the northwestern bastion had long been abandoned, and all the Norse were now on the road, some five hundred men.

They still outnumbered us.

"Merewalh," I ordered, "time to release your horsemen." I leaned over the inner rampart. "Finan? Did you see Eardwulf?"

"No, lord."

"Then we're not done."

It was time to take the battle outside the walls.

Merewalh led two hundred horsemen into the fields to the east of the Norsemen. The riders stayed a good distance away. They were a threat. If Sigtryggr tried to retreat to Brunanburh he would be harried all the way and he knew it.

Yet what choice did he have? He could throw men at the walls, but he knew he would never capture Ceaster by assault. His only chance had been treachery, and the chance was gone, leaving fifty or sixty of his men dead in the street. A dozen of Finan's men were moving among those corpses, slitting the throats of the dying and stripping mail from the dead. "A good day for plunder!" one of them called cheerfully. Another pranced down the blood-soaked stones wearing a helmet crowned with a great eagle's wing.

"Was he mad?" Stiorra asked me.

"Mad?"

"Sigtryggr. To come up these steps?"

"He was battle-mad," I said, "and you saved my life."

"I did?"

"He looked at you and it distracted him just long enough." I knew I would wake in the night and shiver at the memory of his sword reaching for me, shiver with the certainty that I could never have parried the speed of his attack, shiver with the sliver of fate that had saved me from death. But he had seen Stiorra and he had hesitated.

"Now he wants to talk," she said.

I turned and saw that a Norseman was waving a leaf-heavy branch. "Lord?" Finan called from the gateway.

"I've seen it!"

"Let him come?"

"Let him come," I said, then plucked Stiorra's sleeve. "You come too."

"Me?"

"You. Where's Æthelstan?"

"With Finan."

"Was the little bastard in the shield wall?" I asked, shocked.

"He was in the rear rank," Stiorra said, "you didn't see him?"

"I'll kill him."

She chuckled, then followed me down to the barricade. We jumped into the street and stepped over the fallen masonry and the blood-laced bodies. "Æthelstan!"

"Lord?"

"Weren't you supposed to be in the church?" I demanded. "Did I give you permission to join Finan's shield wall?"

"I left the church to piss, lord," he said earnestly, "and I never meant to join Finan's men. I was just going to watch them from the top of the logs, but I tripped."

"You tripped?"

He nodded vigorously. "I tripped, lord," he said, "and fell into the street." I saw that Cengar, the boy he had rescued, was protectively close to him, as were two of Finan's men.

"You didn't trip," I said, then clipped him around the ear, which, because he was wearing a helmet, hurt me a lot more than it did him. "You're coming with me," I said. "And you too," I added to Stiorra.

The three of us walked under the arch, stepped around the bodies with their heads crushed by rocks, avoided the puddles of shit, then Finan's ranks parted for us. "You two are coming with us," I said to Finan and my son. "The rest of you stay here."

We walked thirty or forty paces up the road. I stopped and cupped my hands. "You can bring two men!"

Sigtryggr brought just one man, a great beast of a warrior with broad shoulders and a broad black beard into which was woven the jawbones of wolves or dogs. "He's called Svart," Sigtryggr said cheerfully, "and he eats Saxons for breakfast." Sigtryggr had a strip of linen tied about his missing eye. He touched the bandage. "You ruined my good looks, Lord Uhtred."

"Don't talk to me," I said. "I only talk with men. I brought you a woman and a child so you can speak to your equals."

He laughed. It seemed no insult touched him. "Then I shall

talk to my equals," he said and bowed to Stiorra. "Your name, my lady?"

She looked at me, wondering if I really wanted her to conduct the negotiations. "I'm not saying anything," I spoke to her in Danish, and spoke slowly so Sigtryggr would understand. "You deal with the boy."

Svart growled at the word "boy," but Sigtryggr put a hand on the big man's gold-bound arm. "Down, Svart, they're playing word riddles." He smiled at Stiorra. "I am the Jarl Sigtryggr Ivarson, and you are?"

"Stiorra Uhtredsdottir," she said.

"And I took you to be a goddess," he answered.

"And this is the Prince Æthelstan," Stiorra went on. She spoke in Danish, her voice distant and controlled.

"A prince! I am honored to meet you, Lord Prince." He bowed to the boy, who did not understand what was being said. Sigtryggr smiled. "The Lord Uhtred said I must talk to my equals and he sends me a goddess and a prince! He honors me!"

"You wanted to talk," Stiorra said coldly, "so talk."

"Well, lady, I confess matters have not gone as I wished. My father sent me to make a kingdom in Britain, and instead I meet your father. He's a cunning man, is he not?"

Stiorra said nothing, just gazed at him. She stood tall, proud, and straight-backed, looking so like her mother.

"Eardwulf the Saxon told us your father was dying," Sigtryggr confessed. "He said your father was weak as a worm. He said Lord Uhtred is long past his best, that he would never be at Ceaster."

"My father still has two eyes," Stiorra said.

"But not as beautiful as yours, my lady."

"Did you come to waste our time?" Stiorra asked. "Or did you wish to surrender?"

"To you, my lady, I would surrender all I have, but my men? You can count?"

"I can count."

"We outnumber you."

"What he wants," I spoke to Finan in English, "is to withdraw to his ships without interference."

"And what do you want?" Finan asked, knowing that our conversation was really for Stiorra's benefit.

"He can't afford another fight," I said, "he'll lose too many men. But so will we."

Sigtryggr did not understand what we said, but he was listening closely, as if some sense might emerge from the foreign language.

"So we just let them go?" Finan asked.

"He can go back to his father," I said, "but he must leave half his swords behind and give us hostages."

"And give us Eardwulf," Finan said.

"And give us Eardwulf," I agreed.

Sigtryggr heard the name. "You want Eardwulf?" he asked. "He's yours. I give him to you! He and the rest of his Saxons."

"What you want," Stiorra said, "is a promise that we won't stop you returning to your ships."

Sigtryggr pretended to be surprised. "I never thought of that, my lady, but yes! What a generous thought. We could return to our ships."

"And to your father."

"He won't be happy."

"I shall weep for him," she said scornfully. "And you will leave half your swords here," she went on, "and we shall take hostages for your good behavior."

"Hostages," he said, and for the first time did not sound confident.

"We shall choose a dozen of your men," Stiorra said.

"And how will those hostages be treated?"

"With respect, of course, unless you stay on these shores, in which case they will be killed."

"You will feed them?"

"Of course."

"Feast them?"

"We will feed them," she said.

He shook his head. "I cannot agree to twelve, my lady. Twelve is too many. I will offer you one hostage."

"You are ridiculous," Stiorra snapped.

"Myself, dear lady, I offer myself."

And I confess he surprised me. He also astonished Stiorra, who did not know what to say, but instead looked to me for an answer. I thought for a moment, then nodded. "His men can return to their ships," I spoke to her in Danish, "but half will leave their swords here. They have one day to ready the ships."

"One day," she said.

"Two mornings from now," I said harshly, "we will bring Sigtryggr to his fleet. If the ships are afloat and ready to sail with their crews on board he can join them. If not, he dies. And Eardwulf and his followers must be given to us."

"I agree," Sigtryggr said. "May I keep my sword?"

"No."

He unbuckled the sword belt and gave it to Svart, then, still smiling, walked to join us. And so that night we feasted with Sigtryggr.

Æthelflaed arrived the next day. She sent no warning of her coming, but her first horsemen appeared in the mid-afternoon and, an hour later, she rode through the South Gate leading more than one hundred men, all on tired horses white with sweat. She was in her silver mail, her whitening hair ringed with a silver circlet. Her standard-bearer was holding her dead husband's banner, the flag showing the prancing white horse. "What happened to the goose?" I asked her.

She ignored the question, staring down at me from her saddle. "You look better!"

"I am better."

"Truly?" she asked eagerly.

"Healed," I said.

"God be thanked!" She looked up at the clouded sky when she said that. "What happened?"

"I'll tell you soon enough," I answered, "but what happened to the goose?"

"I'm keeping Æthelred's banner," she said brusquely, "it's what Mercia is used to. Folk don't like change. It's hard enough for them to accept a woman as their ruler without imposing more new things on them." She swung down from Gast's saddle. Her mail, her boots, and her long white cloak were mud-spattered. "I hoped you'd be here."

"You ordered me here."

"But I did not order you to waste time finding a ship," she said tartly. A servant came to take her horse, while her men dismounted and stretched tired limbs. "There's a rumor that Norsemen are coming here," she went on.

"There are always rumors," I said dismissively.

"We heard a report from Wales," she ignored my flippant comment, "that a fleet was off the coast. It might not be coming here, but there's empty land north of the Mærse and that might tempt them." She frowned, sniffing the air and disliking what she smelled. "I did not scour Haki from that land just to make space for another pagan warlord! We have to settle folk on that land."

"Sigtryggr," I said.

She frowned. "Sigtryggr?"

"Your Welsh spies were right," I said, "Sigtryggr is the warlord who leads the Norse fleet."

"You know about him?"

"Of course I do! His men are occupying Brunanburh."

"Oh God," she flinched at the news. "Oh God, no! So they did come here! Well that won't last! We have to get rid of them quickly."

I shook my head. "I'd leave them alone."

She stared at me in shock. "Leave them alone? Are you mad? The last thing we want is Norsemen controlling the Mærse." She began striding toward the Great Hall. Two of her priests scurried behind carrying sheaves of parchment. "Find a strongbox," she talked over her shoulder as she went, "and make sure those documents stay dry! I can't stay long," she was evidently talking to me now. "Gleawecestre is calm enough, but there's still much work to do there. Which is why I want those Norsemen gone!"

"They outnumber us," I said dubiously.

She turned around fast, all energy and decision, and jabbed a finger at me. "And they'll be reinforced if we give them any more time. You know that! We must get rid of them!"

"They outnumber us," I said again, "and they're battle-hardened. They've been fighting in Ireland, and men learn to be vicious there. If we're to attack Brunanburh I'd want another three hundred men, at least!"

She frowned, worried suddenly. "What's happened to you? Are you frightened of this man, Sigtryggr?"

"He's a lord of war."

She looked into my eyes, evidently judging the truth of my words and whatever she saw must have convinced her. "Dear God," she said, still frowning. "Your wound, I suppose," she added half under her breath, and turned away. She believed I had lost my courage and as a consequence she now had another worry to add to her many burdens. She walked on till she noticed the swords, shields, spears, mail coats, helmets, and axes that were heaped by the Great Hall door beneath Sigtryggr's banner of the red ax which was nailed to the wall. She stopped, puzzled. "What's that?"

"I forgot to tell you," I said, "that the battle-hardened men attacked yesterday. They killed three of our men and wounded sixteen, but we killed seventy-two of theirs, and Sigtryggr is our hostage. We're keeping him till tomorrow when his fleet sails back to Ireland. You really didn't need to come! It's very good to see you, of course, but Merewalh and I are quite capable of dealing with big bad Norsemen."

"You bastard," she said, though not in anger. She looked at the trophies, then back to me and laughed. "And God be thanked," she added, touching the silver cross that hung at her breast.

That night we feasted with Sigtryggr again, though the arrival of Æthelflaed with so many warriors meant that the meat was scanty. There was ale enough, and the steward provided skins of wine and a large barrel of mead. Even so, Æthelflaed's presence meant the mood of the hall was more subdued than the previous night. Men tended to talk more softly when she was in the hall, they were less liable to start fights or bawl their favorite songs about women at the tops of their voices. The mood was made even more somber by the half-dozen churchmen who shared the top table, where Æthelflaed questioned Merewalh and myself about the fight at the North Gate. Sigtryggr had been given an honorable place at the table, as had my daughter. "It was her fault," Sigtryggr said, nodding toward Stiorra.

I translated for Æthelflaed. "Why her fault?" she asked.

"He saw her and was distracted," I explained.

"A pity," my daughter said coldly, "that he was not distracted for longer."

Æthelflaed smiled approvingly at that sentiment. She sat very straight, keeping a watchful eye on the hall. She ate little and drank less. "So she doesn't get drunk, then?" Sigtryggr said to me sourly, nodding at Æthelflaed. He was sitting across the table from me.

"She doesn't," I said.

"My mother would be wrestling with my father's warriors by now," he said gloomily, "or else out-drinking them."

"What is he saying?" Æthelflaed demanded. She had seen the Norseman glance at her.

"He complimented you on the wine," I said.

"Tell him it is a gift from my youngest sister, Ælthryth."

Ælthryth had married Baldwin of Flanders who ruled territory south of Frisia, and if this was Flanders wine I would rather have drunk horse piss, but Sigtryggr seemed to like it. He offered to pour some for Stiorra, but she refused him curtly and went back to her conversation with Father Fraomar, a young priest in Æthelflaed's service. "The wine is good!" Sigtryggr pressed her.

"I shall help myself," she said distantly. Alone among my family and followers she seemed immune to the Norseman's appeal. I certainly liked him. He reminded me of myself, or at least of the man I was when I had been young and headstrong and had taken the risks that either end in death or reputation. And Sigtryggr had charmed my men. He had given Finan an arm ring, praised my warriors' fighting skills, admitted that he had been well beaten, and had promised that one day he would come back to take his revenge. "If your father ever gives you another fleet," I had said.

"He will," he said confidently, "only next time I won't fight you. I'll look for an easier Saxon to beat."

"Why not stay in Ireland?" I had asked him.

He had hesitated before answering and I suspected a jest was coming, but then he had looked at me with his one eye. "They're savage fighters, lord. You attack and beat them, and then suddenly there's another horde of them. And the deeper you go into their land the more there are, and half the time you can't see them, but you know they're there. It's like fighting phantoms till they suddenly appear and attack." He half smiled. "They can keep their land."

"As we'll keep ours."

"Maybe, maybe not," he had grinned. "We'll row down the Welsh coast now and see if we can't capture a slave or two to take home. My father will forgive me a lot if I take him a clutch of new girls."

Æthelflaed treated Sigtryggr with disdain. He was a pagan and she hated all pagans except for me. "It's a pity you didn't kill him," she said at the feast.

"I tried."

She watched Stiorra rebuff every effort Sigtryggr made to be friendly. "She's grown well," she said warmly.

"She has."

"Unlike my daughter," she sighed, her voice low now.

"I like Ælfwynn."

"She has a head full of feathers," she said dismissively. "But it's time you found Stiorra a husband."

"I know."

She paused, her eyes looking around the hall that was lit by rushlights. "Æthelhelm's wife is dying."

"So he told me."

"She may be dead by now. Æthelhelm told me that the priests have given her the last rites."

"Poor woman," I said dutifully.

"I had a long conversation with him before I left Gleawecestre," Æthelflaed said, still looking down the hall, "with him and with my brother. They accept what our Witan decided. They also agreed to leave Æthelstan in my care. He will be raised in Mercia and there will be no attempt to spirit him away."

"You believe that?"

"I believe we must guard the boy," she said tartly. She looked at Æthelstan, who was with his twin sister at one of the lower tables. His royal birth meant he should have eaten at the top table, but I had spared him the conversation of Æthelflaed's priests. "I believe my brother means the boy no harm," she went on, "and he insists there must be no enmity between Wessex and Mercia."

"Nor will there be, unless Æthelhelm gets ambitious again."

"He overreached himself," she said, "and he knows it. He apologized to me, and very graciously. But yes, he is ambitious, so perhaps a new wife might distract him? The woman I have in mind will certainly keep him busy."

It took me a moment to understand what she was saying. "You?" I asked, astonished. "You're thinking of marrying Æthelhelm?"

"No," she said, "not me."

"Then who?"

She hesitated for a heartbeat, then looked at me challengingly. "Stiorra."

"Stiorra!" I spoke too loudly, and my daughter turned to look at me. I shook my head and she went back to her discussion with Father Fraomar. "Stiorra!" I said again, but softer this time. "She's young enough to be his granddaughter!"

"It isn't unknown for men to marry younger women," Æthelflaed said waspishly. She glanced at Eadith, who was sitting on a lower table with Finan and my son. Æthelflaed had not been pleased to find Eardwulf's sister in Ceaster, but I had defended Eadith's presence fiercely, saying I owed her my recovery. "What else?" Æthelflaed had asked sharply, a question I had ignored, just as Æthelflaed had since ignored Eadith. "And Æthelhelm is in good health," she continued now, "and he's wealthy. He's a good man."

"Who tried to kill you."

"That was Eardwulf," she responded, "who misunderstood Æthelhelm's wishes."

"He would have killed you," I said, "he would have killed Æthelstan, and killed anyone else who stands in his grandson's way."

She sighed. "My brother needs Æthelhelm," she said. "He's too powerful to be ignored and he's too useful. And if Wessex needs Æthelhelm, so does Mercia."

"You're saying Wessex is ruled by Æthelhelm?"

She shrugged, unwilling to admit it. "I'm saying that Æthelhelm is a good man, ambitious yes, but effective. We need his support."

"And you think sacrificing Stiorra to his bed will get it?"

She winced at my tone. "I think your daughter should be married," she said, "and Lord Æthelhelm admires her."

"You mean he wants to hump her," I growled. I looked at my daughter, whose head was bowed as she listened to Fraomar. She looked grave and beautiful. "So she's to be a peace cow between Mercia and Wessex?" I asked. A peace cow was a woman married between enemies to seal a treaty.

"Think on it," Æthelflaed said urgently. "When she's widowed she'll inherit more land than you can dream of, more warriors than you could hope to raise, and more money than Edward's whole treasury." She paused, but I said nothing. "And it will be ours," she added in a low voice. "Wessex won't swallow Mercia, we'll swallow Wessex."

There is a story in the Christian scripture about someone or other being taken to the hilltop and offered the whole world. I do not remember the tale now, only that the idiot turned it down, and, at that feast, I felt like the idiot. "Why not marry Ælfwynn to Æthelhelm?" I asked.

"My daughter isn't clever," Æthelflaed said, "Stiorra is. And it needs a clever woman to manage Æthelhelm."

"So what will you do with Ælfwynn?"

"Marry her to someone. Merewalh perhaps? I don't know. I despair of the child."

Stiorra. I gazed at her. She was indeed clever and beautiful, and I had to find her a husband, so why not find her the richest husband in Wessex? "I'll think about it," I promised, and I thought of the old prophecy that my daughter would be the mother of kings.

And so it proved.

Dawn. A small mist on the Mærse was broken by the dark shapes of twenty-six dragon-ships that rowed slowly to hold their place against the flooding tide. Sigtryggr's men had kept their word. The ships were ready to sail, and Brunanburh was ours again. The only Norsemen left ashore were Svart and six others who guarded Eardwulf and his three remaining followers. I had wanted Eardwulf handed to me on the day of Sigtryggr's defeat, but he had fled too quickly, though he had only got as far as one of the Danish halls on Wirhealum, where Sigtryggr's men had discovered him. Now he waited for our arrival.

I brought Finan, my son, and twenty men, and Æthelflaed was escorted by a dozen more. I had insisted that Æthelstan ride with me to Brunanburh, while my daughter had also wanted to see the Norsemen leave, and so she had accompanied us, bringing her maid, Hella. "Why did you bring a maid?" I asked her.

"Why not? There's no danger, is there?"

"None," I said. I trusted Sigtryggr to keep his promise that there would be no fighting between his men and ours, nor was there. We met Svart and his few men close to the half-finished burh, where Sigtryggr dismounted from his borrowed horse. Svart brought him his sword, and Sigtryggr looked at me as if asking for permission to take it. I nodded. He pulled the blade from its scabbard and kissed the steel. "You want me to kill the Saxons?" he asked, nodding toward Eardwulf.

"I do my own work," I said, and I swung myself from the saddle and was amazed that there was no pain.

"Father," Uhtred called. He wanted to do the killing.

"I do my own work," I said again, and though there was no pain I took care to lean against the horse. I gasped as if the agony had come back, then I pushed off the stallion's flank and limped toward Eardwulf. The limp was a pretense.

He watched me approach. He stood tall, his narrow face expressionless. His dark hair, no longer oiled as it used to be, was tied with a ribbon. There was a few days' growth of beard on his long chin, his cloak was dirty and his boots scuffed. He looked like a man who had suffered fate's blows. "You should have killed me," I said, "at Alencestre."

"If I had," he said, "I would rule in Mercia now."

"And now you'll rule a Mercian grave," I answered, then drew Serpent-Breath. I grimaced, as if her weight was too much for me.

"You'd kill an unarmed man, Lord Uhtred?" Eardwulf asked.

"No," I said. "Berg," I shouted without turning around, "give your sword to this man!"

I rested on my sword, placing the tip on a flat stone and leaning my weight on the hilt. Behind Eardwulf was the unfinished burh, its long earthen wall topped now by thorn bushes that made a temporary palisade. I thought the Norsemen might have burned the church and stables, but they stood unharmed. Svart and his men guarded Eardwulf's followers.

Berg trotted his horse forward. He glanced at me, then drew Ice-Spite and tossed the blade onto the dew-wet grass by Eardwulf's feet. "That," I told Eardwulf, "is Ice-Spite. Cnut Longsword's blade. Your sister tells me you tried to buy it once and now I give it to you. It almost killed me, so see if you can finish the job."

"Father!" Stiorra called anxiously. She must have believed Eardwulf and Ice-Spite were more than a match for me.

"Quiet, girl. I'm busy."

Why did I choose to fight him? He was going to die whether I fought him or not, and he was dangerous, half my age, and a warrior. But it is reputation, always reputation. Pride, I suppose, is the most treacherous of virtues. The Christians call it a sin, but no poet sings of men who have no pride. Christians say the meek will inherit the earth, but the meek inspire no songs. Eardwulf had wanted to kill me, to kill Æthelflaed and Æthelstan. Eardwulf had wanted to rule, and Eardwulf was the last vestige of Æthelred's hatred. It was fitting that I should kill him and that all Saxon Englaland should know that I had killed him.

He stooped and picked up the sword. "You are in mail," he said, and that told me he was nervous.

"I'm old," I said, "and wounded. You're young. And Ice-Spite has pierced my mail once, so let her do it again. She's a magic blade."

"Magic?" he asked, then looked at the sword and saw the inscription.

†VLFBERH†T

His eyes widened, and he hefted the sword.

I lifted Serpent-Breath and winced as if her weight was gnawing at my ribs. "Besides," I went on, "you'll move faster without mail."

"And if I kill you?" Eardwulf asked.

"Then my son will kill you," I said, "but for all time men will know that Lord Eardwulf conquered Uhtred." I made the "lord" into a sneer.

And he came for me. He came fast. I carried no shield, and he swept Ice-Spite at my unprotected left side, but it was little more than an exploration, an attempt to see if I could parry, and I did not even need to think about it. The blades clashed and Serpent-Breath stopped Ice-Spite dead. I took a pace backward and lowered my blade. "You won't kill me with a cut," I said, "even Vlfberht's blades won't cut mail open. You need to lunge."

He was watching my eyes. He took a step forward, his sword rising, and I did not move, and he stepped back again. He was testing me, but he was also nervous. "Your sister," I said, "tells me you fought in the rear rank of the shield wall, never in the front rank."

"She lied."

"She was lying," I said, "lying in my bed when she told me. She said you let other men do your fighting."

"Then she's a whore and a liar."

I grimaced again, slightly bending at the waist as I used to do when the pain struck suddenly. Eardwulf did not know I was healed, and he saw Serpent-Breath drop even lower and he stamped his right foot forward and rammed Ice-Spite fast at my chest and I turned to one side to let the blade slide past me and then I punched him in the face with Serpent-Breath's heavy hilt. He staggered. I heard Finan chuckle as Eardwulf brought the sword back in a swing, again to my left side, but there was no force in the cut because he was still recovering from the lunge and from my blow and I just raised my arms and let the blade hit my mail. It struck just above the wound and the mail stopped the blade and there was no pain. I smiled at Eardwulf and flicked Serpent-Breath so that her tip cut open his left cheek, already bloody from the blow I had given him.

"If your sister whored for anyone," I said, "it was for you."

He touched his left hand to his cheek and felt the blood. I could see the fear in him now. Yes, he was a warrior, and not a bad one. He had trapped Welshmen on the Mercian border and driven them away, but his skill had been at laying ambushes or avoiding ambushes, at out-thinking his enemies and attacking them when they thought themselves safe. He had doubtless fought in the shield wall, protected by loyal men on either side, but he had always fought in the rear rank. He was not a man who took delight in the song of the swords.

"You whored your sister to Æthelred," I said, "and made yourself rich." I flicked Serpent-Breath again, aiming at his face, and he stepped back fast. I lowered the blade. "Jarl Sigtryggr!" I called.

"Lord Uhtred?"

"You still possess Eardwulf's money? The treasure he took from Gleawecestre?"

"I do!"

"It belongs to Mercia," I said.

"Then Mercia must come and take it," he answered.

I laughed. "So you won't go home empty-handed after all. Did he steal a lot?"

"Enough," Sigtryggr said.

I cut Serpent-Breath at Eardwulf's legs, not a serious blow, just enough to drive him back a pace. "You're a thief," I told him.

"That money was given to me." He took a pace forward, his blade rising, but I did not react to the threat and he stepped back again.

"It was gold that should have been spent on men," I said, "on weapons, on palisades, and on shields." I stepped forward and gave him a back-handed cut that simply drove him away. I followed, sword raised, and by now he must have known that I was not hurting, that I was moving easily and quickly, though I sensed that I would tire fast. Serpent-Breath is a heavy sword. "You spent it on oil for your hair," I said, "and on baubles for your whores, on furs and on horses, on jewels and on silk. A man, Lord Eardwulf, dresses in leather and iron. And he fights." And with that I attacked him, and he parried, but he was so slow.

All my life I have practiced with a sword. Almost from the time I could walk I have held a sword and learned its ways. I had been wary of Eardwulf at first, assuming that he would be faster than me and cunning in his sword-craft, but he knew little more than to cut and lunge and desperately block, and so I drove him back, pace by pace, and he watched my blade and I deliberately slowed my blows so that he could see them clearly and parry them, and I wanted him to see them because I did not want him to look behind. Nor did he, and when he reached the edge of the ditch I quickened my cuts, slapping him with the flat of Serpent-Breath's blade so she did not wound, but just humiliated him, and I parried his feeble counterattacks with thoughtless skill, and then I suddenly lunged and he went backward and his feet slid on the ditch's mud and he fell.

He landed on his back in the ditch's water. It was not deep. I laughed at him then and stepped carefully down the slippery slope to stand at his feet. The onlookers, both Saxon and Norse, came to the ditch's edge and looked down at us, and Eardwulf looked up and saw the warriors, the grim warriors, and such was his humiliation that I thought he would weep. "You are a traitor and an outlaw," I said, and I pointed Serpent-Breath at his belly and he raised Ice-Spite as if to strike at her, but instead I brought my sword arm back and then I cut. It was a massive cut given with all my remaining strength, and Serpent-Breath met Ice-Spite and it was Ice-Spite that broke. The famous blade broke in two just as I had wanted. A Saxon blade had broken Vlfberht's best, and whatever evil Ice-Spite might have harbored, whatever sorcery was hidden in her steel, was gone.

Eardwulf struggled backward, but I stopped him by thrusting Serpent-Breath at his belly. "You want me to cut you open?" I asked, then raised my voice. "Prince Æthelstan!" I called.

The boy scrambled down the ditch's side and stood in the water. "Lord?"

"Your verdict on this outlaw?"

"Death, lord," he said in his unbroken voice.

"Then deliver it," I said and gave him Serpent-Breath.

"No!" Eardwulf shouted.

"Lord Uhtred!" Æthelflaed called in a high voice.

"My lady?"

"He's a boy," she said, frowning at Æthelstan.

"He's a boy who must learn to be a warrior and a king," I said, "and death is his destiny. He must learn to give it." I patted Æthelstan's shoulder. "Make it quick, boy," I told him. "He deserves a slow death, but this is your first killing. Make it easy for yourself."

I watched Æthelstan and saw the firmness on his young face. I watched as he moved the heavy sword to Eardwulf's neck, and watched his small grimace as he rammed the blade down. A fierce spurt of blood landed on my mail. Æthelstan kept his eyes on Eardwulf's face as he thrust a second time, and then he just leaned on Serpent-Breath's hilt, keeping the blade in Eardwulf's gullet, and the drab ditch water turned red, and Eardwulf thrashed for a time and there was a gurgling sound and more blood pulsed to swirl in the water, and still Æthelstan leaned on my sword until the thrashing stopped and the ripples subsided. I hugged the boy, then took his face between my hands to make him look at me. "That is justice, Lord Prince," I said, "and you did well." I took Serpent-Breath from him. "Berg," I called, "you need a new sword! That one was no good."

Sigtryggr held out a hand to pull me from the ditch. His one eye was bright with the same joy I had seen on Ceaster's ramparts. "I would not want you as an enemy, Lord Uhtred," he said.

"Then don't come back, Jarl Sigtryggr," I said, clasping his forearm as he clasped mine.

"I will be back," he said, "because you will want me to come back."

"I will?"

He turned his head to gaze at his ships. One ship was close to the shore, held there by a mooring line tied to a stake. The prow of the ship had a great dragon painted white and in the dragon's claw was a red ax. The ship waited for Sigtryggr, but close to it, standing where the grass turned to the river bank's mud, was Stiorra. Her maid, Hella, was already aboard the dragon-ship.

Æthelflaed had been watching Eardwulf's death, but now saw Stiorra by the grounded ship. She frowned, not sure she understood what she saw. "Lord Uhtred?"

"My lady?"

"Your daughter," she began, but did not know what to say.

"I will deal with my daughter," I said grimly. "Finan?"

My son and Finan were both staring at me, wondering what I would do. "Finan?" I called.

"Lord?"

"Kill that scum," I jerked my head toward Eardwulf's followers, then I took Sigtryggr by the elbow and walked him toward his ship. "Lord Uhtred!" Æthelflaed called again, sharper this time.

I waved a dismissive hand, and otherwise ignored her. "I thought she disliked you," I said to Sigtryggr.

"We meant you to think that."

"You don't know her," I said.

"You knew her mother when you met her?"

"This is madness," I said.

"And you are famous for your good sense, lord."

Stiorra waited for us. She was tense. She stared at me defiantly and said nothing.

I felt a lump in my throat and a sting in my eyes. I told myself it was the small smoke drifting from the Norsemen's abandoned campfires. "You're a fool," I told her harshly.

"I saw," she said simply, "and I was stricken."

"And so was he?" I asked, and she just nodded. "And the last two nights," I asked, "after the feasting was over?" I did not finish the question, but she answered it anyway by nodding again. "You are your mother's daughter," I said, and I embraced her, holding her close. "But it is my choice whom you marry," I went on. I felt her stiffen in my arms. "And Lord Æthelhelm wants to marry you."

I thought she was sobbing, but when I pulled back from the embrace I saw she was laughing. "Lord Æthelhelm?" she asked.

"You'll be the richest widow in all Britain," I promised her.

She still held me, looking up into my face. She smiled, that same smile that had been her mother's. "Father," she said, "I swear on my life that I will accept the man you choose to be my husband."

She knew me. She had seen my tears and knew they were not caused by smoke. I leaned forward and kissed her forehead. "You will be a peace cow," I said, "between me and the Norse. And you're a fool. So am I. And your dowry," I spoke louder as I stepped back, "is Eardwulf's money." I saw I had smeared her pale linen dress with Eardwulf's blood. I looked at Sigtryggr. "I give her to you," I said, "so don't disappoint me."

Someone wise, I forget who, said we must leave our children to fate. Æthelflaed was angry with me, but I refused to listen to her protests. Instead I listened to the chanting of the Norsemen, the song of the oars, and saw their dragon-ships go downstream into the thinning mist that covered the Mærse.

Stiorra stared back at me. I thought she would wave, but she stayed still, and then she was gone.

"We have a burh to finish," I told my men.

Wyrd bið ful āræd.

Historical Note

Æthelflaed did succeed her husband as the ruler of Mercia, though she was never proclaimed queen of that country. She was known as the Lady of the Mercians, and her achievements deserve to be better remembered in the long story of England's making. The enmity between Æthelflaed and Æthelred is entirely fictional, as are the Witan's deliberations that led to her appointment as ruler. There is no evidence that Æthelhelm, Edward's father-in-law, attempted to remove Æthelstan from the succession, though the doubts about Æthelstan's legitimacy are not fictional.

King Hywel existed and is known to this day as Hywel Dda, Hywel the Good. He was an extraordinary man, clever, ambitious and able, who, in many ways, achieved for Wales what Alfred hoped to achieve for England.

Sigtryggr also existed, and did attack Chester, and did lose an eye at some point in his storied career. I have probably brought that attack forward in time. The anglicized spelling of his name is Sihtric, but I have preferred the Norse spelling to avoid confusion with Uhtred's faithful follower, Sihtric.

I am grateful to my good friend Thomas Keane, MD, for describing Uhtred's miraculous recovery. Doctor Tom never claimed it was likely, but it is possible, and on a dark night with the wind behind you and a whisky inside? Who knows? Uhtred is always lucky, so it worked.

Uhtred's son is also lucky in owning a sword made by the smith who marked the blade with the name or word:

†VLFBERH†T

Such swords existed, and a number remain, though it seems the blades were so valued that some fakes were made in the ninth and tenth centuries. A man would have to pay a vast sum for such a sword because the steel of a genuine Vlfberht blade was of a quality that would not be matched for a thousand years. Iron is brittle, but smiths had learned that by adding carbon they turned the iron into steel that would make a hard, sharp, and flexible blade that was much less likely to shatter in combat. The usual way of adding the carbon was to burn bones in the smithy fire, but that was a hit-or-miss process and left impurities in the metal, yet, some time in the ninth century, someone discovered a way of liquefying the iron-carbon mix in a crucible and so produced ingots of superior steel. We do not know who that someone was, or where the steel was made. It seems to have been imported to northern Europe from either India or, perhaps, Persia, evidence of the long reach of the trade routes that also brought silk and other luxuries to Britain.

No place in Britain is more associated with the making of England than Brunanburh. It is, truly, the birthplace of England, and I have no doubt that some readers will object to my identification of Bromborough on the Wirral as the site of Brunanburh. We know Brunanburh existed, but there is no agreement and little certainty as to the exact location. There have been many suggestions, ranging from Dumfries and Galloway in Scotland to Axminster in Devon, but I am persuaded by the arguments of Michael Livingston's scrupulous monograph *The Battle of Brunanburh, a Casebook* (Exeter University Press, 2011). The battle that is the subject of the casebook is not the fight described in this book, but the much more famous and decisive affair of 937. Indeed Brunanburh is the battle that, at long last, will complete Alfred's dream and forge a united England, but that is another story.

About the Author

BERNARD CORNWELL is the author of the acclaimed *New York Times* bestsellers *1356, Agincourt,* and *The Fort;* the bestselling Saxon Tales, which include *The Last Kingdom, The Pale Horseman, Lords of the North, Sword Song, The Burning Land, Death of Kings,* and, most recently, *The Pagan Lord;* and the Richard Sharpe novels, among many others. He lives with his wife on Cape Cod.